Protector of the Union

This is a work of fiction. The characters, incidents, and dialog are drawn from the author's imagination and are not to be construed as real.

Any resemblance to actual events or persons, living or dead, is entirely coincidental.

Join us to learn about our books: https://woodenhookstudios.com

Edited by: Alane Kochems

ISBN: 979-8-9900459-8-9 (Paperback)

ISBN: 979-8-9900459-7-2 (Ebook)

Protector of the Union

Book One of the Felgenland Saga

By

Eric C. Holtgrefe

Wooden Hook Studios

Also by Eric C. Holtgrefe

— Stories in the Felgenland Saga:

Love and Honor in the Felgenland

— The Corpus Ad Astra Adventure Series:

Book One: Innocence Lost

To My Father, our family's mighty protector, thank you for your wisdom and military service.

To my Wife and Children, your love, patience, and support made this all possible

Psalms 23:4-6

The men from Earth call me a dictator. I can no more dictate how to live to the lowliest man in the Union than I can command the masses to follow me! No, I say all I can do is protect, and protect I shall! When I came to Stahlburgh, the men of Hansaburgh tried to continue to call me an "Emperor". I said to them, "No! I am a Protector... a Protector of the Union."

— Protector of the Union Karl I
Commentaries on Utopias; and How They Should Be Served

Prologue

Count Heinrich Karl Adolphus-Wilhelm von Machthaber zu Hinterland stood watching as the old *Schirmherr* or protector lay dying. The old man's skin was ash gray, and he lay on the hospital bed with his hair a greasy mess. The protector was unkempt and Heinrich guessed that the protector's courtiers had purposely kept away the nurses.

The courtiers were vultures who now stood around watching the old man die. The old man was beyond medical care. The reaper was coming for him no matter what the doctors did. All the assembled eyes were aglow with dreams with the succession after the protector's death. There were two main groups, the doves, who stood at one end of the large room, and the hawks who stood on the side where Heinrich watched. This would be the first time the Union electors chose a new protector. The courtiers assembled around the dying protector were anxious to know the result. For the electors, this was the one chance to elect the next protector. All assembled waited for the old man to die to see how the voting played out.

The protector's eldest son and Primus, Ruprecht, entered. The tall, seventy-year-old man looked much like the old protector, Ruprecht was the soft-spoken leader of the doves and interested primarily in the arts, industry, and science. The doves wished to maintain the current peace with the Terrans. A peace where trade and culture would determine who would champion humanity in the rim, or as those in the Union called the frontier, the Felgenland. The doves were quick to ignore the Terran war machine. Their ancestry stemmed back to the first human who beat his sword into a plowshare. The doves ignored the score of systems that suddenly had "revolutions" where new leaders happily marched to the Terran drum.

Ruprecht leaned over and said something to his centenarian father, but returned upright when his younger brother, Raimond, entered the room. Unlike Ruprecht, who looked like the aristocratic families of Hansaburgh, Raimond looked more like his late mother, the patroness, Julia of Protelan. Raimond's face would not be out of place in Havskrun, the Protelani capital city. Raimond didn't just have the Protelani looks, he had their same determinism and pragmatism. He was Secundus in the Cognatii which were the ten candidates eligible for election to the office of Protector of the Union.

Raimond strode boldly to his father's bedside. Ruprecht bowed to his father and turned to face his brother. The brothers embraced, more for the courtiers than out of love. Both men looked grimly at each other. They knew the time had come when one would become the protector and the other would be made a grand duke in the hinterland and shuffled off to his country estate and silence.

Raimond broke the embrace and produced a small cloth. He began wiping down the old protector's face and hair. The gesture was a token to the old protector's dignity. Instead of being happy at his son's brief cleaning, the old protector frowned at him.

The protector then spoke to Raimond, but Heinrich couldn't hear what the protector whispered. Then, the old protector cast a wicked look at Heinrich and the hawks, silencing those who had been muttering to each other. In earlier years, guards and terrible judgments would have followed that look. That was Karl's way: swift, brutal, and final. Karl had conquered the disparate tribes of Stahlburgh. He united all the people in a grand union and gave them a brutal peace. Well, Heinrich thought, that was what the legends told. Karl's ruthless demeanor gained him the epithet "the Iron Fist". People only spoke of Karl that way in a hushed whisper far from his presence. Nowadays the

"Iron Fist" was more apt to vent his rage on his nurses, whom he berated daily even though they did their best with the old man.

The large doors to the protector's chamber opened again. Grand-Duchess Signe Bosdottir von und zu Haldersmere entered with a score of other Dynasts. Signe's pearl-gray eyes were ablaze. Heinrich had known Signe for years. She was his father's friend. The excited look could only mean one thing as the grand-duchess was also the steward of the election. Signe was the final arbiter and her duty was to announce who would be the next protector. All that was necessary was the current protector's death.

"I'll leave soon enough you bastards," Karl said, his voice hoarse and sickly. A nervous murmur ran throughout the two groups. Sycophants muttered and mumbled oaths wishing the old protector to live for a thousand years. Karl coughed.

"Be silent! I know whom you've selected, and you'll get what you deserve," Karl said, his voice becoming hale.

"You all yearn for the fire and sword! Like stupid children you want to climb the high mountain. You want to put your face in the cold whipping wind that is fate. I've tried to stop you from touching the hot stove. It seems I've been too easy on you all. Like a loving father, I kept the four horsemen from your door. But you have not listened! Now you revel in the breaking of seals and prepare a banquet for when the riders come! I warned you! To fight Terra is to hasten our demise! I thought I taught you to choose reason over madness. Malcolm and Jesus take me for I have failed!"

"Father, please," Raimond said pained at the old man's anger and frustration.

"Wait your turn! This is still my time. You'll be the protector soon enough," Karl said. "You don't think I saw your little coup? I saw the seeds of your plan when you realized you were the younger son. When you are the protector, grip the wheel tightly, my son. These vultures will all try to take the power away from you. If you let them, they'll sail this ship of state into a black hole bringing nothing but chaos and self-destruction!"

The Grand-Duchess's face contorted in fury. Heinrich realized that she suspected that one of the electors had leaked the final results.

"No, Signe, no one talked," Karl said, noting the woman's fury. "I've been the patron of this Union for decades. You didn't think I would know which way you all would leap? Ha, don't be foolish! I have known the machinations of the least peasant to the grand dreams of the foremost families."

Karl coughed and blood trickled down the side of his cheek and stained his bed. Nurses checked his vitals on the machines beside the bed. Raimond and Ruprecht closed their eyes at seeing their father, the great protector, in so much pain.

After clearing his throat, Karl said, "Now, I will venture past the edge of the universe. I go to a place where I am the servant and the King of Kings is my master. I will finally see Malcolm, my friend, face to face. I leave to reunite with my long-lost love, Julia. Keep the Union —if you can! I never wanted to be here! It was pure foolish luck I landed here and the will of the Allfather that I became protector!"

The old man coughed and medical monitors chimed their ominous tones. The old man went still as his chest slowly lowered as he let out his final breath. After decades of vigorous activity, the body of Karl, first Protector of the Felgenland Union was still. His soul passed from the universe.

Heinrich felt the tears form at the corner of his eyes. All his life, Karl was there, a constant like the rising of the Holstensonne. Heinrich smoothed down the jacket of his Assault uniform. The cold reality spread over the hushed gathering—the "Iron Fist" was no more. Their father was dead.

In her loudest command voice, forged by years of yelling orders in the Union Navy, Signe shouted, "The protector is dead! By the will of the Allfather, long live the protector!"

"Long live the protector!" the gathering responded. Heinrich had taken up the cry, but who was the new protector? Karl had seemed to think the electors voted in Raimond, but was the old man correct? Signe moved determinedly to stand before the Secundus, Raimond.

Signe dropped to her knees, spreading her elegant dress out like a young bride for a photo. She turned her steel gray head upwards and shouted, "Protector of the Union, my honor is to serve! Long may you live!" Heinrich felt the electricity in the room. The hawks had won!

"Long live Protector Raimond!" the hawks shouted joyously. The election had gone their way. The Union had chosen the warrior over the artist. Now, the hawks would get their war with Terra. Either Terran aggression or a declaration of war from the parliament would transform the cold conflict into a hot war. Then, the military factories would start twenty-five-hour-a-day production. Unemployment would be forgotten as the need for labor would become paramount. The Parliament would give vitamins and meat to the small, sickly Assault, the Union's ground force, readying those warriors for the fight. The Union Navy, singing of mighty ships and grand battle lines yet sailing the stars in glorified garbage scows, would get their due too. Interceptors would roll out from the factories, and the space docks would build behemoths of tremendous fury. The war machine would awaken like King Arthur to save the Union.

"Grand-Duchess, as is our way, lead me to the cathedral for the investiture," Raimond said.

There was a cheer from the hawks, led together by Grand-Duke Alasdair Campbell, the foremost defense contractor, and Marquess Aidan MacCarthy, whom people called "the architect of the Union Navy" and Campbell's rival. Both men hoisted Raimond on their shoulders and marched through the doors, which were high enough to let Raimond to pass even on the tall men's shoulders.

The first protector died on the thirteenth of November, an ominous and unlucky date for a change of power. Heinrich noticed the room had cleared. All that remained were sincere mourners of the late protector.

"Congratulations, Henry, my friend! Your father has beaten the odds! I wish you congratulations too, as you are now the Union's heir presumptive," said Wilhelm *Markgraf* Bruckner of Bruckland. Wilhelm embraced his friend and fellow Assault officer. Heinrich patted his friend on the back and released the embrace. Heinrich hadn't realized what the election would mean for him. With Karl's death, Heinrich had unexpectedly moved from Sextus to Primus. He was the first of the Cognatii and the leading candidate to become the next protector. All eyes would be watching him now.

"Thank you, Will," Heinrich said flatly. Heinrich should have been excited, but he couldn't muster the enthusiasm. Wilhelm looked concerned at his friend's dour attitude.

"Look, I have to go to the investiture and give my oath. We can talk later. Don't be so upset when duty calls. As the protector's son, you'll make Major faster than I will," Wilhelm replied with a smile. Henry looked forlorn, rather than happy. Wilhelm bowed slightly, turned, and left. Heinrich knew he should follow Wilhelm, but he couldn't leave his grandfather just yet. If he walked out of the chamber, his grandfather's death would be real. His father would be the Protector of the Union, and he'd be the best candidate for heir. Heinrich watched as the remaining people began to disperse.

An older woman sat next to Karl's deathbed. She wore a long, black widow's dress. She sat crying and muttering to the corpse. A young lady in a Union Navy uniform stood next to her and offered the woman a tissue. Heinrich guessed the young woman was the old woman's granddaughter, since she was close to Heinrich's age.

"Grandmar, are you well?" Heinrich asked the old woman as he approached. He used the familial 'grandmar' as was customary amongst the Felgenlanders.

"Aye... Karl was such a grand man! He was always kind to me. He sponsored my son for a commission in the Assault. After my son died, Karl gave him a posthumous knighthood. After that Karl showed me great kindness. He would always write to me, concerned how I fared. I know Karl is with my Lewie and the Allfather now. I know I shouldn't be sad, but I wish he could have stayed with us just a bit longer," said old woman softly, tears staining her cheeks.

Heinrich nodded and said, "As a boy, he used to hold me in his lap. I would come to the villa to see him, and he chased me with water pistols in the warmth of the summer. His council would scowl at him for playing, and beg him to return to their weighty conversations. My grandfar would laugh at them and wink at me. I know I will never miss him even as much as you do, but I offer my condolences nonetheless."

"Primus," the old woman said, forgetting her sorrow and becoming the loving mother she once was, "My guess is that you will miss him more."

Heinrich leaned forward and gave the old woman a grandson's kiss on her cheek. She smiled and Heinrich said, "Of course, Grandmar, of course."

Heinrich straightened. It was time to face his destiny. He began silently preparing himself for the emotional journey to the investiture. He turned to leave, but the young Naval officer blocked him. While speaking with the old woman, Heinrich had completely ignored her. Now he looked at her as she blocked him from the exit.

The officer stood a half of head shorter than Heinrich in her oyster gray uniform and low-heel boots. Heinrich nodded to the woman, expecting her to move. As his head bobbed he noticed the broad wing emblems of an interceptor pilot above the pocket on her jacket.

She said, "My condolences, Primus, on the death of your grandfather. His like will never be seen again in this universe." Her soprano voice carried a timbre of command and force, but was appropriately respectful for the heir of the Union.

Heinrich hated this dance. He suspected the woman wanted

something from him. He would have to be gracious, and entertain her request. He then realized he didn't know her name. He checked her nameplate, it said, "MacDonald." She was a descendant of the first clan to settle on Stahlburgh, the MacLeod-MacDonalds.

Heinrich would have to watch himself with a member of such a powerful dynasty. Heinrich had been raised in the country as a boy, and then sent off to school as a youth. He hadn't needed to learn to swim in the ocean of the court nor learn the games of courtiers as Sextus.

He worried about making a mistake on the credentials of the woman, if she held a dynastic rank, or carried a title. Instead, he relaxed and decided to address her by her rank and surname.

"Thank you, Star Lieutenant MacDonald, you do me a great kindness," Heinrich replied.

"As you have shown my aunt, Primus, she is a poor creature living in her manor since the death of her son, my cousin Lewis. The protector was all she had left," Lieutenant MacDonald said.

Heinrich nodded and pulled a clean handkerchief from his pocket. He presented the embroidered handkerchiefs to the young woman and said, "Please accept this, on your aunt's behalf, that she may always dry her tears when she thinks of Karl, my grandfather. She may call upon me any time. Together we can talk of her days with my grandfather."

The naval officer blushed and hesitated before eventually taking the handkerchief. Heinrich felt stupid and embarrassed—his actions were an ancient tradition—until he watched the officer put the item in her small gray purse. His embarrassment faded as he realized the officer was safekeeping the item. Was the gift an unintentional treasure from the event?

Heinrich had followed the tradition because his grandfather had done similar actions countless times as Heinrich was growing up.

"Thank you, sir," Lieutenant MacDonald said turning her attention back to Heinrich. "Now with your leave, sir, farewell."

Heinrich nodded and stepped around the woman. If she had wanted anything else she made no attempt to stop Heinrich as he moved toward the door, stopping briefly to turn and see the two women with his dead grandfather.

Heinrich hesitated a heartbeat before he pushed through the doors. Behind him lay the Union's comforting past. As he traveled through the dim corridors of the protector's villa, Heinrich knew the dark foreboding future lay before him.

Part One

The War Begins

CHAPTER ONE

Primus and Peasant

A Cage of Gold

The day was gray and wet with a soft rain that drifted into people's faces and slowly soaked their clothes. Henry tried to focus on the Grand Minister of the Commons as she spoke from a dais in front of the main steps into Saint Malcolm's Cathedral before his grandfather's funeral service. Henry's parents disturbed him with their running commentary on the second minister's speech.

"You're sure she and Labor will go, Raimond?" asked Marta von Machthaber, Henry's mother and, now, Patroness of the Union. She was a canny politician who had maneuvered her husband to victory in his recent election. Candidates could not electioneer due to the selection protocols. However, spouses had no such injunctions.

Henry looked at his mother's steel gray hair that was immaculately coiffed and pulled into a side part up-do. She was a handsome older woman. She would give him a side glance every so often with her coppery brown eyes. Henry noted her cream complexion was made up with a modest makeup palette for the funeral. Additionally, she wore a full black dress that covered her from chin to ankle. Henry tried to not feel cynical about his mother's appearance. The public funeral was all theater. She, like his father, had known the old protector's remaining tenure was short. No one was sad at this funeral, except Heinrich.

"Yes, dear. I must dissolve the Parliament," said Raimond as he interrupted Henry's thoughts. "She and Solidarity don't have the votes to stay in power. Besides, she was riding out her predecessor's term. She may be popular in the polls, but the press uses such biased polling.

Who can tell what the Commons will do? That said, our internal analysts report that she is out and the Liberal Federalists will be in. Everyone says when she is out, she will be go... and go for good."

Henry wondered why his mother wanted the woman's blood. Henry should have reasoned out his parents' plans, but he had no energy to do so. Henry was disgusted by the political speeches and the speakers' grandstanding when they should have focused on his grandfather and his grandfather's accomplishments.

Heinrich looked to his brother Mathias, who cradled Henry's nephew, Rolf. The baby played with a tassel from Mathias's uniform, while Mathias's wife, Tanja, looked on impassively.

The wild thought occurred to Henry that Mathias could become the protector. Mathias smiled grimly, shaking his head 'no.' On a day like today, Mathias knew Henry's thoughts. Like his brother, Mathias was not interested in speeches and grandstanding either.

"Finally, she's done. Now, it is my turn at the podium," said Raimond.

The protector left his family and strode from his place to the podium. The journalists snapped pictures from their camera drones. The light was blinding. Other drones used small mapping lasers for the holocast images. Seeing his father standing at the podium tall and proud, Henry felt a small surge of pride. The new protector was one-hundred-and-ninety centimeters tall, a few centimeters taller than his average subject. He wore a plain Prussian-blue Assault uniform and a round officer's cap, emblazoned with the Union's heraldic dragon in front of crossed Anderson-Campbell pin rifles. The cap shielded the protector's hazel eyes from the mist and the drones' flashing lights. The protector's pants had a large silver stripe on the sides, the only mark of difference between the protector and an Assaultman.

Raimond looked out amongst the gathered, and he rubbed his freshly barbered face. Then he took his hat off and put the hat down softly on the podium. The action convened Assault regulations. His bald head was freshly shaved. As protector, Raimond could have had a mane of flowing hair grown in the best labs. Instead, Raimond desired to show that even the protector must accept the Allfather's will.

Since Karl's death, the press had used the protector's bald head as a sign Raimond was a war monger. Some idiot from the *Glückstadt Nexus Times* even commented, "The new protector keeps his head shaved in extreme Assaultman fashion, like at any moment he would climb into a drop capsule to put his jackboot on an enemy's throat.' These attacks infuriated Henry and his family since the headlines were a clear indication that the offending papers were just upset with the election's outcome.

"My sisters and brothers," the protector said interrupting Henry's thoughts, "for we are all a family, bound in Union. I come as a humble servant, to mourn for our lost father—a man who united us as a people. Together, we find purpose in our traditions, freedoms, and religion—things that the Terrans would forbid. Only the Allfather gives us the freedom to be who and what we are. We do not need permission nor do we have to conform to any Terran standards. Our Union is the last hope for freedom for humanity as we are the counterbalance to the rapacious Terran Directorate. We must awaken from our slumber! Come to your senses. The concept of freedom is only a heartbeat from being lost! Before my father died, he decried the fact that those who supported me wished to go to war. He said, 'You all yearn for the fire and sword! To climb the high mountain and put your face in the cold wind of fate.' These are the stern words of a father who doesn't wish to see his children hurt."

The protector paused for effect, before continuing. "But what must we do when a neighbor covets our property and would strip us of our rights and traditions? Do we not climb mountains to see the best way forward? Is not dangerous freedom preferable to peaceful slavery? Have we desired anything but the freedom to chart our own course in the eternal darkness of the cosmos?"

The Assaultmen nearby began a loud chant. The sergeants attempted to silence them, but the junior officers joined the shouting.

"Allfather! Union! Protector!" The chant became a grunting orchestra of approval. The pitch of the calls changed as a Navy detachment joined its brothers. The chant spread across all assembled. The Dynast hawks and their retainers joined the call. The commoners then joined in the chorus. Finally, the doves joined! Henry and his family picked up the cry.

Raimond had tears in his eyes, and his voice broke slightly as he said "Follow me! Today, we mourn our father. Tomorrow, we will gird ourselves to meet those who wish to deny us our Allfather-bestowed rights!" The protector turned and left the dais. He climbed a set of stairs and entered the large main doors of the Cathedral of Saint Malcolm.

The chant continued, others started to shout the Union's motto, "Unio omnia obligat!" Henry felt caught in the crowd's rush. At that moment, he would have crawled naked over broken glass for the Union. His father had, at least temporarily, united the people for the coming war with Terra. He remembered how at the end of "nightmare week" his tired and depleted squad had to lift a three hundred kilo log. Individually, none could carry the load even at when fresh. But after the forging of "nightmare week," the squad would, together, lift and hold the weight. Henry realized the protector had started forging the Felgenlanders into a nation that could support the trials of the upcoming war with the Terran Directorate.

Mathias looked to his brother with a grim smile, "Time to put that Assault training to good use, right, bro?"

"Mathias, look somber, the bloggers are photographing us," Marta said. "We don't need a headline that shows you grinning like a fool at this event."

"This was supposed to a be grandfather's funeral," Henry said to Mathias.

"Yes, but we know if he were here as a younger man, he'd have been the first one chanting," Mathias said. "Grandpa hated the Terrans more than anyone else I have ever met. Yes, he'll be missed, but the Terrans signed their death warrant at Asimov."

Heinrich nodded and brushed the now sleet off his brother's uniform. Mathias bore the ceremonial rank of colonel-in-chief, or *Stabsoberst,* of the Fifteenth Stahlburgh Rifle Regiment. Henry too was colonel-in-chief, only of the Ninth Regiment. Per tradition, Henry and Mathias were made ceremonial colonels at their father's ascension. Henry and Mathias still held their regular commissions. Henry was a captain or *Hauptmann* in the Seventy-Second Grenadiers. While Mathias, who was four years younger, was a lieutenant, or *Leutnant*, in the First Lochiel Dragoons.

Henry suddenly realized the crowd's chants were fading. The Dynasts had begun to enter the cathedral, and the moment they had felt collectively was over.

Henry eyed the cathedral. The structure had always given him an uneasy feeling. The cathedral was built on a place called the "Rock of the Saints" where the tyrants had slaughtered their enemies, real and perceived. After the protector had rid Stahlburgh of those evil people, the catacombs became the resting place of the Union's honored dead.

Henry hated entering the cathedral, he always thought he heard voices from the crypts. Some cried out in anguish, but others called out in ethereal joy.

Today, when Henry entered the cathedral was quiet. Henry had a sudden feeling that his grandfather's passing had silenced the voices, perhaps only for today. Henry felt sadness as he followed his mother to the protector's pews in the private balcony above the masses below. These were the pews his grandfather had occupied on Sundays, and religious ceremonies. Henry half expected to see the old man appear, in his resplendent Assault uniform.

Henry remembered being in the cathedral for a wedding. Today,

Henry could only think of his grandfather and his own change in station. As Primus, he was now in training as a servant to the people, his people. If he was worthy, he would be chosen to protect them... one day.

Henry looked at the massive crucifix hanging above the altar. Christ looked from his cross, his throne, forlorn and pained. The look reflected his heart. Henry directed his gaze below to the right of the altar where a small chaplet had the eternal burning flame of Malcolm. Malcolm had brought the Felgenland back to God, yet his reward was to be crucified and then burned on his cross.

A long procession of priests, reverends, vicars, and deacons filed into the cathedral and interrupted Henry's thoughts. After the clerics came the commoners. The procession was yet another sign of Henry's future. He watched the lines of people. As protector, he would spend the rest of his life in service to these people. Henry felt frustration at being the heir of the protector. He was supposed to be Sixtus, and after his uncle's, supposedly assured, ascension, Henry would have moved off the list of the Cognatii altogether.

Henry's angst was stemmed by the appearance of the arch-cardinal, his cousin, at the end of the long procession. The chief cleric paced in with acolytes and he swung a burning brand of incense that billowed smoke. Even stories above the procession, Henry smelled the earthy, deep scent.

"By our God, the Allfather of the Universe, his son, Jesus the Son of Man, and the Eternal Holy Spirit, we pray for our lost spiritual father, Karl, our late protector, anointed by the Allfather and Malcolm to lead us these many decades," the arch-cardinal said.

"Saint Aaron of Nebraska," the arch-cardinal said.

"Pray for us," Henry and the congregation responded.

"Saint Augustine of Hippo."

"Pray for us."

"Saint Balthazar of Arcadia."

"Pray for us."

"Saint Blaise."

"Pray for us."

"Saint Clara of Mars," the arch-cardinal said. Henry suddenly realized this would be a full Central Orthodoxy funeral. He'd be stuck listening to the entire litany of saints. Henry felt smothered by the cloying incense. As the service continued, he felt better after the air conditioning came on and cleared the incense. By the time the consecration and communion came, Henry had control of his unhappiness. By the final blessing, Henry had relaxed. Whatever was bothering him had disappeared. He considered whether he wanted to stay in the Bundstadt or head to what he considered was his home, his father's *Schloss* in the country.

"Henry, Mathias, you are dismissed," said the protector. "Your mother and I will remain to pray for my father's soul."

Henry and his brother stood. Mathias looked to his wife who now held their son. She too stood and they left. Henry looked again at the cross. He crossed himself and then left via another corridor.

"Phew! I thought you'd never get bored enough to leave, Primus!" said Henry's valet when Henry strode out into the corridor. The valet fell into step with his master.

"Have some respect, Johann," Henry said, "you, of all people, need more boredom and more church services."

"That is not why your parents selected me as your valet and bodyguard, sir."

"They selected you, Johann *Markgraf* Strass of the March of Kildromey, because you are a high aristocrat, from a leading, yet neutral, dynasty on Lochiel and a single man."

"Exactly," Johann said, "I am an irresponsible companion, far more likely to get you to bed a high-born wench! Then your parents get the male heir they want to cement the dynasty! I'm an agent of destiny!"

Henry scowled at his valet.

Johann continued, "Of course, the heir needs to be a boy, since the Felgenland still has trouble believing women can vote or lead. I am an enlightened man. I prefer an aggressive take-charge female. One who knows just what she wants when she sees me. I love when she climbs my volcanic cliff face just like old General Schwarzenrode at the Battle of the Landing, and then she comes around to my rear for some good hammer and anvil action."

Henry looked at the valet, disgusted. The man had just compared his illicit behavior to the maneuvers at the Battle of the Landing. The battle that had facilitated Henry's grandfather, Karl, the victory over the old tyrants. After the Battle of the Landing, Karl created the Union. Johann was a known libertine and carried his reputation as a cad as a badge of honor.

"Do you wake up in the morning, Johann, and think 'Maybe today I will clean the vomit off of my liege's uniform?'"

"No, sir," Johann said. "You are an Assaultman and can hold your liquor but only passably, you lightweight."

"My vomit would come from your predilection to share your perverted sex life with me," Henry said.

"Technically, sir, the vomit would come from your mouth."

Henry fumed silently. Johann had an irritating ability to find Henry's metaphorical red button and break his finger pushing it.

"I'll be driving to *Schloss* Machthaber at Greiff-im-Wald. You are dismissed until I return to the capital," Henry said.

"Understood, sir. Although I'd advise that the ladies of the capital have much more to offer than the barnyard maiden you must have stashed in the sticks," Johann said.

"What you are calling 'the sticks' is the village that has been my home for twenty-five years. Get lost before you offend me even more."

Johann did not respond, but bowed slightly, smiling. He straightened, turned, and left. Henry knew the valet was happy to be able to slink off to some gutter to find a companion, preferably of questionable morals, with whom to spend the night.

Henry navigated through the cathedral's labyrinthine halls, chambers, and alcoves. He knew them by heart from the many religious ceremonies he attended growing up. After several minutes of walking, Henry appeared at the top of the stairs to the darkened subterranean parking garage. He descended the four flights of stairs that were reserved for the protector, aristocracy, and politicos. The stairs ended in the garage where the very important persons had parked their vehicles. Stepping off the stairs he was stopped by an Assaultman in his dress uniform who challenged Henry.

"Leaving so soon, Primus?" asked Alasdair *GroßHerzog* Campbell of Inveraray and the Argylle Islands.

"Yes, your grace. I'm leaving for my country estate. Please inform the protector that I will return early in the morning," Henry responded. "Now stand aside and let me pass this checkpoint."

GroßHerzog Campbell wore an Assault uniform with silver shoulder boards. On the shoulder boards were the double acorns and laurel wreath of an *Oberstleutnant,* or lieutenant colonel. On Campbell's left collar was a medallion of silver showing a heart in front of crossed Anderson-Campbell pin rifles, on the right was a silver number two. Henry remembered the heart emblem belonged the Second Stahlburgh Rifles, the Line Guards. The Line Guards defended the protector, the protector's family, and the capital city. The *Kreigskanzler*, the War Chancellor of the Union hand selected Line Guard's officers from the best of the aristocracy. The enlisted were chosen on merit and excellent conduct. A Line Guard position was a duty that always led to something greater. The middle-aged Campbell looked at the Primus and asked, "Where is your valet, sir?"

"I dismissed him," Henry said. "Why? Do you expect trouble today?"

Campbell paused, his face stoic. A moment passed while Campbell looked pensive. He then said, "No, sir. My instinct, as commander of the Battalion of the Presence, is to be overly cautious. I've held this position for ten years, and guarded your grandfather. But, times have changed. Now, I must bend to new wills. I cannot stop you, of course. You are free to your own leisure and counsel. Please allow me to at least send an Assaultman with you. He will return with you tomorrow or via military transport the day after."

Henry hadn't wanted to get stopped by the Line Guards, doubly so by their commander. Henry studied the lieutenant colonel. Campbell was representative of many of the Dynasts: dour, tradition-bound, stern, and uncompromising. Henry suspected the Assaultman was a "minder" and did not want to be chaperoned in his own home. While seemingly cautious, Henry suspected Campbell had ulterior motives. The Campbells had reputations as notorious social climbers, and rapacious businessmen and women. Besides, this was the Bundstadt, the Union's capital city. If Henry wasn't safe here, he was not safe anywhere.

"No, thank you, your grace," Henry said, "I will take an unmarked hovercar and drive out the secondary exit. I don't require an escort detail. I will keep a low profile."

"Are you certain, sir?" Campbell asked. The lieutenant colonel seemed to be probing the kind of man he was. Henry paused. He considered that perhaps the cautious Line Guard was merely covering his backside if, by some quirk of fate, there was trouble.

"Positively certain, your grace," Henry replied. Campbell nodded and stepped aside to allow the Primus to pass the checkpoint. Henry went to the motor pool and collected a key fob from a vending machine. After finding the plain black hovercar, Henry climbed into the driver seat and pressed the ignition. The fans whirred to life and Henry programmed the driving computer's destination for his *Schloss.* He'd decided to maintain control until he was on the main parkway out of the capital. Henry mused that the countryside would be a peaceful respite from the capital. The hovercar exited the secondary parking entrance and burst out into Kocher square. Henry looked up, admiring the statue of Lena, his revered ancestor. The one-hundred-meter statue was a magnificent work his grandfather had erected after forming the Union. Henry marveled at the statue of his grandfather's great-grandmother. The statue of Lena stood defiantly holding the flame of freedom in her right hand while casting off the shackles of slavery with her left.

Henry focused on driving as he merged into traffic. In the flow of hovercars, Henry grew bored with driving and moved the control dial to full auto. Then, he disengaged the driver's couch from the controls. The driving computer was following the plotted route. Henry was free to lounge, sleep, watch a video, or sample something from the mini-bar while the driving computer dealt with the heavy capital city traffic. Henry was about to roll the couch around to take a nap, when he noticed an older hovercar threading dangerously through traffic. He re-engaged the couch and took back the vehicle's control from the driving computer. Henry's Assault training made him cautious of such a reckless vehicle.

The older hovercar moved parallel to the driver's side of Henry's vehicle. As the vehicles matched speed, the older hovercar's passenger side window opened and Henry saw a balaclava wearing man lean out of the window and raise a shoulder-mounted, rocket-propelled grenade (RPG) launcher. The man aimed the weapon.

Henry slammed on the brakes. The traffic behind him honked and swerved around him. Before speeding past Henry's vehicle the man fired the weapon. The rocket-propelled grenade missed the driving compartment but sliced through the gravity pressed armored casing around the engine and battery of Henry's vehicle. The warhead, meant for a tank or armored personnel carrier, entered and exited the vehicle's engine block. The round finally hit a marble plinth on the roadside and exploded. Henry gripped the wheel as he saw the control panel on the hovercar go dark. Henry fought the vehicle's controls as the hovercar skidded across the road and slid into the middle of an open plaza.

"Come on, come on! Just a few more meters!" Henry said. Henry tried to will the hovercar to reach the plaza's other side where he could find better cover. The car finally halted as the power to the fans died.

Henry didn't waste any time. He knew that he couldn't stay and wait for help with the assassins still active. Henry's training kicked in, and he needed to move. He rotated his arm and pressed the emergency alert on a new item given to his family by Huegel Electronics. Worn on the forearm, the device was a streamlined tablet with GPS tracking that was supposedly accurate on every Union world. The Huegels had cheekily branded the device the "Electronic Vambrace Information Liaison" or EVIL for short. Henry pressed the release latch and push the driver's door, but nothing happened.

Henry quickly climbed over the hovercar's center console to the passenger side. He pushed against the door as he pressed the release. The door budged, but only a little. Henry needed more force. Henry pressed the release, braced himself, and pushed the door with his entire body. The passenger door scraped as metal rubbed on metal, but the door opened with a groan. Henry climbed out and quickly scanned the plaza. The assassin's vehicle had spun around a roundabout and collided with another vehicle. A half dozen assassins piled out of the wreck and began shooting as they made their way towards him. Henry started running when he heard the report of their weapons opening fire.

The guns thrummed with an ack-ack-ack sound that Henry had heard before—on Asimov. He instantly identified the sound of the guns as a Terran-made Armnikov-2347 or AN-47. The light machine gun was cheap and mass produced in the Earth's mega-factories.

The assassins were less than a kilometer away making Henry well within the AN-47's range. Henry realized he had been staring at the enemy instead of moving. Battlefield survival doctrine dictated that staying anywhere longer than three seconds under rifle fire would get you killed.

Henry ran for one of the long square plascrete pay toilets that appeared every hundred meters in rest plazas like the one Henry had crashed into. Henry was maybe thirty meters from the toilet, but the building seemed light years away. Henry ran and then slid behind the bunker-like public toilet. Running, he'd heard the enemy's slugs skipping along the pavement behind him. Henry checked his EVIL, realizing it was only three minutes since the RPG had hit the hovercar.

Henry was safe for the moment behind the toilet. He'd stay there just long enough to find his next bit of cover. Henry peered around the corner to determine where the assassins were. Cars crashed into each other as the assassins fired hassium rounds at anyone or anything that moved. Henry realized that this wasn't just an attempt on his life but a concerted effort to sow terror and chaos in the capital. Henry decided next his piece of cover was a small plinth that connected to a guard rail. Henry hopped up and ran toward the plinth. Closing the distance, he dropped behind the small decorative platform. Catching his breath, Henry pressed his EVIL, and said, "This is TEUTONIC PRINCE. I am under fire! I've activated my emergency tracker and request immediate help."

While waiting for a response, Henry searched for his next spot of cover. Suddenly a pressure wave knocked him back. A mortar had exploded twenty meters from his position. Adrenaline flooded his system as Henry scanned the plaza and the road for the mortar crew. He couldn't find the enemy but he did see all the casualties that the terrorists created. Men and women lay bleeding out, cars burned, hassium char and slug-holes peppered the facades. A small girl lay dead, still clutching her doll, mere meters from the Primus. The plaza was a charnel house. Henry's stomach turned, even though he had seen his share of death on the battlefield.

From the western parkway, terrorists started swarming the road.

They all wore dark balaclavas and black tactical jackets with black trousers and boots. Henry quickly counted forty terrorists. The terrorist moved methodically down the street shooting anyone who was still alive. Seeing the carnage, Henry wished for an Anderson-Campbell 2350 Mark 4 pin rifle, the Assault's main battle rifle. Even with a rifle, Henry realized he was no match against forty enemies. Yet he yearned to payback the terrorists for all their death and destruction.

The terrorists moved another twenty meters closer to Henry's position, but then scattered into anti-air formation. Henry briefly glanced up as the wind kicked up on the street. A Union Navy dropship appeared overhead. The dropship's waist turrets started belching tracer pins temporarily causing confusion with the terrorists and halting their mayhem. The dropship's belly ramp thumped open. Henry watched expectantly for Assaultmen to belay into the plaza. Seeing nothing from the dropship's belly, Henry decided to move to a fountain with a large base thirty meters away.

Henry popped up and ran. The terrorists bent on his death left cover to fire at him. The dropship immediately returned fire ending the lives of those who dared attack.

Henry reached the public fountain. The pavement was pitted from the shelling. A loud explosion made the ground quake as the dropship fired a missile, presumably at the mortal crew. Henry took the explosion to run towards another spot, farther away. As he stood to run, Henry tripped and tumbled on the cratered pavement. He fell three meters from where he had been. He felt white hot pain in his left ankle. He scrambled to stand and cover the distance back towards the fountain's cover, but the terrorists surged forward after he tried to stand but couldn't. The dropship picked off a half dozen, but the terrorists scented his blood and would not be denied. Henry watched in anguish as they approached. He hoped that they would kill him quickly. He had no desire to suffer the ignominy of being a prisoner.

The terrorists charged to within ten meters of his position. Henry tried to crawl away, but the terrorists were going to overtake him. Henry steadied himself for what would come next. He hoped that after his death the dropship would end every one of these monsters. He closed his eyes as the hassium rounds, hastily fired, landed around him. He heard the ack-ack-ack of the AN-47s ring in his ears along with the whine of the dropship guns. He opened his eyes and looked at the terrorists. He would die like a man. The terrorists in haste and excitement began to clump up. Henry prayed to the Allfather for a rifle. With a pin rifle he would have mowed down the fools who ran at him shoulder to shoulder and back to front like sheep.

As the terrorist closed to five meters, they started falling as green bohrium rounds poured into their amateur attack formation. Henry watched in amazement like he had conjured their deaths by magic.

A squad of Line Guards materialized around the Primus. Time dilated as Henry watched the remaining terrorists come closer and he heard the soft clicks of the Line Guards' rifles. The deadly bohrium quickly cut down the front rank of terrorists. The scene reminded Henry of farmers with scythes cutting wheat during the fall harvest.

The Line Guards wore Assault battle suits with exposed wires and all manner of LED lights. The rainbow lights pulsating across the battlesuits hypnotized Henry. Henry recalled hearing about a special project that could cloak a warrior. Apparently, these were the prototypes.

The Line Guards' squad leader began to move and signaled the squad to advance. The leader fired into the mass of terrorists until his rifle's magazine went empty and then switched to his service pistol as he continued to advance. A terrorist shot at the leader with a slug thrower. The leader shrugged off the slug rounds. His squad advanced to almost point-blank range practically firing their weapons in the terrorists' faces.

Henry crossed himself and offered thanks to the Allfather. The Line Guards today were avenging angels who cut down the mayhem-causing terrorists. The fighting ended as the remaining terrorists raised their arms in surrender.

One of the Line Guards came forward, and asked, "Primus, are you all right?"

"Other than a sprained ankle, yes," Henry said. Henry scanned for the Assaultman's rank and added, "color sergeant."

"Colonel is coming over to you, sir," the color sergeant said. The sergeant dropped to one knee and checked the Primus' ankle.

"I'm going to give you a painkiller. You'll be able to stand on the ankle, but you'll need a doc to check out the injury, sir," the sergeant said. Henry nodded, and the sergeant jabbed the Primus with a small battlefield anesthetic. Henry stood as the squad leader approached.

"ID check please, sir," the squad leader said. As Henry approached the leader's chest plate had the small battlefield emblem that designated its wearer as a lieutenant colonel.

Henry nodded, and said, "Ready for check, colonel."

The lieutenant colonel asked, "First question, what is your paternal grandmother's middle name?"

"Thora, for her mother," Henry replied. The man checked the response on his battlefield hardened EVIL.

"Confirmed. Second question: please give me your military identification number."

"One-one-seven-bravo-November-six-nine-three-nine," said Henry rattling off the numbers with ease.

"Confirmed. Third question: what was the name of your first pet, and what species was the pet?"

"Theodoros, he was a miniature schnauzer," Henry said with a pang of sadness, as he thought of the long dead puppy.

"Confirmed," the squad leader said, raising his visor and exposing Alasdair Campbell's face. Campbell put his hand on his helmet, trying to jam the helmet's ear-bud deeper into his ear to hear the faint radio chatter.

"Yes! We have him! Yes! We have a confirmation! Blast it, Obersturmheim! I just confirmed him!" Henry guessed Campbell spoke to the Procurator-General Erich *Herzog* Obersturmheim, the Line Guard regiment commander.

"Yes! Tell the Lord Protector, that he is fine! Yes! Yes! We captured thirteen of them! No, General. Yes, we'll convene the tribunal! Wait, why would I hand these *scum* to a civilian court? Yes, we're assembling now, sir. Campbell out."

During his call, Campbell had repeated himself several times and sounded like he was trying to explain the situation to a child. Henry had heard the rumors that the general was well past his prime and knew his father planned to request the general's resignation.

"Primus, would you be so kind as to bear witness at this military tribunal, since you were a victim," asked Campbell.

"Wait... Why not send these butchers to a court of law?" Henry asked, surprised that Campbell planned to hold an immediate military trial. Outside the Union home planets, tribunals, courts-martial, and extra-judicial proceedings were common. However, Stahlburgh had not seen martial court proceedings since Karl's Unification War.

"Orders from on high, sir," replied Campbell laconically. The squad lined up the thirteen surviving terrorists in front of the colonel. Henry crossed himself at the unlucky number. He wanted to be done with this affair and headed to the countryside, where he knew he would be safe, personally and politically.

The Line Guards forced most of the terrorists to their knees while two large guards led the first terrorist to stand before the colonel.

Two Assaultmen bearing captain's acorns arrived. Henry suspected Campbell had summoned the men over the radio. Campbell plus the two captains were the three judges required for the tribunal. Henry nodded inwardly, Campbell was strictly following the Articles of War. Two more Assault officers appeared while the enlisted Line Guards began to cordon off the area. With the fighting over, the crowds began gathering. Most wanted to see what was happening, but some of the onlookers began shouting at the Assaultmen.

"Kill those butchers!"

"The bastard Assaultmen started this chaos!"

Campbell coolly ignored the shouts. He shut his faceplate and turned on his external speakers.

Campbell said, "Ensign Trochter will advocate for the defense, while Ensign Bergdorf will advocate for the protector."

"Aye, sir," both men replied via their external speakers.

"Ensigns Trochter and Bergdorf, have either of you won a case in a civilian court of law?" Campbell asked. Henry remembered this from his battlefield law class at the Academy. The Articles of War were explicit; in a tribunal one side couldn't have an unfair advantage. An Assaultman who was a civil legal advocate and an officer could use the tribunal to dominate his less experienced opponent.

"No, sir," replied both men.

"Ensigns Trochter and Bergdorf, have you been briefed and participated in a tribunal before?"

"Yes, sir, I took the class at Steinthal," Trochter replied.

"Yes, sir, I remember battlefield law at the Academy," said Bergdorf.

"The tribunal has three officers as judges and the required advocates. Therefore, I hereby declare this tribunal lawfully assembled," said Campbell.

"State your name," Campbell said sternly.

The man spat on the ground and said, "According to the Treaty of Fomalhaut, I am a prisoner of war. I am a dissident and I do not agree to be judged by the 'so called' protector's lackeys. I demand acceptable counsel!"

"You were caught committing acts of terrorism against the Union's citizens. You are not members of a foreign military nor are you partisans. You did not fight under a lawful banner, and you targeted civilians. We are still tallying the number of people you have murdered

—all in cold blood. Now, quit arguing! How do you plead?" Campbell said.

"Not guilty!" replied the man. The rough looking man gave an ugly and smug smile. Henry waited to see if the tribunal would defer the matter to a civilian court. Henry had puzzled out the terrorist's gambit. The terrorist was attempting to abuse the Union's laws to escape the tribunal's swift judgment. The terrorist knew public opinion always swayed a civilian court. In the urban and political courts of the Bundstadt a civilian judge's need for reelection would be a good hedge against the terrorists receiving a death sentence from the courts. Henry realized quislings had coached the terrorists.

"Per the protector's edict, this tribunal will move forward in its proceedings," Campbell said. Henry looked surprised at the bold move. The protector could use edicts to pass judgment, but only after a declaration of emergency by Parliament.

"By what edict, bootlicker?!" asked the terrorist, spitting on the ground at Campbell's feet.

"The Edict of Order, declared by the first protector, Karl, in Anno Domini 2269. The Parliament has never rescinded the emergency conditions that generated the edict; therefore, the law remains valid," Campbell said.

Campbell then looked at Henry, "In the absence of the protector, the edict provides that the Primus, or other Cognatii, may validate the tribunal's authority. The edict has survived many challenges over the years in the Union's supreme judicial court. Therefore, tribunals are considered constitutional. Now, does the defendant have any other questions?"

Henry felt betrayed. If Henry assented to the tribunal, and Campbell's obvious desire to try these terrorists, Henry would be giving the man a blank check. Campbell would become judge, jury, and perhaps even executioner. Henry remembered his father talking about how edicts required a great deal of political capital to enact.

Would his father, the new Protector of the Union, be able to deal with the political fallout Henry's assent could create?

The terrorist's face showed his worry, and he said, "Mercy, Primus! I request mercy!"

Before the terrorist spoke, Henry had been hesitant to give Campbell his assent, but the craven terrorist's plea enraged him. At that moment, Henry could only envision the dead girl, killed by these monsters who showed her no mercy. The girl was only slightly older than Henry's nephew, and—escaping justice—these monsters would have rejoiced at the Bundstadt's destruction and her murder.

"Lieutenant Colonel Campbell, you can proceed," Henry said. He would be damned before he let these monsters run to a politically influenced civilian court.

"Judges, do you need to hear any arguments from the advocates?" Campbell asked.

"No, sir," the two officer judges stated. Henry nodded; the officers of the tribunal were equally upset at the cowardly terrorist's pleas.

"Unfortunately, the use of lawfare against this tribunal leaves me no room in sentencing," Campbell said. "Judges, what is your verdict?"

"Guilty," said the first captain.

"Guilty," said the second.

"I concur, the prisoner is guilty. Advocates, any objections on form or order?" Campbell asked.

"The protector's advocate is satisfied," said Ensign Bergdorf.

"The defender's advocate can find no argument in which to exonerate his charge. In other circumstances, I would request the tribunal consider mercy in its sentence. However, we must maintain an orderly society. Therefore this tribunal must make an example, so all know that no one is above the law," said Ensign Trochter.

"Agreed. Prisoner, this court has no choice but to sentence you to immediate execution for your role in the slaughter of people of the Union. Say your prayers and prepare to meet your maker," Campbell stated. Henry weighed what was happening. He knew he should be irritated at being used by Campbell, but Henry also felt the terrorist had violated something sacred when he tried to escape his crimes.

"Please, no! I don't want to die," the terrorist screamed.

"Sergeant, perform your duty!" Campbell said. One of the Line Guards next to the terrorist pulled the terrorist away from Henry, the advocates, and judges. The terrorist continued to cry. He begged for mercy and shouted that he was being framed for murder. The cries excited the crowd. Some of the louder crowd members began fighting with each other. Henry began to worry the mob would grow larger than the Line Guards could manage. The crowd's yells halted when the terrorist was pushed by the sergeant, face first, against a nearby building's concrete foundation and shot in the back of his head. Henry watched as the blood from the terrorist sprayed all over, and the corpse bled out on the city concrete.

"The rest of the accused, take note, we shoot mad dogs," Campbell said. "Next prisoner, we have twelve more proceedings."

The remaining terrorists continued the same gambit the first had attempted. Henry tried to find sympathy for the terrorists, but grew numb to their cries. Henry began to become more irritated with Campbell who had used him. Henry acknowledged Campbell was in a way performing some small act of justice. However, Henry also realized the press would go after him and his family, not Campbell.

The undertakers were the only happy ones at the sight of thirteen dead terrorists, since they would get quite a nice sum from the Protector's Villa to bury the corpses. Henry looked at the terrorists' bodies stacked neatly in body bags along the sidewalk. The proceedings and executions had been swift. All thirteen terrorist fools sounded like robots each repeating the same arguments. Henry couldn't understand why one of the terrorists hadn't tried another tact. Were the fools so programmed they couldn't think for themselves?

Naturally, halfway through the tribunals the press had arrived. Henry smirked. "Concerned citizens" had likely "notified" them so they could report on how this massacre was the Assault's fault. Henry thought sourly of how the press believed his father was just a militarist jackboot.

Shortly after the news corps' arrival, independent bloggers and audcasters crowded around the press corps. Campbell had paused sentencing to expand the cordon and eject the journos from within earshot of the immediate tribunal site. Some of the more stubborn, or stupid, journos had locked their heels and refused until Campbell had threatened to arrest them. When the journos retreated to a designated press space, they stopped their cries of "liberty of the press!" Campbell was no fool. He owned several estates and didn't want the news to whip up an angry mob of peasants that would burn his beautiful homes to their foundations.

Having performed his duty, Henry began to look for an exit. During the tribunal proceedings, armored personnel carriers had appeared ferrying Assaultmen, both constabulary guards and Line Guards into the area. Henry spied a waiting transport and moved towards it. The journos sensed the show was over and noticed one of their quarry was escaping. The news men and women began to shout questions at Henry.

"Primus! What was your involvement in this incident?"

"Were you involved in the fighting?"

"Is that one of the protector's hovercars smoking over there?"

"Machthaber, can we get a statement?"

Henry attempted to ignore the reporters. Colonel Campbell gave orders to two Line Guards to escort the Primus to the APC. The men strode next to Henry protectively. Henry noted the Line Guards protected him from the reporters like the news men and women were terrorists also.

"Henry!" called one of the journalists, "*Yaist News—Felgenland*, can you confirm whether the Assault planned this atrocity?"

Campbell moved behind Henry, opened his face plate, and leaned in to Henry. He said, "Wisdom is being silent, sir. Do not give them the opportunity or they will just drag your name through the gutter."

Henry felt instantly insulted. Henry was in this position because Campbell had used him. Henry figured the press would blame him and his family. Moving forward, Henry decided he wasn't going to listen Campbell's advice. The journo's question, made Henry's blood boil. The Line Guards had stopped the terrorists' mayhem. Then the tribunal had taken out the remaining garbage. Henry wasn't going to let the press write their own history!

"Out of my way," Henry snapped, breaking free of the Line Guards.

Henry moved closer to the journo. The news man stood, like a red caped matador flagging a bull. The journalist smiled as Henry approached. The news man was middle aged but had a boyish face. Henry recognized him. The news man was an anchor on a corporate network until a scandal forced him to become an independent journo. Henry tried to remember the incident. Henry's parents had discussed the news man at length after he went independent. Henry recognized he had gone too far into the journo's trap to escape without embarrassment.

"I'm sorry, who are you with," Henry asked.

"I'm Carl Tuckson, I'm an independent with thirty million followers. I see you are pretty distraught, sir. Are you alright? Can you tell me what happened here?"

Henry paused, but then said, "Ah yes, I remember. You interviewed my father before the election. You were fair in your questions."

Tuckson smiled and said, "Good to know! Can I have a statement?" The other reporters crowded around the journo with their recording devices out hoping to catch some of the conversation.

Henry nodded and said, "Terrorists surrounded the streets and attacked this plaza. Like many others, I was trapped in the war zone.

Thankfully, Lieutenant Colonel Campbell and the Line Guards stopped the terrorists and prevented more death and destruction."

"I see," Tuckson said, "Anything else?"

"Yes, the Line Guard's heroism was the only thing that stood between these terrorists and the rest of the city. The Guards' quick response and bravery prevented the terrorists from murdering more people."

"Primus! What about the terrorists' summary executions?" asked another journo. Henry debated his next statement. He could easily blame Campbell, who had shamelessly used him to hold the tribunals.

"I validated the tribunal," Henry said. The statement wasn't the best response, but Henry was being honest. "The Edict of Order from 2269 still stands. Colonel Campbell did his job. He remains, as always, a loyal Assaultman of the Felgenland Union."

The gathered men and women went crazy. Journos started yelling all manner of questions at Henry. The roar of discordant voices prevented Henry from understanding any of the questions.

Otto Weber, the Villa's majordomo, used his large frame to push Henry past the journos. Weber's push was firm but respectful, and Henry knew Weber was acting on the protector's orders. Weber's commanding voice called out, "No more questions! Can't you see the strain on the Primus! I assure you, the Villa will issue a statement soon."

The press continued to badger the majordomo, who continued to coolly stress that neither he nor the Primus would make any additional comments. Henry entered the APC and Campbell followed. Henry knew Weber would remain until he left, then the majordomo would meet him back at the Villa. Henry sat on the bench seat and the colonel sat down next to him. The APC's ramp closed and the engine revved. Henry was leaving the site.

"You are a bloody stupid, boy," the colonel said pulling off his helmet.

"You're welcome, Campbell," Henry said flatly in response.

"You never engage with those press mongrels! You should have never given the terrorists an opportunity to begin with! I offered to have an Assaultman escort you! Instead, what did you do? You almost got yourself killed! You pompous little brat!"

"I don't answer to you," said Henry. "Just do your job and stay out of my way! I'm not my uncle! I can handle myself in a fight!"

Henry grew more annoyed by Campbell's attitude the longer he sat there. The man had seriously overstepped his station. Worse, now Campbell felt like he could give an order to the Primus, the heir and first citizen of the Union!

"Listen," said the colonel arrogantly. "I'm only trying to help you! You are Primus! You need to think about more than yourself! What happens next time the terrorists attack you? Next time, our enemies may put you into a spot from which you can't escape! You think the terrorists were acting alone? The Terran Directorate will use every method to try to take you, or other Cognatii, out. You are now a symbol of the Union's future! You need to stop being so reckless!" Henry felt like the social climbing noble had stepped on his pride.

Henry waited a moment and then said, "Thank you, Campbell. I believe we are done now."

The lieutenant colonel snapped his helmet on and proceeded to ignore the Primus as the APC rolled through the city.

Henry noticed the buildings increasing in height. His heart sank as he saw the looming spire of Saint Malcolm's Cathedral through one of the small tactical windows. He was headed for the Protector's Villa. It was the last place he desired to be at this moment. The meager light disappeared as the APC entered the Villa's subterranean garages. After a few minutes the APC stopped and its rear hatch opened. Two Line Guards stood waiting; they saluted as the lieutenant colonel exited. Henry waited a moment for Campbell to disappear and then exited. The Assaultmen again snapped to attention. Henry went to the private elevator for the protector and his family. An Assaultman now guarded the elevator. He snapped to attention as Henry approached. The lift appeared and Henry entered. The elevator's console scanned Henry's EVIL and the doors closed. A moment later, the elevator moved upwards.

The doors opened, and Henry's mother stood before him visibly upset. She rushed forward and embraced him. She said, "What were you thinking! You could have been killed!"

"Mother, I am all right. The terrorists were sloppy and thankfully the Line Guards arrived just in time."

"My son, never do something so foolish! I mean it! Don't ever do that again! You now owe that man a favor! You don't think he will use that favor against you?"

"Where is my father?" Henry said breaking his mother's embrace. He now realized why she was so upset. Henry had expended his parent's political capital. At the moment, he was tired and didn't feel like being insulted by his mother. Henry's ankle throbbed and all he wanted was to go to his bed and rest.

"The protector is handling this mess," she responded. "Your actions have complicated things. He will need to accelerate our timetables! That means we will need to offer favors we never planned to offer. Henry, Henry, what a mess!"

"What do you mean, mother? There was no mess."

"Oh yes, this is a mess!" the patroness said, "The *Glückstadt Nexus Times* has already published a story with the headline 'Power Mad Primus Kills Peasants!' This is the headline citizens in our most populous city will read in the morning. Your father is consulting with his privy council on damage control."

Henry felt his rage rising. Damage control? The terrorists had slaughtered hundreds! Now, the press was using his title to sell purposely salacious articles! Murdered innocents immediately forgotten for quick corporate profits!

"We can deal with the press later," The protector said entering the room. “We have our own press. Not every paper is hostile towards us. Now, Henry, are you all right? USIS’s Domestic Branch has already issued a report from the camera feeds from downtown. USIS’ report said you did well, considering the situation.”

“Yes, sir. Thank you,” Henry said.

“Oh no, don’t misunderstand me. I’m not impressed by your actions, son. Due to this incident you’ll have to spend a few more weeks here on Stahlburgh,” The protector said.

“But! I’m slated to deploy with the MjGAs. I’ve been training for almost six months for the insertion on Nakdong!”

“We’ve canceled that operation. Look, I can’t let you leave now, son. The press will say I’m secreting you away,” said the protector.

“Sounds like you have more for me, father,” Henry said. He dearly loved his parents, but at times he felt like their lowest priority.

“Yes, you owe Lieutenant Colonel Campbell a thank you. I’ve announced a banquet and ball in his honor.”

Henry frowned.

“What, son?” his father asked.

“You know I dislike banquets and balls of honor,” Henry said.

“Why?” his mother asked, “There will be ladies there and you can invite your friends.”

“Mother, the fêtes are full of boors and sycophants. No one is real or truthful at those events,” Henry said.

“Yes, but they allow us to spread favor and patronage,” the patroness said. “Plus, you can repair your image with the press. All of that is important as one of the Cognatii.”

“I see I am to be punished, though I have done nothing to deserve it,” Henry replied

“Mind yourself,” his father replied. “This is not the country anymore. This place has ears.”

Henry had been having a fight about matchmaking with his parents since he turned seventeen. His parents often dangled him out as a prize to sycophants with their even less than charming daughters. Now, instead of the country folk, Henry was to be the prize of the urban burghers and their self-centered daughters.

"As you wish, sir," Henry said, becoming equally laconic. He knew when his parents were unhappy.

"If you were married, you would have a wife to share your burdens," Henry's mother said. "Look at your brother."

Henry frowned; he hated these discussions the most. The pressure to marry had been intense as his grandfather grew increasingly ill. Henry's parents wanted him to find a woman to cement an alliance. They constantly suggested candidates and Henry rejected them. Henry liked women. He just detested his parents' choices. Many of the women were beautiful but without substance. Most were vain and selfish. The rest of the women in private were crude or boorish. Henry's foremost objection was that he wanted to choose his spouse. After all, he would have to live with the woman for the rest of his life barring unforeseen circumstances.

"Go to bed and get some rest," the protector said as he dismissed his son. The protector knew there was no sense in creating more family drama so late in the day.

Henry bowed, and reflexively headed for the elevators to his parent's previous apartments.

Otto Weber intercepted Henry. Weber was like an uncle to Henry. The man had been a part of the Protector's Villa for as long as Henry could remember. When Henry and Weber were younger, Henry would demand to ride on the man's broad shoulders and Weber would oblige him. Weber would pretend to be the noble steed for Henry's chivalric knight. These days, Weber was a man whom Henry could confide in, knowing that Weber valued his integrity more than his life.

"This way, Primus. You are now the master of the Protelan Suite," Weber said.

"Weber, you can still call me Henry."

"I know, Primus," Weber said, "but I find your new position in the Cognatii thrilling. If you would prefer, I shall continue to call you Henry in private."

"I suppose I understand," Henry replied.

"I know all this must be difficult for you," said Weber softly. "You don't recognize the honor you have received."

"No, I don't really, Weber," said Henry.

"Follow me to your new apartments. Perhaps, I can offer you some perspective, since I've served your family for over sixty years."

"I didn't know that, Weber," Henry said.

"I started when I was a toddler," Weber said with a wink. Henry laughed.

"Now, some perspective." Weber led Henry to the elevator to the Protelan Suite. As they approached, the lift doors opened and both men entered.

"When Karl came to Stahlburgh, the tribes here were one step above raving primitives. He brought an iron rod to the lawlessness. He bound us all together and we became the Union. This is a fact I believe young folks like you have forgotten." Henry nodded and listened. He had missed the majordomo's lessons when he was in the country. None of the *Schloss'* servants had the majordomo's grace or charm.

"Karl, Allfather—send him to heaven—did not just bind us. He sorted us as he structured the Union. No one man, not even the protector, can control us all. We are a giant cooperative enterprise. Everyone had value to the old protector. He never called a man or woman a peasant. He was a wise father. Now, your father, our new protector, must find his tenor. I doubt he will have to wait long to discover it. The Terran Directorate senses weakness in the Felgenland, and the Terrans seek to test him. I pity their foolishness. If there is one man in the Union you never want to try, it is your father."

"Really?" Henry said, surprised at Weber's strong statement. The majordomo was obviously a loyal fan of the protectors and their family. Growing up, Henry wasn't sure whether that was just Weber looking out for his job.

"I once heard a story about him. When he was just a young officer he walked into the jungles of Heinlein on Tau Ceti with his platoon. The MjGAs were there fighting a pirate king who'd set himself up in a complex deep in the jungle. Just when his platoon was to strike the complex, the MjGAs were discovered by a poor boy from a nearby village. Your father's commander, whose name I will not reveal—to not speak ill of the dead—ordered the boy's death. The commander sat in orbit over the planet, and wanted to continue your father's mission. However, your father refused. Yes, he was Secundus, but your father's commander was a hero of Karl's conquest and a man with tremendous political capital."

"What happened?" Henry asked.

"The platoon released the boy. The boy told the pirate king. His forces discovered the MjGAs and killed many of those men. Your father fought a rear-guard action and many more would have died if not for him. The MjGA commander finally evacuated the platoon, and like all our covert operations, the government disavowed the mission. Even then, men knew not to test your father's mettle. The Terrans are fools if they think the new protector is made of anything other than Stahlburgh steel."

The elevator stopped and the door opened ending Weber's story telling. The majordomo exited. Henry exited and followed the majordomo towards the Protelan Suite. The apartments were at the end of a long, opulent hallway. Paintings of all sort hung on the walls to either side. The paintings were gifts from the Dynasts and the artists the Dynasts patronized. An expansive canvas labeled *MacLeod's Landing on Stahlburgh* made Henry stop as it caught his eye. Weber opened the suite doors, but Henry stood in front of the canvas and said "Weber who gave us this painting?"

Weber turned and scanned the oil painting, "That came from

Martin Fraser almost eighty years ago. It was a gift to Karl on your uncle's birth. Do you like it?"

"The composition is striking, yes," Henry replied.

"When *Graf* Gilbraith-on-Heather is next at the Villa, I will prompt an introduction. Kenneth is, well, not a fan of your father. However, he is a connoisseur of fine art and probably has all of the pertinent details on the painting, which will make for a charming conversation."

"Wait, he doesn't like my father?" Henry asked. Henry had never met anyone who disliked his father. Admittedly, Henry moved in small, carefully selected circles.

"Yes, he's a Violet in the House of Dynasts," Weber said.

"Oh, how odd," replied Henry.

"This way, Primus. Or, do you need to mount your noble steed? Mind you, I am no longer the stallion I once was," Weber said with a smile.

Henry laughed. Weber always had a way of cheering him up, "No, just the apartments."

Weber entered, the Protelan Suite had belonged to Henry's uncle when Ruprecht was Primus. With the succession, the apartments became Henry's. The oversized front room was designed for entertaining. The twelve-meter-by-eight-meter room was red velvet and gold. The apartment was opulent, baroque, and not to Henry's taste.

"Do you require anything more, Primus? I will have servants bring up your luggage from your parent's apartments. I apologize for not having the suite ready for you at the coronation," Weber stated as they entered.

Henry hesitated. He wanted to ask Weber for more stories of long ago. Instead, Henry realized how selfish that would be, as the man was always pulled in a million different directions. Weber never complained nor showed any sense of urgency; he focused on being with the people who were in his presence.

"No, Weber. Good evening," Henry replied. The majordomo bowed and shut the door as he exited the front room.

Henry looked over his cage. There was an ostentatious chandelier on the ceiling, and a carpet with a sumptuous pile, the texture showed a subtle variation in the overall crimson color of the apartment. Dark Mahogany cabinets and small tables lined the walls. The suite's creator had designed the decor for show. However, Henry felt embarrassed by the gaudiness. His upbringing was much simpler and less ostentatious.

Henry moved to the right and entered the small corridor that led to the southern facing rooms. Henry examined each of the six rooms one by one. There was a nice drawing room, an office, a billiards room, and three fine bedrooms complete with en-suite bathrooms.

Henry then returned to the front room and decided to inspect the other rooms off the northern corridor. There were eight rooms on the left side including a small shrine or chaplet with an altar facing eastward, a salon or small dining room, a small library, and a soaking room with oversize step-down hot tub. One room was not a room at all, but a door to a small exterior rooftop garden. Returning inside, Henry discovered there was a small bedroom for his valet, and a pair of penthouses with luxurious bathrooms.

Henry realized these two suites had belonged to his aunt and uncle. He entered the more masculine looking room, intending to claim the room as his own personal space. He sat on the large bed. The penthouse room looked like the owner had hastily vacated. The sheets were folded and arranged in piles at the end of the bed. The ornate glass covers bore hand prints from servants who had hurried to clean out the drawers. Henry realized that his uncle had probably not suspected that the election would go against him and hadn't bothered to gather up any clothes or possessions until after the Grand Duchess of Haldersmere announced his brother's selection. The hasty departure was a lesson to Henry. If he lost the election, he should be ready for his change of station.

"But now, here I am," Henry said to the empty room. He looked around. There was a window, the bed, a dresser, an armoire, and two night-stands. On the wall across from the large over-sized king bed was a console that displayed the Villa's emblem. With a word Henry could summon any member of the palace staff to cater to his wildest of whims. Of course, his jailers—his parents—may not approve of some of those whims.

"There are worse prisons," Henry said, trying to cheer himself up. Growing up, he had few responsibilities. His grandfather's funeral had changed everything. Now, he was living in the fishbowl. The door banged open startling Henry.

"There you are!" shouted Henry's valet.

"Really, Johann," Henry said, "we are no longer knocking?"

"Nope," Johann said, "I've come to fetch you for a fitting for the Campbell banquet. Dress blues, or rather blacks, I never can tell the damn Assault uniform color unless I've been drinking."

"The color is Prussian blue. I don't know how you can keep your commission," said Henry.

"Easy, I'm rich. I bribed my way up the ladder," said Johann. "I started in the volunteers and Daddy got me a regular commission. You really need to learn how to play the game, sir. Now, let's move. The patroness sent me on this errand, and I will not cross her."

Henry stood and moved toward Johann and the door saying, "Are my things here? I'd prefer a fresh set of clothes. Since I will be staying here indefinitely."

"Fantastic! I'll move my things into the other big room here," Johann began but was cut off.

"No, Johann. You get the valet's room. The other room is reserved for my intended," said Henry.

"Not bloody likely that will happen soon," muttered Johann.

Henry didn't have the energy to fight over the comment. After ensuring the valet would choose the servant's bedroom, Henry moved into the front room. A portly tailor and the tailor's assistant, a young man of perhaps seventeen, stood in the front room.

"Primus, we will measure you, and fabricate your new uniform in time for the gala tomorrow," the portly tailor said.

"Excellent," Henry said, "a finely woven prison uniform," With that, the tailor began taking his measurements.

Nakdong Part One

"Corporal!" said the ensign. Jurgen ignored his officer. He pointed his rifle at the second man in the line of "revolutionaries"—pro-Terran partisans. The revolutionaries were anti-Union irregulars that had been part of the Nakdong government coup.

"Wulf, officer says stand down," said the staff sergeant, a man named Hertzog.

Jurgen cursed his luck. He was in position and ready. Now, he'd need to let the revolutionaries go. Jurgen was tired of stalking the partisans but not doing anything. They had been playing cat and mouse with this column for almost two days.

"Yes, ensign, Wulfjaeger reporting," said Jurgen over the squad communications net.

"I'm glad Hertzog told you to stand down. You almost caused an incident," said the ensign. "Next time respond to my ping, understood?"

"Aye, aye, sir," said Wulfjaeger. Jurgen knew the ensign meant the statement to be a request, but men had been hanged for disregarding less important orders.

Jurgen was sure that Hertzog would dress him down when they got back to the barracks. In the meantime, Jurgen watched as the guards marched onward, oblivious to the Assaultmen in the jungle.

Checking he'd closed his comms, Jurgen hissed, "Lucky day for you bastards."

Jurgen glanced rightward to the pro-Union counter revolutionary partisans, known as the "contras." Jurgen was in charge of the contras.

Maricela, their leader, met Jurgen's gaze with her zombie-like eyes. Her visage briefly changed to an almost begging look as if to say, '*why are you not killing the revolutionaries?*' She suddenly turned to the marching enemy column and promptly brought her rifle up. Before Jurgen could do anything, she starting firing.

"Who is firing?!" Hertzog bellowed over the comms.

"By Malcolm's ashes," Jurgen swore switching his comms to voice input. "The contras are shooting! They're going after the revolutionaries!"

Jurgen could almost smell the smoke coming from the ensign, Thom Laakso. Jurgen figured the officer was just gun shy, since the squad had been avoiding attacking the revolutionaries.

"Set your fields of fire and attack," replied the ensign. The statement shocked Jurgen. He then checked the battlefield and began firing into the enemy's position. Maricela and her companions were shooting their pin rifles like hell was coming at them. They downed the end of the column that Jurgen had allowed to pass. The attack shocked the enemy, but the enemy's ranks wheeled around to flank Jurgen's unit. Jurgen was busy firing his rifle slowly and steadily. He remembered his foot positioning and to lead his target.

'Keep the pressure constant. Don't slap the trigger, stay in the game! Keep your head on a swivel,' Jurgen thought to himself. The enemy came closer and one of the squad's traps exploded. The enemy's center fell after the blast. The revolutionaries stopped momentarily and the contras charged forward with Maricela shouting something in Libertadese.

"Squad, charge!" shouted the ensign. Jurgen shook his head in wonder. Did the ensign put on his big boy pants today?

"It's aye! Aye! Hooray!" shouted Hertzog. The sergeant jumped up from their position and gave the cry in an attempt to motivate the squad.

"The Assault leads the way!" said Jurgen and the rest of the squad.

They hopped up and followed their staff sergeant. Jurgen started firing as he ran forward. The contras had moved only five meters before they took cover. Hertzog ran past them. The enemy blunted the staff sergeant's charge with overwhelming fire. Hertzog fell dead. Jurgen looked at the staff sergeant's body, the hassium rounds had killed him instantly.

"They're reacting! Get the heavy down! Drop covering fire!" Laakso shouted, breaking into Jurgen's thoughts. The charge didn't have the effect Laakso had wanted, and now, Jurgen was fighting for his and his buddies' lives.

"Two by five, move!" shouted Sergeant August Sutcliffe, the next most senior non-commissioned officer. Jurgen stopped his charge and crouched behind a large jungle tree. He rolled around the trunk to face the enemy and took some shots. He then rolled back waiting for orders. Behind the three-meter trunk, Jurgen knew he was behind good cover. Jurgen checked for the contras. They were his responsibility, and they had stopped a few meters behind him huddled under makeshift cover.

"What's the play, Auggie?" asked an Assaultman over the squad comms.

"We're going to get the heavy down here and give these fools a beatdown," August said on the squad channel.

"Get set! We're going to push again once the heavy is down," said the ensign. Jurgen silently cursed all the times he wished his officer would engage the enemy. Whatever motivated Laakso now, he was committed to the combat. Jurgen put those thoughts out of his head for a moment as the enemy started shooting at his position.

"Hi, cuties," said a female voice over the squad comms channel, "You need a Sister of Athena to help you poor boys? Looks like you are in a spot trouble!"

Suddenly an interceptor buzzed the area knocking Jurgen, his squad, and the enemy to the ground with its jet wash.

"Yes, ma'am," said Laakso over the squad channel. A bright blast appeared about ten kilometers to the west as a surface-to-orbit missile rocketed out from an enemy battery. The missile chased the interceptor.

"Just a second, honey," said the pilot. "Got to tell a missile I'm busy washing my hair. Be a dear and sing the Navy Song for me to cheer me on. I'll be back before the second verse."

Jurgen couldn't sing the Navy Anthem with a rifle pointed at his head. Fortunately, Auggie spoke up. "I got this..."

Jurgen listened as the sergeant sung in his clear Irish tenor.

"Like Valkyries we ascend,
Bearing our warriors, hand in hand,
This duty never ends,
We soar high, united we stand.

"Sailing forth, we are the light,
Sisters of Athena, we fight!
Defending all, our solemn chore,
For Union's call, forevermore!"

Jurgen watched as the interceptor broke left and dove. The pilot dropped chaff and countermeasures. The missile shot past the interceptor, unable to handle the turn. The missile flew off as it lost target lock and disengaged.

"Good job, cutie! I'm sending you poor boys a little gift as a thank you. Now, y'all might want to hunker down!" said the pilot. The interceptor turned and shot back towards Jurgen's unit. Jurgen watched as the interceptor launched an anti-personnel missile. He stopped looking at the interceptor and hit the deck. For a split second, Jurgen could see the bright exhaust from the ammonium-nitrate-and-aluminum-filled missile. Then, his helmet blacked out, protecting his vision as he flattened out even more. Jurgen didn't dare look up, as he waited for the impact. When the interceptor's missile hit, there was a loud boom, then shrieking wind, and the ground quaked. Jurgen felt the heat from the explosion wash over him. The explosion's fiery intensity was warm but bearable, and his suit's air conditioning turned on to counter the heat. He suddenly worried about the partisans who weren't wearing any battlesuits.

"She dropped the missile too close; I'm getting cooked!" shouted one of the Assaultmen.

"Now now! I dropped it right where it needed to go, silly boy. Your battlesuit will keep my missile from burning your beautiful Spartan body. Don't forget to say thank you to STELLAR SERAPH if you ever come up to where we Amazons live," the pilot said.

"Thanks, SERAPH, much appreciated," Laakso said after a pause. "Get up, set up fields of fire! The enemy may not have taken that on the chin like we expected! Check on our wounded."

"Aye aye!" the squad replied in unison. Jurgen stood up and watched as STELLAR SERAPH shot a few larger missiles at the surface-to-orbit missile battery's location. The jungle sounds returned to his ears, and he checked the area in front of him. He had to immediately turn his head as SERAPH's missile impacted sending another bright light that overloaded Jurgen's faceplate. Again, the jungle went silent. Jurgen realized that his helmet had cut all external microphones because of the ear popping explosion. His vision returned and he checked the area in front of him. Where once was lush jungle now was a blackened crater. Small flames flicked over the crater. Charred human remains lay near the edge of the blast radius.

Before he could check on the contras, they raced past Jurgen. He used his external speakers to yell at them, but they ignored him. The counter-revolutionaries charged towards the remaining enemy.

"Hertzog's dead, sir. We've got two others wounded, but they can walk," came over Jurgen's comms. Concerned about his charges—the contras—he squelched the channel. Jurgen dropped his rifle, allowing the Anderson-Campbell 2350 to dangle on his body from its sling. He searched a utility pocket for his zip cuffs since it looked like taking prisoners was on his dance card today. However, his search was in vain, as Maricela and her contras began executing the survivors. Jurgen watched with apprehension as the counter-revolutionaries shot the enemies — some in the back of the head, some in the face.

"*Penedeharr*," Maricela said every time she shot one of the enemy.

"Wulfjaeger, stop them," said Laakso on a point-to-point communication. "We might get intelligence out of the prisoners."

Jurgen watched as the trio of counter-revolutionaries finished off the last survivor. He gave them high marks for efficiency.

"Too late, sir," Jurgen replied, "they did them all."

"Explain to them moving forward that we're keeping prisoners," said Laakso.

"Yes, sir," said Jurgen. He wanted to ask what changed, why they were suddenly fighting, but decided against saying anything to the ensign. That was a discussion with Auggie back at the forward operating base.

"Yo, Auggie, how'd you know that song?" asked one of the Assaultmen over the channel. "I'd be cooked if SERAPH had asked me to sing it."

"Wasn't always an orbital infantryman. After basic I had a nice posting as a marine," responded the sergeant. "Got cushy details like guarding the Navy's showers and the officer ladies' bedrooms."

"Who'd you piss off?" asked another one the squad.

"Don't know. Ship sailed into the dock and I was off to the Ninth. I rolled up just before we all hit the dropship down to Nakdong in August," said the sergeant.

Jurgen smiled. He had been with the Ninth Stahlburgh Rifles since he'd left basic eighteen months ago. He had been a part of the staging and ramp up to the move to Lalande 21185. After several weeks on a transport, Jurgen and the Ninth had landed on Nakdong almost fourteen months ago. At first, they were teaching the Nakdong military how to be all they could be. Then, they spent several weeks locked in a barracks due to civil unrest, while the Lalande government fell. After the fall, the Ninth moved via Armored Personnel Carrier and truck to Jeonbuk on the southern continent.

Nakdong was only one of five habitable planets in the Lalande system and had been spared the worst of the fighting when the system government fell. As a result, refugees and partisans fled to Nakdong. Assault High Command decreed that the Assaultmen of the Ninth were now a "military advisory unit" to the counter-revolutionaries in the bloody civil war.

"Fall in," said Laakso. "Cut the chatter. We're packing up."

Jurgen stopped wool gathering to watch as two of the Assaultmen hauled Hertzog's body onto a Robotic Mobility Unit for Logistics and Equipment, the RMULE. The RMULE carried all the extra bohrium magazines, extra rations, and any other logistics or gear the Assaultmen needed. Jurgen turned and hand signed to the partisans they needed to follow. Maricela nodded, her face hollow. She and the other two fell in behind Jurgen. Jurgen didn't know their names. He only knew Maricela's because when the partisans became his problem, she saluted him and said her name.

"Wulfjaeger, take point," said Auggie, as he stood in the middle of the unit next to the RMULE.

"Aye, aye, sergeant," said Jurgen as he hustled to the front of the squad. Jurgen hated point duty. Being the first in the line meant he had to be doubly on the bounce.

"Jurgen," said an Assaultman via point to point.

"Yeah, what Roscoe?" replied Jurgen to his friend, Corporal Roscoe Cannon. Roscoe was Bravo fireteam's lead. Jurgen envied his friend, as he didn't have to deal with the contras.

"What gives? Why are we now fighting? Yesterday the ensign couldn't sneak away fast enough from a fight."

"Don't know," was all Jurgen said.

"Ask the partisans, dummy," said Roscoe. Jurgen had become the one squad member designated to speak to the partisans. Any time the Assaultmen wanted information from someone other than an NCO or officer, they'd ask Jurgen to ask the partisans.

Jurgen turned on the point connector that hooked into the headset that Maricela wore under the open pot helmet. He'd rarely used the point to point, since Maricela never talked unless she was swearing at the enemy. He'd rely on the built-in translator to switch between Felgenlander *Neu-Englisch* over to her language, a creole of Processing Age Esperanto, English, Spanish, and Chinese.

"Maricela, what's going on?" asked Jurgen.

"We're marching," Maricela replied.

"No, like with the conflict," said Jurgen, trying not to sound too frustrated. The one-hundred-fifty-two-centimeter woman trudged along. She wore the open body plates and helmet of a Nakdong military officer, complete with the Chinese symbol for one "一." Underneath the armor she wore a plain green jacket and pants tucked into army boots. Her face was dirty and whenever Jurgen opened his faceplate, he could catch a whiff of her noticeable body odor.

"We just killed some bad *penedeharrin*," she replied. "Were you sleeping in that tin can?"

"Hold," called the ensign. Jurgen threw up his hand to signal a halt. He turned to Maricela and popped his faceplate, braving the smell. Jurgen knew the ensign was checking the map and he had a few minutes. He wanted to know what Maricela actually knew, and that always meant showing his face to the woman.

"Why are we killing revolutionaries today," Jurgen asked her flat out.

"They didn't tell you?" said Maricela passively in accented *Neu-Englisch*. Jurgen hadn't realized she spoke his language.

"Tell us what?" Jurgen spoke slowly for gravity and so that Maricela could understand him without a translation system.

"The Union declared war on Terra and their *penedeharrin* boot lickers!" said Maricela with a ghastly smile. It was the first time Jurgen had seen her more animated than the zombie look she usually wore.

"Thanks," said Jurgen, shutting his faceplate. As if to underscore the discussion, a flash message appeared on Jurgen's heads up display.

> "FLASH TRAFFIC! FLASH TRAFFIC! To all Union Military units… At 0900 Nakdong universal time the Parliament of the Felgenland Union and the Protector of the Union declared war on the Terran Directorate. All military personnel are to leave Terran space and assume arms against our enemy. For Victory! By the grace of the Allfather, Victory!"

"What did the partisans say?" Roscoe asked.

"Read the traffic," said Jurgen.

"By Malcolm's beard! It's true? We're at war?"

"Yup," was all Jurgen could manage.

"That explains the interceptor pilot," said Roscoe. "Those Valkyries are usually too busy flying reconnaissance to help us out."

"Okay, keep moving, we're looking for a branching trail in about three hundred meters," said the ensign to Jurgen.

Jurgen was too busy keeping his head on his swivel to do much other than grunt in response. Roscoe kept chattering about medals, honors, winning stars, crosses, and dining with the protector. Jurgen soon tuned Cannon out as he trudged along. He wanted to ask if the regimental command would allow a dropship pickup since they were at war.

"We have to make up time, Jurgen, so pick up the pace," said Laakso on the point to point. Jurgen wanted to ask why, but settled for an "Aye, sir!"

Wulfjaeger started marching faster, and after a few minutes of a brisk hike the squad came to a small clearing in the jungle. The clearing was about thirty meters and encompassed a crossroads of two rough jungle trails.

At the cross' center someone had staked a toddler to the ground. When the child saw the soldiers, he began to cry. Jurgen was about to rush forward when he felt Maricela tug on his rear grab handle.

"Don't do it."

Jurgen halted.

"Sir, we've got a civilian in front of us. Holding to talk to the contras," said Jurgen on the command channel.

"Roger, I'm moving forward," said Laakso. Jurgen turned and popped his faceplate.

"We have to move the kid, get him to safety," said Jurgen.

"No," said Maricela flatly. Jurgen got irritated at her. What kind of woman was she that she wouldn't help a child?

Jurgen turned to move towards the toddler, but another contra grabbed him.

"*La gato jumps en el cielo, mientras los amigos 吃 tacos y dance, senor!*" said the small dirty man. Well, that's what Jurgen thought he said, until his translation system spoke.

"Sir, the boy is a living trap set by the revolutionaries."

"Christ and the Prophet save us!" swore Jurgen. Laakso approached and the trio and Wulfjaeger.

"Report," said Laakso popping open his faceplate.

Jurgen pointed to the kid and said, "Kid's a booby trap."

Wulfjaeger had never seen his officer even blink, but Laakso's left eye teared up as he looked back from the scene with the toddler. He turned and started to move forward.

"No," said Marciela to Wulfjaeger. Jurgen shrugged; he couldn't order the officer to do anything.

"Hey, buddy," said Laakso shutting his faceplate. He moved closer.

"No, no *Penedeharr*!" said Maricela moving forward, trying to stop Laakso. Laakso pushed her aside gently and moved to the child. The small boy mewed. Maricela ran back to Wulfjaeger.

"He will die," said Maricela. The officer looked around at the scene. Jurgen wasn't sure what Laakso intended, but he saw Laakso pulled out his external canteen and offered it to the child. The boy hastily accepted and drank the liquid. That was the last thing either experienced as a small chirp sounded and a large explosion took out Assaultman and toddler in a huge fireball. Jurgen felt the heat, but he and the partisans were far enough away to just observe the spectacle. There was nothing left of the child or the officer.

"By Malcolm's ashes!" shouted Auggie over the command channel. "What in all the galaxy was that!?"

"Laakso," said Wulfjaeger. "You're in command now, Auggie."

"My lucky day," said Auggie unhappily. "Next time I see those bloody revolutionaries I'm killing them really slowly, for Laakso."

Maricela nodded, hearing the exchange. She said, "Now you fight like contras!"

Jurgen suddenly realized why Maricela and her companions had executed even the minorly wounded revolutionaries. Jurgen knew the monsters who rigged the baby deserved so much more for the sake of justice. Sadly, Jurgen thought, only the Allfather would be their judge.

"Get moving. Laakso would want us safe back at the base," said Auggie.

Jurgen moved forward and crossed himself when he passed the scene of Laakso's demise. All the men following him crossed themselves as well.

"Why did he do that?" said Maricela over the communications link. Apparently, Laakso's actions had puzzled the contra.

"I don't know? I guess he couldn't tolerate the child's suffering," said Jurgen. He wasn't entirely sure why Laakso had done any of the things he did today. He just hoped that he and Laakso would meet again at the resurrection. Then, Jurgen could ask the man what his motivations were.

"That baby, she not the worst the guards do," said Maricela brokenly. Jurgen wasn't sure if she was having trouble with his language or if Maricela was having trouble expressing something deeper. Jurgen wondered if Maricela had experienced something worse. He wondered if someone close to her had experienced something. He didn't dare to ask either. He continued to keep an eye on the trail for more traps.

After a few minutes of silence, the squad came to a large hill and everyone began the hump to the top. The chatter on the public channel, "the speakeasy," went quiet. Jurgen realized everyone in the squad was exhausted after the fight and were focused on pushing up the hill.

Jurgen relaxed when he reached the summit and saw it was as bare as his cottage's pantry. Where below there was thick jungle, this hill—a rocky outcrop really—didn't even have grass.

"Let's not linger," said Auggie as he reached the top. Out of nowhere, an interceptor buzzed the squad and knocked them down.

"Malcolm's ashes!" swore Auggie. "We've got an enemy interceptor! Set for action!"

The Assaultmen scattered. Some headed down the trail, while others retreated back into the jungle from where they had just come. Jurgen ran towards the edge and momentarily paused searching for some cover. A small ledge was a meter below him. He dropped down on the ledge and hugged the cliff face.

"Flash traffic! Calling air control on *USWC Spirit of Lena*. We need a Sister of Athena, pronto!" said Auggie.

"You boys getting into trouble again?" responded a voice over the squad channel.

"SERAPH! Thank the Allfather," Auggie said.

"Hey, SERAPH you going to introduce me to your Assault

friends," asked another pilot.

"Boys, meet my wing-gal, LUNA JETSTREAM," said SERAPH.

"Pleasure," LUNA said. "Aw blast! We grabbed two more, you break right!"

"Sorry boys, work calls," said SERAPH. Jurgen felt the two interceptors pass over as each streaked towards opposite sides of the horizon. Three hostile interceptors followed immediately after them.

"Well, we're the last thing those pilots will care about! Let's move down the trail!" ordered Auggie. Jurgen paused to watch the fireworks in the sky for a moment, but then climbed off his ledge. He moved with a purpose and was at the head of the squad on the trail in moments.

"Kill the chatter! We need to keep the squad channel clear for the Navy so the ladies can give us a sit rep on those hostiles," said Auggie.

"Dang it, SERAPH! They're not getting the message!" said LUNA over the comms.

"Drop down and do a nap of the planet, we'll drag them into the Shuwa Bay kill zone!" said SERAPH. Jurgen could hear the stress in her voice.

"What are you going to do?" LUNA asked.

"I'll go for the ceiling; I have a friend who owes me a favor!"

Jurgen and his squad mates dashed into the thickest part of the jungle.

"Halt, get the electronic counter-measure screen off the RMULE!" ordered Auggie. Jurgen huddled next to the RMULE and signaled the partisans to join him. The loud crack of an interceptor made Jurgen jump.

"Going orbital," said SERAPH. "Calling *USWC Advantage*, Thomasin you in the CIC?"

"Aye, STELLAR SERAPH, Pullings here," said another female voice.

"I have two unwelcome suitors on my tail. Can you give them a wrong number?" said SERAPH. "Remember, you still owe me from that boy we hid in our room at Lichtburg!"

"*Advantage* is tracking them! Firing in three... two... one... Ball-four away" said Thomasin noting she shot computerized drone missiles. Jurgen looked skyward through a break in the canopy. The heavens flashed and a small dash of light streaked across the sky from what he assumed was the spacecraft.

"We're even now, Hannah! The smart drones have your hostiles."

Cannon pulled the screen around the unit, blocking Jurgen's vision. The squad was now electronically, thermally, and visually a hole in the universe.

"Impact. Splash one hostile," said Pullings.

"Still have one more," said SERAPH. "I'm doing a negative pull!"

"*Advantage* engaging broadsides!" said another, older, woman's voice.

Jurgen could almost imagine the large flash across the sky as the *Advantage* fired an entire battery of anti-ship weapons. Jurgen vaguely remembered the lesson from basic on interceptor versus war craft combat. Basically, the cliff notes were "don't." The interceptor was designed for nimble operations, while the space war craft were veritable giants next to the small piloted craft.

"Aye, aye, captain," said SERAPH. "Splash another hostile! Thanks Goldilocks!"

"That's Captain Sternfahrer, and you don't have a lot of room to talk SERAPH, you're a brighter shade of blond than I am," Sternfahrer said.

"Ugh, SERAPH," LUNA cut in, "I could use some help!"

"Duty calls, *Advantage*," SERAPH said.

"We're almost three klicks from the Shuwa Bay apron," said Auggie. "Let's give the girls a moment. Once we've confirmed no more hostiles, we'll move forward."

Jurgen heard the loud crack of the interceptor shooting high overhead. His HUD noted the interceptor noise was off at the western horizon. Jurgen figured it was the enemy chasing LUNA's interceptor. SERAPH's interceptor rocketed overhead with a loud thundering roar.

"Break left, LUNA!" said SERAPH.

"Breaking!" LUNA responded. "He's shooting!"

Jurgen listened as LUNA's instruments gave a warning siren as the hostile's missile shot towards her.

"Fox-four away," said SERAPH.

"Breaking away!" said LUNA. "That's a kill, SERAPH! Watch out!"

LUNA shouted as SERAPH's missile passed by her and destroyed the hostile. Jurgen kept hearing the siren warning that was the pilots' dread—missile lock.

"No, the missile has me in lock!" said SERAPH in a panic. "Help! I'm hit! I've lost my stick, and the panel is red," Jurgen heard the siren warning turn to an annoying klaxon sound over SERAPH's comms.

"Hannah! Get out of there!" said LUNA.

"Ejecting!" said SERAPH. Jurgen could tell the pilot was in a panic by the tone of her voice.

"By the Prophet!" said Auggie. "They got her!"

"Don't worry, sweetheart," said SERAPH a moment later. "I'm not dead yet. I've cleared the interceptor with the eject pod. I'll be down with you cuties in a moment."

"Flash traffic, Flash traffic! *Spirit of Lena* air control, we have a pilot down! Repeat! We have a pilot down!" said LUNA.

"Roger," said the calm voice of the military air controller. "Return to base, LUNA JETSTREAM. Ground control says there is a hostile fighter squadron headed your way."

"Aye, aye, ma'am," LUNA said, "Sorry, Hannah! I gotta bug out!"

"Get going, Lana! No sense in sticking around. I'll be fine."

Jurgen and the others in the squad stood up. Everyone had been listening, but no one knew what to do.

"Flash traffic, Flash traffic! *Spirit of Lena* air control calling all Assault units! We have a downed pilot and cannot send a rescue. We need a hero. Any of you Spartans willing to aid a lady?" said the military air controller.

"*Spirit of Lena,* this is Fifth Squad, Hotel Company, Ninth Stahlburgh. We're close. We'll go get her!" said Auggie.

"Aye, Hotel Company. You're tagged on the rescue. Godspeed!" said the *Spirit of Lena* air controller. Cannon and his fireteam started pulling down the ECM netting.

"I'm hitting the jungle canopy. Let me flash my locator. Come get me, my jungle lords!" said SERAPH. Jurgen's HUD flashed as SERAPH's beacon appeared.

"Okay, I want volunteers. Who wants to go get SERAPH?" asked Auggie.

"I'm in, she sounds hot," said Roscoe. His helmet turned to Jurgen and Wulfjaeger could almost telepathically hear Roscoe begging Jurgen to go too.

"I go," said Maricela. "She killed many—how you say? Butt-holes, today!"

"Well then, Wulfjaeger you're on too," said Auggie.

"Wait, Auggie! The rest of the partisans," said Jurgen in vain. Auggie interrupted Jurgen.

"I've got the other two contras, Wulf. You, Cannon, and your girlfriend are going. Any other volunteers for the fireteam?" said Auggie.

"I'm in, Auggie! She saved my bacon; I'd like to call us even," said one of Jurgen's newer squad mates. The Assaultman was slightly younger than Jurgen and had graduated from basic a class after him. His name was John Clayton, but everyone called him "Metal Kid" as he listened to ancient Heavy Metal music almost constantly. Between Cannon, Metal Kid, and Jurgen, Jurgen was the ranking Assaultman.

"Any other takers?" said Auggie. When no one responded, Auggie said, "Your show, Wulf. See you back at the base."

Jurgen then said to Maricela, Cannon, and Metal Kid, "Let's go, the Assault leads the way!"

Auggie said to the rest of the squad, "Fifth Squad, move out!"

The two Assaultmen and Maricela formed up on Jurgen's six and the group started bushwacking through the jungle. Every now and then Jurgen would check the marker. The beacon was off, but the HUD remembered the position. After an hour of pushing through the underbrush, Jurgen stumbled into a clearing, and halted. He flashed his beacon so SERAPH could locate them provided she had a connection to the GPS and Union military communication network.

"Hang tight, SERAPH," broadcast Jurgen as the others caught up with him. Maricela was panting, but she looked more animated than usual.

"I'm here waiting for you, dreamboat," replied SERAPH.

Jurgen still heard the nervousness in her voice. He hand-signed to move forward and turned to continue barreling through the thick jungle. The HUD said SERAPH was about six hundred meters away. Jurgen felt better about her being within range of his weapon. He would have said something, but he was expending one hundred percent of his effort pushing through the vegetation getting to the pilot. He took his eyes off the jungle to check his map, and as he did so, he tripped on a tree root and fell into a massive jungle bush. As he started to get up, he felt the jet wash of an interceptor and saw hassium rounds pass over him.

"Hey, Corporal! We've got company!" said Metal Kid over the fireteam channel. Jurgen rolled trying to extract himself from the bush. The alien plant had hooked into his forward grab handle. He turned his head up for a moment and saw a small five-man revolutionary hunter team. Jurgen was sure they were looking for SERAPH. His four team members to five enemies weren't bad odds. Jurgen also wanted some payback for Hertzog and Laakso.

"Give me a sit rep!" said Jurgen.

"I've got three on me, Corporal," said Metal Kid.

"Engaging!" said Cannon. "I got two."

That was the five. Jurgen waited for a break in Metal Kid's fire to see if any hassium rounds were still flying. Since the revolutionary hunter team continued to fire, Jurgen decided on one big push to free himself from the plant to get into the fight. Jurgen got his legs underneath him and pushed. The firing stopped for a moment as the revolutionaries reloaded. Jurgen popped up from the bush and saw he was fifty meters from the three enemy soldiers. Metal Kid didn't have a good firing angle on the revolutionaries; however, Jurgen's current position flanked the bad guys.

Jurgen reflexively fired. His first shot killed the point man. Jurgen swung his rifle to take out the next revolutionary. He fired a quick three burst, and that revolutionary went down. The final revolutionary spun to take aim at Jurgen. Hassium pins landed haphazardly around Jurgen's legs as the revolutionary panic fired at Jurgen's position. Jurgen cursed his luck. He had gotten the drop on two of the men, but the third one would get him.

As the man tightened his aim, Jurgen trained his rifle on the target. The revolutionary hesitated. Jurgen didn't. He took aim and pulled the trigger. Jurgen's shot missed. A moment later the man dropped over. Maricela appeared behind the fallen revolutionary holding a bloody combat knife. Jurgen could see through his sight that she wore her ghastly smile. Jurgen took his head off his scope and checked for other enemies.

"Jurgen, got a bit of an issue here," said Cannon.

"Roscoe!" said Jurgen. He quickly checked Cannon's location marker and started running towards him.

"I'm good, I think," Cannon said. Jurgen tried to hurry, but it took him almost ten minutes to move through ten meters of underbrush.

Jurgen finally broke free to see that Cannon sat on the ground in a small open space. Roscoe's rifle had cracked in half and sat on either side of the Assaultman. Jurgen scanned the area; to the north were two dead revolutionaries.

"Got me in the leg. I think it's a clean shot, but my dancing days are over for a while," said Roscoe. Jurgen hurried to Roscoe's side to begin battlefield first aid. Jurgen checked his friend for wounds, running his hands over Roscoe's battlesuit. Sure enough, Jurgen felt a hole in the left leg of Cannon's battlesuit. Jurgen saw the hassium pin had gone through the leg cauterizing the wound on Cannon's thigh.

"How're you feeling?" said Jurgen. He worried the hassium pin had ripped up something internally and Cannon was bleeding out under the skin.

"Like I got shot! Help me get up," said Cannon stiffly. Roscoe tried rise on his own but grunted and fell back.

"No good! I can't put any weight on my leg!" said Roscoe.

"Don't say, 'Leave me behind!' or I'll deck you," said Jurgen.

"Who me? Hell no," said Roscoe popping his faceplate. "I want to see what the pilot looks like!"

"Metal Kid, get over here," said Jurgen. After a moment, Metal Kid and Maricela appeared.

"Help Roscoe up. You three are going back to base," said Jurgen. Metal Kid nodded. Jurgen expected Maricela to refuse but she went to Cannon's side while Metal Kid went to the other. Together, they were able to get Cannon up and moving.

"You dog!" Cannon said to Jurgen, "You did this on purpose!"

"What? Didn't volunteer and forced the bad guys to wound you? The battlesuit's trauma drugs are making you loopy, Roscoe!" said Jurgen.

"I want a headcam shot. I've never met a real-life Valkyrie!" said Cannon, slurring his words. Jurgen had been joking about the meds, but it looked like the suit had doped Roscoe pretty heavily.

"Sure. Now get moving or Maricela and Metal Kid will have to haul you back on a stretcher," said Jurgen.

Roscoe leaned in and said, "Too late."

Cannon started to topple, and Metal Kid said, "Hold on to this rifle!"

In one swift motion, Metal Kid tossed the pin rifle to Maricela while he lifted the sagging Cannon in a fireman's carry.

"Let's go," Metal Kid said, moving towards the base. Maricela followed along dutifully.

"Metal Kid, you make it back and I'll call you Metal Man!" Jurgen said.

"Get the girl, and, I'd prefer just Metal!" said Metal Kid over the fireteam channel. Jurgen's HUD showed that the trio was already ten meters closer to base.

The enemy had gotten the drop on Jurgen too many times today. He'd not let the revolutionaries get the drop again. He checked his HUD, the beacon's last flash showed SERAPH still almost six hundred meters away.

"Sure, no problem. Got to sneak past a jungle full of guards, grab a Valkyrie, and get back to base. Provided she's okay, this is all doable," said Jurgen to himself. He spent the next few minutes picking his way through the dense underbrush, until he came to a jungle opening. An expansive jungle pool sat smack dab between him and the pilot.

"Glad this suit is pressurized and sealed," said Jurgen as he entered the water and started swimming. Looking out over the water, Jurgen realized the pool was actually a small lake.

"You still with me, dreamboat?" SERAPH sounded tired and scared.

"Yes, ma'am," said Jurgen. "Just taking a little swim."

"The jungle is full of teams looking for me," said SERAPH. "I can see them all over the place."

"Yeah, I got delayed when we ran into one," said Jurgen.

"You okay, dreamboat?" SERAPH asked.

"Fine, ma'am," said Jurgen. "My buddy, Roscoe, got hit. He and the rest of my fireteam are heading back to base." There was silence for a moment.

"Thanks for coming for me," said SERAPH.

"Can't leave you, ma'am. The Assault never leaves a man behind, much less a Valkyrie," said Jurgen.

"I really hate that the press call us that," said SERAPH. "It just sells those stupid skin magazines."

"Never looked at them, ma'am," said Jurgen.

"Really? You're a terrible liar, dreamboat," said SERAPH. "Call me SERAPH or Hannah. Ma'am is my old, married wing commander."

"Just respecting the rank, SERAPH," said Jurgen. He was halfway across the pool. The lake water was up to his chin. If he ducked, he'd blend into the lake. The star Lalande was going down, and nightfall was coming.

"Tell me more about how you avoided looking at the Valkyrie mags. My little brother had a stack of them under his bed. I think he poached them from Dad, but Mom just threw them all away when she found them," said SERAPH.

"I don't know. I was from a poor family. We could barely afford food, much less anything..." said Jurgen.

"Decadent?" she suggested.

"I was going to say as luxurious as a magazine full of scantily clad women," replied Jurgen.

"Okay, what did you do then, poor boy?" said SERAPH.

"Lots of things. Most weren't approved of and all focused on getting a handful of griffins," said Jurgen. His feet touched the bottom of the lake's bed. Jurgen was almost to the other shore.

"Still no magazines? Not even a peek?" asked SERAPH. She was sounding really scared now that the star was dipping under the horizon.

"No, I had a girlfriend. I couldn't afford her, but I at least got to see the real thing every now and then," said Jurgen. He smiled. If Jenny saw him now, she'd be laughing. She'd scold him and tell him he was no good. Jurgen pushed the thought out of his head as he saw flashlights coming from the jungle in front of him. The torch beams scanned the area. Jurgen ducked low in the water, hoping to look like a jungle log on the surface of the lake.

"What happened to your girlfriend? You said you had one," asked SERAPH.

"Broke up with me, got engaged. She's probably married by now, to a prissy gentry boy," said Jurgen.

"What a dunce!" said SERAPH. "Say, what's your name, dreamboat?"

"Jurgen."

"Dashing, like the young engineer in Neuklang's virtual reality opera *Der Singularität Szyklus*. He was my favorite character, even though the opera companies usually get a mezzo-soprano to play the role," said SERAPH.

"Never saw the opera. I think I was named for my father's younger brother," said Jurgen.

"Your uncle?" said SERAPH. Jurgen waited and watched as the revolutionaries' torches scanned around the lake. Jurgen held his breath, but a few moments later the torches all turned into the jungle and left the lakeside.

"Never met my uncle. He ran off to seek his fortunes and never came back to Tavishire," said Jurgen. His HUD showed SERAPH's last position was only one-hundred-and-fifty-meters away.

"Gotta go silent, Jurgen," said SERAPH. Jurgen crawled from the lake, with vines and other organic matter clinging to him and forming an impromptu ghillie suit. Jurgen rushed from the lake's shore and into where the vegetation thickened. Jurgen straightened as he blended into the foliage. Screened by the light jungle Jurgen checked his HUD. He was approximately one hundred meters from Seraph's position.

"I'm almost there," said Jurgen.

"Sorry, Jurgen. I've moved," said SERAPH. "My position was getting too hot. The bad guys discovered my ejection pod and parachute."

"Can you flash me a beacon?" asked Jurgen as he moved forward. The light jungle stopped abruptly and turned into a plantation. From the lack of jungle, Jurgen suspected the owners had recently left the plantation and the jungle was attempting to retake the land.

"Repeat, can you flash me a beacon?"

Jurgen saw he was fifty meters away from SERAPH's last beacon. Jurgen weighed his options and decided cross the open ground, risking detection. As he strode through the abandoned plantation, Nakdong's small white moon rose on the horizon. Jurgen looked up; the white moon illuminated the whole area. Jurgen noticed Nakdong's dull red moon was waning in the sky. Jurgen hadn't bothered to learn their names; now he wished he had.

At twenty meters from the beacon, Jurgen saw the escape pod. The pod looked like the front cockpit of an interceptor. This one looked like it had been beaten by every club in the jungle. Jurgen dropped prone as his external speakers alerted him to the sound of footsteps.

Jurgen hoped the vines and lake's organic matter would help conceal him. He moved his rifle like a periscope scanning the area. The suit's electronics projected the rifle's scope picture onto his faceplate. The scope showed a five-man team moved towards the pod. The first three stood watching while one revolutionary, possibly the leader, entered the pod. The fifth revolutionary looked like he was on watch. Suddenly there was a commotion as two more men appeared with a smaller form between them. The smaller form held its hands against its head.

"Malcolm save me!" said Jurgen. "SERAPH, if you are captured, can you pat your head?" The smaller figure lifted its hands and gave its helmet a tap.

Jurgen rolled slowly on his back and cut his comms.

"Allfather, I don't often converse with you, but for the love of Malcolm and your son, the Christ, can you cut me a break today?" Jurgen prayed.

Jurgen's HUD then started. He watched as the words came across his screen.

> "Flash traffic! Be advised naval operations for "VIKINGRAID" are now underway. All Assaultmen must return to base and report to the rally point."

Jurgen rolled back on his belly. A series of bright flashes lit up the night. The Navy was shelling orbital batteries and sending their "rods from the gods" down onto revolutionary-held facilities. Jurgen watched as the flashes distracted the revolutionaries. Four peeled off from the pod and ran into the jungle. Jurgen wasn't sure if they had panicked, were under orders, or were attempting to get reinforcements. Three to one odds were better than seven to one. Jurgen knew that the Allfather must have opened a window. Jurgen popped up to a kneeling position, aimed, and shot the leader who had turned his attention to SERAPH. The shot was worthy of an expert shooter, and he blew the leader's head off. The two subordinates froze in shock. Jurgen wasted no time. He trained his sights on the nearest and quickly double tapped the trigger. The revolutionary dropped to the ground. SERAPH turned and pulled a survival knife from her pressure suit's arm. She expertly stabbed the other guard in the neck, dropping him. Jurgen ran to her position.

"Are you okay?" he asked.

"Yes, they just found me," SERAPH said as she grabbed her confiscated survival rifle from the downed revolutionary.

"Let's go!" said Jurgen. SERAPH checked the rifle and chambered a round. He tagged the beacon that showed the Assault base on Shuwa Bay on his HUD. He and SERAPH were almost five kilometers away. He started towards the point and then checked to see that SERAPH was right beside him. She wore a gray pressure suit that looked like an armor-less version of the Assault's battlesuit. SERAPH's pressure suit wouldn't stop small arms fire—or even an angry stick—but it could keep the pilot protected from the jungle's less desirable biological elements. They jogged for a few minutes until the underbrush slowed their progress. Jurgen worried he and SERAPH were going to have to bushwack through more dense jungle, but suddenly they hit a paved jungle highway.

"Blast! We hit the Western Highway," said Jurgen. He looked up and down the highway nervously.

"Is that bad?" asked SERAPH.

"Yes, very bad," said Jurgen. "I had hoped we'd track to the south and avoid the dang thing!"

"Huh, how so?"

"The road isn't a straight line. I don't think Nakdong actually has a kilometer of straight road. But, even as crooked as the road is, the Western Highway is heavily patrolled by the revolutionaries." As if on command, an antiquated military jeep appeared on the road. The jeep rolled down the highway with four soldiers in its seats.

"I only get one break today, eh, Allfather?" Jurgen said as he raised his rifle and shot the driver. The jeep veered and dropped off the road, hitting an embankment, and forcibly ejecting its passengers. The three remaining soldiers did not move after they hit the ground. Jurgen didn't waste time determining if their necks were broken; he just seized the opportunity.

"Come on!" He moved to the jeep, hopped in the driver's seat, and put the wheeled vehicle into reverse.

"I should drive. I'm the pilot!" said SERAPH as she moved towards the driver's side.

"Good point," said Jurgen as he shifted to the passenger seat. "Now I can provide over watch! Get in! Drive to the east!"

Jurgen pointed in the direction they needed to go and SERAPH put her foot down on the accelerator. He wasn't sure what electronics SERAPH's suit had, but she didn't ask for directions. Jurgen figured SERAPH's suit must have had a GPS map or way point to the Assault base. She got the jeep oriented and did not spare the accelerator.

"This thing is still on the ground," Jurgen said as SERAPH took a sharp turn too quickly.

"Don't remind me," SERAPH responded. "We'd be back at base if this thing could fly!"

Jurgen watched as the meters to the way point ticked down. After several hair-raising minutes where Jurgen was happy his rifle had a sling and he'd found a handle to grip, the road widened and straightened out.

"We're getting close! We are almost at the Shuwa Bay apron!" said Jurgen. The Assault base was a virtual fortress, and it sat on the end of the peninsula that protected Shuwa Bay. The Navy guarded the area by orbit while several thousand Assaultmen guarded the base on the ground. The peninsula was a perfect defensive spot but terrible as a staging area for offensive operations. As they got closer, Jurgen heard an announcement on his external speakers.

"Unknown vehicle, slow your speed and proceed to the checkpoint! This is Bravo Company, First Lochiel Dragoons. You have entered a restricted zone!"

SERAPH slowed the jeep, and Jurgen looked for a Bravo Company Armored Personnel Carrier. A small hill started to move in the darkness and Jurgen realized it was an APC. He pointed his microwave comms at the APC and flashed a request to connect signal. The APC accepted the signal.

"Corporal Wulfjaeger, Fifth Squad, Hotel Company, Ninth Stahlburgh Rifles, and STELLAR SERAPH reporting back to base.

We've had revolutionaries chasing us," Jurgen said.

"Been expecting you, corporal," said the APC operator. "Charlie Company picked up some of your fireteam in the jungle a few klicks from here."

Jurgen relaxed. Cannon, Maricela, and Metal Kid had made their way back to base safely.

"Glad to hear that. Can you direct us?" asked Jurgen.

"Even better, we're going to drive you. Slow the vehicle and I'll send Lance Corporal MacIntosh over," said the operator.

"Stop the jeep," said Jurgen. SERAPH didn't argue and slammed the brakes. Jurgen could see an Assaultman running towards them. The Assaultman climbed into the driver's side as SERAPH hopped into the back.

"Geez, you could have met me at the APC. I haven't run like that since basic," said MacIntosh.

Jurgen laughed. "Blame the Angel; she's the pilot."

MacIntosh put the jeep into drive and started speeding to the base.

"Wait! You're a Valkyrie? Wow! I'm driving VIPs today," MacIntosh said.

"Yes, sure am, cutie," SERAPH said. Jurgen could tell her anxiety had evaporated and she was returning to form.

"I'm not that cute," said MacIntosh awkwardly, as he weaved between checkpoints and barrier gates.

"Oh, I think you all look like Lukas Stahl. I loved him in the *Last Message*. He made my heart melt," SERAPH said. Jurgen smiled; the *Last Message* was a girl's movie. The film was a love story. The part Jurgen had heard about was where the man read all the electronic messages to the woman he loved as she slowly lost her mind to Kronenberg's syndrome. Jenny had relayed the entire plot to him once; yet another reason he should have left her sooner.

"I don't look even close to Lukas Stahl," MacIntosh said, "Besides, I remember him from his portrayal of Caspar Röist in *One Eighty*

Nine."

"That was an epic movie," said Jurgen. He remembered the historical action movie about the Swiss Guards who defended the Vatican against overwhelming odds during the sack of Rome. Jurgen had skipped meals for a week to see the movie with Olrich. Both felt the movie was worthy of a little starvation.

"Yeah, I saw the actors' training regime for *One Eighty Nine.* I don't believe any of their abs were painted on for the movie," said MacIntosh. The trio was close to the main barracks. Things were hopping on the base; foot and vehicle traffic were thick. Dropships were in a holding pattern above, and interceptors flew patrols overhead.

"Me either, but I am a connoisseur of Lukas' abs," said SERAPH. "They are the closest thing I've seen to perfection in this universe."

"Well, when I park this jeep, can I get a cam shot of you, ma'am?" asked MacIntosh. Jurgen smiled; the man had guts.

"I'll show you mine, if you show me yours," said SERAPH.

"Deal," said MacIntosh. "But once the helmet comes off, you'll demand I put it back on. My own mum thinks I'm ugly."

SERAPH didn't respond as the jeep pulled into a large transport hub. In seconds, MacIntosh had parked the jeep and gotten out of the vehicle.

"Ugh, I need to do my makeup and hair. I neglected them both, not knowing that getting captured was on my dance card. So, be nice, boys!" said SERAPH. She pulled off her helmet showing her matted, pinned blond hair, lightly tanned face, blue eyes, and full lips. MacIntosh snapped his picture, and Jurgen did likewise for Cannon.

"Wow, ma'am, you're hotter than Sophie van der Meer," said MacIntosh.

"Thanks, but she is way prettier than I am," said SERAPH. "Now pay up, boys, I want to see what my rugged heroes look like."

MacIntosh took off his helmet. Jurgen wasn't a good judge of male looks, but the lance corporal wasn't supremely ugly. He had typical Lochiel features and other than needing a shave, didn't look like he was abnormal.

"Oh, you're good looking," SERAPH said, "I was a little concerned at how much you downplayed your looks, but you look like a boy I dated in secondary."

MacIntosh straightened with a little pride at being good looking enough.

"Thanks, ma'am, much appreciated. Thanks for the photo too! I'm printing it and putting it up on my honor board in the barracks. Farewell," said MacIntosh as he saluted and turned to find his unit.

"All right, your turn. Pay up," said SERAPH turning to Jurgen. Jurgen popped off his helmet, trying to hand comb his sweaty blond hair.

"Uh oh, Herr Stahl has competition," said SERAPH. "You should have been an actor. You're beautiful!"

Jurgen laughed. "I've got better things to do with my life, but thanks. Coming from someone so comely, that's quite the compliment!"

SERAPH put on her helmet, and Jurgen followed suit. Then, she saluted Jurgen, who, in shock, returned the salute.

"Um SERAPH, I'm only a corporal. I'm supposed to salute you. Your bio says you're a sub-lieutenant. You float up there with the Allfather," said Jurgen.

"I don't know about that, corporal. My feminine intuition tells me you may fly higher than I will before things are over," said SERAPH. Jurgen was about to respond when a dropship landed drowning out communication over the external speakers. SERAPH and Wulfjaeger both turned to look at the ship. The door opened and another pilot in a pressure suite came running.

"You made it back, SERAPH!" said the figure over her speakers as she approached.

"LUNA!" said SERAPH, "What happened?"

"I bugged out. I was chased all the way to the vacuum line by the enemy! The hostiles were all set to get some Union Navy interceptors until I crossed into the thrust line," Luna said.

"What happened then?" Seraph asked.

"The *USWC Aptitude* showed up with anti-interceptor batteries all prepped. The flight tried to turn around, and *Aptitude* got two before the rest figured out how to piss off," said LUNA angrily. "Who is your friend?"

"Oh, this is Jurgen. He's not my friend; he's my hero!" SERAPH said leaning against Jurgen in a pantomime of seduction. Jurgen suspected, in their suits, the gesture looked more comical than anything else.

"Is he cute?" LUNA asked.

"Very," SERAPH said.

"So, hey there sodger, you want to show me yours if I show you mine?" asked LUNA. Jurgen wanted to laugh. If Roscoe or any of his other squad mates were here, they'd have buckets of saliva pouring out of their suits as they scrambled to go face-to-face with the Valkyries.

"Sorry, LUNA. Thanks, but I've got to pass. I've got a wounded friend I need to check on," Jurgen said.

"Your loss," said LUNA a bit sullenly.

"Don't worry, Lana," said SERAPH. "I've got Jurgen's cam shot. You and I can put a hardcopy up on our bunk later."

"Well, then," LUNA said. Jurgen realized the pilots had dismissed him. He snapped to attention and saluted them. They returned the salute and he turned heading for the hospital. He didn't move more than five meters when Metal Kid appeared.

"Come on, corporal! Sergeant sent me to find you! We've got fifteen minutes until the briefing," said Metal Kid, or rather now, Metal. Jurgen had hoped for a respite, or even the luxury of a shower. Instead, he followed Metal to the spacious Quonset hut that doubled as a general briefing space and mess hall.

Metal and Jurgen sat waiting. After a few minutes of sitting comfortably in his air conditioned battlesuit, Jurgen drifted off to sleep.

"Come on Wulf, wake up," said Auggie banging on Jurgen's chest plate. Wulfjaeger was up and at attention in a second.

"At ease," said Auggie. "You were so peaceful we hated to wake you."

"So, you wrote something on my armor?" said Jurgen.

"Nah, we're infantry we can't write, only draw," said Auggie.

"Gee, thanks," said Jurgen. Metal stepped forward and said, "Don't let the sergeant rib you. I got your back. No one drew anything on you."

"Now that sleeping beauty is awake, I need all eyes on me. We're going to be working in tandem with the First Stahlburgh Rifles, plus the Second and Third Dragoons on this one. We're taking hill one-five-five, which is the second highest peak in the landing zone. We need to hold it at all costs. We're down top and the ensign, plus Cannon who, even wounded, wanted in on the fight. The contras are going to be with us and will provide back up."

Jurgen looked around to see the contras standing in the back. Maricela looked almost alive at the thought of killing more guards. She smiled her ghastly smile at Jurgen, which made him shudder.

"Now, any questions?" asked Auggie.

"When do we roll out, sergeant?" asked Metal.

"We're up on the bounce at zero seven hundred. Thankfully we got a reprieve since we just came in from the field. Load up is at zero eight hundred local. This one is the real deal, so get some rest," Auggie said. "Anything else?"

No one said anything.

"Fifth Squad!" Sergeant Sutcliffe said, "attention!"

The squad snapped to attention.

"Fifth Squad will hold the line! Remember, men, five is our honored number. Like the wounds of Christ, we will bear all suffering!" Auggie said. The speech was his version of a motivational speech and Jurgen felt his blood start pumping.

"It's aye! Aye!" started Auggie.

"Hooray!" responded Jurgen and the rest of the squad.

"Get ready, sack out. Dismissed!" said Auggie. The men filed out heading to their barracks. Jurgen looked towards the hospital. As he did so, high up in the sky an interceptor broke the sound barrier and traded missiles with an another enemy interceptor. A klaxon sounded and the base got even busier. Engineers started running to and fro checking the artillery batteries and the surface-to-orbit automated missile batteries. Jurgen started trotting towards the hospital. He wasn't going to let a chance to check on Roscoe slip by again. He walked in and went to the counter.

"Cannon," he said to the nurse on duty. The civilian woman nodded and pointed to the corridor to the east. Jurgen headed down the eastern corridor and found Roscoe in the first room, sleeping on the bed.

"Roscoe," said Jurgen popping his helmet and gently shaking the man.

"He out," said Maricela, startling Jurgen. She had slipped in behind Wulfjaeger, silently and cat-like.

"I just wanted to say goodbye," said Jurgen.

"You tell him later," said Maricela. Jurgen was unsure what that meant and stared at the woman.

"You have, an aura?" She said unsure of the word. "You will kill many *Penedeharrin* tomorrow. I know."

"How do you figure?" asked Jurgen. He was mesmerized. For whatever reason, Maricela was opening up to him.

"God, or what you call Him, the Allfather told me so," she said.

"He's been incredibly hard to get on the phone," said Jurgen.

"No, He going to give you how you say... wreathes and stars?" Maricela said.

Jurgen sat and thought, the laurel wreath on an Assaultman's shoulder boards meant a senior officer or a general. Jurgen couldn't figure how even the Allfather could make a woodland trash peasant like himself a general. That was a rock so big even the Allfather couldn't lift it.

"When I was in the *Cámaras mortuorias*, what my people called the dungeons that the *Penedeharrin* caged us in after the takeover. I saw Him, my beautiful Jesus. He came to me as I was being tortured. He said I had his... authority... to get revenge. They abused me, but I never cried. My father told me never to shed a tear, and that all my pain would be washed away when my beautiful Jesus comes again. They killed my father while I watched."

"I'm sorry," said Jurgen.

"For what? You didn't do anything to me. You and your people have helped mine. We are bound in the blood of the *Penedeharrin!*"

A silence ensued, while Jurgen and Maricela listened to Roscoe's breathing and the beep of medical instruments.

"So, wreathes and stars?" Jurgen asked.

"Ahh... Si... Jesus said I would meet a man with hair the color of Lalande's rays, a blond wolf, and he would fly high, like an..." Maricela paused. She couldn't seem to find the word.

"An eagle?" asked Jurgen.

"No, the creature on your nation's *escudo*..." Maricela said.

"Huh? What the dragon?" said Jurgen, selecting the supporter with which most of the Felgenland identified.

"No, not the snake, that is the sign of *il Diablo*, the other one," said Maricela.

"The griffin? That's the emblem of the Protector of the Union!" said Jurgen. A peasant like him had big dreams if they wanted to wear such an august symbol. The griffin was a symbol of the Chancellery, the Protector's Villa and the protector's estate *Schlosses* in the countryside, and, of course, the Union's highest military award, the Golden Segreant Griffin.

"Si, you will fly high with the griffin," said Maricela.

"Well, okay then," said Jurgen. "I've got to get some rest; I will see you in the morning."

"Si, we are killing *Penedeharrin*. I will be ready," said Maricela. "You go, I stay with Mr. Gun. He did good job killing today."

"Cannon," Jurgen said, "It is Cannon."

"Si, si," said Maricela. Jurgen left and made his way through the crowds to his bunk in the barracks. Jurgen toyed with the idea of a shower, but instead decided to sleep in his battlesuit. That way he could maximize his sleep time and still be ready on time. He hit his bunk and tried to zone out but he fretted about the morning. After tossing and turning for a bit, sleep overtook him.

CHAPTER TWO
Directorate-Union War

Three Times Fate

Henry awoke, showered, dressed in a robe, and ordered an opulent breakfast. He had been up late as servants had delivered his possessions piecemeal. The experience was surreal. With the addition of knick-knacks and other personal items, the Protelan Suite almost felt like home. So much so, that Henry debated whether he should even redecorate. He was about to eat another biscuit with chocolate and hazelnut spread when Johann slammed open the door and entered the dining room. Today, Henry was ready, as he had heard the valet stumbling around in the corridor.

"Okay," was Johann's greeting. "You need to fire the scullery maid. She's a bad influence."

Henry recalled the young woman. She was just eighteen and from a small village in the Valley of the First Farmers. She was as gentle as a dove and always quiet around Henry.

"Why is that?" Henry asked, expecting the worst.

"She got me drunk, and after that, I think she may have done unnatural things to me," said Johann.

"I doubt you need much help getting drunk, Johann," Henry replied. "As for unnatural things, I thought you liked activities like that."

"No, no. Not those types of unnatural things. I woke up and well, I feel cursed."

"Are you sure you aren't just hung over?" asked Henry.

"Yeah, that too," Johann said, "I had a moment when I was in the toilet..."

"Not today," snapped Henry, "I am eating. If you really have an issue, see a doctor or a priest."

"Yes. I'm talking to the future protector. When you're the Allfather's anointed you can just ask him to pardon my sins. I promise I'll stop sinning and become a devout and holy man," said Johann. "In the meantime, that witch gave me an odd rash."

"Look, I am having a carefree and opulent breakfast. Save any medical details for later. Now, you're welcome to join me or wander off to attempt respectability. You need to get your act together. We're off to the Protelan embassy. I just got Weber's message with today's agenda," said Henry. "After that, we're going to the new museum opening, and if we're on time, I will arrive in the House of Dynasts to hear some of the arguments on the Terran Directorate war proposal."

"Oh, Allfather, how boring!" said Johann. "Malcolm guide me home."

"I'm surprised you call to the Allfather. I always thought you preferred calling to the infernal side," said Henry. He felt like he was winning the verbal sniping contest with his valet today.

"Yeah, but only at night," Johann admitted. "Everyone depicts angels as interceptor pilots, but from the little I remember from my Sunday school, other than Miss Foster who taught me many other subjects..." Henry frowned at Johann to dissuade further conversation on that topic.

"Um, yeah... Angels are dudes. Not that I have a problem with that, but the way the Bible describes them, they aren't much fun. They turn folks into salt and chase them with flaming swords and what not. Whereas demons, they're pretty much into all the fun stuff: vanity, gluttony, greed, wrath, envy, and let's not forget the best one, lust!"

"You know Johann, I doubt even as protector I can guarantee salvation for you." Henry replied skeptically.

"It's all good. I'm on the Saint Augustine path. One of these days I'll give up my wanton wastrel ways and become a saint too." Johann said.

"Like today?" Henry asked.

"Not looking too good for today, and tomorrow's forecast isn't much better either," said Johann who then snatched Henry's orange juice glass and swallowed every drop. The valet placed the empty back in front of Henry who immediately moved the cup away from him, as if the glass were radioactive.

"Get dressed," Henry commanded. Johann snapped to attention and then wobbled out of the small dining room. Moments later, Henry could hear the loud sounds of his valet throwing up. Henry rolled his eyes at the sound, stood and procured a new glass, and poured himself more orange juice.

Henry dressed himself. The valet was supposed to dress Henry, but he had given up on Johann doing anything proper—or job related—weeks ago. At zero nine hundred, Henry's chauffeur messaged that the car was ready and waiting for him.

"Let's go, Johann," said Henry. Johann came out in a nicely pressed Class A uniform, hair combed, clean shaven, and presentable.

"Before you ask about my appearance, are there women at the embassy?" Johann asked.

"Yes," Henry replied. "Still, don't get any ideas. You'll cause an incident. All of the women there work for the ambassador, who also is female."

"Good, I am glad I didn't cleanup for nothing," Johann replied. "Also, challenge accepted, I've never seduced an ambassador before."

Henry rolled his eyes at the valet as he left the apartment. He looked once again at the MacLeod oil painting. The pause allowed the valet to catch up and then both men waited for the elevator. The lift doors opened and they entered; Henry hit the button for the garage.

"Is she pretty?" Johann asked.

"Is who pretty?" Henry replied.

"The ambassador, duh," Johann said.

"I don't know. She's in her sixties at least," said Henry.

"Okay, that ups the challenge in some ways, and makes things easier in others," said Johann.

"Forget it, Johann," said Henry. "We need to keep the Protelani happy. They are close allies, major trading partners, and in general a favored nation."

"You're worried the ambassador won't get her money's worth? I never get complaints, just hate mail."

"Ugh, Johann, I really don't want to know." The doors opened, and the duo walked to the waiting hoverlimo. An Assaultman quickly hopped out from behind the steering wheel to open the door for the Primus.

"Good morning, Primus," the young man said. Henry entered the hoverlimo and waited for Johann to enter. The valet stood chatting with the driver.

"Johann, get in here," Henry said. At the rate they were moving, Henry wouldn't make it back to the Villa until midnight. Johann entered and the driver shut the door.

"The Protelan Embassy, sir?" the driver asked.

"Yes, what's your name?" Henry asked.

"Krueger, sir," the Assaultman said.

"What is your rank, Krueger?" the Primus asked.

"Sergeant," Krueger replied.

"Thanks, Sergeant Krueger," the Primus said.

"You're welcome, sir," the driver said, as he focused on his job.

"Nice kid. He's from Lochiel too, but the other side of the world. I thought he was related to a girl I knew, but he's not." Johann said.

Henry nodded, trying not to encourage the valet. He powered on his EVIL and began to review the documents the *Staatskanzler*, the State Chancellor, Russel Bertrand-Hoyt, had provided him. The documents outlined the visit, which was intentionally cordial. Henry and the Protelani would discuss military matters. The Protelani would ask for things. The Primus should be noncommittal but pleasant. As a last resort, the Primus could tell whomever asked that the Union Government would consider the matter.

The limo sped forward. They passed Kocher Square, the Lena statue, and an expansive park called simply "Union Park." The limo then turned on to *Botschaftsstrasse* or "embassy row." Henry thought Union Park was nicely kept, but rather plain for the real estate it occupied. Henry mused about what he could do about with the park, should the electors choose him as protector. Henry realized that subconsciously he had begun to accept that he might be the protector one day. Today, the thought wasn't that bothersome.

The hoverlimo pulled into the drop off spot at the Protelan embassy. There was a fancy wall, with a nice wrought iron fence. A small guard shack sat behind the wall. The wall had text stating "The Sovereign Territory of the Protelan Republic, Welcome to our nation!" A luxurious, marble walkway led from the drop off area to the embassy building.

Henry and Johann stepped out of the hoverlimo and two female Protelan Navy officers greeted them. The Union had copied the Protelan Navy's design of an all-female Navy, perhaps even more successfully than the originator. Johann looked like the cat who ate the canary as the Navy officers scanned him and Henry.

Henry looked at Johann and mouthed, "Behave."

Johann shrugged as if to say he wasn't doing anything.

"You and your servant are cleared to proceed, sir," the naval officer said. Then she and her fellow officer saluted him. Henry returned the salute, and he and Johann started walking side by side towards the embassy building on the marble path.

"She wants me," Johann said.

"You think most of humanity wants you, Johann. News flash, that's a delusion. Most of humanity only wants you to go away," Henry said.

"She mentioned me specifically," Johann said.

"She called you 'my servant,'" Henry said.

"Ah, yes, but did you hear how she drew it out," said Johann.

"You're imagining things. Stay frosty, we're not in the Union right now," Henry said.

"Good, I hate that place. They are after me for unpaid parking tickets," Johann said. Henry was about to scold his valet when a tall man appeared.

"Good day, Primus. I am Major Bjorn Halvorsen of the Protelan Space Marines," Bjorn said, snapping a salute. Henry returned the salute. The space marine was almost ten centimeters taller than Henry. Protelan had less gravity than Stahlburgh, and her people were all tall. He had a broad frame, unlike the naval officers whose figures looked like fashion models. His dirty blond hair was cut in a short, military style. He had steel gray eyes and a stern visage.

"A pleasure, I am Primus Heinrich von Machthaber and this is my valet, Lieutenant Johann *Markgraf* Strass of the March of Kildromey," Henry said.

"Good day," Bjorn said with a slight bow to Johann.

"So, um, where's the ambassador?" Johann asked.

"She was detained on important internal business," said Bjorn. "I will be your host for your tour."

"Excellent," Henry said, scowling at the valet.

"Shall we enter the embassy?" said Bjorn. The trio entered and Bjorn escorted them into a conference room. Military photos, mainly of naval ships, were proudly hung around the room. Bjorn sat at the head of the table.

"Please feel at home," Bjorn said casually, as he gestured towards a refreshments table at the back of the room. The table contained mainly Protelani fare – various types of salted and pickled fish.

"Um, is this it?" Johann asked.

"Yes, did you expect someone else?" Bjorn asked.

"Um, no," said Johann as he slumped into his chair sullenly.

"Well, then, to business," Bjorn said. He and Henry spent most of the hour discussing military affairs between the Union and Protelan. Johann sat there bored before eventually pulling out a tablet to watch a movie.

"And we'll expect a shipment of Anderson-Campbell pin rifles, 2350 model fours," said Bjorn. "We're a practical people and know the Union isn't ready to sell their best weapons to us... yet."

"We'll take that under advisement. Alasdair Campbell and his company will need to agree to the order, which, provided there isn't an export control concern, shouldn't be an issue," said Henry. Sure, he could be putting Campbell in a bind, but after the fiasco yesterday. Henry didn't really care.

"Last item," Bjorn said looking very serious, "My government wants a military exchange."

Henry couldn't see any harm in the request. Plenty of other militaries had sent representatives to Stahlburgh before.

"Sure, I'm probably speaking out of turn on this one, but I can't see any issues. When do you want to do the exchange and for how long? Does your government have candidates in mind?" Henry asked.

"I'll send a memo to Protelan Navy Headquarters, and they'll get back with me. Let's talk next week, if that sounds acceptable?" Bjorn asked.

Henry stood, extended his hand, which Bjorn took, and said, "Yes, thanks." Henry turned to Johann and found his valet asleep.

"Sir, about your man... I don't wish to offend, but he seems a little useless," said Bjorn. Henry smiled. The Marine's comment certainly raised his standing in Henry's book.

"He is. It's hard to get good help these days," Henry said. Bjorn laughed and Henry joined him. Johann cracked open an eye, and said, "We done?"

"Yes, let's go. Major," Heinrich said snapping to attention.

"Primus," Bjorn said, also snapping to attention. "Next week, I promise."

"Best of luck. If you have the same red tape we have, well, I won't hold a delayed response against you," Henry said.

"Honestly, the red tape is worse. We're smaller, so there really is no excuse," said Bjorn with a broad smile.

"Again, all the best," said Henry.

"Allow me to escort you two," Bjorn said. The trio left and saw nary a person in the embassy all the way to the hoverlimo. Johann's eyes darted around like he was looking for state secrets. He was, of course, looking for Protelani women.

The limo stood waiting, with Krueger sitting in the driver's seat. Krueger looked like he was going to hop out but Henry motioned for him to remain in the vehicle. Bjorn opened the passenger compartment for the two Felgenlanders. Henry and Johann stepped in, and Bjorn shut the door. Kreuger put the limo in drive and waited for orders.

"The new Museum of Union History, sergeant," Henry said. Krueger left the embassy and merged into traffic.

"Museum, sounds lame," Johann said.

"I don't know. Ladies like museums," Henry said.

"Yeah, librarian types who put pencils in their hair," Johann said grumpily.

"I thought you liked a challenge?" Henry asked.

"I do like a challenge. However, librarians are like shooting fish in a barrel," Johann said.

"You can stay in the limo if that suits you," Henry said. Johann made a face.

"No, I like barrel fish too," he replied. Henry laughed inwardly. The limo went several blocks, again passing Union Park, before floating into the museum's parking lot. Krueger dropped off Henry and Johann as close as he could get to the entrance. Dignitaries and honored guests milled about in front of a giant blue ribbon that someone has strung across the entrance way.

"There he is," said a nicely dressed older woman when Henry exited the hoverlimo.

"Primus, I'm Julia Schneider. I'm the museum's chief curator. I am so sorry *Graf* von Adler isn't here, but the director was busy with his own county's business, something about a workers' strike," Schneider said to Henry. The woman was in her late fifties and had an immaculately coiffed head of gray hair.

"Frau Schneider, this is my valet, Lieutenant Johann *Markgraf* Strass of the March of Kildromey," Henry said waving his hand towards Johann.

"Enchanted," said Julia as she presented her hand in a lady-like fashion. Johann merely grasped the appendage, shook her hand, and said, "Pleasure."

Julia turned and said, "This way, sirs."

Henry looked at Johann and frowned. Johann nodded at Julia and made a thumbs down gesture. Henry laughed inwardly. The first woman with whom they spoke to today and Johann turned his nose up at her.

Julia reached the front of the crowd, grabbed the microphone and tapped on it before she said, "Now that our benefactor is here, we will cut the ribbon."

Reporters snapped pictures with bright flashes as Henry, Julia, and the other patrons stepped forward and placed their hands on the handles of a ridiculously large scissors. The cameras again flashed and then a young man stepped forward with an actual pair of scissors and handed them to Henry. Henry cut the ribbon; the museum was officially open.

"Would you like a private tour?" Julia said, looking specifically at Johann.

Before either man could accept, a naval officer approached Henry, Johann and Julia. She wore the Union Navy oyster gray Class A officer's uniform: a bucket hat, jacket with interceptor wings, pencil skirt with black side stripes, opaque gray tights, and black regulation ankle boots with a five-centimeter heel. The officer wore her red hair neatly pinned back in a bun.

"I apologize if I missed the ribbon cutting," the naval officer said.

"No problem, Lady MacDonald," said Julia. "We'll add you and the Director via post processing. Do you know the Primus and his... valet," Julia said stressing the word "valet."

"Why, hello," Johann said, suddenly more animated. MacDonald nodded to Johann, but kept her eyes on Henry.

"I doubt he would remember me, but we've met," she replied.

Henry nodded and said, "A pleasure, star lieutenant, I do indeed remember you." The officer blushed.

"Lady MacDonald is here on behalf of her father, *Grosskoenig* Angus MacDonald, who gave a sizable donation for our exhibit on H. Malcolm MacLeod," said Julia. "Lady MacDonald, you are welcome to join us."

"Yes," Johann said eagerly.

"Only if it won't disturb the Primus. He is the major benefactor after all," Lady MacDonald said.

"Not at all, your company would be refreshing," Henry said.

"Well then," said Julia. "This way, please."

Lady MacDonald walked side by side with Henry, forcing Johann to choose to walk in front of or behind the couple. He chose behind Henry suspected Johann was checking out the rear view of Lady MacDonald.

Julia guided the trio up the short flight of stairs and into the museum, holding the door for all three. All the military officers removed their headgear as they entered.

"Yip!" Johann said softly as he entered.

"What was that, Johann?" said Henry.

"She pinched my butt," Johann said in disgust. Henry shrugged, as if to say, "So what?"

"I am sure it was accidental," Lady MacDonald said.

Johann gave Julia dagger eyes as she maneuvered around the trio. The chief curator began her tour.

"This is the entrance hall. You can't see it today, but we have velvet ropes that will help people queue for check in and ticketing. With the support of your generous patronage, we can offer admission for the low rate of five pfennig. This will allow tourists and locals to come to the museum and discover their heritage. This way, please."

Again the curator motioned the trio forward by the curator and into the main hall, and again as they passed she gave Johann's butt a pinch. Another VIP signaled to the curator who stepped away from the trio and out of earshot for a few moments.

"I'm used to being taken advantage of, but that woman's pinches hurt!" said Johann. Henry just tried not to laugh; Lady MacDonald merely stayed silent. Julia then appeared wearing a new coat of lipstick.

"This is our main hall, where we discuss the Union's founding and Karl's tenure as first protector. We were very lucky to get some artifacts from Hansaburgh, including a one-sixtieth scale model of the Lena statue. The von Saltz family, who initially purchased the model, generously donated it. The model was one of the initial submissions when Karl commissioned the statue that now stands in Kocher Square," lectured Julia.

"I would very much like to see that," said Henry.

Julia nodded and said, "This way, Primus." The curator led the trio into a small display room, that held the statue's model. Henry moved towards the display, and Lady MacDonald followed him.

"The detail is amazing, Primus," said Lady MacDonald. "What an honor to have such an illustrious ancestor!"

"Thank you. Call me Henry, please. Only my parents call me Heinrich, or if I am introduced in more formal circumstances."

"Yes, Henry, and please call me Bonnie. My given name is actually

Beatrix, but everyone in my family calls me Bonnie. Plus, I actually prefer Bonnie."

"Both are beautiful names. Why are you Lady MacDonald? Shouldn't that be your mother?"

"My mother died when I was young. She and my unborn sister got the Martian sweats, and well, you know how things can progress with that."

"I get the sweats all the time," interjected Johann rather inappropriately. Henry looked at his valet.

"Johann, go learn something, somewhere else," Henry said. Henry noted Bonnie's discomfort with the statement and with Johann in general.

"I'm afraid to leave your side, sir," Johann said.

"Get braver," Henry responded. Johann looked for the curator, who spoke with another patron and made a beeline for another exhibit hall.

"I apologize, my valet..." said Henry.

"It's nothing," said Bonnie.

"He wasn't my choice," said Henry.

"I understand," replied Bonnie.

"Again, apologies."

"Let's go to my family's exhibit," said Bonnie, and she tipped her head towards an exhibit hall in the opposite direction of Johann's escape route. Henry followed Bonnie into the hall and saw yet another oil painting of *MacLeod's Landing on Stahlburgh*. The painting immediately drew Henry's attention. He paused looking at the canvas.

"The painting is beautiful, isn't it?" asked Bonnie, noting Henry had stopped moving.

"Yes, breathtaking," said Henry as he admired the details.

"This is a copy. The original is in MacDonald Hall, or as we MacDonalds call it, Dunvegan. The castle is our ancestral estate. My great-grandmother painted the original," said Bonnie with a touch of pride.

"Wait, I thought I had an original," said Henry. "There is one hanging outside my apartments in the Protector's Villa."

"Maybe? According to family lore, there were three originals. Nowadays, there are many forgeries. The story I have always heard was that my great-grandmother was at the landing when she was a young woman. Later, she made three paintings, each slightly different. My tutors were very precise in my lessons on the paintings, as they are a part of the MacDonald legacy," Bonnie said.

"Can you recognize if a painting is an original?" Henry asked.

"Maybe? I've never needed to though. My father had this reproduction made specifically for this exhibit. He had a professor from the University of the Isles at Portree supervise the reproduction."

"What is the history of the painting at Dunvegan?" Henry asked. He wanted to know more about the paintings, and Bonnie's excitement encouraged Henry's interest.

"My family is sure about our painting as my great-grandmother passed it to my grandfather. My great-grandmother was originally Flora MacLeod. She was a cousin of H. Malcolm. Some family legends say she was a pirate as fierce as Grace O'Malley, while others said she was the first weaver and seamstress on Steel, what we called Stahlburgh before the protector. The painting's legend begins when Flora turned sixteen. Her family decided to stop being star rovers and came to Stahlburg." Bonnie stopped; she looked embarrassed.

Henry was hanging on her every word. "Um, why'd they come?"

"Oh, you'll make fun of me," said Bonnie, her pale skin turning crimson.

"No, I won't. Please tell me," begged Henry.

"The family ran out of whisky," Bonnie said softly. Henry tried not to laugh, but the stereotype of the Scots and especially the Sheeplanders was that they didn't get out of bed without a dram of whisky. Henry started to chuckle.

"Go ahead and laugh," Bonnie said with a smile, "I suppose now, the more I think about it, the funnier it does sound. But in my great-gram's defense, Stahlburgh was a wonder. Our world exceeded my family's expectations about habitable worlds. From what I remember, most initial settlement expeditions turned out to be wild goose chases. Not Stahlburgh though."

"So, Flora's family settled here permanently," asked Henry.

"Yeah, MacLeod found Stahlburgh. Family tradition holds that while his ship had landed a time or two previously he'd always stayed on board. This landing was the big one as Flora and her family planned to settle. The soil was good, and the variform wheat would grow, and with that..."

"The whisky would flow," Henry said.

"Yes," said Bonnie. "I'm a bit of a weirdo for a MacDonald. I can't stand the stuff."

"Not really my thing, either, but my people are Germanic. We've always preferred beer," said Henry. "When did Flora paint the pictures? At the landing?"

"No, later, after she met my great-grandfather. That's a completely different tale, though. That one isn't just about H. Malcolm MacLeod, but involves the Prophet Malcolm, the Campbells, and Martin Fraser," said Bonnie.

"Wait! Martin Fraser was the one who gave my family the painting," said Henry.

"Well then, you might have one of the three real paintings," said Bonnie.

"Would you like to see it?" Henry made the offer reflexively, and then started to blush. He had inadvertently asked Bonnie to see his home, and while not exactly asking her over to his place, it was a bit forward for the Felgenland.

"Yes, but after the appropriate time. I don't frequently visit the homes of men whom I've just met," Bonnie said softly. She put a hand on Henry's arm, trying to soften the statement.

"I understand. Please forgive me. I just find this painting to be fascinating," replied Henry looking back at the canvas.

Bonnie blushed and said, "If you want to buy me a coffee, I will consider the matter forgotten."

Henry was about to respond to the suggestion, when Johann appeared. He was disheveled. His uniform was askew, and he had lipstick smears all across his face and neck. He looked like a hunted beast.

"There you are," Johann said with relief. "That woman is a monster! I don't know if I am in love or terrified."

Bonnie pursed her lips and turned red as she tried to contain her laughter.

Henry looked at Johann and raised an eyebrow.

"I know you're thinking, 'He's led her on,' but I swear to you I turned off the smolder! She's still interested!" Johann said. Henry laughed out loud. He never thought that Johann would be hoisted on his own petard, but here he was. Before anyone could say anything more, Henry's EVIL chirped. The message said Krueger was out front and ready to pick up Henry and Johann for their next engagement.

"Bonnie, thank you. Your history lesson was amazing," Henry said. "I'm on a tight schedule today, but I hope to see you again for a part two."

Bonnie gave a slight curtsy and said, "I hope to see you again as well. Goodbye, Henry."

"Bye," said Johann as he looked around frantically. "Quick, before she comes back, let's get out of here."

Johann grabbed Henry and began half dragging the Primus towards the exit. Before they were clear of the museum, Julia appeared.

"Leaving so soon," she asked locking eyes with Johann.

"Yes, Frau Schneider. I have another appointment. Both Johann and I enjoyed our time here immensely," Henry said. Julia just stared at

Johann.

"Well," she said in an almost purr, "you'll have to return."

"Of course, good day," Henry said.

"Oh, Johann," Julia called sweetly, "you forgot your hat."

Henry tried not to laugh as he said, "Better go get your cap, Johann. I'd hate for you to contravene Assault regulations."

Johann approached Julia like a timid kitten. After snatching the hat from her, Johann turned and ran to Henry's side.

"Bye-bye," Julia said blowing a kiss at Johann. As they exited the building, Johann said, "Thank the Allfather. She could have gobbled me up."

"I thought you liked that," Henry said.

"I thought I did too," Johann replied.

Krueger hopped out and opened the door so both men could enter the passenger compartment.

"You look like you had a good time, sir," Krueger said looking at Johann. Johann looked at a mirror.

"Eek! I've been tagged by that succubus!" Johann said. "Quick, get me a clean wipe or a handkerchief!"

Henry chuckled as Johann spent the drive to Parliament scrubbing his uniform and skin. When he finished, his skin looked raw from all the cleaning, but he was lipstick free.

"Are you rethinking sainthood now?" asked Henry.

"Potentially," said Johann as he straightened his uniform. "Since I was too busy avoiding that devil, tell me, what happened with you and that lady chick?"

Henry sighed. "I suppose it shouldn't surprise me that you have already forgotten her name. I was discussing art with Lady MacDonald."

"Art, eh?" Johann said suspiciously. "I think I've called it that before."

"Not everyone is a degenerate like you, Johann."

"Former degenerate. I'm swearing off my former life. Frau Schneider has made me see the error of my wanton ways, well, at least until tomorrow," said Johann.

"I don't think it works like that," said Henry. Johann was about to respond when the two young men saw the angry crowds of people surrounding the parliament building. Henry had expected protesters but the two camps looked ready to attack each other. The token protesters who casually waved signs and chatted with each other had been replaced by passionate true believers ready to fight the other side for their heretical beliefs. One camp held signs saying, "No War!" while the other held signs saying, "Destroy The Directorate!"

"Going to circle around the back way, sir," Krueger said. Henry nodded. He didn't want a repeat of the terrorists and the plaza.

"Gee, some of the folks look fighting mad. I wonder what's happening? I figured the war declaration was a done thing," said Johann.

"Guess we'll find out," Henry said. Both men sat alertly watching the crowds as the limo drove around the building to the private garage. Henry noted the Line Guards were actively patrolling around the building and in the garage. He and Johann exited as soon as the limo stopped.

"Security checkpoint, Primus," the ensign said. "You two know the drill."

Henry and Johann assumed a parade rest stance while the Line Guards searched them.

"I didn't expect any trouble from you, sir, but as you know, orders are orders," said the officer.

"Understood. Can you direct us to the Chancellery elevators?" asked Henry. He had been to the Parliament only a handful of times, and never had mapped the building like he had the cathedral.

"Go straight back and then turn left. If you get lost, my commander will direct you back there," said the Line Guard officer.

Henry and Johann followed the directions, passed the ensign's commander, and found the elevators without issue. Henry and Johann entered the lift. The console scanned Henry's EVIL and Johann's tablet allowing the young men to take the lift to the top floor. Henry noted the elevator went to its destination quickly and quietly. The doors opened to the Chancellery section, which was reserved for the protector, the Cognatii, and the high ministers of state.

"If we give him this power, the protector will drag us all into a war we cannot win! I do not want my poor son, Archibald, sacrificed on the altar of the protector's ego. Even today he spares his son from deployment while preparing ours for the charnel house of war!"

"Gilbraith's time has ended. The speaker now calls Grand Duchess Signe Bosdottir of Haldersmere. You have five minutes for a rebuttal," said the speaker.

"Dynasts, Gilbraith makes good points, if you wish to stick your head in the sand and hope the lion does not eat you!"

Henry watched as the Dynasts erupted in cheers and boos. As a part of the Chancellery, Henry was not permitted to disrupt the proceedings. He could only quietly watch.

The grand duchess continued, "I am sorry, assembled, I had a speech, but after listening to the cowardly pablum Gilbraith has just spouted, I can only turn into... what does the cowardly press call us?"

"The protector's ship wenches!" shouted a young uniformed blond woman. Henry suspected that was Signe's daughter, Astrid.

"Yes, that's right, daughter! As a former *ship wench*, all I can say is that as long as the Navy orbits over Stahlburgh we will defend our home, our kin..." Growing louder, she continued, "And when I was captain of the *Advantage*, we knew that our will to fight would always prevail! Our Navy is ready for every challenge, we are prepared! For the Union's people from death are spared!"

The red and golds started cheering wildly. The blacks were silent, while the oranges and violets booed loudly and shouted, "Jingoism!"

The grand duchess ignored the cries and continued, "If we listen to cowards, yes, I said it—*cowards*—like Gilbraith—we will die in our beds, killed by Terran death squads! I yield the rest of my time to a real man, Alasdair Campbell!"

The chamber erupted in boos and cheers. Henry craned his neck to look at the faction leaders. Alasdair Campbell ascended to the podium. Instead of wearing his uniform, he wore a tailored suit. He carried notes and he waited for the noise to stop before he spoke.

"Assaultman First Class Heinrich Baden... Assaultman First Class Thomas Maynard... Lance Corporal Frederik Schliss... Sergeant Terence White... Lieutenant George Stewart..."

Henry recognized that name! He looked at Johann and said, "He's reading the casualty and killed in action report from Asimov." Alasdair continued reading names for several more minutes and then paused.

"Need I go on, Dynasts? Have you forgotten Asimov?" Campbell said. "My Sister of Athena, Signe, has appealed to your heart as a brave Valkyrie. I could wrap myself in the uniform and claim my Assault service gives me the right to call for war. You all know in what unit I serve, whom I serve, and how my family makes its money. What does the MacDonald call my family? The 'military industrial clan?' I can hear your voice in my head saying that, Angus. Today though I come as a father. My son, Jason, is here today. He wears a uniform too. That is what you do when you are a Dynast. You bleed until the last liter is gone. As a Dynast, you can't send a poor man's son to war while keeping yours home. There is no Union without everyone sacrificing." Some booed and some cheered at this statement. Henry was transfixed. The obnoxious social climber had morphed into an elder statesman.

"We elected Raimond. We know the war will come, whether on our terms or not. I would prefer we push this war into the future. Regrettably, we don't get to know the Allfather's timetable for these events. Moments ago, my vassal, Gilbraith, let his fatherly love cloud his excellent judgment. I understand Gilbraith, my friend, what you said. Kenneth asked why should we put our sons on the bloody altar of war. He asked why did we not seek peace. I ask you, Gilbraith, and all of you whose sons and daughters walk in the land of the living, if we don't fight now, what do we say to the parents of Herr Baden and Herr Maynard? Those two brave men volunteered to fight a rearguard against thousands of soldiers of the Terran puppet government on Asimov. Those men's parents stand here today. Shall we ask them how to vote?" Campbell stopped and all eyes turned to a small, round, old woman. Her face was distraught with grief. At the silence she shouted with the passion of a heartbroken parent, "TO WAR! FIGHT! FOR THOMAS! FIGHT!"

Campbell's eyes watered and a tear rolled down his cheek. "I cannot compete with that statement. I surrender my time."

"The speaker calls on the Great King of the Skye Isles, Angus MacDonald, leader of the loyal opposition," the speaker said. Angus approached the podium. He wore traditional Sheeplands garb of a jacket and full plaid in a MacDonald tartan. His thinning red hair was pressed down, and his thick red beard neatly barbered. Henry watched as the great king ruffled through his notes. A tear fell down the man's cheek.

"My brothers and sisters, I am sorry," Angus said, "To Frau Maynard and all of the other parents, I send my prayers. I cannot comprehend the pain of losing a grown child. To the parents of the lost, I can only say that you must trust in the Allfather. As Malcolm, the prophet, said, 'We all will meet in the eternal age, and all pain will be washed away by the lamb.'" Angus took a moment; the hall was quiet.

Angus shuffled his papers and continued, "Did you know that on the streets of the European Social Commonwealth quoting Malcolm is considered hate speech? In the Australian Commonwealth, the government can fine me fifteen thousand Directorate credits or thirty gold dragons for even mentioning the name 'Allfather!' If I mention Malcolm on Luna, I go to jail for five years. If I say 'Jesus' on Mars, the government can summarily shoot me on the spot. Gilbraith and his party would have made good points, if we were talking about a regime that honored natural, Allfather-given rights. But... the Directorate... does... not! As you all know, I am in opposition to the Gordon government. I preferred the last government where MacDoughall led the Blacks in a majority-minority government with the Oranges. Now, I watch as the Reds and Golds become a super-party dedicated to their causes and industries. And yes, the Campbell and his 'military-industrial clan' sit smack dab in the middle of that alliance. But, record what I say now! I speak to the future so that all generations from here on will know the MacDonald, leader of the Blacks, votes for war! The MacDonald may argue with the other Dynasts, but do siblings not fight the hardest with each other? The Directorate would silence me for speaking my mind. The Campbell may attempt to wheedle away what belongs to my clan, but he has never attempted to silence me! As much as the Campbell is a rival, on Sunday, at the Cathedral of our glorious prophet, I can turn to him and offer him the peace of Christ. One day, Allfather willing, we may both let bygones be bygones. HAVE THE TERRANS EVER SUGGESTED BYGONES BE BYGONES!? NO! SO, I SHOUT TERRA DELENDA EST!" Henry realized he needed to breathe. He had held his breath throughout the entire speech. The chamber was as quiet as a tomb.

"Put me in a dress and call me Susan," said Johann. "Did that just happen? Did the Campbells and MacDonalds just agree on something?"

"TO WAR! FIGHT!" called out Alasdair Campbell. "Fight!"

"TO WAR AND FIGHT!" responded Angus MacDonald. The Dynasts in government began to chant "Fight!" MacDonald's Blacks joined the chant, "Fight!"

"Call a vote!" shouted Angus.

"Call a vote! Call a vote!" the members shouted.

"The speaker calls for a voice vote. All in favor of the resolution to declare war on Terra say 'yea!'"

The chamber roared, "YEA!"

"Opposed?"

A weak mutter of "Nay" returned.

"By voice vote, the Dynasts have ratified the Commons' vote of war. The speaker will now carry the bill to the protector to be signed," said the speaker.

"You will not need to carry the bill far!" shouted Otto Weber.

"Dynasts! I present, the Protector of the Union!"

"Long may he live!" shouted the Reds and Golds. A short moment later the Blacks carried the call. Henry had tears welling in his eyes. His father looked resplendent in his uniform as he climbed the podium. Angus bowed and moved out of Raimond's way.

"I beg your pardon, Prime Minister, Secretaries, and Speaker for this breech of protocol. I am prevented by tradition from speaking in this chamber, but today you have made history. I only wish to place a footnote on your narrative. Never before has the Felgenland Union declared war and never before has a protector needed to sign a declaration of war. As my father said, 'I am a man of peace,' so I say that too. Today, among the leading families, you have made a claim of injury against the Terran Directorate. I am here to deliver that message to the dictators of Earth. Bring the seal!"

The *Kriegskanzler*, the war chancellor, appeared. The man was old, older than the protector and moved slowly due to his age.

"They dug up old Schwartzenrode!" Johann said.

"I'm shocked you knew that, Johann," Henry said.

"I... um... dated... his niece for a while. She was really something!"

"Like Frau Schneider?" Henry asked.

"Yeah, in twenty years," said Johann.

"With this seal, I assent and sign this bill of war. To our foes in the Terran Directorate I say, 'Beware! I have unleashed the Dragon. The sons and daughters of the frontier have spoken!'" Otto Weber's baritone voice started singing the chorus and first verse of "Sons and Daughters of the Frontier," the Union's national anthem.

We hear the echoes of our past,
In the old songs we sing and stories held fast.
We're the sons and daughters of the frontier!
Carrying on Lena's legacy, holding it dear.

In Stahlburgh the heart of the Felgenland, our fortunes aligned,
A union born of hope, we were all entwined.
We're the sons and daughters of the frontier,
In this land of freedom, we hold traditions dear.

Gray skies ignite with starlight at night,
Faith guiding us through darkness as we struggle and we fight.
We're the pioneers, carving out the sky,
United by our freedom until we die!

Between the chorus and the first verse, the chamber resonated. Henry and even Johann joined the singing. The anthem continued to the crescendo:

United together, all our foes will fall,
Assaultmen and the Navy, the Felgenland's wall.
Oh, come you sons and daughters of the frontier!
Remember together, we'll all hold Lena's vision dear!

"Parliament is dissolved for the week!" the protector said. With that statement, the magic suddenly disappeared. The Dynasts who were part of the government crowded around the protector. The Commons government ministers appeared and joined their Dynast counterparts. The Union was going to war. The protector and his council were planning how to send the notice to Terra, with a punctuation mark delivered by the Navy and dotted by the Assault.

Henry and Johann looked at each other like strangers in a strange land. A page appeared with a note.

"Primus, Primus!" the young man said as he handed Henry the note. Henry read the note, which said, "Join me down on the floor, Heinrich - RvM"

"We're joining the government," Henry said.

"I knew the Allfather would reward me for my holiness," Johann said.

"On the floor, not actually joining the government," said Henry as he started down the stairs.

"Wait up. So, I'm not getting made a minister?" Johann asked.

Henry hurried down the stairs and into the huddle of the government ministers.

"Here he is. Ask him," the protector said as Henry appeared.

"Now that we are at war, do you intend to surrender your commission?" one of the government ministers asked.

"What! Why would I do that?" Henry said in surprise.

"A good question," the protector said, "Why did you ask that *Landwirtschaftminister* Grünfeld?"

"Gilbraith said he was being removed from duty. Since we are at war, I seek that the Union shares all hardships equally," von Grünfeld said.

"Gilbraith isn't a minister in our government and does not know about which he speaks," Raimond said. "My son will serve like any plowman's son."

"Of course," Henry said, "I am an Assaultman; I have trained for war."

Raimond nodded at his son.

"You are dismissed, Heinrich," the protector said. Henry bowed and left.

"Drat, I thought you were going to be minister of the treasury, and I could have been your auditor. I would have loved going into all those vaults of dragons and running my hand through all that dirty money," Johann said.

"Johann, you're filthy rich already! Why do you want to be an auditor," Henry said.

"My wealth is tied up in bonds and stocks. It's all digital. There's a thrill to running your hands through physical gold," Johann said.

"Simple, cash the stocks into hard currency," Henry said.

"No way! My accountant would kill me!" said Johann. Henry was about to say something when Bonnie MacDonald appeared.

"Hello, Henry," she said shyly.

"Hello, Bonnie. What are you doing here?" asked Henry.

"I'm meeting my father. Although I saw his speech, I can't believe we're agreeing with Campbells. At this rate, we'll have pigs flying."

"There have been stranger things in the Felgenland," Henry said.

"I'm sure," Bonnie said.

"Oh, about that coffee," Henry said suddenly remembering that he hadn't given Bonnie an answer. She looked at him expectantly. Henry's EVIL chirped.

"Drat, I've got to go, or I'll be late for another engagement," Henry said, forgetting what he was about to say.

"I understand," Bonnie said, "Well, then, I will see you later."

"Yes, farewell!" Henry said, grabbing Johann who was trying to eavesdrop on the ministers.

"Wait! They were discussing logistics! I could make a fortune if I hear what industries they're gearing up to purchase from!" Johann said as Henry dragged him by his jacket.

"You'd end up on a penal colony for insider trading," Henry said.

"No, I could afford the best advocates. I could dodge penal colony time for a good three or four years at least. If I got a sexy, older female judge I could maybe get off with a slap on the wrist!"

Henry pumped his legs. He had minutes to get from the Parliament to the Villa, get the delivered uniform, change outfits and get in the limo.

"Wait! The garage is that way," Johann said pointing. He had finally started walking on his own rather than being dragged along by Henry.

"We're taking the sky bridge," Henry said.

"Uh... We're walking? How peasant chic!" Johann said.

"We don't have time to play in traffic. Krueger is a good driver but..."

"Traffic sucks in the capital?" Johann said helpfully.

"Yeah, not going to argue on that," Henry said. Both men walked across the skyway that connected the parliament building with the Villa and the cathedral. They were almost at the Villa when they reached a checkpoint.

"Identification," said the Assault sergeant manning the checkpoint. Henry presented his EVIL and Johann produced his tablet.

"Cleared," the sergeant said after scanning the devices. Henry entered the Villa and said, "We're not taking the elevator, we'll take the stairs."

"Really? Go without me," Johann said, "I don't do exercise. Remember, I bribe my way out of PT in the Assault. Sure, I can walk, but I absolutely draw the line at stairs!"

"Fine. Stay here. I'll dance with all the ladies at the ball," said Henry.

"Wait! I'm going! I can do some stairs!" Johann said. Three flights later, Johann complained, "I can't do any more stairs! My legs will fall off!"

"Come on! We're almost there!" Henry said.

"If I hadn't walked, I could do these stairs!" Johann said.

After two more flights and a lot of whining, Johann and Henry made it to the floor where the Protelan Suite was located. Henry charged forward but stopped at the painting.

"Come on, Henry! We're going to miss the ladies!" Johann said. "You can get Lady MacCarrotTop to explain what the big deal is about the painting after I find my perfect soul mate for this evening!"

"Her name is MacDonald!" Henry said hurrying into the suite. The uniform hung in plastic on his door. He threw off the older Class A uniform he was wearing and put on the formal uniform. After changing, Henry combed his brown hair and felt ready for the banquet.

"Come on, Henry!" shouted Johann.

"Where are you?" Henry shouted back.

"In the elevator, I've jammed the lift. Close the door on your way out! I don't want riff-raff going through my things!" Johann said. Henry hurried, and Johann released the door just before the elevator's alarm began buzzing.

"Krueger is waiting for us?" Johann asked. He was more amped than a green Assaultmen before a combat drop.

"Yes," Henry said, "You know there's a small ceremony before the ball?"

"Don't care. After the day I've had, I want to see some cleavage and maybe a mini-skirt or two," said Johann.

"What do you mean? Today has been great!" said Henry.

"For you, maybe! I woke up with a rash from that scullery witch's curse! Then, I was almost bored to death at the Protelani embassy. After that, I nearly lost my soul to a demon masquerading as a librarian!"

"She's a curator not a librarian," replied Henry.

"Whatever! Then, I missed my opportunity to be minister of the treasury, and finally, you made me walk and climb stairs!" said Johann. "If I don't see a woman in a barely there gown in the next thirty minutes, I am going to get really upset!"

Henry looked at the valet, slightly worried, and then said, "Calm down. No guarantees, but I am pretty sure one or both of the Falke twins will show up. They're some distaff cousins of Campbells."

"Blond, brunette, or red head," said Johann in a surly voice.

"Depends on the event," said Henry.

"What's their base level of standards for guys?" Johann asked.

"They have no standards, whatsoever," Henry said.

"Perfect, let's go!" Johann said as the elevator opened.

"Then its aye! Aye! Hooray," Henry said following the valet.

"Lust leads the way!" shouted Johann mangling the second verse of the "Marching Song of the Felgenland."

"It is supposed to be, 'The Assault leads the way,'" Henry said crawling into the waiting hoverlimo behind the hard-charging valet.

"Not tonight," Johann said.

"I'm still heading to the MacLeod house, right, sir," Krueger asked.

"Get me to the Falke twins!" Johann said.

"Huh?" Krueger said.

"Yes, the MacLeod house, sergeant," said Henry.

"Yes, sir," said Krueger.

"Make it quick or I'll make sure you're whipped for insubordination!" Johann said.

"You can roll up the window, sergeant," said Henry.

"Thanks, sir," said Krueger as he rolled up the internal window that separated the driver's compartment from the passenger's compartment.

After a few minutes, the MacLeod house appeared. The house was a gigantic estate in the middle of the Bundstadt's eastern suburbs. Whether MacLeod had ever owned the place was debatable. The house functioned as an event center and could be rented. The protector and his family would frequently book the venue as an alternate, non-Villa setting for events. The limo pulled into the wide circular driveway that allowed drivers to easily and safely pick up and drop off guests. Johann banged roughly on the window and Kreuger lowered the glass.

"Sir?" he asked.

"Let me out here! The Falke twins await!" Johann said. Krueger stopped, activated his flashers and remotely opened the passenger door. Johann hopped out and practically ran towards the estate house.

"Look, sir, I can get closer, but there are severe butt-holes clogging up the circle," Krueger said.

"It's fine. I'll walk. There are security cameras, I'll be safe," said Henry. Henry hopped out and began to walk toward the main entrance. Another hoverlimo pulled in front of Krueger and stopped. The door opened and Henry watched a black stockinged leg wearing a cobalt high heel emerge from the vehicle. A sequined royal blue skirt and sparkly blue bodice topped by a coiffed and loosely curled head of red hair followed the leg out of the hoverlimo. Henry moved closer. The woman pushed the curls away from her face to reveal Bonnie MacDonald complete with evening makeup.

"Wow, you look nice," Henry said.

"So do you," she replied. "We've met three times in one day. It must be fate."

"For sure," Henry said.

"So, coffee?" Bonnie asked with a smile.

"Yes," Henry replied. "But we've gone out three times now. That makes us friends by the agony aunts' standards in the news."

"I suppose, I don't really read those columns," Bonnie said. She wobbled a bit and found her footing in her ten-centimeter heels. Henry offered her his arm. She blushed and demurred but then took a step and wobbled again.

"Okay, this isn't what it looks like! I wear pressure boots more than heels these days," Bonnie said.

"I bet all the Valkyries say that," Henry said. She grabbed his extended arm and steadied herself.

"Thanks," she said facing Henry.

"You're welcome," Henry replied softly. He could smell Bonnie's perfume. The fragrance was a mix of vanilla, clove, and jasmine.

"I'm better now. I don't need your arm," she said. Henry kept his arm out if she wanted to release. She flushed a little and said, "I'm going to end up in the society pages as your girlfriend."

"Is that a problem?" Henry asked.

"I don't know? Do you have a girlfriend?" Bonnie asked.

"No, my parents are trying to match me with an 'appropriate' match. What about you? Any boyfriends?" Henry asked.

"I dated a guy, but he shipped out with the First Stahlburgh Rifles," Bonnie said.

"What's his name? Maybe I know him?" said Henry.

"Frank Nordlinger, he's a lieutenant in the First Stahlburgh Rifles. We broke up when he shipped out," replied Bonnie.

"Never heard of him. He sounds like a dumb guy if he broke up with you, Bonnie."

Bonnie smiled and they reached the estate house's entrance.

"Well, we must part ways here," Bonnie said as she released her grasp on Henry's arm. "Otherwise, I *will* end up on the society pages."

"I'm sure they've matched me to worse," Henry said with a smile.

"And much, much better," Bonnie replied. Henry was about to respond when a man staggered up to him.

"You upstarts feel you are better than the rest of us," the man said, liquor on his breath. "My family came here with MacLeod. They sat the foot of the burning cross! Where were your people? Scratching out salt on that worthless rock, Hansaburgh!"

Henry took a deep sigh. "Come on friend, I'll get you another drink."

"No, you turd! You'll do your duty and die like a good boy in your father's war!" the man said.

Henry straightened. He could take insults about his family but wouldn't take insults to his honor.

"What rank were you in the Assault!? How many friends have you lost in combat?"

The man turned red and he looked like he was going to punch the Primus. Henry wasn't worried. Henry passed his hand-to-hand combat training and—like all MjGAs—was rated level five. Henry tensed, ready to fight.

"Oh, Kenny, there you are, I thought I lost you," a thirty-something femme fatale said exiting the estate house. She wore a skin tight body contouring dress that left nothing to the imagination. She put a soothing hand on the angry man.

"I'm sorry, Primus," she said. "My little Kenny is upset he lost his little votesy-woatsy today. I've promised to make it up to him later."

The woman seductively rubbed against Kenneth, who growled at Henry. Henry felt a hand wrap around his arm.

"Let's go in, dear. Our friends are waiting for us," said Bonnie.

Henry looked at Bonnie with surprise. She kissed Henry's cheek, and he could feel the residue of her soft pink lipstick there.

"Wait, who are you?" said the woman hanging on Kenneth.

"I am the scion of the first family, the MacLeod-MacDonalds. Who are you?" Bonnie said. Henry almost expected Bonnie to add the word "harlot" to her statement, her tone was so strong.

"I'm Martha, and just a lowly little ol' Clark," the woman said winking at Henry while petting Kenneth.

"Go away," Bonnie said, as only a Sister of Athena could.

While Martha Clark steered Kenneth inside, he kept his eyes on Henry.

"I'll be watching you boy," Kenneth said menacingly. Before Henry could respond, the voice of Alasdair Campbell said, "I apologize, Primus. *Graf* Gilbraith-on-Heather is a sore loser." Campbell then hesitated when he saw Bonnie's arm around Henry.

"I see you are choosing your side early this evening," Campbell said stiffly. Henry grew rigid, but Bonnie squeezed Henry's arm, and said,

"Why Alasdair, you should remember that we unmarried women are free agents. We have no loyalty to our birth clans. Or, was your wife, Margrethe MacDonald, oops, I mean, Campbell wrong when she said that on your wedding day? How is my distaff cousin? We miss her at our MacDonald clan gatherings."

"After thirty years of marriage, she remains very much a Campbell," Alasdair said sourly. Then he turned to Henry, "If you will follow me, I will ensure your... guest... has a spot at the head table with you."

"Of course, please lead the way," Henry said. Bonnie didn't relax her grasp. She and Henry went hand on arm to their spot at the head table. Henry checked the room; he didn't see Johann anywhere. Henry couldn't decide if that was a plus or a dangerous minus.

Henry helped Bonnie into her seat. She sat next to her cousin Margrethe, while Henry was between Bonnie and Alasdair. The position between the two rival clans gave Henry a greater appreciation for his father and grandfather.

The guests all began to sit down. Henry remembered he was supposed to say a few words.

He produced the printed notes he had received for the occasion, and stood. He took a spoon and gently tapped his wine glass to call the gathering's attention.

"Dynasts, gentry, and other assembled guests," said Henry. "We come now to honor the selfless service of the Grand Duke of Argyll-Inveraray-on-the-Greenwich, Alasdair Campbell. Argyll placed himself at great personal risk to protect not only myself, but the citizens of the Bundstadt. As a result, I am here to offer not only my thanks, but the thanks of the protector, and present the Silver Shield of Honor, for gallantry in duty. Argyll, if you'd please stand."

Campbell stood up. Ever the politician he nodded and smiled politely while Henry pulled out the clamshell with the award. Henry opened the clamshell and Campbell received the award with his left hand. Then Alasdair offered his right hand to Henry to shake. Both men clasped hands, and then separated.

Picking up his wine glass, Henry said, “Now, raise your glasses to Colonel Alasdair Campbell!”

“Here, here!” the assembled said.

Just as Henry took his seat most of the uniformed guests in the assembly stood up and began leaving. Henry knew what the exodus meant. The Union’s military was calling up all the active duty and reserve military members. Henry sat and checked his EVIL. It was powered on and silent. Bonnie’s clutch vibrated, and he knew she just received her orders to report for duty.

“I’ve got thirty minutes to respond,” Bonnie whispered in his ear.

“Thank you for the conversation,” Henry responded.

“A war doesn’t excuse you from a coffee date,” Bonnie said. Henry smiled.

“Be careful and come back for the coffee, I promise we’ll go somewhere special.”

Bonnie nodded and kissed his cheek in front of everyone. Henry stood, helped Bonnie with her chair, and watched her leave.

When he sat down next to Campbell, Henry realized a large number of people had gone. Henry knew that Campbell’s duty station was here in the capital and there was no rush for Alasdair to report. Henry wasn’t sure why his EVIL hadn’t chirped with orders. The Seventy-Second Grenadiers would most assuredly deploy since they were the Union’s special forces regiment.

“You know, I have a cousin that is your age, Primus,” Alasdair said. “If you ever should need a companion for an event, I can ensure her attendance. It seems you are destined for more of these events rather than a troop transport.”

The remark irritated Henry, but he simply nodded. Servants delivering food to the high table distracted Alasdair and Henry took the moment to reflect on Campbell’s statement. Was Campbell being mean? Or, was the man giving Henry some form of court intelligence.

The dinner was a single course since the event included dancing. Henry methodically ate the meal. He hadn't had much since breakfast, yet he didn't want to appear boorish by stuffing his face. When the dancing began Henry just sat at the table. He wasn't the only person who was without a partner for the night. As Henry watched the dancing, a young red-headed man approached the table and stood in front of the Primus. The man performed a head bow, seeking Henry's permission to speak.

"Yes," said Henry.

"May I join you, Primus?" the man asked.

"I see the other MacDonald has now appeared. Late to the party, like all MacDonalds," said Alasdair. The comment intrigued Henry and he nodded "yes" to the man. The man moved to sit in the chair that Bonnie had occupied.

"Good evening, sir. I am Crown Prince Drostan MacDonald, nephew of King Angus and my uncle's heir," Drostan said. "I am here to determine your intentions towards my cousin, Beatrix." Henry paused for a moment. He hadn't intended to appear to have dishonorable intentions with Bonnie.

"I assure you my intentions are strictly honorable. Your cousin and I became acquainted after seeing each other at three separate events today," said Henry.

"Don't worry, Primus," said Campbell, intruding on the conversation, "All of the MacDonalds will sell their womenfolk for a dozen sheep. Marriage is entirely optional."

Drostan eyed Alasdair and said, "We may sell a woman for marriage, but only a Campbell would marry a sheep."

In his peripheral vision Henry saw Margrethe stiffen at the statement. Henry waited, but Margrethe must have decided it was better not to get involved when two Felgenlander men were exchanging insults.

"Oh, the brat wishes to impress the Primus. Watch yourself,

Heinrich. The MacDonalds appear friendly, but if money changes hands, they are worse than Terran bankers."

Drostan's pale cheeks grew red in anger. "I suppose, yes, you must be wary around MacDonalds with your money, Primus, but never turn your back on a Campbell. If you do, you'll find everything you hold dear stolen from you: lands, counties, and favorite aunts."

"Oh, look, Primus, the brat is upset a more prudent clan has taken yet another mismanaged relationship. Don't you have an uncle to wheedle an inheritance from? Now run along, little brat, this table is for responsible dynasties!"

Drostan gave Campbell a stare that Henry had seen before. Henry suspected that if Drostan wasn't in front of a crowd, he and Alasdair would be exchanging blows.

"I didn't stammer. Or, have you been drinking Gilbraith's vassal's brew? The MacDonalds can't get enough of it. Sadly, the whisky makes them as stubborn as the waves they fish," Alasdair needled.

"Campbell, Drostan asked to speak with me. Let him have his say," said Henry. He was tiring of whatever history the two men were reenacting.

Drostan turned to Henry. "Another time, Primus. I will speak with you again without the present boorish company. Goodbye."

Alasdair, emboldened by Drostan's retreat, said, "Go on, you, before you smell up this gathering with your rotten island fish!"

Drostan bowed to Henry, then turned and walked away. Henry relaxed, and a page presented Campbell with a note.

"I must leave, Primus. I am urgently needed at Campbell Industries. Come, Margrethe, I've got to deal with work and I worry for your sensibilities since the drunkards and riff-raff are invading." Then Alasdair bowed and Margrethe stood and gave Henry a curtsy. Then both left, leaving Henry alone at the table. After a polite space of time, Henry used his EVIL to message his valet and driver. He then stood and exited the estate house. Krueger waited in the hoverlimo by the exit. Johann was nowhere to be seen, not that Henry had bothered looking.

"Where to, sir?" Krueger asked. Heinrich debated saying the country, but instead he said, "The Villa. It's been a long day."

"Yes, sir," replied Krueger. Henry mused the man would be happy to get back to the Villa and go off duty.

"Should we wait for your valet?" Krueger asked after a pause.

Henry sighed and said, "Nope, he'll find his way back. He always does."

Viking Raid

"Hit that big fellow again!" the *Freiherr* screamed. Jurgen could feel the lump forming where the brute had slammed his massive fist into his face. He'd have a bruise, but Jenny was used to seeing those now. She certainly liked the meals and the pints they'd bought.

Jurgen moved forward. It was time to end this fight. After all, the brute was making Jurgen burn calories he couldn't afford. The brute was *Freiherr* Thackeray's man, and he looked like a little head attached to a muscular brick. Jurgen had pounded the man in the face a dozen times and the brute just stood there smiling, his incisor-less smile. The brute readied his fists to protect his head.

Jurgen prepared to perform, what recently, had become his signature move: a hard left to the gut followed by a right cross to the face. He'd broken tougher opponents with that move, and he was sure this brute would go down too. Jurgen stepped in with his left, smashing into the brute's softer belly and causing his opponent to double up, leaving his face unprotected. The brute realized the fight was over a split second before Jurgen's right cross connected. After Jurgen's fist slammed into his face, the brute dropped into the mud of the makeshift ring. Jurgen tried to feel bad for the brute, the man wouldn't get any money for losing the fight, but the thought of the winnings kept running through Jurgen's head.

"Good man, Wulfjaeger!" screamed *Freiherr* Donal MacTavish, his backer.

The old *Freiherr*, or baron, was the descendant of the man who named the village, William MacTavish, and the barony or shire,

Tavishire. The shire wasn't much really, just a few farming families, a general store, and a small state church. For Jurgen, Tavishire was the only home he'd known. He was born here, and he'd probably die here. Up to the north on the shire's border was Tauber-over-the-Roten. Tauber-over-the-Roten was in the Valley of the First Farmers. Jurgen figured that if he ever got ahead of his expenses, then he'd go there. If he didn't, well, that was up to the Allfather. Many Tavishire men, including Jurgen's uncle, would disappear seeking their fortune and fame.

"Jurgen, Jurgen!" a shrill little voice yelled through the gathered onlookers who sat smoking pipes or chewing tobacco. Jenny always demanded the real, not synthetic, cigarettes and the woman smoked like a chimney, but never offered one to Jurgen. Jurgen didn't smoke. He'd tried a cheap cigar when he was younger, got caught by his father, and was forced to smoke several until he threw up. That was enough smoking for him.

"What's up, scamp?" Jurgen asked his oldest sister, Mara.

"Mother says you have to come home, now," she said, like only a ten-year-old girl could in her demanding yet factual voice. Jurgen loved the young girl the most out of all his siblings. Only his younger brother, Olrich, could boss him around more than Mara. Olrich spent most of his days as only a fourteen-year-old farmhand could, working the land. All of Jurgen's siblings had to make money; the debts and the rents were crippling his family. Well, that was what Jurgen's mother always said.

Jurgen found his shirt where he'd thrown the garment before the fight. As he straightened to fasten the long-sleeved button down, he felt one of his teeth give way in his mouth. He stooped over to spit it out.

"You need to duck more!" Mara said coaching her brother.

"I do duck! Now, let me collect my winnings and we're off," Jurgen said, turning to MacTavish. Jurgen saw silver and a little gold as money changed hands among the cronies, bookies, and factors that surrounded the old baron. Jurgen knew MacTavish would be in a good mood; the old baron always bet a lot of money on Jurgen.

"Wulfjaeger, my boy," MacTavish said looking at Jurgen as he approached. Jurgen smiled at the "my boy." When MacTavish called Jurgen that, the baron's winnings were especially large.

"I've won a gold dragon from old Mercy here," MacTavish said, pointing to the elder John Mercy, the shire's largest landowner. Mercy was a former Assaultman and had married a Sheeplands' beauty. Other than his wife's premature death, Mercy had everything and his attitude showed it. MacTavish was delighting in making Mercy pay him. Usually money went to a Mercy, not the other way.

"Congratulations, *Freiherr*," Jurgen said. The gold coin with a dragon's image was something that, if Jurgen had no debts, he could see after five years of hard labor. Dragons were a rare sight in Tavishire.

"Oh, and here is your part: one silver griffin and fifteen copper pfennig," MacTavish said. "If you come back tomorrow, I'll double that!"

"Thank you, kindly, sir," said Jurgen taking the money. Half would go to his mother, since she always needed money. Jurgen would spend the rest on Jenny.

Mara walked up and took Jurgen's hand, "Goodbye, *Freiherr*. Our mother needs Jurgen at home."

The baron laughed. "Mara, let me know when you're old enough, and I'll match you to my oldest," MacTavish said loudly. "He needs a tough woman to keep him on the clock!"

"Thank you, sir. Goodbye," Mara said. She was young but had learned—like all commoners—that the nobility, even country barons, were to be shown courtesy. Mara also knew the corollary: avoid the nobility as much as possible.

"Remember what I said, Wulfjaeger," MacTavish said as Mara pulled Jurgen through the crowd.

"I will. Thanks, sir," shouted Jurgen in response.

Jurgen and Mara escaped the crowd from the boxing pit. They then passed the church, carefully crossed themselves at the graveyard, and took the leftmost track to their cottage. The family cottage was deep in the woods.

"What is all this about, Scamp?" Jurgen asked, his mind returning to his sister's message.

"Mother said she would tell you when you get home. She has bad news," Mara said. The matter-of-fact attitude about bad news annoyed Jurgen, but Mara was tougher than Steelwood when she was given a task, and if he was to wait for news, so be it. The duo marched towards the cottage in the distance.

"Is one of the boys hurt? Are Olrich, Freddy, and Duncan alright?" asked Jurgen with a sudden worry.

"They are fine, and Agatha is fine as well," Mara said, naming her younger sister.

"Then the news is about Jenny, right?" said Jurgen as he broke into a run.

"Wait, I'm coming with you!" shouted Mara. Jurgen ran down the track, through a copse of fir trees, before reaching the broken stone fence that marked the cottage's front garden.

"Jurgen, I see you got another bruise today. Johnny Mercy's tractor throw you again?" said his mother from the rocker where she sat by the door. Jurgen had been lying to his mother about the source of his fighting money. His lie was that he worked for the younger Mercy on his farm.

At first, the tale was true. Jurgen had worked on the farm for a day where Johnny continually called him "worthless woodland trash." When Jurgen had enough, he quit. Jurgen had sporadically fought in the village's bare knuckle boxing ring. No longer employed, Jurgen went to the ring during "working hours." At first, the winnings were small, but after several surprise wins, Jurgen's profits enabled him to afford his mother and Jenny.

"No, mum. I was cleaning the stables and Mercy's riding horse kicked me," lied Jurgen. He hated the lying, but his mother didn't appreciate the village fighting ring or the men who participated in the boxing. She would pass the ring and say that "bare-knuckle fighting was almost as bad as joining the Assault." Jurgen always reasoned that at least boxing wouldn't get him killed.

"So, you haven't seen Jenny at all today?" his mother asked. Jurgen tried to puzzle out why she asked.

"Why? Mara said you had bad news," said Jurgen his blood suddenly cold.

"Mother, Mother!" Mara said running up.

"I'm telling him now, Mara. Go wash up for supper," the woman said to her daughter. Mara nodded meekly but before she went inside, she looked at Jurgen and said, "I'm sorry, Jurgen."

Jurgen waited until Mara was inside to question his mother. He hated being treated like a child; he was nineteen. He'd spent two years in backbreaking labor as a conscript for the local count building the roads. He was a voting man on the census rolls. He deserved to know what was going on with his girlfriend.

"Preacher read Jenny and Johnny Mercy's banns today at the service," Jurgen's mother said. "I missed you at church. I always save you a seat in our pew."

Jurgen felt the cold worry turn to hot fury. Jenny had strung him along and now dumped him. She hadn't even had the decency to tell him they were done.

"I always thought your absence was funny, Jurgen. You work straight through the week and also on the sabbath, but old Mercy's hands are always at church on Sunday."

Jurgen realized that his lies had caught up with him. All he wanted to do now was head to the pub. There, Gretchen would smile at him and let him drink as much lager as the few silver coins in his pocket would buy. Maybe if he told her his story, she would give him strong ale at lager prices.

"Well, what do you have to say for yourself?" the older woman asked. The question wasn't gentle. Other than selling eggs, he'd never seen his mother earn any money. Sure, she occasionally cooked, but Jurgen and his siblings did all of the work and brought in most of the income.

"I'm going to the pub to get drunk," snapped Jurgen. He didn't have to explain anything to his mother.

"Just like your father," said Jurgen's mother venomously. Jurgen could feel the hot tears forming at the corner of his eyes. His mother's remark was a low blow. Jurgen's father was small man inside a large man's body. Jurgen and all of his siblings knew that their father drank to make up the difference. When sober, Jurgen's father had been almost human. Jurgen turned and marched past the cottage's front garden, heading towards the village and the pub.

"Jurgen! Don't go!" shouted Mara as she ran out of the cottage door.

"Go inside, now, Mara," his mother said sharply. Jurgen didn't even turn around. He wasn't going to back down to his mother anymore. She was on her own from now on, and the pub was calling to Jurgen. He charged down the track. He neglected crossing himself at the graveyard which held his dead father's grave. Jurgen's mood only lightened as he saw the tavern's shingle. Jurgen knew the shingle well. The sign bore a yellow rooster crowing and "The Golden Cock" in Gothic script. Jurgen was sure there was some subliminal message in the shingle but he was never sober enough to ask Gretchen, the publican.

"Lager me up! Ah hell, give me a whiskey!" Jurgen shouted crossing the bar's threshold.

"Aye, dearie," Gretchen said. "You want: Irish, Scottish, Martian, or Felgenland whisky?"

"Hell, why not try 'em all?" Jurgen feared whiskey, especially Scots whisky. Today, he'd conquer that fear. Jurgen had always avoided hard liquor since whisky had been his father's downfall. When the man died from falling off a ladder, the constable said he reeked like a Sheeplands' still.

"Suit yourself, love," said Gretchen. She placed five shot glasses on the bar. Jurgen picked up the first one and slammed the glass back. After the heat left his throat, he threw back three more shots. He moved left to right along the shots on the bar. The heat built until felt numb all over. Jurgen began to feel worn out and put his head on the bar.

Jurgen jerked when someone slammed a hand on the bar. He lifted his head and saw an Assault sergeant and two other Assaultmen climbing onto the barstools next to him.

"Give us a good strong ale, wench," one of the Assaultmen said to Gretchen.

"Coin first," said Gretchen snidely to the Assaultman.

"Now, now, don't be like that, sweetheart," another Assaultman said. "We're real men, not this peasant rabble. We have money, and a lot more for a dove like you."

"Here's plenty of coin, bar wench," the sergeant said. The sergeant slapped down a recently printed five dragon note on the bar. The note still smelled like the printer. Jurgen looked at the old face of the Primus, the man looked a few years older than Jurgen's grandfather had been when he died. Gretchen's eyes lit up. The bar never made that type of money even during the cattle markets.

"Beg your pardon, gov," said Gretchen. Her toned had changed and she cooed at the Assaultmen.

"Your best ale too, wench," snapped the sergeant impatiently. "None of that watered down peasant swill!"

Jurgen smiled at the Assaultmen's bravado. They looked like wolves among the village sheep. Jurgen realized that he'd never had the temerity to address Gretchen in such a rough fashion. Most of the patrons were polite to Gretchen, who had the power to ban them from being served.

"Folk round here don't much like the Assault, gents," said Jurgen to the Assaultmen.

"Why is that?" the sergeant said stiffly, turning to the peasant who had the pluck to address him.

"Our count is one of them colors that doesn't much fancy the Union," Jurgen said slurring his words ever so slightly.

"He's a Violet?" asked the sergeant.

"Violet, Orange, Black, whatever... He's got us all bowing and scraping, but I'm brave enough to say 'Allfather bless the Union and our protector!' The count can damn me to hell. But I know our protector ain't a bad egg. He's just got his hands tied with the Dyn... the Allfather-forsaken nobles," Jurgen said, unable to say "Dynasts."

"You sound like you've been conscripted," the sergeant said. Jurgen nodded.

"It's a terrible thing that the Dynasts do to you peasants. Karl wanted the life-tax to make people appreciate the Union. Make you work two years in exchange for your franchise. As soon as the life tax was drafted, what did the Dynasts do? Force you poor peasants do back breaking labor," said the sergeant.

One of the Assaultmen said, "Yeah, all I got was bread and water. Damn duke had us out sleeping under the stars for almost two years." The sergeant nodded with a paternal look on his face.

"That ain't nothing," Jurgen said, "I worked road construction for the current count's father. I blew out my knee and barely made a pfennig for two years. Plus, my Da died while I was out on the road and I couldn't leave to attend the funeral," Jurgen said. Jurgen didn't mention he never asked for leave; he still held missing the funeral against his dynast.

The sergeant was about say something when Gretchen interrupted with the Assaultmen's drinks and several gold dragons in change. Jurgen croaked a chuckle thinking about how she must have run across the village collecting bar debts to break the note.

"Get this man a lager on me," said the sergeant gesturing towards Jurgen.

"As you wish, gov," said Gretchen as she poured a beer for Jurgen. She served him the watered-down swill that Jurgen recognized Gretchen used to "slow down" the over-intoxicated.

"No!" the sergeant said. "I said get him a lager. A proper one, wench!"

Gretchen set the poured beer on the back bar, and looked like she was going to back talk the sergeant. The two other Assaultmen looked at her, and she lost her nerve.

"Beg yer pardon," Gretchen squeaked. She poured a rich, intoxicating beer and set it in front of Jurgen.

"Mighty kind, sergeant," Jurgen said gulping half the glass. "Primus Ale, a fine choice. I can see I am going to like you Assaultmen. You've got class. You look like you've seen things. More than this dung heap. You've probably seen the entire galaxy!"

"Hush, love," said Gretchen meekly. Even drunk, Jurgen could feel Gretchen's apprehension. Jurgen was too drunk to determine what unnerved Gretchen about the Assaultmen.

The sergeant was about to respond when his subordinate, who had been in a quiet discussion with his buddy, suddenly shouted in mirth, "And I says, is your hair real? She says 'Yes, you want sticky-sticky or not?' Turns out that her hair wasn't the only thing real on her!"

The two Assaultman's laughter was loud enough to rouse the two old pensioners who sat in the back booth. They stood, in disgust, and left leaving money for their drinks on the table. As they exited, they gave the Assaultmen the evil eye.

"Perkins, mind yourself," the sergeant said in a low growl.

"Aye, sergeant," Perkins said straightening. The alpha had spoken and Perkins looked like a whipped dog.

"I bet you get all the girls, Perkins," Jurgen said. "I had a girlfriend. She left me for that prissy fop, Johnny Mercy. Priest read their banns in the state mass today. Well, good for her! I could barely afford her anyway," Jurgen said. Jurgen looked at the pile of coins that sat openly on the bar. He reached over and plucked a gold dragon off the pile. Jurgen held the coin up staring at the money's detail in the light.

The coin was old, almost as old as he was. The dull coin showed the protector's face. Jurgen flipped the coin. On the reverse was a coiled dragon breathing fire. The dragon was the emblem of the Felgenland people. On the ridge of the coin were the Latin words, "*Unio Omnia Obligat.*" Jurgen struggled to remember what that meant.

Perkins watched Jurgen like an eagle. The Assaultman moved to snatch the coin back from Jurgen, but the sergeant intercepted Perkins's hand and smacked it down on the bar.

"Perkins has a reputation with the ladies, which is saying something. All Assaultmen get the girls. Perkins, tell this young man about that time on Libertad in Lalande?" said the sergeant like a theater director coaching his lead actor.

"Uh, right, Libertad," Perkins said, looking a little strangely at the sergeant. "Oh yeah Libertad, that was some farm girl. We fought some pirates that held her pap's farm. She was grateful and repaid me with a roll in the hay. I really fancied her, shame about the guards..."

"I remember," the sergeant said interrupting Perkins. "I was just your corporal then. She was a beauty too! But that girl on Pentothia, she was a fashion model!"

"Oh, yeah! She was just a bit of fun, sergeant, and heck, she bought the drinks too," said Perkins.

Jurgen was so drunk he had lost track of the conversation. All he could focus on was the coin. He'd never an inclination to steal anything before, but, with the coin in his hands, the temptation crept into his drunken brain. Before the lesser impulses of his nature could force him to act, the pub doors opened. Farm workers and plowmen came crowding in for supper time. Jurgen dropped his hand slightly and returned his focus to the Assaultmen.

"What I gotta do to get a coin like this, sergeant?" Jurgen said, "You came in here and got a lot of coins, plural. I bet you cleaned out the village of coins. Still, you all walk around with coins like this jangling about your pockets. How come?"

"That's our prize money. Some of that money was from killing pirates, some from our last skirmish with one of the Terran Directorate's client states. The Union pays well for success. We're here because we needed a break. Things get boring drinking in the same pub in the Bundstadt," the sergeant said.

"If the capital is boring, you guys must have seen some wonders," Jurgen said.

"Well, if you join up with us for a full term—twenty years—I'm authorized by the protector to pay you up front for your first year of service. Usually we pay only fifty griffins, but I'm feeling generous. I'll give you one gold dragon, that one you are holding there," said the sergeant. Perkins looked like he wanted to argue with something the sergeant said. The sergeant shot Perkins a stern look, and the man turned away. Jurgen smiled, a gold dragon, all his!

"You ain't going anywhere, Jurgen," a young male voice said. Jurgen closed his eyes in annoyance. Opening them, Jurgen put the coin on the bar. He turned around and saw his younger brother, Olrich, standing there. The boy was dirty, but his ginger curly hair and freckles were still visible under the dirt.

"Shut up, Olrich," Jurgen said, facing his brother. "What do you know? You think I want to stay here and lick Mercy's boots?"

"Don't join the Assault! You don't come back! If you do come back, you come back in parts," said Olrich pleading with his brother.

"Boy, we aren't at war with anyone," the sergeant said. "The Assault only keeps the peace for the Union. With no war, no one gets hurt."

Olrich's eyes squinted at the sergeant. Olrich was young, but he knew war was on the horizon. He stared until the sergeant realized he needed to butt out.

"Olrich, you know we ain't going to be anything but woodland trash if I stay here. If I go off, I'll get me a pocket full of change like this. Then even prissy Johnny Mercy will come over and plow my lands for me," Jurgen said. His brother just gave him puppy dog eyes, a silent plea not to go.

Jurgen's dander rose and he said, "Hell! They made old man MacAllisdair not only a general, but a baron. There is a damn column with a statue of him in the capital," Jurgen said. "Remember, we all had to memorize that for our history class in the school house."

"All the hands know about *Freiherr* MacAllisdair," Olrich said. "They say he ain't right in his head! He don't leave his house!"

"You mean his estate," Jurgen said. "Hell, if I had that large a house I'd never leave either. I could run game through the halls and shoot them in my front room."

The sergeant nodded and the Assaultmen started laughing. Olrich looked at his brother, then the Assaultmen. He realized his cause was lost.

Olrich quickly hugged his brother, trying not to cry. He said, "I love you, Jurgen. Mara found me and told me about Jenny. I know you ain't coming back, even if you live! Don't forget Mara or me!"

Jurgen stood awkwardly and hugged Olrich for another few seconds before breaking his embrace. Jurgen turned to the sergeant and slurred, "I'm in! What do I got to do?"

"The coin is yours, after you swear on the Gospel of Malcolm. You are a stater right?" the sergeant asked.

"Hell yes. Ever since my mother's father baptized me. But, I ain't a particularly good one," Jurgen said.

"We're not here for your soul, just your body. Swear on the book, then we'll all take a drink to the health of our protector," the sergeant said. "After that we will be off to wealth, fame, glory, and women."

Jurgen fingered the gold coin. He traded his life for it so easily. Would the trade be worthwhile? He gave the coin to his brother and patted the boy on the head.

"Run along now," Jurgen said, "Give this coin to the old woman. Tell her I got really drunk and decided to be a real man so I joined the Assault. Tell her I had no other choice since she didn't like me boxing."

"I will," Olrich said tears in his eyes. "I'll never forget you!"

Jurgen buried his emotions deep; he didn't want to cry in front of the Assaultmen. Jurgen gave a stern look to his brother. The boy turned and ran out of the bar.

"Where were we sergeant?" said Jurgen. He was starting to lose his peripheral vision from the alcohol.

"The oath and a toast," said the sergeant as he pulled out a dog-eared copy of the Gospel of Malcolm. Red spots had stained the black book's cover. The small tome looked worn and the book had been read in all sorts of conditions.

"Raise your hand and repeat, 'I... your name... swear on the grave of the Prophet that I wish to join the Assault,'" the sergeant said. "No need for other witnesses as there are three Assaultmen who will vouch for your oath."

The sergeant said the last part as he shot a glance at the publican. Gretchen stood there watching, red faced and angry. However, she kept her mouth shut.

Jurgen straightened, put his hand on the book, and said, "I, Jurgen Wulfjaeger swear on the ashes of the Prophet that I wish to become an Assaultman!" Jurgen bowed and kissed the book.

"Now! To our protector, long may he live!" said the sergeant. The sergeant then raised his glass and downed his expensive beer.

"To Karl, I know they call you 'the Iron Fist,' but today, you are the best son of a bitch in this galaxy!" Jurgen said. He downed the rest of his beer and grabbed the remainder of Perkin's strong ale. He slammed down that beer too. The alcohol quickly overwhelmed Wulfjaeger, and he tilted forward into the waiting arms of the Assault sergeant.

Grabbing Jurgen, the sergeant said, "Perkins, give me a hand. We got the only dog in this pack of sheep. I'll let Lieutenant Huegel know this is the best we could do. The peasants here are nothing but worn-out pensioners and scrawny youth. The rest are sheep. Let's get back to the barracks."

Jurgen woke suddenly from the dream. He hadn't dreamed about the day two years ago when he lost Jenny and joined the Assault in months.

"Joke's on Jenny," he said to himself. "She's stuck making Mercy babies, and I'm off on adventures in the galaxy."

Jurgen looked at the time. Like clockwork, his body had woken him ten minutes before his alarm. He debated whether he would use his suit's waste bladder or pop his seal and use the latrine. The Assault had designed the suit for extended operations and he could relieve himself at any time. He wasn't sure how long he'd be in the field and decided to keep the bladder empty for an emergency. Besides, Jurgen reminded himself that his suit always reeked for a while after he did his business. He popped his helmet off and wrestled with the suit's front and rear hooks.

"I got you, corporal," Metal said. The kid had been hovering next to Jurgen since they got back from SERAPH's rescue.

"Thanks, Metal," said Jurgen. "Call me Jurgen or Wulf. You've earned it."

"Sure, Wulf," said Metal, "since we're using our superhero names."

Jurgen laughed. He never had thought of himself as anybody special. The thought of being a spandex-clad crime fighter seemed absurd. Jurgen would have said something more, but his bladder urgently reminded him of more pressing concerns. He quickly moved to the latrine. There was a queue, but it moved quickly. Jurgen did his business, washed his hands, and splashed water on his face. His chin wouldn't pass muster with its whiskers, but otherwise he was still relatively clean after yesterday's ordeal. He stepped out of the latrine.

"Wulf," said Auggie as Jurgen exited.

"Sergeant," said Jurgen, stopping and acknowledging the NCO.

"With Cannon out, I'm putting you in charge of his fireteam. I'm moving Metal Kid in with you, since he's been following you around. He'll take the place of Messer, whom I am moving onto fireteam charlie. The contras remain with you as well, no getting away from them. Besides I think their leader has a crush on you."

Jurgen scowled. "I hope you're joking, sergeant."

Auggie nodded. "I am, but she certainly follows you around. Anyway, that's the good news."

"What's the bad news?" Jurgen asked.

"You get RMULE duty," Auggie said. Jurgen's face must have shown his displeasure because Auggie continued. "Don't get upset! The RMULE is going to be the most important thing we take. The robot will be fully loaded with supplies and a portable sat comm. We're all getting linked up with division and General Meagher for this one."

"Wait! Meagher? I thought he was out because of Asimov," said Jurgen. Jurgen remembered the general's court-martial after the action on Asimov. Meagher had created the battle plan that had failed spectacularly. Assault High Command had roundly condemned the general during his court martial calling him a renegade and butcher. The instructors at basic had required Jurgen's class to watch the court martial.

"I didn't ask. My guess is that with the new protector and the war, 'Fighting Mad Meagher' is back in high command's good graces. He'll monitor the fight, and the RMULE is our life line to him and help. You're the most reliable NCO I have, so you got the job. If we make it through VIKINGRAID, I owe you a beer. Sound good?"

"Aye, aye, sergeant," Jurgen said. He wanted to quibble that a beer wasn't worth the price of watching the baggage train, but orders were orders.

"Let's suit up and load up," Auggie said. Jurgen and Auggie went back to the large common sleeping area in the barracks. Metal and another Assaultman stood there waiting for Jurgen.

"Aha, he's here. I am sure you remember Assaultman First Class Ismail Ackbar. He's the squad medic," Auggie said.

Ackbar snapped his heels together. He was in his battlesuit and ready to go.

"Ready for duty, corporal," Ackbar said.

"At ease," Jurgen said. "Metal help me with the suit."

"I got you, Wulf," said Metal. Together they took several minutes to put the suit back on Jurgen. After popping on the helmet, and hitting the lock, Jurgen could hear the radio playing "Sons and Daughters of the Frontier," the Union's national anthem. He felt relaxed; the subliminal messaging was working to keep him loose for the upcoming fight.

"Hotel Company!" called *Hauptmann*, or Captain, Hans von Richter over the company's command comm.

"Platoon!" called out the first and second lieutenants over their platoon comm.

"Squad!" called Auggie over the squad comm.

"Move out!" the captain said. Jurgen and his fireteam moved out of the barracks and onto the tarmac. There in front of an APC was the RMULE, Maricela, and her two fellow contras.

Jurgen looked up in the early morning sky. A Union Day fireworks display in the Bundstadt would have paled in comparison. Interceptors zipped across the sky, and clouds of drones floated around the base, providing a screen against enemy intelligence gathering.

"Stop gawking and load up!" Auggie shouted. Jurgen snapped out of his trance and saw the 3rd Lochiel Dragoons had loaded the

RMULE. Jurgen looked at the cartoon painted on the vehicle's side. The image showed a cowboy standing there and scratching his head, with a bubble that said "Horse? What Horse?"

As he entered the APC, the corporal who supervised the RMULE loading handed Jurgen his rifle. As Jurgen's hand made contact with the rifle, his battlesuit linked to the rifle's electronics. Jurgen's HUD showed the rifle had a full magazine and that the extra magazines were full. Jurgen was combat ready. Jurgen then checked his HUD's RMULE menu, which showed totals for the supplies and extra ammo loaded on the RMULE.

Jurgen threw the rifle sling around his body and sat down. His service pistol banged against his chest plate, and Jurgen checked the ammo on the pistol and its magazines. The HUD showed the weapon and extra magazines were full. A loud blast sounded in the distance, which Jurgen's suit silenced to protect his hearing.

"Wulf, this is Auggie," Sutcliffe said.

"This is Wulf. I hear you Auggie. What's up?"

"I'm going to run the squad comm through your helmet and into the sat comm on the RMULE. You'll lose a channel, but you'll also hear all the comms for VIKINGRAID. If the general or any other higher up needs the squad, I need you to stay frosty for that call," said Auggie.

"Aye, aye, sergeant," said Jurgen. '*Great*,' Jurgen thought, '*I'm now the radioman too.*'

"We're moving out," said the APC's driver as the vehicle's hatch closed. The loading corporal plopped down next to Jurgen.

"Ever been in an APC before?" the corporal asked.

"Yeah, once, in basic," Jurgen said. "You guys are braver than I am."

The corporal laughed. "You say that like this is a rolling coffin."

Jurgen didn't respond; the corporal had guessed his thoughts.

"I think you orbital infantry are the brave ones, either rappelling from a dropship or being blasted from space in a capsule. That is too much falling for my tastes. Besides, short of a RPG or tank round, this APC can take a ton of abuse. If a round hits hard enough to get in here, well, then, it will be over quick for me. Y'all have to deal with all that garbage and you don't have gravity-pressed cermetal protecting you, well, except for your suits," said the corporal. "Name's Flaterty, but they all call me Wayne, like the ancient cowboy actor on account of my first name being Marion."

"Hey, Wayne. I'm Jurgen or Wulf," Jurgen said. "Say, what's up with the cowboy cartoon on the side?"

Wayne laughed, stopping for a second as the APC bounced hard. The vehicle had cleared the main gate and was speeding along a track in the jungle. Occasionally, the APC would echo with a loud tink, as small arms fire hit its hull.

"That's Wyatt, our mascot. He's a horseless cowboy, just like the rest of us," Wayne said. "We're officially the Third Lochiel Dragoons, but unofficially we're called 'the unhorsemen' since we're dragoons without a horse. What about your unit?"

Jurgen said, "We're the Ninth Stahlburgh Rifles. Back in the War of Unification, Karl asked our commander, old Schwartzenrode, what the regiment was called. The old man thinks he's going to play a trick on Karl and so he says the regiment is 'Liberty's Longest Love.' Without missing a beat Karl declared the Ninth was known as 'Violence Regiment.'"

"Why'd he say that?" Wayne asked.

"'Cause old Schwartzenrode constantly talked about how violence and liberty are inseparable. Said they were lovers—you couldn't take someone's liberty without violence and you couldn't protect your liberty without violence. The old general was a warrior poet," Jurgen said.

"Sounds like it," Wayne replied. The APC bounced again, and then its engines revved up, the APC lurched forward.

"Get your guys ready, Wulf," Wayne said. "We're thirty seconds to drop off."

"You aren't sticking around?" Jurgen asked.

"Nope, we're off to marker seventy. We need to plug the road or the enemy will run a tank battalion through that gap," Wayne replied. He punched Jurgen on the chest plate. "Best of luck to ya, brother!"

Jurgen slapped Wayne's suited arm and said, "You too! See you back at the barracks!"

The APC abruptly halted and the ramp dropped down with a loud *thunk.*

"Go, go!" shouted Jurgen into his comm. Wayne hopped out first. Jurgen saw the tracers from the APC's main guns blasting into the jungle. Red hassium tracers returned. Wayne moved three meters from the APC and prepared to drop the RMULE. Jurgen saw Wayne get cut in half by an RPG that buzzed straight through his waist. The APC's main gun turned and poured fire in the direction from which the rocket grenade came.

"We've got anti-tank weapons and heavy fire! Get out and get a kill zone set up," screamed Auggie over the squad net. Jurgen jumped out of the APC and grabbed the controller to release the RMULE from Wayne's dead hand. Jurgen saw the RMULE was half unloaded from the APC. Quickly looking at the controller, Jurgen flipped the toggle for the auto-unloader to finish dropping the RMULE.

"Ackbar, get this Assaultman's body back on the APC," Jurgen said.

The Assaultman first class said over the fireteam's channel, "Aye, aye, corporal!"

Ackbar drug the two parts of the valiant dragoon's body back into the APC just as the autoloader retracted back into APC. RMULE ejected and autoloader onboard, the APC's rear buttoned up as the APC starting rolling out.

Jurgen took a moment to orient himself to the chaotic conditions. The squad was in a small clearing on the top of a large hill. Jurgen's internal compass told him he faced the southeast. He moved forward until the jungle track was ten meters behind Jurgen. The APC had dropped his squad and the RMULE on a curve in the jungle track. A hassium round buzzed past him bringing back to the battle.

Thirty meters in front of his fireteam was a gentle gradient heading down into the jungle plain. The enemy was attempting to climb the hill from the southeast, which meant the landing zone was behind Jurgen to the northwest.

A message displayed across his faceplate, "Sat-link connection in 5... 4... 3... 2... 1... CONNECTED."

"We're hooked in Auggie," Jurgen said. Jurgen pulled his rifle close and began shooting down the hill. He wouldn't hit anything, but the covering fire might make the enemy less aggressive.

"Good, get your team to dig in... Belay that! Get down!" Auggie shouted.

"Down!" Jurgen said as he dropped. His external speakers cut out a split second later, but the noise was so loud the rumble reverberated through his helmet. The noise, like a bullet train's whistle, was the sound of an incoming artillery round. A heartbeat later, there was a large explosion and fireball floating up from the jungle below.

"Get up, get set, and dig in! We've gotten a quick respite!" Auggie said. As the sergeant's voice quieted, Jurgen heard the back channel from the rest of the fight filtering in. Ackbar and Metal moved to Jurgen's position, setting up for action.

"One-hundred-and-fifty-first interceptor wing, move to the southeast to provide air cover. We've got elements there that are exposed," a calm Navy air traffic controller said.

"SERAPH and LUNA on it," a familiar voice replied. A moment later, Jurgen and his two fireteam members felt the jet wash as SERAPH and her wing gal buzzed the hill.

"Sorry cuties!" said SERAPH as she shot past. Jurgen ignored the chatter for a moment as he and other squad mates pulled auto-diggers from the RMULE and dropped their diggers into position. Jurgen watched as his machine began to work. In the chaos of the APC drop, Jurgen lost the contras. He decided to focus on digging his position, the contras would have to find him.

"Metal! Provide over-watch!" said Jurgen.

"Got it, Wulf," replied Metal.

"Ackbar, get the RMULE! Move the robot closer so we can get it into the bunker after the diggers finish," Jurgen said. The auto-digger had dug a meter and a half foxhole in the ground since he issued orders. Jurgen pulled up the digger's command screen and extended a T-shape forward from the digger's position. The digger would add a trench where Jurgen and his fireteam would take up defensive positions. Ackbar returned a moment later with the RMULE.

"Enemy sighted, firing!" Metal said over the team channel. Jurgen heard the soft echo of other Assaultmen reporting the same thing.

"Here they come, Fifth Squad!" Auggie said. "Time to show them why we're Violence Regiment!"

Jurgen watched as the auto-digger made the front trench deep enough for the fireteam to climb into. He and Ackbar maneuvered the RMULE into the protected rear of the trench. Then Jurgen and Ackbar climbed over the RMULE and forward into the foxhole. Metal paced a few meters towards the hill's edge and popped off a few rounds. Scores of hassium rounds returned his fire, and Metal ran back to the trench. When he reached the foxhole he hopped into position to the left of Jurgen.

"LUNA break off!" said SERAPH. "We've got company!"

Jurgen looked up to see the Union interceptors go their separate ways overhead. To Jurgen's right, in the distance, was a small mountain. Jurgen panned over to the mountain with his rifle scope. The battlesuit auto-magnified the picture. Jurgen could see Assaultmen lined up to defend the peak. Around Jurgen, the rest of Fifth Squad started firing. The enemy was approaching the squad's position, but he couldn't see any yet. He fired off the rest of his magazine and swapped in a new one.

"Get the kill zone set!" an officer shouted on a muted channel. Jurgen realized he hearing the RMULE radio chatter from the mountain to his right. Jurgen remembered that the mountain to the right was labeled "Hill One."

"Sergeant Weimar! Get your men set!" the officer said.

"Aye, aye, Lieutenant Nordlinger!" the sergeant replied.

"Head on a swivel," Jurgen said to his team. The hassium rounds from the enemy below stopped. After checking the kill zone in front of him, Jurgen looked to the sky, worried the enemy interceptors were about to drop a bomb on his squad. Jurgen saw five enemy interceptors were trying to approach Hill One, and his position. The enemy would move towards the mountains but LUNA and SERAPH's interceptors would block them. The Union interceptors would attempt to get in the enemy's six o'clock and shoot them down. The aerial fighting was becoming a standoff. The enemy interceptors couldn't engage in a bombing run, and the Union interceptors couldn't drive off the enemy. Suddenly the enemy interceptors changed tactics.

"I've got one that has lock!" screamed SERAPH. Jurgen looked up to see a Union interceptor with an enemy on its tail. Jurgen's attention changed as he heard the unmistakable sound of artillery passing overhead. Before he could say anything, the jungle below the squad erupted in flames. As the smoke cleared Jurgen could see the large mass of enemy force swarming from the jungle below. The enemy was giving the battle their all and trying to play "king of the hill" with the Union.

"Enemy firing!" SERAPH said. Jurgen watched as an enemy interceptor fired a missile.

"I'm hitting the ceiling," said SERAPH. Her interceptor turned ninety degrees upward and its afterburner thundered.

"No Hannah! You'll black out!" LUNA screamed. Jurgen's heart stopped. He knew the pilot and he felt dread at the other's call. SERAPH's interceptor dropped chaff, flares, and drones on its way into low orbit. Two more enemy interceptors broke off to give SERAPH chase, leaving LUNA to fend off two.

"Ha, bye-bye!" LUNA said as she maneuvered behind one enemy and fired two missiles. LUNA's missiles raced out and hit the enemy's craft before exploding against the enemy's engines and left wing. The enemy interceptor pilot ejected from the tumbling fighter craft before it crashed into the jungle and exploded.

"Blast it! Hannah, where are you? I need help!" LUNA said.

Jurgen wanted to call out for SERAPH, but Metal's voice brought his eyes to the slope before him.

"Incoming enemy, Wulf!"

The enemy battalion in front of the Ninth started cresting the hill; drone swarms hung in the air above them. Jurgen reached into a utility pouch on his waist and threw up a hand full of seed-like drones to provide a counter screen. As he tossed the drones, red hassium pins flashed past him.

"Engaging," Metal said, firing back. Jurgen started depressing his rifle's trigger. Jurgen only got a few shots off when an enemy interceptor buzzed their position and knocked the fireteam down. Before Jurgen could get up, an explosion and fireball rained down from above him.

"Got him," said SERAPH over the channel, "I'm coming back! Hang in there, Lana!"

The explosion was a brief respite from the enemy fire. As Jurgen got back up and into position, the enemy restarted their climb up the hill. Metal's rifle started spitting out pins; every ten bohrium pins including a green tracer. Ackbar leaned into his rifle. His mic was on and Jurgen heard him whispering.

"May the prophets, Isa, Muhammad, and Malkum, peace be upon their honored names, guide my shot," Ackbar said before pulling his trigger. Jurgen didn't have time to dissect the theology of a New Age Muslim venerating what Jurgen considered to be his religion's saint.

Jurgen looked down his sight. The enemy was within thirty meters and trying to set up a heavy weapon. Jurgen shot at the crew and slowed their progress when he killed their leader. Metal's rifle flashed and Ackbar's muttering reassured Jurgen his team was working.

"This is Meagher. I need a field report," the general said over the division comms.

"This is Nordlinger," an officer said, "We're getting rushed! Weimar and Schmidt have blunted the rush, but we could use some help, General!"

"Combat air traffic control, AURORA GUARDIAN requesting a run to help the Assaultmen," an interceptor pilot interjected. Jurgen had to ignore the channel as the enemy battalion charged his position. He sprayed the enemy as they came forward. He continued to fire, so focused on the enemy so much that he was surprised when his magazine showed empty. He quickly ejected the spent magazine and swapped in a fresh one. He charged the rifle and began firing again. The enemy was almost on top of his team.

"They're coming up, Auggie," Jurgen said, aiming his rifle at the lead soldier and firing. Metal was still shooting, and Ackbar was saying his prayers with the squeeze of a trigger as an amen. The enemy's shots became more accurate as they closed the distance. Jurgen felt a smack against his shoulder. He expected pain, but the shot must have been a glancing hit.

"They got me," Metal said calmly as he continued to fire.

"Metal, can you fight?" Jurgen said.

"I'm still in, Wulf," Metal said as he shot his rifle in rapid succession at three of the enemy soldiers. Ackbar stopped praying, and ran over to check Metal's injuries.

"He's good, shot in the shoulder," Ackbar said. As Ackbar returned to his spot in the trench, the jungle in front of the fire team ignited in an explosion that knocked Jurgen back.

"This is Fifth Squad, Hotel Company, Ninth Regiment. We need air cover," Auggie said over the general comms. "We've got an incoming tank!"

"Roger, I've got you cuties. LUNA, stop playing footsie and let's help our beautiful Spartans down there!" said SERAPH. The enemy paused as a giant fireball exploded below Hill One.

"AURORA GUARDIAN reporting a successful drop. LUNA, SERAPH, got room for a third?" said AURORA GUARDIAN.

"Sure, though now we're a joke," SERAPH said pausing for a moment, "A blond, a red head, and a brunette fly into a dogfight..."

"Hey, I'm raven haired!" LUNA said. The three Union interceptors flew over Jurgen's head, high enough to avoid a back blast. One of the interceptors broke high and pulled an inverted loop lining up behind an enemy interceptor. Jurgen watched realizing the enemy hadn't expected the maneuver. The Union interceptor fired a missile and it arced out hitting the interceptor between its engines.

"That's three!" SERAPH's voice called out. "Two more and you all are buying me drinks on the *Lena*!"

"You got lucky, Hannah," LUNA said.

"More enemy climbing the hill," Metal said. Before Jurgen could react, the entire front of the trench exploded into sand, dirt, and rock shrapnel. The blast tossed Jurgen like a toy thrown by an angry child. He hit the ground and had the air knocked out of his lungs.

"Breech! Teams three and four, get over there and cover the hole!" Auggie shouted. Jurgen wanted to say he was good to fight, but he struggled to breathe. He saw spots and felt like he was going to pass out.

"Hang on boys, I'm going to hit that tank," said AURORA GUARDIAN. "Ladies, it's been a slice of heaven. Breaking off."

Jurgen's lungs finally started to function, and he gulped air. AURORA's interceptor passed over Jurgen and started dropping munitions on the enemy's position over the hill. As Jurgen's vision cleared he saw a fireball rise from below the crest of the hill forty meters away.

"Hang in there Fifth Squad, I'm sending reinforcements," Meagher's voice said over the comms channel. Jurgen finally had enough oxygen in his system to stand. He surveyed his position. The blast had tossed him thirty meters from the crater that used to be his trench. The enemy were now meters away from crater.

"AURORA, no good! Repeat, no good! That tank is still moving," said Auggie over the channel.

"Alpha Company, jump!" came a new voice over the channel. "General, I'm on the tank and the rest of the company will push the enemy back. Come on, you apes! Do you want to live forever?!"

Jurgen had trotted forward a few meters to engage the enemy, when he realized his rifle had melted into slag. Jurgen realized the RMULE would have a replacement and the tank blast had miraculously spared it. Unfortunately, the RMULE was now between him and the enemy. Jurgen thought about making a run for the RMULE, when three MjGAs dropped down in front of him. The large, mechanized armored units belonged to the Union's special forces. Jurgen watched as the MjGa's jump jets cushioned their descent.

"Watch out there, Assaultman!" said the lead mech operator. "Follow me in, I'll get you to your RMULE or my name isn't Will Bruckner!"

Jurgen used the MjGA as cover. The operator started clearing the enemy from the crater around the RMULE with his armor's shoulder mounted minigun.

"Bruckner's Broncos, charge!" said the officer. "Seventy-Second bring death like the Fourth Horsemen you are!"

The three other mechanized armor units moved forward clearing the remaining enemy. A tank blast hit one of the armored units. Jurgen charged forward and grabbed a spare rifle off the RMULE. As his suited hand contacted the rifle, it synced to his battlesuit. Jurgen crouched behind the RMULE, and fired at the enemy. On his left, Jurgen saw Metal at the edge of the crater, still hunched over firing.

"Ackbar!" Jurgen shouted.

"Hey, AURORA, I see you missed the tank! I think that means you owe us all a drink!" said Bruckner. Jurgen watched as the operator lined up a launch tube on his armor. Moments later a large bohrium pin shot out from the launch tube and hit the tank.

"Okay, stud. Tell you what, you paint him with a laser and I'll get him on this run," AURORA purred.

"Use your big girl guns," said Bruckner. "I just hit that beast with a bohrium lance and the tank didn't even flinch!"

"Oh, I love using my big girl guns! Step back or you'll literally be hot stuff, stud," said AURORA.

"Down!" Bruckner said. He and the other armor unit dropped into a push up position, the robotic looking armor flattening as much as the boxy forms would allow.

"Down!" shouted Jurgen. He and Metal crouched in the small crater. A moment later Jurgen saw AURORA's missile heading for the tank below.

Jurgen's externals went silent and his faceplate became opaque. His suit's Geiger counter display spiked, and an orange radiation warning flashed across the HUD.

"I do so love it when a woman goes radioactive," said Bruckner. "Looks like this sector is going to be hot enough for a while that you boys won't have a ton of trouble. General, where do you want us Fourth Horsemen? We're ready to roll on."

"I need you over with the First! Nordlinger's squad is getting mauled," the general's gruff voice said over the comm.

"Ackbar, report," Jurgen said as soon as his faceplate became transparent and the Geiger counter started to quiet.

"Here, corporal," said Ackbar. "I'm elbow deep in Auggie's guts."

"Prophet's ashes," Jurgen said. "Auggie, you in command?" Auggie didn't respond.

"Metal, let's move! Auggie is down," Jurgen said. The Assaultman next to him didn't move. Jurgen hit the emergency release on Metal's helmet. Blood splashed out as Jurgen rolled Metal onto his back. Metal's shoulder and chest plate had taken a dozen hits. Metal had a frozen grim look on his face; Jurgen closed the man's eyes.

"Auggie is dead, corporal," Ackbar said.

"Manzini, Prost, Meier, Fisher, Murphy, any other team leads, report," Jurgen said. Static came over the squad channel. Jurgen climbed out of the crater and looked around. Looking out to the north, Jurgen saw falling stars. No, Jurgen corrected himself, dropships filled the skies over the valley. Jurgen looked down the hill into the jungle from which the enemy force had emerged. The only thing he saw down there was a large crater and burned bodies at the edge of the blast. A high radiation alert cautioned Jurgen from moving forward. In this sector of the battle, the Union had stopped the enemy.

"Weimar, fall back," Nordlinger's voice came over the general channel. "General, we have three battalions assaulting our position! We need help!"

"Coming in for a run," said SERAPH. "You cuties better hunker down."

SERAPH's interceptor buzzed Jurgen's hill and then followed the terrain's nap. She fired several missiles into the enemy forces and created a super-hot wall of flame, which slowed the advance. As SERAPH began to climb towards mountain's summit, an enemy missile appeared from behind the mountain.

"Watch out, Hannah!" said LUNA. LUNA crossed SERAPH's path. The missile switched lock to LUNA's interceptor.

"No, Lana!" SERAPH shouted, as the missile impacted head on with LUNA JETSTREAM's interceptor, detonating and destroying LUNA and the spacecraft instantly.

"That helped, thanks, Valkyries!" Nordlinger said. SERAPH's interceptor shot over the mountain and veered to the right.

"Time for some payback!" said SERAPH. Jurgen could hear the anger in the woman's voice. Jurgen watched as the Union and enemy interceptors wheeled around the horizon. There were two enemy interceptors to SERAPH's lone fighter. Scanning the horizon, Jurgen could see more enemy interceptors, flying northward. The enemy was trying to enter the airspace where the Assault were moving from landing to their staging points.

Jurgen checked the RMULE and replaced the magazines he had reflexively burned through in the firefight. He grabbed two more spare magazines, and replaced the half full magazine in his rifle.

"Fifth Squad, report," an officer said over the squad channel.

"Wulfjaeger here, sir," Jurgen said.

Jurgen looked around. Metal was dead. The remains of the other fireteams huddled in their trenches while Ackbar triaged and treated casualties.

"What's your status? I can't raise Sutcliffe," the officer asked.

"We're out, sir. We cannot fight," Jurgen said.

"Roger, hold tight," the officer replied.

"Aye, aye," Jurgen said. He watched as the two enemy interceptors came closer to his hill. There were plenty of Union interceptors, but they were all busy in other sectors. The enemy interceptors began their approach. Jurgen shrugged. Unlike Metal, this would be a quick death. When the interceptors were a kilometer away, SERAPH's interceptor popped over Hill One.

"Got you two snakes!" She shouted as she rapidly fired four missiles.

Jurgen watched as the missiles traveled the distance in a heartbeat and reduced the enemy to metallic mist.

"That was for Lana!" said SERAPH as she turned her interceptor skyward, "*Lena* this is STELLAR SERAPH, I am out of armament and requesting a refuel and rearm."

“Roger, STELLAR SERAPH. Head back to base,” the controller said. Jurgen took a deep breath, the beautiful Amazon was heading back to safety, at least for the moment. Then Jurgen panicked. Where were the contras?!

He searched for the contras and returned to where he remembered them disembarking the APC. There, he found the body of one. A hassium round through the contra’s helmet had killed the man instantly. Jurgen found the other one on the other side of the dirt track. Numerous hassium rounds riddled the small man’s chest plate with holes. He lay there peacefully like he was asleep. His face looked joyful. Jurgen crossed himself and continued to look for Maricela. He couldn’t find her. He started walking back to the RMULE’s position.

He stopped to watch the continued fighting for Hill One.

Jurgen’s stomach rumbled and so he checked his chronometer. The time was almost nineteen hundred local. He had been fighting for hours, yet to Jurgen it happened in a flash.

He fumbled into a utility pouch and came up with an MRE bar. Jurgen flipped open his faceplate and shoved half the bar in his mouth. Then, he slurped some water from the suit’s canteen system. The jungle smelled of a fetid mix of cordite, napalm, and death. He flipped the faceplate down and scanned the mountain. The fighting was still strong. He thanked the Allfather that the enemy hadn’t realized how weak his position was. If they had, Fifth Squad would have been dead or captured.

“This is STARDUST STRIKER and NEBULA NOVA moving into position,” a female voice said over the channel. Jurgen watched as two new interceptors took up position over his sector of the battlefield.

“Fifth Squad, Hotel Company, be advised Alpha Company, Second Battalion, of the Fifteenth is on their way to reinforce,” a voice said over the division channel.

“Aye, aye,” Jurgen said. He turned to stand next to the RMULE and stumbled over a burnt pile of leaves. As he looked down, he realized he was stepping on a human form - Maricela. She had burns along her right arm and pin rifle shots, but she was still breathing.

"Ackbar, I've got wounded!" said Jurgen. He hefted the woman in a fireman's carry and ran to the triage area. He gently placed Maricela next to Ackbar, whose battlesuit dripped with blood. Ackbar nodded. He checked Maricela's pulse and then got to work. The light from the star dimmed and Jurgen could see the hassium tracers shooting up the small mountain to the west. He wanted to feel like he should run over there and take up a position, but his heart wasn't in fighting. He was tired and numb. Jurgen sat down next to Ackbar, who had stopped for a moment to move the RMULE closer to facilitate easier access to the medical supplies.

"*Muertos Penedeharrin!*" Maricela mumbled after Ackbar injected her with some drugs. She continued, "*Yo pagará tu por tu crueldad, mi vengos vin, nǐ huì kàndào!*"

Jurgen leaned his back against the RMULE's legs and closed his eyes.

Jurgen jumped as someone thumped his helmet. He looked around frantically. He had fallen asleep.

"Whoa, calm down, corporal," a sergeant said. "We've loaded up your casualties, and graves registration will be here shortly. The Fifteenth has this hill now."

Jurgen wanted to punch the sergeant, but took a deep breath. Off in the distance Jurgen thought the local star was setting.

"Did we win?" Jurgen said.

"Yes, the Fifteenth rolled in around midnight local. We set up here since this hill was undefended, just in case," said the sergeant.

"Wait, midnight? What time is it?" Jurgen asked.

"Zero six thirty, the worst of the fighting on Hill One died down after the Twenty Seventh reinforced the First," said the sergeant. "You are the last of the Ninth that we're evacuating. Since you weren't wounded, we put you last on the evac schedule. I was waking you so you could load up." Jurgen realized he was watching a star rise.

Jurgen nodded. "Thanks, sergeant. Go get Fifth Squad some payback!"

"Aye, will do, corporal," the sergeant said. Jurgen looked around. A dropship sat thirty meters from his position in the middle of the hill. The scene was radically different from the day before. The fighting had burned away most of the foliage and pock marked the ground with craters.

A Navy warrant officer signaled Jurgen to hurry over. He picked up his pace, entered the dropship's bay, and found a seat. The hatch sealed and Jurgen popped his helmet. There were three other Assaultmen in the bay. They all looked at Jurgen.

"Is there a problem," Jurgen asked.

"No," one of the Assaultmen said. He continued to stare at Jurgen. The other two stopped staring and began to talk.

"You hear about that fight on Hill One? I heard that the enemy threw a division against the First," the one said.

"Really? Sergeant said a guy named Weimar took out half of the enemy that crawled up there, said there was bodies everywhere. Weimar and his fireteam killed a company with knives and bayonets alone," the other said. Jurgen sat back as the third Assaultman continued to stare.

"What?" Jurgen said.

"You're unlucky," the Assaultman said. "They said your whole squad died, yet you are still walking around and without a scratch."

Jurgen looked down at his armor. The plates were cracked and dented. He was sore, and every muscle screamed like he'd been doing hard core PT for days. He didn't feel like he had gotten off without a scratch.

"I took my share of punishment," Jurgen said.

"I think you're a reaper, a veritable angel of death," the man said. Jurgen had heard rumors of "angels of death," men who were so unlucky whole entire units died around them. Jurgen remembered Pappy, a staff sergeant who'd been his battlefield mechanics instructor in basic. Pappy had lost both legs and an arm when the Terrans bombed the Union colony of Blackwater. People had called Pappy an "angel of death" because somehow he had survived the attack. Pappy said that the whole thing was nonsense. Jurgen tried to forget the title and ignore the men. After a fifteen-minute flight, the dropship landed on the Shuwa Bay tarmac. Jurgen grabbed his helmet and walked off the dropship.

Part Two

The Time Between

CHAPTER ONE
One Door Closes

November turned into December, December into January. Then came February. Finally, March roared like a lion. Henry had been in the capital for over four months, and he hadn't gotten a call to report for duty. At the new year Assault High Command informed him that they put him on inactive duty. When he inquired about his change in status, High Command told him he was inactive due to being in an "unassigned" state.

Henry had asked his father, when he saw him—a rare occurrence with the war—when he would deploy. His father had reassured him that Assault High Command would activate him "soon." Today was the twentieth of March and a Friday. Henry always had dinner with his parents on Friday. Today, Henry vowed to find out what he would really be doing, and would he ever go back to being an Assault officer?

Not that Henry had been idle. He was a veritable dynamo — opening museums, hosting banquets, and corresponding with foreign militaries. Major Bjorn Halvorsen had contacted him after the Union declared war and said that the Protelan bureaucracy had moved uncharacteristically fast in deciding in their exchange officers between Protelan and the Union. Halvorsen said he'd be leading the Space Marine contingent. Now, all that remained was for Assault High Command or the Admiralty to select their candidates for the exchange; a function frustratingly outside Henry's portfolio.

When Henry wasn't kissing babies, he was babysitting Bjorn. Not that the massive Space Marine was a chore to watch. Bjorn was athletic and enjoyed sports. The Union with its large influx of Scots had a plethora of top-notch golf courses, and Henry found himself on the links with the Space Marine more often than in a conference room.

Henry worked hard to convince Halvorsen to bring the Protelan Navy—and their Marines—into the war on the Union's side. Halvorsen was always eager to fight. However, the protector had complained during past Friday dinners that his government had received only reluctant responses from Bjorn's civilian counterparts.

Henry sighed and threw off the covers on his bed. He was bored. To fill his time, Henry had redone the Protelan Suite. He replaced the gaudy reds and golds with an alabaster marble that came from somewhere in the Sheeplands. The walls still bore the von Machthaber coat of arms every three or four meters, but this was done with a few centimeter mosaic embedded in the walls. Henry updated the furniture to a more contemporary style.

Johann had become a more active valet, after he had slunk home from the banquet. Johann never mentioned whether he had attained the Falke twins' legendary company. Henry hadn't asked the man, and Johann did not raise the subject. Rather, the valet began to do actual work. Henry suspected Johann's clan was pressuring him to marry and return to their estates. But, for whatever reason, Johann became a sober and quite dour companion.

"Good morning, sir," Johann said knocking and entering Henry's bedroom.

"Good morning, Johann," Henry said. Henry stood and waited for Johann to hand him clothing, which Henry would then wear. This was their routine, and after weeks of this equilibrium, Henry felt like this had always been the status quo.

"I don't know if you heard, sir, but *Graf* Gilbraith's son, Archibald, died in a tragic hovertruck accident in the Sheeplands," Johann said. "The poor *Graf* has taken ill and is in a terrible state."

"Are the maids gossiping with you again, Johann?" Henry asked.

"No, I read it in the news," Johann responded in a subdued manner. Henry looked at his valet with surprise.

"What? I read the paper, yes," Johann responded. "I feel as I am now an older man, and I must understand what is going on in our glorious Union."

"Johann, do I need to have USIS scan you to determine if you are a Terran spy?"

Johann looked utterly disgusted with Henry and said, "No, but if it makes you feel better, I will submit to a scan, sir."

"I can finish up here. Why don't you take the day off," Henry said. "I am sure there are companions that would happily get drunk with you, the scullery maid, for instance?"

Johann shook his head. "I am afraid I can't do that. Can you keep a confidence, sir?" Henry started to worry; Johann had a secret?

"Aye," Henry said, nodding for effect.

"After the banquet for Alasdair Campbell, I had an encounter with your mother. She, Layla, Serena, and I had a discussion."

"I take it Layla and Serena are the Falke twins' given names?" Henry asked.

"Yes," Johann said.

"Well, what did my mother say to you?" Henry asked.

"She dismissed the Falke twins explaining to them that they were never to set foot in the Villa again. After they hastily departed, she sat me down and lamented that she couldn't outright have me neutered as I am needed to carry on a dynasty. I took a deep sigh of relief at that statement, but then she told me she had a much better punishment for me."

Henry could imagine his mother having such a conversation with the wayward valet. He kept his mouth shut and forced himself to not laugh for fear the valet would not reveal his secret.

"Ah, so, go on," Henry prodded.

"She said she could arrange a marriage for me. I think she said the phrase a 'make you a matrimonial gelding.' She would match me with a woman of low means and ugly appearance. As our wonderful religion does not permit divorce, I could be attached to such a creature for many decades. Since she is the patroness, a powerful woman, and my mother's best friend, I considered her proposal with all due seriousness."

Henry was about to burst out laughing. He covered his amusement by staring at his uniform jacket's buttons. When he could control his laughter, he solemnly said, "Go on."

"I took the prerequisite pause to show consideration and assured the patroness that I was her humble servant. Then she informed me that I no longer worked for you but for her."

Henry went from laughing internally to raging. The valet was his personal servant, and now, his parents were removing Henry's little remaining control over the valet. Henry stood silently glaring at his armoire.

"If the standing closet is annoying you, I can take a fire axe to it, sir," Johann said, looking at the focus of Henry's anger.

"The closet is a stand-in for someone else," Henry replied.

"Uh huh," Johann said. "Anyone I know?"

"Most assuredly," Henry said. Henry was about to continue when there was a knock on the door. Johann quickly went to the front room to admit the guest.

"Henry," Johann said. Henry was still fuming when he entered the front room in his uniform jacket, trousers, and bare feet. Standing there with a large grin on his face was the Field marshal of the Assault.

Henry went to attention, locked his heels, and said, "Sir."

"At ease, nephew," said Field marshal Padraig O'Cruadhlaoich.

"Thanks, Uncle Paddy," Henry said. His uncle came forward and briefly embraced his nephew before both men stepped back to chat.

"Well, how's life in the Villa?" Padraig asked.

"Terrible. I do nothing but kiss babies and have my valet threatened with becoming a eunuch," Henry said.

Padraig laughed. "My older sister's handiwork I assume. She has her threats, but her bark is worse than her bite, especially if Raimond can reason with her."

Henry sighed. "Hopefully you are here on behalf of my request."

"What request, Henry?" Padraig asked. Henry almost lost his grip on his temper. All these months and Assault High Command hadn't even considered his request for active duty!

"I want to go on active duty. I'm an Assaultman; I've trained for this war my entire career, Uncle Paddy."

Padraig's face darkened, and he said, "You know that won't happen. Your father and your mother—especially your mother—want you safe here on Stahlburgh. Mathias will deploy. We'll send him to Lalande as a Marine or in the First or Ninth on some guard duty. You're too important."

"Then, by the Allfather, discharge me!" Henry said angrily.

"I can't do that either. Your discharge so early in the war would be a terrible optic. The press would cry 'Why is the Protector of the Union's eldest son not serving!?' Unthinkable, especially as it was Raimond who initiated this conflict. Violet party fools, like Gilbraith, would have a field day with that news especially since Gilbraith himself has a terrible secret," said Padraig. The man trailed off suddenly stimulated by another thought.

Henry's rage abated at the hint of court gossip, especially since Gilbraith-on-Heather had insulted and threatened him at Campbell's banquet.

"Do I have to beg?" Henry said with a smile.

"Only a little," Padraig said with a smile. He waited a moment to tease Henry but then said, "After VIKINGRAID, the news service ran a series of articles on a Sergeant Maximilian von Weimar. The face looked familiar, so I had our friends at USIS do what they do best."

"I remember that Assaultman. The press christened him 'Maximum

Carnage.' He and the rest of his squad left bodies strewn all over that mountain. What did USIS discover? Is he Gilbraith's illegitimate child?" Henry asked.

"Even better, USIS confirmed Maximilian is Kenneth's natural second son. The men are estranged, but that's not important now since Kenneth is dead," said Padraig.

"Wait! Johann said he was merely sick," Henry said. The valet nodded.

"A lie, Kenneth died a week ago. With the war, we need total support from Stahlburgh's first families. Alasdair Campbell told your father that the Fraser clan appears to have a contested inheritance between Kenneth's son and his nephew. If the new *Graf* Gilbraith were an Assaultman, your father could change the Frasers' allegiance from the Violets to the Red or the Gold parties in government. Therefore, I was ordered to discharge Sergeant Weimar."

"Was that wise? Kenneth's actions don't appear to show someone who had his priorities in the right order," Henry asked.

"Wise? We'll see. Only time will tell," said Padraig.

"Well, then, since Assault High Command has discharged Weimar to the House of Dynasts, shouldn't High Command also discharge me to the Chancellery?"

"No, that's out of the question," Padraig said. "Your mother would skin and wear me like Hercules wore the Nemean Lion."

"Doubtful, you don't have an impenetrable hide, sir," said Johann. The field marshal simply stared at the valet. Johann bowed and excused himself.

"Well, maybe this new Gilbraith would appreciate some friendly advice from the Primus on how to be a Dynast?" Heinrich said.

"Well..." Padraig said, inwardly cursing that he confided in his nephew.

"I'd happily welcome back Maximilian. Or, does he prefer Max, I wonder? I am sure as he is an Assaultman and Sheeplander he is fond of hunting and fishing. Do you think he'd care to join me, Uncle? We could become fast friends over fishing, shooting, hunting, drinking, and discussing Union politics. Especially, the topic of how the protector, the patroness, and Assault High Command conspired to cashier Weimar and then railroaded him into becoming his father's successor. I could advise Gilbraith on favors he could extract from the protector and patroness to keep his discharge a secret. Perhaps instead I can offer Gilbraith a better deal? His father was a Violet. They seem like a party that could be on the rise with the proper patronage," said Henry, trying his hand at reverse psychology. To Henry and the other Machthabers the Violets were the direct opposite in their beliefs.

"You wouldn't dare. The Violets are strongly against the war and the Union," Padraig said, his face turning red in anger.

"Oh, I'd dare. Fortunately for you and my parents, I am a mercenary. My discharge is necessary for my discretion," said Henry.

"Impossible," said Padraig with resignation. Henry then switched tactics.

"Fine, then put me in the war. I don't care where. If you need a sergeant to fill Weimar's post in the First, I'll give up my commission and go," said Henry. "I am bored and want out of this place, Uncle."

"No promises, but I'll see what I can do. Nakdong is progressing. The Assault has almost taken the planet. High Command would like to call the mission complete, except that we can't eliminate the enemy high command. Once we end the resistance in the Lalande system, we'll push forward to L 98-59. USIS has been shouting that the Terrans are massing there. Your aunt Siobhan and I have some reservations about charging into L 98-59. Another story for another time, I suspect. In the meantime Henry, promise me that you'll stay away from the new *Graf* Gilbraith. If you do, I'll see what I can do about a billet," Padraig said.

"Of course," said Henry with a smile.

"I worry about you, my nephew. This place is making you quite sly.

I used to be able to spin you around in a web of fantasy, but now I feel like you are the spider," said Padraig.

"A bored prisoner only has a dream of escape, Uncle," said Henry.

"Well, I'll try to bake a cake with a key, but no guarantees on when I can arrange delivery. In the meantime, you are welcome to come observe the war from Assault High Command. Be sure to wear your colonel-in-chief epaulets when you show up. A mere captain isn't going to get past the guards," said Padraig. "Now speaking of High Command, I have to go. Your mother asked me to visit you. I would have come sooner if I had suspected you were up to so much mischief."

"Goodbye, sir. Remember the terms of our bargain, and I'll remember mine," Henry said, snapping his bare heels together. Padraig nodded and smiled. The field marshal then turned and left the apartments.

"He's gone, right?" Johann said peeking out from the southern corridor.

"Yes, Johann."

"Good! I feel the winds of freedom, and you know what that makes me want to do?" Johann said.

"I don't know. Polish my shoes?" Henry asked.

"No, have the Falke twins over for dinner and breakfast. You can polish your own shoes now," Johann responded. "The patroness has forgotten the first rule of combat: never underestimate an Assaultman's resourcefulness."

Henry was only slightly irritated with his valet; Johann was returning to his true debauched nature. As Henry had suspected, the weeks of diligence were just an act on the valet's part. Johann assumed that if Henry were serving, Johann would no longer be his valet. Instead, an enlisted batsman would fill that role for the Primus. Henry pondered what Johann would do free of any responsibility.

Henry's thoughts changed to dinner with his parents. He turned to put on his socks and shoes. He had to get through a day of kissing babies, but tonight he would try to change his parents' minds. Would his knowledge of a potential scandal with the Fraser be a large enough lever to move his father and mother?

Henry moved through his day with a zeal he hadn't had in a long time. When evening came, he, Johann, and Krueger were all happy to return to the Villa. Henry left the car and went to the elevator to the protector's public apartments. The elevator doors opened and Weber stood at the controls.

"Primus, what a nice surprise," Weber said. "Please allow me, sir."

"You know I always have dinner with my parents on Fridays, Weber," Henry said with a smile.

"Oh, today is Friday, isn't it, sir," Weber said. "You'll forgive me, my days blur together as you can imagine. This Villa doesn't run itself, and I only know the day if we are attending service." The elevator began moving.

"Well, tonight I hope to secure a promise to fight in the war," Henry said, testing the waters with the majordomo since Weber seemed to have a good grasp of the Machthaber mind.

"Your father has mentioned the topic often. I applaud the example. Everyone should be in uniform. I may not appear so, but I am a veteran. In those ancient days, my service was little more than guard duty for your grandfather. Perhaps, those were merely simpler times."

"I mean to leave the Villa," Henry said. He often wondered if the elevator moved at the speed of the majordomo's will.

"Is something not to your liking, sir?" Weber asked.

Henry debated his next statement. He wanted an honest opinion and decided to put his faith in a man who always seemed to be there for him no matter the circumstance.

"I'm irritated I'm being used as a pawn in my parents' game. I should be building my fame as an Assaultman, not opening museums and playing nursemaid to a foreign military officer. These are not the duties of either an Assaultman or a special forces officer," Henry said.

"You are right, Primus," Weber said, with a pause. Henry waited for the rest.

"Those are not the duties of an Assaultman or a special forces officer, but they are the duties of a protector in training." Weber said. If there was more to Weber's thought, the elevator doors opening ended it.

"Bye, Weber," said Henry.

"*Guten Appetit*, Primus," said Weber. Henry moved through the public apartments and into his parents' private apartments. Henry noticed that his parents had also remodeled. Gone was the gaudy gold and crimson wall paper. In its place was wood paneling and flooring with finely woven red and gold accent rugs. Henry moved through the private front room and to his parent's private dining room.

Opening the door, Henry saw his parents seated at the table. While Henry had a lot of latitude when speaking to his parents in private, he was still bound by the customs and traditions surrounding the protector—like any other Felgenlander. In the Villa, someone was always near and listening.

The protector sat at the head of the two-meter table, while the patroness sat at the foot. Henry approached and sat down at the protector's right hand. Henry waited his for parents to guide the conversation. Once the servants had cleared the meal, things would become more private and casual.

"How have you been this week, my boy," asked his father.

"Well enough, Father," Henry responded. "I opened the Museum of the Sheeplands in Balquidder; I stood for photos with wounded Assaultmen at the Union Veterans Hospital; and I made an appearance at the cathedral for Jason Campbell's wedding."

"All good things," the patroness said. "Did you meet anyone interesting?"

"No, not really, Mother," Henry said passively, "just the usual petitioners looking for something. Since I am merely Primus, I tend to tell them I will carry their messages to you."

"Anything of note?" the protector said.

"No, the usual: appointments, favors, and as always money," Henry said.

"Heinrich dear, favors are the protector's currency," the patroness said. "We use favors as important levers to motivate people."

"I'm sure they are," said Henry. Henry waited. His mother was winding up for a long lecture. However, servants appeared with dinner. The dinner was baked chicken with a side of Stahlburghian beans, and Hasselback potatoes. The patroness' hunger was stronger than her desire to lecture, and she became silent as the three ate.

"Do you know anything about the Sheeplands, my son," asked the protector, as the servants cleared the dinner.

"A bit, I was friends with a Sheeplander when I was actually serving as an Assaultman," said Henry.

"Tell me about him," asked the protector.

"George, he is a baron. His family has a profitable distillery. They make a pretty good whisky called *The Royal Neep*. George claimed the drink was quite popular with the Sheeplanders. Why? Are we entertaining someone important, father?" Henry asked.

"No, I'd like to have a familiar drink in case I have to invite a new Sheeplander *Graf* for a visit," said the protector.

"Like Kenneth's son?" Henry said seeing his opportunity. Henry saw the jolt his comment gave his mother. The patroness then looked questioningly at the protector.

"What? He's your son as well. Did you think he wouldn't find out? This Villa has more ears than a maize field," said the protector. Henry smiled inwardly. He would let his parents wonder how he found out that secret.

"I think it's time we accelerate your education. I want you to attend the weekly protector's briefings with me. Your security clearance is sufficiently high as an Assault officer," the protector said.

"Aye, aye, sir," Henry said, like an Assaultman addressing an officer.

"This dinner is more informal than that, Heinrich," said the protector. The patroness was obviously irritated at Henry's knowledge and attitude. She put her fork down and said, "It is also high time you find a wife. Saint Malcolm himself warned that an unmarried man was a danger to civilization."

"And yet, the Prophet never married," Henry replied to his mother. She looked at Henry with a stare that could cut steel.

"Heinrich, you have become a wild little boy," she said to him.

"One could also say I have become a strong, independent man, who is not ruled by his mother. Many of the women I associate with decry a man who cannot separate himself from his mother," Henry shot back.

"Those trollops aren't interested in marriage," the patroness replied coolly.

"You mean the endless parade of women you 'motivate' by slyly holding me out as a potential match? All so you two can gather favors while you seek the 'perfect advantageous match?'" said Henry becoming angry.

"Enough," growled the protector. "We are a happy model family, remember?"

"Now Heinrich, have you met anyone of note?" said the protector. Henry looked angrily at his father. The protector added, "My question is fair. Your mother and I are curious."

Henry sighed. "I had met someone just before the Union declared war. She and I seemed potentially well matched, but then the Navy gave her deployment orders."

"What was her rating and designation, my son?" said the patroness, her interest piqued.

"She is a star lieutenant and an interceptor pilot," said Henry.

"I suppose if you are settling for, what do the papers call them again, dear?" the patroness asked her husband.

"The protector's ship wenches," the protector said.

"A ship wench, yes... I suppose if you are settling for a ship wench then an interceptor pilot is better than some wrench turning trollop," said the patroness.

"Mother, listen to yourself," Henry said. "You sound as bad as the electronic slag that is called our mainstream news."

"An astute observation," said the protector. "Your mother worries that the ruthless, and yet, stupid journalists will capitalize on any entanglements. These are the same people who have for years lauded the doves even though those fools hid their heads in the sand."

"Is she from a Dynastic family?" Henry's mother asked.

"I'd prefer not to say since she has not communicated with me since she left," Henry said. "I wrote her, but she hasn't written back."

"That's not unusual. The Navy is slow in sending communications from the front," the protector said.

Henry's mother softened, and said, "I suppose I didn't expect you to want a more dynamic lady. Your father and I have attempted to find a traditional match from a Dynastic family, who would meekly stand beside you. I see you seek a woman who may outshine you. At least you're looking in the traditional cadre of the hawks. I don't think your father or I could accept a daughter-in-law who came from the theater or—Allfather forbid—a movie actress!"

"Yes, I agree. An actress is almost as bad as an advocate or muckraker," said the protector.

"Have you read our paper recently, Heinrich," the patroness asked. Henry knew the paper to which she referred was the *Felgenland Mirror*. The paper was part of the O'Cruadhlaoich news service, a popular holocast and news site.

"No, Mother," Henry responded. He wondered what she would say next.

"The war's first ace, Hannah DeBeck, will be in the capital. If you are amenable, we could arrange a meeting," said the patroness.

“No,” Henry said flatly.

“Why not? She’s pretty, she’s an interceptor pilot—since that’s your type now—her family is one of the middle classes, and she’s a war hero,” said the patroness with irritation.

“And everyone would say, ‘There goes Heinrich with his war hero wife! She wears skirts and so does her husband who never fired a pin rifle during the war’ or ‘She’s more a man than he is, since she killed five of the enemy whereas he didn’t even dare set foot on an enemy world.’ No, thank you,” Henry said.

“Patience, both of you,” the protector said. “Now, Marta, Heinrich’s point is valid. A war hero wife would—currently—over shadow his stature. However, Heinrich, when you are protector, a wife who served would bring the loyalty of many Navy households.”

The protector paused to let his point sink in. Then, he cleared his throat and continued, “Now, with regards to Frau DeBeck, I think it is worth considering a coffee date. She is an attractive war hero. The Navy has been promoting her story to entice young women to enlist. If her orbit were to rise so high that she was seen having coffee with the Primus, well, what better incentive? She’s a nice enough young lady. I have met her several times.”

Henry’s gut told him that Hannah, even if she was the last woman in the Union, was not the type of wife he wanted. When he envisioned his ideal lady, his imagination always pictured Bonnie MacDonald. The fantasy was an odd since as he had only spent a few hours with Bonnie.

“I will pass on Frau DeBeck. I’d rather talk about shooting a rifle at an enemy. I believe Assault High Command is ignoring my messages. Is that on account of either of you?” Henry said. The patroness looked insistently at the protector. Henry realized both of his parents had been preventing him from deploying.

“You two did not!” Henry said angrily.

“Wait, son. You need to hear us out,” the protector said.

"You have five minutes or I call the *Glückstadt Nexus Times* or *Yaist News-Felgenland* and give them an exclusive interview," threatened Henry.

"You wouldn't dare," the patroness said.

"Sure, I would! I'd suggest the interview could be titled, 'Protector uses his influence to spare son from dangerous war duty!' or perhaps it should be properly titled 'The patroness...'"

"Enough!" the protector roared. Then, standing he shouted, "Weber! Weber!"

"Here, sir," said Weber appearing almost instantly.

"Clear the kitchens and send up our USIS detail. Heinrich has forced my hand," the protector said.

"Yes, sir. I did warn you he was unhappy," Weber said as an aside before leaving.

"What's this all about?" asked Henry.

"Your mother and I have a confession. The information is top secret and we need to have USIS sweep the room for bugs first," said the protector. A five-man team of USIS techs appeared. They wore clean suit gear, and Henry couldn't determine age or gender for any of the members. They scanned the room with their tools and set up tripods with electronic devices which began blinking in unison.

"Your EVIL, sir," one of the techs said to Henry. Henry removed the device and the tech placed the EVIL outside the tripods.

"You are secure, Lord Protector," the lead said. "There are no bugs nor spy devices here. You are a hole in the universe."

"Thank you, Smythe. You are all dismissed; you can collect the devices in the morning," said the protector. The USIS team left.

Weber appeared, and asked, "Do you need anything further, sir?"

"No, but please stay as an impartial witness," said the protector.

"Yes, sir, but you know I am not impartial," said Weber.

"Fine, you are retained as Heinrich's advocate then," said the protector with a half-smile. The patroness put her face in her hands.

Henry wasn't sure if it was in frustration or something else.

"After Karl's funeral," Raimond said, "you were attacked." Henry nodded; he rarely thought of the incident. However, as if summoned, Henry recalled the child who had died clutching her doll.

"The press described the incident as a case of domestic terrorism, completely isolated from anything else in the universe. But that was simply not the case," said the protector.

"From the USIS reports, the number of Felgenlanders who that wish to see the Union's end are so few they can't shake a rifle much less field a platoon of terrorists," said the protector.

"The Terrans attacked me," Henry concluded.

"Yes," said the protector. "Quislings aided the attack, but the Directorate sent in a team to kill you."

"The Directorate has made it a priority to kill you, Heinrich," said the patroness. "Those godless animals want to kill you as a way to get to us, to your father."

Henry realized his mother had been crying. Henry wasn't sure why a foreign power was trying to assassinate him. To Henry the Directorate's assassination attempt seemed desperate or crazy. The Cognatii weren't vital to the government's functioning, unlike the ministers, Dynasts, or the protector.

"Why? What purpose would my death serve? We're not a monarchy. Mathias would just become Primus."

"That's not how Terra sees our Union, sir," said Weber gently.

"That's right. USIS has given me a score of gold boxes with your name mentioned by dozens of nefarious contacts. The USIS Synthesis Division has several teams tracking down Terran operatives and puppets inside and outside of the Union," said the protector. "There are a dozen dangerous leaders of violent separatist groups seeking your head. The main one is code named 'MAMMON' and he was behind the attempt on your life."

"Well, what better place for me than the Assault? We've done a thorough background check on all the personnel. I should be as safe as I can be," Henry said.

"MAMMON is only half of the problem. There is a mercenary unit that the Directorate has hired to find and kill you if word gets out about your whereabouts on the battlefield," said the protector.

"What your father isn't saying is that Assault High Command cannot guarantee your whereabouts would remain secret enough to protect you," Weber stated with a bow towards the protector.

"Yes, precisely. The Terran Maxim of Defense has boldly called for your head, along with the heads of the MacDonalds, Campbells, Gordons, Frasers, and Buchanans. She screams and howls like a banshee for assassins, spies, terrorists, and separatists to kill us all. We've had to keep you from your duty. The press has cooperated, some willingly and others under threat. None of this is public knowledge," the protector said.

"I am sorry, my son," said the patroness. "We've tried to shield you, and instead we've strangled you in a smothering embrace."

Henry stood and went to his mother, who looked up from her tears. Henry took out his handkerchief and dried his mother's eyes. Henry could tell the knowledge had worn down his mother.

"I'm sorry, Mother," Henry said, "I never realized when Father became protector the stakes would be so high."

"We didn't tell you the stakes either," the patroness said. "You are right; you are not a child anymore."

"Consider this the beginning of your apprenticeship in earnest, and, if fortune changes, we can talk about your deployment. I agree with you, Heinrich, you need to be on the battlefield—in a role that gives you glory, but doesn't put you in undue danger," the protector said. All assembled fell silent.

Weber waited a moment and said, "Do you need anything else, sir?"

"No, Weber," said the protector.

"Good, I have to eject the Falke twins. The valet brought them into the Villa. Shall I give the man a good thrashing, sir?"

"No, his mother has been informed of his poor behavior. He will be leaving the Villa in the morning," the protector said. Henry wasn't sure if he was sad or happy at the thought of Johann leaving.

"Very well, sir," Weber said bowing and leaving. Henry had never realized how tied into the Villa the majordomo was. Weber was apparently the dominant force in the Villa and knew the whereabouts of everyone down to a mouse in the pantry.

"Your mother and I will retire now," said the protector. "Remember, in the morning we will begin your lessons. Some day you will do the same with your son."

"Or daughter," said the patroness. "No sense in putting off for another generation something that needs to happen: a woman leader, a protectoress."

"I prefer protectrix," the protector said, "but that's getting ahead of ourselves. Our son has not found his lady. Perhaps tomorrow he may wake with an eye for marriage and the joys of living a settled life. But I also recognize that when I was his age I sought glory on the battlefield. A life like that is at odds with marriage. Now, goodnight my son."

"Goodnight, Father and Mother," said Henry. His parents came over and each gave him a gentle hug. The patroness then embraced the protector lovingly. He put his arm around his wife. Henry felt drained. He decided to head to his apartments. He stood, grabbed his EVIL and exited the protector's apartments. He then approached the elevator. As he got closer, the door opened. Henry expected Weber to be in the lift, but it was empty.

The elevator closed and began moving. Henry felt strangely calm for a man with a price on his head. He mused on how he and the scions of the first families of Stahlburgh were all on a Terran hit list. A tiny thought in the back of his mind suggested that perhaps the hit list could bind the first families together.

Henry went over the list. Angus MacDonald was the High King of the Skye Isles, a broad archipelago bordering the northern circle of Stahlburgh. Angus also had significant vassals across Eisenwald and Lochiel. The MacDonald clan commanded the fealty of hundreds of sub-clans and minor houses. The MacDonalds in their isles were a nation practically unto themselves. They supported Karl as a way to prevent the Campbell from becoming Protector of the Union. The Directorate would love to kill Angus or his heir, Drostan. Henry remembered Drostan as the man who was so concerned about Henry having ill intentions towards Bonnie. Henry suspected that he would need to pay Angus a call, and Henry wanted to ensure Bonnie was all right as he had not heard from her. Henry owed the woman a coffee after all.

The lift door opened and Henry exited. Thinking of Bonnie, he saw the expansive oil on canvas painting. He studied its details before examining the others in the collection. Some were of pastoral scenes he couldn't place, while others were of personages he should know but didn't.

On the corridor's right side was the picture of MacLeod's landing. Across from that painting hung another expansive oil on canvas painting of an Assaultman in one of the earliest battlesuit prototypes. The Assaultman held a banner with the black and gold stars of Hansaburgh. Behind him, a battle raged against the old tyrants, the Ó Gallchobhoir clan, whom Karl exterminated or drove into ignominy and exile. The Assaultman stood on the Ó Gallchobhoir clan's banner, which lay in the mud. Henry turned on his EVIL and used it to scan the picture. Within moments a short summary appeared on the EVIL.

> This is the oil and canvas of "Alaric Campbell's Victory of the Vanguard." The canvas is a symbolic portrayal of the seventh Grand Duke of Argyll-Inveraray-on-the-Greenwich in his fight to secure the landing zone of Karl von Machthaber (first Protector

```
of the Union) at the Battle of the Landing.
The original now hangs in the Protector's
Villa, a gift from Alasdair Campbell, eighth
Grand Duke of Argyll-Inveraray-on-the-
Greenwich.
```

That was the Campbells, a clan that was ancient, martial, and very powerful.

Henry didn't need to muse much on Alasdair. He was the president and chief executive officer of Campbell Industries which was vital to the war effort. The Campbell was a high-ranking officer in the Line Guards. Killing Alasdair would be a huge blow to the war effort, even if Henry wasn't fond of the man.

Henry then looked at the next largest painting. The oil painting was of a medieval knight bowing to a king. Below the large painting was a smaller painting that depicted a man standing in similar pose bowing in front of Karl. Henry scanned the large painting with his EVIL.

```
Adam Gordon pays homage to Robert the Bruce.
This is an original painted by the fifth Duke
of Huntly-on-the-Aberdeen. The original oil on
canvas is on display in the Protector's Villa.
```

Huntly-on-the-Aberdeen was a duchy to the east of the Sheeplands on Stahlburgh. Henry mused how the Gordons were yet another military clan. However, the leading Gordon, Alexander, was the current prime minister. He had been elected as the president of the House of Dynasts upon Raimond's succession. Henry had been introduced to a niece or cousin, but the woman was not nearly as interesting as her relatives. Alexander's death would put a large part of Stahlburgh into turmoil as well, since the Gordon clan—like the MacDonalds—was intimately connected to a large number of other clans. Additionally, Alexander was, by all appearances, an able politician and a natural leader.

There remained only two large paintings in the corridor that Henry had not examined. He surmised one would be for the Frasers and the other for the Buchanans. One showed the image of a mighty oak centered alone in a pastoral meadow. The other was of a man in seventeenth century armor with a large white curly wig. Henry was stumped, yet, he felt using his EVIL would be cheating. If he were to become protector, he would need to know the august lineages of the houses and clans he had to protect.

Weber appeared, apparently drawn to the Primus standing in the corridor, and said, "Are you all right, Primus?"

"Yes, Weber," said Henry. "I'm studying a little art history. My house is so young and unimportant compared to some in the Union."

"Oh, sir, how I wish I could dissuade you from those thoughts. What your house lacks in antiquity, it makes up for in dynamism. Take the MacDonalds. They came here first, and then allowed over the decades newcomers to supplant them. The Campbells have always been second: second to arrive, second in command, and second in people's thoughts. The Gordons are a spectacular house, spectacular villains and spectacular heroes. One branch, fought against your grandfather, while the other branch, were allies, but also kin-slayers. It is only after Karl's ascension that the Gordons have 'righted the ship' so to speak.

"The Oak of the Buchanans looks strong. Presidents and prime ministers provide an honored heritage, but the strength is only bark deep. Without Karl's protective hand, the Buchanans would have perished in the days of house warfare and chaos." Henry nodded realizing the oak painting belonged to the Buchanan. That meant the last piece was...

"Then there are the Frasers. Martin Fraser who lost a hand to the Ó Gallchobhoir tyrants for a sliver of the burning cross of Saint Malcolm. Martin was a dashing man, who was a patron's patron. He renovated his estate and made a great house that is one of the jewels of

Stahlburgh. He called the house the "Bonnie Dundee" after Claverhouse. That's the subject of the painting which was Martin's gift. Sadly, Martin's children, grandchildren, and even great-grandchildren have been lackluster descendents. Martin's strength seems to have faded. If the Frasers can find another Martin, then out of all the first families, the Frasers have the potential to be as great as the von Machthabers."

"But my family has nothing in comparison to these others," said Henry interrupting.

"What?! You are the great-grandson of Lena, Stefan, Rolf, Karl, and the others who gave these families their freedom! Your heritage is the frontier! Your family is the Union! If your grandfather were here, he'd whip you for uttering such nonsense!" said Weber, agitation rising through his usual calm demeanor.

"I apologize, Weber. I've had a long day," said Henry.

"Aye, sir, I understand," Weber said, returning to his usual self. "Forgive my outburst. I have seen much of your family's history, but you are still very young. If you get the chance, you should go to Hansaburgh. The families here only look impressive while on Stahlburgh. Atop the mines and marble of the old capital world, the von Machthabers' shadows are long and deep. I still marvel that your grandfather picked Stahlburgh as his capital world. I suspect the statue of Lena here cemented his decision, but only he knows that answer. Now, good night, sir."

"Goodnight," Henry said. Weber left, and Henry once again looked at the artwork. The paintings were a veritable fortune. If the MacDonald's painting was an original then the canvas would be priceless by itself. Displayed on the walls were some of Stahlburgh's most cherished histories and stories. Turning to enter his apartments, Henry realized that in a century or two, one of his grandchildren could be marveling over a portrait of him. The thought was sobering. Would he be a hero or a villain?

Henry noted a mess in the front room. He ignored the spent bottles. The servants could clean up after his ex-servant in the morning. He went to his bedroom and turned on the light. His bed was a mess, and in the center was a very drunk Johann. Henry realized the sheets, mattress, and frame would now need to be irradiated to clean and disinfect them. Henry turned off the lights and headed for what was, previously, his aunt's room. The room was a bit musty, but clean, and the bed was ready and unoccupied. Henry stripped off his uniform and crawled naked under the covers. He slept dreamless, restful sleep.

"Help! I'm being abducted!" screamed Johann. Henry jumped out of bed ready to fight. Henry saw it was early morning by the Holstensonne's faint light. Henry quickly dressed, minus socks and shoes and then opened the door to see a half-naked Johann struggling against two burly footmen.

"Johann, you're fired," Henry said. "You're being escorted out. The staff will send your things to your family's hall."

"Oh, come on Henry, you must be joking!" Johann said.

"You've failed time and again, and my parents are tired of you," Henry said. "You yourself said that you worked for the patroness, remember?"

"But you were going to get your freedom, and me, mine!" Johann said.

"I have gotten what I wanted. Now, you are getting your freedom. As the barmaids say, 'You don't have to go home, but you can't stay here,'" Henry said. After all of Johann's antics, Henry was tired of the man. Sleeping in and trashing Henry's bed was the final straw.

"Come on, give me another chance," said Johann as the footmen started to move him.

"We're done," Henry said. "Go home and sort yourself out."

"Henry, wait. If I go home, Mother has said she'll contact my cousin, General Heath Gordon, and get me a posting in the Second Division. They are slated to head to the next front once Nakdong wraps up!" Johann said in a panic.

"I think some time at the front will help build your character. Remember when the enemy fires at you, you should duck. Move him along. He's been trouble long enough," Henry said. The footmen nodded and lifted the struggling noble.

"Come on, Henry! Don't do this to me! Henry!" Johann hollered as he left. Henry went back to his temporary room. The antique clock showed it was zero six thirty. Henry decided to crawl in dressed and get another hour or two of sleep. He awoke a half hour later to a knocking on the apartment doors.

"Coming!" Henry shouted, hopping out of bed and moving towards the door.

"Good morning, Primus," said Weber as Henry opened the door.

"Good morning, Weber. Please come in," Henry said. Weber strode in followed by a team of maids in formal black uniforms, two workmen, and a young man in a tailored red and gold embroidered suit. The maids went to work cleaning, and the workmen entered Henry's bedroom. The young man stood next to Weber and looked like a miniature majordomo.

"After some discussion with your parents, I have put forward my nephew, Markus, as a candidate for your valet. He has turned seventeen and volunteered to serve his conscription here. I am hoping it is a start to his career in service," Weber said. In all the years Henry knew Weber, he never knew Weber had a nephew much less a brother or sister.

"Hello, Markus. Are you a Weber also?" Henry asked.

"Hello, Primus," Markus's voice cracked with nervousness. "No, I'm a Fleming."

"Like the woodcutting corporation," Henry asked.

"Yes, sir," said Markus nervously. "My father and his brother went into business together. Sadly, my uncle died on the job, but my father has done well."

"And you decided service was better than being an entrepreneurial lumberjack?" Henry asked. Weber smiled at his nephew, who look like he was being tortured.

"No, sir!" said Markus. "My... my... older brother is getting the firm." Markus looked to his uncle who nodded.

"I wanted to enter service. My Uncle Otto... I mean Weber... He talks so highly of you and your family. I wanted to serve and to be part of the Union's history," said Markus.

"Fair enough," said Henry. "I suppose you'll have to pass the patroness's interview, but as far as I'm concerned you can start right now."

"Well, then its settled, sir," Weber said. "I was able to gain assurances from your parents that if you were in favor of my nephew, then you would be the ultimate arbiter of his employment. He is your man after all, sir."

"Welcome aboard, Markus," said Henry. "Or, do you prefer Fleming? I am happy to call you by either your surname or given name." Markus looked at his uncle who nodded and closed his eyes.

"Um... Markus, sir! Uncle Otto is a bit old fashioned. I wouldn't remember to respond to Fleming even though it is my name," Markus said.

"Fair enough. First, fetch my clothing for today. I'll need my Class A's, the ones with the Colonel-in-Chief acorns," Henry said.

"Yes, sir," Markus said with the precision of an Assaultman. He then left to enter the Primus' rapidly crowding bedroom.

"He's hard working. The nerves will fade," said Weber.

"I have no worries. In a few years, he'll play stallion for my son, I'm sure," Henry said. Weber's eyes started to tear, but he bowed at the statement nonetheless.

"I expect nothing less," said Weber straightening, "Now, do you require anything, Primus?"

"No, Weber. Thank you," Henry said.

"For what, sir? I am only doing my duty," Weber replied.

"That will be on your tombstone, you know," Henry said.

"I do not deserve that honor. But, if that is what is said of me, I shall rest in peace," Weber replied. "Now with your leave, I have a half dozen other details to address." Weber bowed and left. Markus returned carrying Henry's formal uniform with his captain's acorns.

"Is this it, sir?" Markus asked nervously.

"No. I'll show you the right one; we all have to learn sometime," said Henry.

"Even you, sir? You're a mighty Assaultman and Primus. I find it hard to believe you didn't pop out of the protector's head ready to take over," said Markus. The statement was slightly forward for a new valet, but Henry suspected years of coaching from Otto gave Markus fodder for his remark.

"Ask me that after today. Like you, I start a new job today. Wish me luck," said Henry.

"Best of luck, sir," Markus said. Henry smiled. Markus wasn't as independent as Johann, but the young man had potential. After twenty minutes of training, some questions, and some answers, Henry was ready to leave. Krueger signaled he was ready to retrieve Henry.

"Shall I go with you today, sir?" Markus asked.

"I'm afraid that today you get to stay," Henry said. "When USIS clears you, you'll be able to attend these type of meetings. Until then, keep the home fires burning."

"Yes, sir," Markus said. Henry turned and left. Markus followed behind to shut the doors, which he did roughly on Henry's tail. Henry rode the elevator down and climbed into Krueger's waiting hoverlimo.

"No Johann today, sir?" Krueger asked.

"No more Johann forever," Henry said. "Now, off to the Ring."

"Roger, heading to USIS Headquarters," said Krueger.

Henry pulled up his schedule on his EVIL. His father had sent him the itinerary for the day. First stop was USIS, then Assault High

Command, and finally the Admiralty.

After an hour and a half the landscape became one of scrub country enclosed by tall fences with barbed wire and plastered with warning signs. The limo slowed as Krueger stopped at the checkpoint. The driver flashed his credentials, and rolled down the rear window for the guard to check the rear passenger compartment. The guard nodded and motioned the vehicle through the checkpoint. The small access road went over a hill and to a large circular building. The building was called "the Ring," and was the nerve center of the Union Special Intelligence Service.

The hoverlimo drove to the main entrance and parked behind the half dozen cars that belonged to the protector and his entourage. Henry exited the limo and put on his officer's cap.

"Good morning, sir," a middle-aged man said approaching Henry.

"Good morning," Henry said.

"I'm Division Chief Ewan Fraser. I'm the head of the Subversion Division," Ewan said. Ewan shuffled a portfolio case from his right hand to his left to shake Henry's hand.

"Right, you're the spies who deal with terrorist groups," said Henry while he shook Ewan's hand. Ewan retracted his arm and stiffened, obviously insulted, but after a small pause he said, "No, sir. I am an intelligence officer. My job is to help dissident groups overthrow the Directorate puppet governments."

"Oh, I beg your pardon," Henry said. "I'm afraid my Assault training has colored my world view."

Ewan relaxed and said, "I remember those days, and yes, my former brothers have low opinions of intelligence officers. However, if they knew the lengths we go to get the vital intelligence they need, they might give us our due."

"I'm here for that today," Henry said.

"Well, then, I'm glad. Follow me," Ewan said. He and Henry went to the main entrance where a woman stood. She was around Ewan's age and held a VIP badge.

"Primus, this is my wife, and deputy, Molly," said Ewan, introducing the woman.

"A pleasure, Frau Fraser," Henry said with a nod.

"No, the pleasure is mine, Primus," said Molly excitedly, "I was so thrilled when the Director selected our team to brief you. This is literally the most exciting day I've had here, well except for when I started!"

"What about the day you met me?" asked Ewan quizzically.

"Oh, and that one too," said Molly absently.

"Molly, dear, the Primus's badge," Ewan nudged. Molly fumbled the badge. Henry took off his hat and Molly tried to put the badge over his head, but instead struck Henry in the face with the cheap chain lanyard.

Molly then dropped the badge as she tried to hand the card to Henry. She then bent over. At the same time Henry reached down for the badge. Both of them almost cracked heads as Molly snatched the badge and straightened. Frustrated, Ewan snatched the badge from Molly and gently handed the ID to Henry.

"Thanks, Molly. See you later," Ewan said.

"Nice to meet you Frau Fraser," Henry said.

"Bye-bye, Primus," Molly said, curtsying before she turned and left.

"Now that you are properly badged, we can begin our tour," Ewan said. Ewan and Henry entered the building and were immediately presented with logo emblazoned glass turnstiles, a fancy entrance for VIPs.

"After you, sir," Ewan said. Henry entered and badged through the turnstile. The process was similar to the many times Henry had entered compartmented facilities in forward operating bases. Ewan followed and they entered the "dog and pony show" corridor, which proudly displayed all the awards and successful operations where USIS was a key player.

After the corridor, Ewan led Henry to a small history museum. Henry wandered around the museum looking at the photos. One caught his eye, an action in the Republic of Cygnus. His father stood there in a battlesuit minus his helmet being briefed by a young man in civilian clothes. The picture bore the caption, "Lacheln briefs the Secundus before the operation."

"What's this about?" asked Henry.

"Ah, I was going to show you that one. That's obviously your father. He was one of our best Assault operatives. We obviously need you, as there are times the Assault and Navy can get into places that we cannot. With your father is one of our legends, Georg Lacheln. He's someone I'll introduce you to, if there is time," Ewan said. Henry had known that his father had been on USIS-requested missions. However, he hadn't realized his father was so involved with USIS that Raimond's photo would hang in the USIS museum.

"If you're ready, I'll take you on the rest of the tour," Ewan said. Henry then spent the next half hour visiting each office and learning the office's function. Ewan started at the museum and went clockwise around the ring. First stop was the Directorate of Research, which Ewan explained worked in a government-corporate partnership to build items destined for intelligence gathering.

The next stop was a large server farm that belonged to the Directorate of Cybersecurity. Ewan mentioned that the farm was constantly working on factoring and refactoring quantum encryption methods. All of the protection effort was taxing as the Union had outlawed artificial intelligence. The two men continued the tour.

They stopped outside a door that was labeled "Directorate of Production" which Ewan explained was where analysts evaluated data and wrote the intelligence reports. Production then transmitted the reports to the various USIS customers like the Assault, the Navy, the government, and the Protector's Villa for action.

The two men then continued along the building's curve until they reached a bank vault door, where a large sign said "Directorate of Operations."

"What's in here?" asked Henry.

"That's Georg's division, Synthesis," replied Ewan. "They are the central nervous system of the entire organization. You can only go in by invite."

"Ever been in there?" asked Henry.

"Yes, twice," said Ewan with a smile. "My office is nicer."

Henry smiled, and the two men continued through the Directorate of Operations and back at the Directorate of Administration where the tour had started.

"Now, we're off to the Director's office, where we'll join the main briefing. Hopefully, I've detained you long enough to avoid the boring stuff," said Ewan with a wink. "Follow me, please, sir." The two men strolled a few meters through Administration until they came to a posh office. The office's nameplate said, "Director James Graham, USIS".

Ewan and Henry entered the office, and went into the director's conference room. Inside, the protector sat at the head of an expensive looking table and officials, both civilian and military, flanked him on either side. His father nodded slightly to Henry as he entered.

"Next brief, please," said the protector.

An older man looked at the new arrivals and said, "Fraser, perfect timing. You're up."

"Aye, Director," Ewan said, dropping his portfolio notebook and heading to the holo-projector.

"As you all are aware, we sponsor six disparate groups on Mars. They all seek the same thing: removal of the Maxim of Mars and the Terran Directorate-client government. However, the six groups can't stand each other. They all see each other as rivals. Enter Jerry Slomong. He's a financier who can broker a temporary truce among the groups and unify them to take out the Terrans."

"Wait!" a civilian said from the back of the room. "We have signals intelligence that the Martian client state put Jerry on a kill list. Every police unit, guard force, and military member is looking for him. If the regime catches him, he's a goner. How are we going to extract him with all that heat?"

The director looked at Ewan, who was trying to suppress a smile. A short overweight balding man wearing a cheap suit pinched the bridge of his nose and groaned in frustration. He straightened and put on a pair of glasses. Henry suspected the man was a nerd that USIS kept in a basement office out of sight.

"Seriously, MacKintyre," said the man suddenly. "The protector is here and we're now finding out that someone leaked Jerry's identity?"

"Sorry, Georg," said the man identified as MacKintyre. "The Union Navy only gave us the signal collection this morning. At their fastest, the Navy still takes weeks to get the data even though we have a rough blockade on Sol."

"Well, if you'd do your damned job!" said Georg, but was cut off by Graham.

"Chief Lacheln, watch your language! We have the protector here," Graham said.

Henry recognized Chief Lacheln as an older version of the man he'd seen in the photo with his father.

"James, you should know better," said the protector. "A foul word won't hurt my sensibilities. As Georg knows, I've said my share in the past." Lacheln nodded to the protector as an apology.

"I'll need a plan to extract Jerry Slomong. We'll get him for you, sir," said Graham, looking to the protector and then Ewan. Ewan was enjoying the interplay and didn't look phased.

At the director's look Ewan said, "Relax, gentlemen. We already extracted Jerry. His name is now George, George Reynolds. He's currently on Eisenwald in a safe house. We are planning to move him to the covert site, once I can secure the grounds."

"Excellent work, Fraser," Graham said.

The protector nodded as well and said, "What's the next step?"

"Well, sirs, I need to ensure the landowner will support the camp. He's a former Assaultman, and he's got land aplenty. I'd need at least three hundred griffins a month to make the deal work though," Ewan said.

"Three hundred!" Graham spat, "that's the entire monthly budget for collection division!"

"We need that site," Lacheln said. "I've got a half dozen operatives that will need Martian-resistance support."

"Fifty is all I can spare," Graham said. The protector leaned over and began speaking to one of his entourage.

"Ewan, who is the landowner?" asked the protector. "Maybe we can bring some leverage against him?"

Ewan looked like a kid caught with his hand in a candy jar. Graham looked at Ewan with a stare that said "answer or no more promotions."

"My cousin, Maximilian Fraser."

"The new *Graf* of Gilbraith-on-Heather," said one of the entourage.

"Gilbraith," one of the USIS civilians said, "can we trust him?"

"Do you have something, Olson?" Graham asked.

"Yes, Domestic Branch has been monitoring his late father's, Kenneth's, actions. Kenneth was involved with someone we believe to be part of the Ultras."

"Ultras?" asked Henry, speaking out of turn.

"Ultra-Violets, they are the terrorists who claimed responsibility for the attack on the Primus, colonel," the civilian said.

"Aha. Thank you, sir," Henry said.

"Hendrik, that was the Primus," Ewan said.

"My apologies, sir," Olson said looking like he'd been electrocuted.

"Don't apologize," Henry said. "Can we trust Gilbraith if his family has connections to the Ultras?"

"Max and Kenneth have never gotten along. Max is loyal to the Union, sir," Ewan said. Henry nodded. Again, things hinged on this new peer. Henry wondered if he had made the deal with his uncle in haste.

"If he goes for the offer, we're in business," Ewan said. "Of that, I have little doubt."

"Are you sure, James," the protector said to a member of his contingent.

"Sir?" Graham asked, his interest piqued by a comment Henry missed.

"It seems Kenneth was heavily in debt and behind on road construction in the Sheeplands," said the protector as casually as if Kenneth had an unpaid parking fine.

Olson blurted out, "Sir, the roads in the Sheeplands are always atrocious!"

The man who had whispered to the protector locked eyes with Olson. The older man had a deep fire in those aged eyes that caused Henry to sit up and notice. Henry thought he heard a feral growl coming from the man. The man spoke slowly in a deep voice.

"The roads are merely a lever to move the man. I will entrust the task of making the man jump to my son, Daniel. He is an auditor. We will get this Maximilian's support by carrot or by stick."

"Exactly, *Markgraf* von Huegel," the protector said. It was the same tone the protector used when training his dogs.

The room erupted in noise and Graham said, "Enough, we'll discuss this later. Get back to work." The room cleared, and Henry was alone with his father.

"What was that all about? And who is *Markgraf* von Huegel, Father?" Henry asked.

"A very useful, very dangerous man," said the protector. "That's for another time though. What did you think of USIS?"

"I'm impressed," said Henry.

"Don't be. The Terrans have cities full of people like this. We're behind on the intelligence front almost as much as we are on the military front, which is where we are headed next. You asked good questions. I also overheard Ewan singing your praises, to the director, on his way out. Having USIS in your corner is a good thing, during an election for protector. Director Graham is an elector, as are several intelligence officers who were made barons for their service. They won't advertise their association, but they will know what this place feels about you. Let's go. We still have more to do today," said the protector.

Father and son walked to the posh main entrance of the Ring. There Director Graham stood waiting to collect their badges. The protector thanked the director. The director nodded. Henry could tell by body language the man wanted more from his father, but hesitated.

"Now we're off to familiar territory, Assault High Command," the protector said after saying his farewells to the USIS director.

"Shall I ride with you, or do we need separate vehicles?" Henry asked always willing to get a private moment with his father.

"Most of the contingent was only with me for USIS. We'll ride together in my vehicle. I'm sure we'll see others later at Assault High Command," said the protector.

"Yes, sir," Henry said, heading to the protector's hover limo. As he approached the vehicle, a color sergeant with a nameplate that said 'Daniels' got out and opened the door for him. Henry and his father entered the vehicle and took off their hats.

"Now, we'll find out whether I need to send more regiments to Nakdong. Hopefully, if Mars becomes a tinder box, Nakdong, and the rest of Lalande will fall to our forces. Then we'll move to a new system."

Henry nodded. The hoverlimo accelerated forward leaving USIS behind.

Nakdong Part Two

Jurgen read the duty sheet. He had guard duty again. He was stuck at the base again. He knew only part of the problem was him. The Ninth Stahlburgh Rifles had taken a beating, and General Meagher was still trying to assemble the remaining pieces into a functional military unit. The First wasn't in much better shape, but due to dumb luck, the regiment had taken fewer losses than the Ninth.

After VIKINGRAID, Jurgen's fellow Assaultmen had declared Jurgen an "angel of death" and refused to serve with him out of fear.

The only ones who associated with Jurgen were Maricela and Ismail Ackbar. Maricela and Ismail didn't get along for religious reasons. Maricela didn't believe in either Muhammad or Malcolm and was quick to call both infidels. Ismail believed in both, as well as a host of other holy men. Ismail also believed Maricela was an unclean woman due to both her hygiene and her lack of a male chaperone. Jurgen suspected Ismail could have forgiven Maricela for not having a chaperone but really detested her body odor. Either way, Jurgen was stuck with the oddballs. The Assaultmen with whom he used to associate, well the ones who survived, no longer gave him the time of day.

"Look. There is an opening for a sergeant in the First," Ismail said pointing out an open slot.

"Who is the officer?" Jurgen asked.

"A Captain Nordlinger," said Ismail.

"I don't know him," Jurgen said. Jurgen was desperate to get back into the fight. Even Ismail had been on a patrol in the jungles. After

VIKINGRAID, Jurgen wasn't assigned to jungle patrols. The official reason was that the Ninth's I Battalion was still trying to "balance the marbles" and that there wasn't equipment or a squad for Wulfjaeger. Jurgen thought that explanation might be accurate, but couldn't confirm it. Enemy artillery had killed his company commander, Captain von Richter. Richter's lieutenants had also been killed along with the captain. An enemy interceptor had killed II Battalion's leader —Major Neidermeyer. That meant the only officer between Jurgen and General Meagher was the colonel and CO of the Ninth Regiment, Friedrich Eisenhower. Unfortunately, an enemy sniper wounded Eisenhower and the colonel was in a hospital bed. The room was two down from where Cannon had been.

The Navy evacuated Cannon right after VIKINGRAID. Cannon wrote Jurgen said he was already on Stahlburgh. Roscoe said he processing through a medical discharge.

Jurgen didn't envy the man, as Cannon would be visiting dead Assaultmen's families while waiting for his release. Cannon had written Jurgen a message that had gotten through the censors and told him of a heart wrenching visit to Metal's mother. Cannon presented the older woman the Union flag and she completely broke down in tears. Roscoe said that she was utterly alone now, as her husband had passed away a few years ago. Roscoe hadn't shared any more stories after that. He just sent a message saying he was out. Jurgen knew that the visits had to be hard on Cannon.

After VIKINGRAID, there were days when Jurgen would wake in a cold sweat worried the tank was going to run him over. That was a dark dream. He'd get up, shower, and head to the mess hall where everyone avoided him. Maricela would eventually join him odor wafting, and give him her ghastly smile. It was like she knew his dreams and was welcoming him to the brutal nightmares club.

"You going to kill today?" she asked, finding Jurgen. If Jurgen had been around other Assaultmen, they might have teased Jurgen that she was his girlfriend. At least, being a pariah meant that he was left alone.

"Nope, guarding the base," Jurgen said.

"*Que se jodan kun ruan zhi tiuj malkuraĝuloj*," Maricela said in her native tongue. Jurgen didn't know what she said, but suspected she made an offensive assessment of his leadership. She hated being stuck with Jurgen on guard duty. He suspected that she was considered "damaged goods" as well, and no one higher up wanted to deal with her care and feeding. Jurgen was about to hit the chow line when a sergeant entered the mess hall and blew a shrill whistle.

"Attention," the sergeant shouted. Jurgen and the rest of the Assaultmen snapped to attention. An officer strolled in wearing a battlesuit but no helmet.

"At ease," the officer said. "Listen up, I'm Major Wilhelm Bruckner, out of the Seventy-Second. I've been granted the authority to assemble a squad for a special mission. I'm not going to sugar coat this one gram. This is a suicide mission—full stop. I've got a hunch I know where the enemy HQ is located, but command is still wary since they got a black eye with VIKINGRAID. So why am I here? Well, command said I could assemble volunteers and go looking for the enemy HQ, provided I didn't steal anyone's Assaultmen. Ninth's I Battalion told me that this is where they are keeping the unassigned survivors from VIKINGRAID, and so I am here to ask, 'Who wants some payback?!'"

Jurgen remembered the crazy special forces officer from VIKINGRAID. He piloted the Mech that painted the tank from hell for the Navy to drop a nuke on it.

"I'm with you, major," Jurgen shouted. He hadn't even made a conscious decision to volunteer. The urge had come from somewhere deep and primal. The mess hall looked at Jurgen shocked. Maricela was the only one who was happy; she cheered loudly like a lunatic.

"I see the corporal and the contra here are the only ones with a set of stones. Any other takers or is I Battalion right and this is truly the island of misfits," Bruckner said.

"I volunteer," Ismail said.

"That's three. I need close enough to sixteen to call this a squad. Any other takers?" asked the major. No one else volunteered.

"Fall in you three," the major said. Jurgen moved forward along with Maricela and Ismail. Jurgen hadn't even gotten breakfast. The major turned and left the mess hall. Jurgen, Maricela, and Ackbar followed, as did the sergeant who had proceeded the officer.

"Folks, this is Sergeant Joachim Krause, and he's man enough for a fireteam," said Bruckner.

"Don't forget it, sir," said the sergeant.

"Sir, is it true this is a suicide mission?" Jurgen asked.

"You getting cold feet, corporal," asked Bruckner.

"Nope, I just wanted assurances from the conductor on where the train was headed, sir," Jurgen said. Bruckner laughed. The major had to stop walking he was laughing so hard.

"What's your name, son?" asked the officer asked straightening and walking again. Jurgen smiled at being called son, the major was only a few years older than him.

"Wulfjaeger, sir," Jurgen said.

"Fantastic, I always wanted a wolf," said Bruckner. "Glad to have you, Corporal Wulf. If we survive this, I'll make sure you get sergeant!"

"Thanks, sir, but I only want payback," Jurgen said. The major approached the First Regiment's barracks and mess hall.

"Me too! Last stop, we're going in to see if the First is mad enough to stop feeling sorry for themselves. I lost two of the best operators in the whole damn Assault in VIKINGRAID and three more in subsequent sorties. The whole blasted tenor of Nakdong is wrong — not that the press would tell you that. We're fighting last century's war. I'm here to kick the brass in the pants and convince them to modernize their tactics. Then, I'll lock heels and say, 'Aye! Aye! Hooray!'"

Jurgen smiled. He liked this officer. Bruckner was like Laakso, but only if Laakso had been cloned with half of his DNA swapped with that of a medieval crusader.

"Krause!" shouted the major.

"Yes, sir," replied the sergeant.

"How many we got? I'm not good at math, since I'm an officer and all," Bruckner said.

"We got eight with these three, sir, counting you and me," said Krause.

"We're eight short. Well, introduce me and wish me luck," Bruckner said as he entered the First's mess hall.

"Attention!" shouted Krause as he entered. Jurgen, Maricela, and Ismail marched in tow with Bruckner who strode in like a general.

"At ease," said Bruckner. "Listen up, I'm Major Wilhelm Bruckner, of the Seventy-Second. Command is letting me select the baddest Assaultmen who want to volunteer for my special mission. I'm not going to sugar coat this one gram. I'm on a suicide mission to take out the enemy leadership. I'm absolutely positive I've got their coordinates, but command is still wary since they got a black eye with VIKINGRAID. Now, I am marching in here and asking you all, 'Who wants some payback?!'"

"Hell yeah, major," a captain said stepping forward. "Captain Nordlinger, ready to serve! The Assault leads the way!" Ackbar looked at Jurgen and smiled. This was the captain who had an opening in his squad.

"What's your beef, captain? I didn't expect another Academy brother to decide to take a one-way train," asked the major.

"I just lost an entire fireteam to an 'intelligence error.' I am getting damn tired of having my men stick their necks on the chopping block, let's get some and make it count," Nordlinger said. Six other men approached.

"We're with the captain, major," one said. The major looked at the

Assaultman. The Assaultman and his comrades snapped to attention.

"Corporal Andrew Tobias," Tobias said saluting, "and with me are Mueller and Vogel."

Bruckner returned the salute and then turned to the other fireteam.

"Corporal Enrico Andreas," Andreas said saluting, "these are Dunne and Brennan."

"We are short one, sir," Krause said.

"I'm in, major," said a sergeant first class. He wore a battlesuit and held a partially full foam cup of coffee in his one hand and his helmet in the other.

"What's your name, son?" asked the major, even though the sergeant was demonstrably older.

"Sergeant First Class Francis Holzhauser, most folks call me Hot Dog," Holzhauser said.

The major laughed out loud and said, "Is that cause you're a Frank?"

Holzhauser made a gun with his loose coffee cup fingers and went, "Pew pew."

"Okay Hot Dog, you're top. Krause, give the count to Hot Dog," said Bruckner. Jurgen didn't know about the discipline of his new unit, but he liked the cut of its jib.

"Okay top, we've got this lot plus three more, AFC Werner, Lance Corporal Boyle, and Lance Corporal White. This here is Wulf, Crazy Contra girl..."

Maricela locked her heels, saluted, and said, "Maricela."

"Okay, Maricela, then we have..."

"AFC Ackbar," Ismail said locking his heels and saluting. The others made their salutes and introductions.

"Let's get to the rally point. Command is going to get impatient. I'll transmit IDs to Fighting Mad Meagher; he's the one who is letting me go on this goose chase. I guess he's hoping I don't come back, then he has one less headache," Bruckner said. Bruckner marched his crew along the tarmac toward a waiting APC.

"You couldn't scrounge us up some of those Mecha-jaegers, eh major?" asked Hot Dog.

"Yeah, I tried that. Most of them are in repair. Some chowder-head didn't send any repair parts when they made this thrust. The mechs are sitting in some grease monkey shop waiting on parts that are sailing from Stahlburgh. We're 'borrowing' an APC. The Second Lochiel won't even know the vehicle is gone. Besides, when we return, we're either dead or covered in glory," Bruckner said.

"The Glorious Dead, I like that," said Hot Dog.

"All right, Glorious Dead, grab battlesuits, pin rifles and," said the major stopping.

"You aren't going to believe this. Meagher isn't letting us go. He says the deal is off because we've only got fifteen Assaultmen," said Bruckner in frustration.

"Wait, sir, I see another recruit. What's your name, son?" Hot Dog said to no one. "You're AFC Töricht Mann, eh? Well welcome aboard, AFC Mann! There's our sixteenth, sir."

Bruckner smiled at the German name Töricht Mann, which translated roughly to "foolish man." Then he started entering the fictional Assaultman's information. It was a gamble whether command would notice the deception and stop the mission. Across the tarmac sat an open Spacecon with weapons and suits. Jurgen and Ismail headed towards the supplies. As they started off Hot Dog shouted, "Get your girl a suit too! She might as well be our AFC Mann! Move your butts!"

Jurgen and Ismail broke into a run. Once at the Spacecon, both men grabbed suit bottoms. Jurgen's suit had been unrepairable after VIKINGRAID. He hadn't been issued a new one since the enemy couldn't mount an effective attack on the base.

Jurgen pulled off his boots and quickly stepped into the suit and pulled the lower section up to his waist and slid the suspenders onto his shoulders. Jurgen then grabbed the top half from its cradle and pulled it over his head. Ackbar came over, wearing the bottom half of his suit, and helped Jurgen seal the midsection.

"Back is good, corporal," Ackbar said, grabbing his top half. Seeing he was suited up, Maricela approached Jurgen.

"Suit?" she said. Jurgen latched Ackbar's back and patted him on the shoulder letting him know he was good. Jurgen then began to help Maricela into a battlesuit. While overall, the suit was a bit big and bulky for the slender woman, Jurgen had to give the bottom a tug that lifted Maricela for a moment to get the suit past her hips and derrière. She would have a tough time getting out of the suit.

"Is no problem. They bury me in the suit," Maricela said looking at Jurgen's face. He smiled and Maricela smiled back. Her smile looked almost natural and human.

"Quit playing with that girl and get her moving! We're waiting on you slowpokes!" yelled Hot Dog.

"Hey man, can I get a photo?" asked a long-haired man in a flowered shirt. The man had appeared while Jurgen put on the battlesuit.

"What are you? A journo," Jurgen asked as he helped Maricela with the top. The top was loose and went on easily.

"Yeah, man, but I'm not a corporate drone, like I am independent," the man said. "Now about that photo, dude."

"Sure, who you with?" Jurgen said. The man started taking photos with an ancient camera that hung on a lanyard around his chest.

"Possum Press," the man said.

"Never heard of them," Jurgen said as he tucked Maricela's dirty hair into the back of the suit's collar, so she could secure the helmet.

"Them? It's just me, man. I'm Possum," the journalist said.

"Are you cleared to go into the combat zone?" said Jurgen. Jurgen grabbed a helmet and put it on.

"Yeah, like no, man, the screws are keeping me here because my totally not made-up credentials didn't clear their systems. It's totally unfair as the military systems are totally stacked in favor of the corporate drone types who got all sorts of dudes and dudettes that can vouch for them," Possum said.

"Hey top, can we take a journo with us?" Jurgen asked.

"Who's he with?" asked Hot Dog.

"Possum press," Jurgen replied.

"Never heard of them. He's welcome to come along," replied Hot Dog.

"You're in, Possum," Jurgen said on his externals.

"Thanks, man, you are like, the best ever," Possum said. "I've never been on a patrol before. Where are you dudes and dudette headed?" Jurgen wondered if he should make up a story. Possum stood there impatiently.

"We're on a suicide mission to kill the enemy brass," Jurgen said, opting for the truth.

"Far out! You know I was just talking with my financier—my girlfriend. She's a trust fund kid from Fomalhaut and has been checking up on me. Anyways, I said to her this morning, Astral Clarity —that's her far-out beautiful name—I think that the universe is going to send me somewhere important today. She was like, 'Far out, I was drinking lotus water last night and totally had a vision you'd be winning a Nova Award for your next column!'"

"Grab your pet, the girl, and the rifles, and get over here! We're tired of waiting for you. The APC is rolling your way!" said Hot Dog.

"You got any armor, Possum?" Jurgen asked, interrupting the man.

"No, man, I don't do guns and armor! I'm totally like a pacifist!" said Possum. Jurgen wasn't sure what a man who called himself a pacifist was doing in a war zone. Any journalist or other civilian that wasn't wearing battle rattle in a combat zone was a few jacks short of a card game.

"Awesome," said Jurgen. "Get in the APC."

The APC rolled up and dropped the hatch. Jurgen saw a crowded interior. The major sat in the command seat, and Nordlinger sat in the weapons cupola. One of the AFCs was in the driver's compartment and nine other Assaultmen sat on the benches. Hot Dog stood manning the door.

"Get in! I ain't rolling out a red carpet," said Hot Dog.

"Wow, you guys, and gal, look so rugged, can I get a picture?" Possum said.

"Only if you're quick," Hot dog said. Jurgen and Maricela grabbed seats. Possum put the camera up to his head and took the shot. As soon as Possum finished Hot dog yanked him into the APC. The APC started rolling, simultaneously closing its hatch. Possum sat next to Jurgen.

"Aw, man, this always happens to me. We have to go back, man!" Possum said.

"No can do. Why you want to go back?" Jurgen said.

"Man, I totally forgot to take the lens cap off! I totally blew my shot," Possum said.

"Tough break," Jurgen said. Possum began bemoaning how the universe hated him. Jurgen muted the man, paying attention to the radio chatter. The major had patched them all into his command channel, worrying that at any minute the operation could be canceled.

"Heading for the main gate," the driver said.

"Command, be advised this is operation GLORIOUSDEAD. We are requesting to exit the gate and head into the jungle," Bruckner said. There was silence. Jurgen could almost envision the command staff looking for the appropriate paperwork.

"Roger, GLORIOUSDEAD. You're cleared for egress. Good hunting," the radio operator said. The gates opened, and the auto-turrets panned away from the road.

"Whew! That worked," Bruckner said.

"Course it worked," said Hot Dog. "My buddy at command, Master Sergeant Holmes, owed me one. You got your suicide mission now, major."

The major looked at the command tablet and ignored Hot Dog. He said, "Take a right at the next goat path... Yes, now!"

The APC swung wide as the driver turned it to catch the angle and hit the track. The Assaultmen in the back bounced up and down on their benches.

"Whoa, I guess seat restraints do save lives! I thought that was just corpo-propaganda!" said Possum latching his restraints after taking a tumble.

"We're on this track for the next few hours," said the major. "I'm napping out. Wake me when the trail gets too tight for the APC."

Jurgen was going to try to nap out too. He always hated the time between whether it was the time between combat, traveling, or leaving places. It didn't matter, Jurgen hated waiting for the action. He put his head back and closed his eyes.

"Finally, I got it working," Maricela said, communicating on the point-to-point. "Are you sleeping in there, blond wolf?"

"I was trying," said Jurgen raising his head to look at Maricela. "What do you need?"

"I wanted to say thank you. Jesus said I will not survive this fight," said Maricela.

"Thank you for what?" Jurgen asked. He purposely side stepped the statement about not coming back.

"You have always been kind to me, blond wolf," said Maricela. "I want you to know I am Maricela Feng-Ling Solara. My father Javier Xiang-Wu Suno was the prime minister..."

"Of Lalande," Jurgen said. "I had no idea."

"Listen, blond wolf, you have given me what I hoped for: a way to avenge my father. If I fall before the end, you must kill Xiomar Zhan-Li Esperanza, the tyrant who tortured my father and me. He is the *penedehin* Terran puppet who ruined our worlds. If he dies, I go to my sweet Jesus a happy woman. Esperanza will burn for all eternity for what he has done to my people," said Maricela said.

"Esperanza, got it," said Jurgen.

"Promise me," said Maricela.

"I promise," said Jurgen.

"Pledge it on your Malcolm!" insisted Maricela.

"By Saint Malcolm's ashes I will end Esperanza if you do not," said Jurgen.

"*Bueno, multan dankon*!" Maricela said in her native tongue. Her helmet disconnected and she laid her head back.

Jurgen put his head back and thought about the mission. When he died, his younger brother, Olrich, would get all the victory pay, a stipend, and the rest of Jurgen's benefits. The thought comforted Jurgen. His younger brother was a smart kid. He'd probably use the money to set up in a trade or go to university. Olrich would then help Mara either with a dowry or by aiding her education. His younger siblings would have a much better life than he ever had. As far as legacies went, that was a pretty good one for useless woodland trash who was never going to amount to much. Jurgen began to feel sleep approaching.

"Oh, sorry, blond wolf. I forgot. My sweet Jesus says you are going to survive this mission," said Maricela. Jurgen shook his head, unbuckled, and stood up. He looked around the APC. Nordlinger was busy tracking with the APC's weapons while the rest of the Assaultmen were sacked out. Like any military member, an Assaultman knew to nap whenever he didn't need to do something else.

"Can't sleep?" asked Hot Dog. The sergeant first class stood by the door, hanging on the safety bar.

"No. What about you, sergeant?" Jurgen said.

"It's just Hot Dog, now," the sergeant said.

"Fair enough, call me Wulf," Jurgen said.

"Will do, Wulf," said Hot Dog. "I can't sleep. Hell, I can't even sit down. I always get the shakes before a drop or an action."

"Really?" Jurgen asked.

"Yeah, in basic they sent me to a bunch of doctor-officers. They ran a bunch of tests on me and sent me to a specialist. At first, they thought the shakes were some rare form of Isaac's Syndrome or a palsy. I figured they were going to drop me, give me a medical discharge, but then they sent me to a head shrinker named Colonel Joseph O'Brian. The colonel gave me a bunch of tests, asked me about my mother, and all that." Jurgen listened. He had never been to a doctor until he joined the Assault much less a psychiatrist.

"Well, what did the colonel say," Jurgen asked.

Hot Dog started laughing, "The colonel comes back after the interview and says I'm a racehorse. The colonel says he saw a previous case and was calling the shakes 'Rico's Syndrome' after the other fella. Colonel said I was cleared for duty and that my shakes are a form of nervous excitement. Says my id likes... hell... even *loves* combat, and like a racehorse eager for the track, my lizard brain wants to get in and mix it up."

"That's odd," Jurgen said. He remembered all the times he had been under fire and how after the initial engagement there was a sort of euphoria about the violence. Maybe Jurgen's id liked combat too?

"Yup. After a few years and a lot of firefights, I just sort of went with it. That's when they started calling me Hot Dog in earnest."

"You getting the shakes now?" Jurgen said.

"Like an epileptic riding a mad cow on top of a coin operated Eridani mattress," said Hot Dog. "This is the big one. I can feel it in my bones, and I am ready to kick some tail."

"Wulf, spot me on the cupola," said Nordlinger.

"Yes, sir," Jurgen said.

"I'm just Nordlinger now, rank went out the window once we left the base," said Nordlinger.

Jurgen waited as Nordlinger climbed down from the cupola

platform and then he climbed up. The switch only interrupted the turret's scanning the jungle for a moment. The track was tight, with the alien jungle crowding in on both sides of the road. Jurgen realized that the odds of an ambush were high, and the thought of being attacked kept him vigilant while at the station.

Occasionally, an interceptor would pass overhead. They all bore Union markings. After VIKINGRAID, the Union Navy had hit the local interceptors' runways and spaceports hard. The few spacecraft that floated above never stuck around to fight, as the Union Navy would dog-pile the enemy. Every so often, Jurgen could hear the pilot's chatter and how they bemoaned the lack of dogfights. Before VIKINGRAID he would have happily joked with them. Now, he remembered how SERAPH, the pretty pilot he had saved, almost bought the farm, and LUNA JETSTREAM's sacrifice for her wing gal. The lack of an enemy to fight wasn't something about which to be sad. Rather, it signaled that victory on Lalande was around the corner.

The APC bounced and Jurgen focused on the track. He checked the chronometer on the instruments. He had been manning the guns for almost two hours.

"Wulf, hop down. We're going to have Tobias spot you," Bruckner said.

"Aye, aye, major," Jurgen said, climbing down. Tobias climbed into the cupola, fresh and ready.

"We've got a little more than hour and we'll be at the hard part. Get some shut eye," Bruckner said. Jurgen found an empty spot on a bench, strapped in, and put his head back. He immediately closed his eyes and went to the blackness of sleep.

"Up! Up! Up!" Hot Dog shouted. To underscore the command, the APC's turrets started shooting.

"Wulf, you, the contra, and Ackbar need to get out and flank left! Andreas you and your fireteam hop out and move right!" said Hot Dog. Possum was up as well, camera in hand.

"Oh man, this is going to look so groovy!" Possum said as he pulled the lens cap off his camera and started snapping pictures. The APC ramp lowered and the jungle was in a low twilight from a slow eclipse. Red hassium tracers buzzed past the APC's rear hatch.

"Move! Move!" said Krause. "We're going to back you up once you get your butts out there!"

Jurgen grabbed his rifle that had fallen next to where he was sleeping, and ran for the exit. He spun left, popping out from the APC a moment after a hassium round had whizzed by. He checked his cover options and saw a large, uprooted jungle tree about ten meters from his current spot. Jurgen began firing towards the direction from which the enemy was shooting and ran. The APC's miniguns started firing a heartbeat later. The guns made a high, loud whine as they ejected thousands of bohrium pins into the vegetation. Jurgen ran to the trunk and crouched down. He saw the track had ended. All that lay before them was thick, unending jungle. Another shape stacked next to him; it was Maricela.

"We'll be going down into the bunkers soon," Maricela said, "*Vaya con Dios, amiko, shàngdì bǎoyòu.*"

"May Malcolm the Prophet intercede with the Allfather for your vengeance," Jurgen said. He had a feeling this would be the last thing he said to Maricela, provided the woman's divine premonitions were true. She jumped up and ran forward into the jungle.

"Don't just sit there, move!" said Krause. Jurgen stopped wool gathering, hopped up, and ran forward. Pushing through the vegetation, he fell about three meters onto concrete. He caught his breath and stood up scanning the area. The concrete bunker was merged into in the dirt and designed to be undetectable from orbit. Five meters ahead was door into the bunker. On either side of the hatch were auto turrets that began to aim at Jurgen.

Before Jurgen could react, someone pushed him and Jurgen fell into a roll. When he stopped, he saw Ackbar had pushed him out of the line of fire. Ackbar tried to crouch as the auto-turrets opened fire, but the hassium rounds separated the leg from his body.

"Grenade out!" shouted Krause, who tossed the projectile at the turrets. The grenade landed and rolled under one turret, exploding. The other turret then trained its fire on Krause. The turret's fire went through Krause's chest and killed him instantly.

"Lance out," cried Andreas as one of his fireteam shot a bohrium lance at the remaining turret. The lance sheared through the turret's base and then kept going. The Glorious Dead had neutralized the turrets.

"We've got two more doors, and we're down Ackbar and Krause," said Hot Dog.

"Okay, time to split up. Wulf, you and Andreas' team take this door. I'll take the left most door with Hot Dog, Werner, Boyle, and White. Nordlinger and Tobias' team will take the rightmost. Understood?" Bruckner shouted.

"Aye! Aye! Hooray!" said Hot Dog. Jurgen stood and with the rest reflexively chanted, "The Assault leads the way!"

Jurgen moved forward and took the last spot as Andreas, Dunne, and Brennan stacked up on the center door.

"Setting charge," said Dunne. "Clear!"

Bang! The breaching charge blew the door and Dunne, Brennan, and Andreas charged inside. Jurgen waited a heartbeat and then followed.

"Watch out, it's a trap!" Bruckner's radio signal became fainter as Jurgen went deeper. The four Assaultmen were flying down the industrial stairs. A loud explosion sounded and the stairwell rocked. Brennan tripped and fell. Dunne caught Brennan when Brennan rolled into him.

"Hold," Andreas said. Brennan and Dunne stood on the stairs and shook off the tumble. Jurgen and the rest waited for several heartbeats to see if anything else would happen.

"Grenade out!" Andreas said, throwing the projectile underhanded down the stair well. A second later the grenade exploded.

"I hope that cleared anybody waiting at the bottom. Now, follow me," Andreas said. He started running down the stairs again. After a few seconds, they reached the bottom. The stairs ended in a corridor with a large vault door.

"Dunne, set the charge!" Andreas said. Dunne ran forward and planted the breeching charge.

"Get back!" Dunne said, running back to the bottom of the stairs. The rest of the team climbed up a few steps, and Dunne pushed the plunger. Bang! The bunker echoed with the blast and the team ran forward. Brennan grabbed the door, and Dunne stacked up, with Andreas behind him and Jurgen last.

"Go!" Dunne said over the fireteam channel and Brennan opened the door. Dunne charged forward firing, but didn't move more than a meter as he was shot through the heart with a red hassium tracer.

"Grenade out!" Brennan said, throwing the projectile into the smoky room. The grenade popped and the firing stopped.

"In, in, in!" said Andreas. Brennan charged forward firing into the smoke and dim light. Jurgen followed them, his faceplate swapping between low light and normal. Three revolutionary guards lay dead in the room. What the grenade had missed, Andreas and Brennan had finished. Looking forward down the corridor, the concrete ended becoming a catwalk above a warren of pipes and valves.

"Clear," Brennan said, Andreas echoed and then Jurgen confirmed by repeating "clear."

"Looks like we're getting closer. Move forward," Andreas said, "and Brennan step lively."

Brennan moved forward onto the catwalk and immediately began firing down through the grating. Red hassium tracers came up from the space below, several hitting Brennan. Brennan fell onto the catwalk. Andreas stepped forward and shot into the space below.

Then, he pulled back to the concrete and swapped magazines. Jurgen checked his rounds, he had thirty-two left in the magazine.

"I'm grabbing Brennan, provided I can get the rat shooting at us from below!" said Andreas. He leaned over and shot through the grating and then snatched Brennan's front grab handle and pulled. Jurgen moved forward and grabbed Andreas and pulled him. Together both men pulled Brennan to safety. The Assaultman was out cold, but his vitals showed he was stable. Jurgen saw several holes in Brennan's battle suit where the rounds had gone clean through.

"Just you and me, Wulf," Andreas said.

"Did we get the enemy below?" Jurgen said.

"Don't know," Andreas said. Jurgen made the hand sign to stay still and pulled a grenade from his utility pouch. Andreas's suited form nodded.

"Grenade out!" Jurgen said, pulling the pin and under handing the grenade toward the gap between the pipes and the catwalk. It bounced on the pipes and then fell below. A second later all hell broke loose. The explosion rocked the immediate area, and the catwalk disintegrated as flames shot from the broken piping.

"You want to keep going?" asked Jurgen.

"Aye, give me a second." Andreas stood and grabbed an extinguisher, which he used on the pipes. The foam smothered most of the flames.

"I think we can chance that catwalk now," Andreas said. "I'll try to jump the gap and hit the catwalk over the gap. If I make it, follow me over."

"You bet," Jurgen said. Andreas went to the edge, and shot down into the blackness. When no rifle fired returned, he slung his rifle, and stood back. Andreas rocked his body, ran, and leaped. The corporal's jump carried him over the gap to the damaged catwalk. His body slammed into the metal grating. He quickly scrambled up and motioned Jurgen to follow.

Jurgen stood, slung his rifle and stepped back. He too rocked his body and prepared to make a running leap. Jurgen dashed forward and jumped. A second later he hit the catwalk, and the metal whined as it tore away from the supports in the ceiling.

The sound was the last thing Jurgen heard before he and Andreas fell. Jurgen hit the ground and passed into blackness.

When Jurgen awoke every muscle in his body screamed in pain. His HUD registered several punctures, and his rifle showed as nonfunctional. He rolled, causing searing pain to travel up from his left calf to his left shoulder. He sat up, crying out in pain as he popped his left arm back into its socket.

Jurgen turned on his helmet's exterior light, the infrared vision had apparently suffered from the fall and wasn't working. Standing up, he surveyed the spot he where landed. Andreas's form lay twisted next to him. Andreas' rifle laying in front of the Assault corporal.

Jurgen looked at the corporal and feared the worst. He patted Andreas roughly on the shoulder trying to rouse the man. It was no use, Andreas was dead. Jurgen saw that a section of the catwalk had broken his own rifle in two. Jurgen leaned over to pick up Andreas' rifle and felt pain shoot up and down his back.

"Not doing so well," Jurgen said. He ejected Andreas' magazine from the rifle and cycled in one off his belt. Amazingly, Jurgen's battlesuit was able to recode the weapon, giving him information on the rounds the magazine carried. Seeing only twenty rounds in the magazine. Jurgen then grabbed all of Andreas' spare magazines and reloaded the rifle.

"Assault leads the way," Jurgen said to himself. He started to walk forward, but realized he wasn't picking up his left foot all the way. Something wasn't working on his left side. The pain started becoming sharper and deeper.

"Time to get some better living through chemistry," Jurgen said, punching the auto-medic button on his suit. He went from pain to a state of euphoria. Jurgen trudged forward, almost tripping on the burned corpse of the enemy who had been so eager to shoot at Andreas and Brennan.

"Hah, hah, sucks to be you," Jurgen slurred with a wicked giggle. He moved past the corpse and continued onward.

The blackened pipe network ended in the concrete alongside the blast door to the bunker's next compartment. Jurgen continued onward several meters from where he fell. Jurgen moved through the blast doors and into a plain gray concrete corridor.

Jurgen knew he was getting close as came into a large conference room. The conference room had sand tables and other systems designed to facilitate command and control. All over the room were smoking holes from pin rifle fire. There were a handful of bodies in the room, including an Assaultman lying face down on the ground. Jurgen hit the release on the helmet. Pulling off the helmet, Maricela's dirty black hair poured out. He rolled her over. Her chest plate had half a dozen hassium shots through it; she was dead. Her eyes were closed and her face had a peaceful, almost angelic, smile. Jurgen looked around. There was a hole from a giant explosion that Jurgen moved through. As he crouched to pass through the hole, his leg began to spike with pain.

"Time for more pain meds," Jurgen said with a giggle. He hit the button and began moving as he felt the pain blockers take effect. His vision started to blur, but he could see a trail of blood painting a path for him.

"Time to find who killed Mari..." said Jurgen slurring the words and lurching forward. He passed through the hole and into a what appeared to be a planning room. Electronics and papers lay everywhere, but the blood trail continued past the equipment and into another hallway.

"If I find you, I am going to murder you!" Jurgen said half drunk and half enraged. He reached the end of the room and noticed that the trail had lightened. Whoever had been wounded had gotten medical treatment. Jurgen tried to focus through the drug fueled haze. The trail led down a three-meter-long corridor and turned right. Jurgen moved along the corridor and turned the corner. A shotgun blast immediately knocked him down.

Jurgen stood up. The blast had cracked his faceplate, but the HUD showed multiple red spots indicating where the blast had hit him. Jurgen pushed forward anyway. He had to continue. At the far end of the hall was a small room with an auto-doc cradle. Completely visible inside the cradle was Maxim Xiomar Zhan-Li Esperanza, the Terran puppet in charge of the Lalande system. Esperanza lay, feet towards Jurgen, in the cradle. The auto-doc was stitching his guts and left shoulder back together. In Esperanza's right hand was a still smoking shotgun.

"If you let me go, you will be rewarded!" said Esperanza. "I have friends on Earth. They will give you money, power, women! Anything you want! Your name will be celebrated as a wise Felgenlander! A man who realized the Union was lost!"

Jurgen put his rifle to his shoulder and fired at Esperanza, wounding him in the right shoulder. Esperanza dropped the shotgun.

"You fool! The Union is done for! Your petty dictatorship will fall! As the Union crumbles from the inside, the Terrans will destroy your colonies! Right now, my allies are massing a fleet on L 98-59 that will destroy your pathetic little Union! The Terrans have an entire battalion on Stahlburgh ready to nuke your protector and parliament!"

Jurgen's mind blurred. He wouldn't be able to function much longer with all the drugs his suit had injected into him. Swaying, Jurgen remembered he needed to do something. His eyes snapped open from his micro-doze.

"Pledge it on your Malcolm!" Maricela had insisted on something. He tried to remember.

"Esperanza! Esperanza! Wake up, Blond Wolf!" Maricela's voice was in his ear, but she was dead and happy. Jurgen wanted to close his eyes and die. Death would be so easy. His mother was right about him; he wasn't going to amount to anything.

"Fly high with the griffin! Blond Wolf," Maricela said in his ears. "Remember!"

Jurgen's eyes snapped open. Esperanza stood, shotgun in hand. The auto-doc had patched up the dictator—including the wound Jurgen had given him. Esperanza shot Jurgen again and again. Wulfjaeger staggered back, his HUD showed red all over his body.

"Fly high with the griffin. Blond Wolf," Maricela's voice repeated. Jurgen straightened. He didn't want to keep going, but he had promised Maricela on the Prophet's ashes. Breaking a promise like that would mean eternal damnation.

"Just die, fool!" said Esperanza.

"You first," said Jurgen raising his rifle. He remembered his lessons from basic. Stance, breath, control the weapon, slide your finger, don't slap the trigger, and double tap. The pins shot out from the rifle and connected dead center in the target.

Esperanza looked shocked and then fell backward. A giant hole appeared in his chest where his black heart had once been. Jurgen dropped his rifle. He was so tired.

He remembered the days during his conscription, when he'd drop to the ground and just sleep. He decided that's what he'd do now. He dropped to his knees and rolled backwards into the blackness.

"You did well, Blond Wolf! I will see you again at the last judgment," Maricela's voice said. He wanted to shoo her away. He just wanted to sleep.

Jurgen awoke in a hospital room. He looked around for Esperanza, the bunker, the Glorious Dead. Had it all been a dream? Maybe he had been wounded in VIKINGRAID and was still in the hospital.

"He's awake, sir," said an Assaultman standing guard. An officer entered. It took a moment, but Jurgen realized the officer was Captain

Nordlinger.

"Wulfjaeger, you're back with us," the captain said. "The doctors weren't sure if you'd pull through and didn't want to get our hopes up." Jurgen stared at him for a moment. Then the events came rushing back to him.

"How long was I out?" Jurgen said.

"Days," Nordlinger said.

"What happened?" Jurgen said.

"Well, we all went into our own doors, Bruckner and Hot Dog immediately hit a barracks full of troopers. The major and Hot Dog were cut down as soon as they entered. The others got some of the bad guys. Then someone detonated an explosive and the whole section collapsed. No one made it out," Nordlinger said, pausing for a moment.

"That's awful! The major was a hard charger. He'd have done well with general's laurels. I liked Hot Dog too, but he was going into the mission for the glory," said Jurgen.

"Well, the good news is that my team got down deep into that cavernous underground fortress and retrieved a ton of intelligence. Possum hitched up with us and got lots of photos. He's now a minor celebrity himself. He's been bugging me about whether you're awake yet. He said he needs a photo of you to complete his 'Nova award winning article,' whatever that means."

"What about Ackbar?" Jurgen said.

"What about me, corporal?" Ackbar said coming in on crutches. Ackbar was missing a leg but otherwise looked unharmed.

"I saw you get hit by the auto-turrets, like Krause," Jurgen said.

"Yeah, the sergeant and I caught the blast. *Mashallah*, I was spared. I only lost a leg, and..."

"Give me a moment, Ackbar," Nordlinger said, "I haven't gotten to that part yet."

"Aye, aye, sir," said Ackbar. He took a seat and listened.

"There he is," said an Assaultman in a battlesuit as he entered the room. The Assaultman hit the quick release on his helmet revealing Brennan's face.

"Welcome back, corporal. I am glad to see you pulled through. You were really low on blood when they grabbed you. I doubt you remember, but you and I were right next to each other on the medical evacuation dropship."

"What happened? How did I get here? All I remember is shooting Esperanza and then sleeping," Jurgen said.

"I was getting to that part," said Nordlinger. "My team and I cleared our section. We met no resistance. We then double-timed it back to the surface, looking to get to the major's location. The major's door had cratered. Then we checked your door and ran forward until we hit the area around the catwalk. Brennan lay there wounded so we got him ready for evac."

"Chicks dig scars. They'll love me," Brennan said with a wink.

"Then we roped down and found Andreas' body. After that, we followed the carnage. We moved into the mess that was in the command center," said Nordlinger.

"That was all Maricela. She slipped by my team and got down there first," said Jurgen solemnly.

Everyone paused and after a moment Nordlinger said, "She has become famous too. Possum wrote a glowing article on her heroism and sacrifice. The locals are calling her '*Zìyóu de libereco*' or the 'Angel of Freedom.' I swear to the Allfather they are building a statue to her in El Esturia on Libertad. But I'm saving the best for last."

"Attention!" A loud NCO's voice shouted. The room, crowded already, snapped to attention. Jurgen wanted to hop up, but his body screamed at him in random jagged pain. Fighting Mad Meagher, general of the assault and theater commander on Nakdong entered.

"At ease," he said. He then turned to Nordlinger. "This him?"

"Aye, aye, general," said Nordlinger.

"Hello, son. How are you feeling?" the general asked Jurgen.

"Ready for duty, general," Jurgen said.

"No, you aren't, kid, but I appreciate the polite lie," said Meagher. Then to the rest he said, "Give me a moment with the kid, please."

The room cleared faster than a Tavishire bar on Sunday. The general was left alone with Jurgen.

"Nordlinger said you were instrumental in finding and killing Esperanza. For that, the Union owes you everything. He had been eluding me for months. Bruckner, tough kid that he was, had a hunch, but Nordlinger said you were the one leading the team in the tunnel," Meagher said.

"No, general. That was Andreas; I was the rearguard," Jurgen said.

"Same difference. That journo has been writing about this whole action, and you're all set to be the hero. He's called you the 'Lion of Lalande,' and the corporates have already picked up on the name. You're now a full-fledged hero, Wulfjaeger."

"I just did my duty, general," Jurgen said suddenly embarrassed.

"I know, son. You don't think I have a few actions under my belt where I hung onto a unit for dear life and came out of the scrape with more fame and fortune than I should have gotten?"

"No, general. You're a bona fide legend," Jurgen said. The general laughed a good long belly laugh.

"Legends are made by the survivors. But I heard what you did, how you kept going. Docs weren't shy in telling me how many liters low you were coming in here. Tobias and his men lined up to give blood. You're damned lucky too — you're AB+. Now, you've got the blood of the Glorious Dead flowing in your veins."

"Yes, general," Jurgen said at the pause.

"I came here to see you, to congratulate you, and to ask if you remember anything Esperanza might have said. Intel has combed through that barracks. Hell, I had the combat engineers tear open that third tunnel. But you were the last one with Esperanza. I want to know if he said anything to you before you killed that sick twist," Meagher said.

"Yes, general. He offered me everything, but I shot him..."

The general laughed. "Good for you, son. Go on."

"He got angry and said the Union would fall and that the Terrans were massing."

The general's eyes grew grim and he nodded, "Massing where?"

"Near L 98-59. Esperanza said the Union would fall from the inside and the fleet would take us from the outside," Jurgen said.

"Excellent work, son," said Meagher. "Now, last thing then I'll let you rest. I've got the Golden Segreant Griffin here. The protector and parliament commanded me to give this to you. The GSG has only been given fifteen times in the history of the Assault, and all of those were for the Unification Wars. The protector himself has touched this medal. It belonged to Field Marshall MacAllisdair. He surrendered his own GSG for you. MacAllisdair gave it up voluntarily, he felt like it would mean more that way. MacAllisdair said he was honored another boy from Tavishire received the award, also since you are its first recipient in this war. A high honor as my old CO doesn't praise many people these days."

Meagher opened a battered and scuffed clamshell and removed the dull, aged award. The griffin stood in an attack pose, claws red from blood, beak in mid roar.

"Fly high with the griffin, Blond Wolf," Maricela's voice echoed in his mind as the general placed the award around Jurgen's neck.

Jurgen's eyes teared up. "Thank you, general."

"No, thank you, son," the general responded softly. "You're headed back to Stahlburgh, Sergeant Wulfjaeger. When you get back there you'll get some R&R have some pictures taken, sell war bonds, and what not. After that, whatever assignment you want is yours — Dragoons, MjGAs, or even the Academy. Now, I've got mop up actions to oversee, and then we're going to load up with the Navy for the next big battle."

"Yes, general," Jurgen said.

"Farewell, Wulfjaeger. If you keep killing the bad guys, I'll be cashiered into retirement. What a wonderful universe that'd be," Meagher said, leaving. Jurgen could hear the division sergeant major calling for attention as the general left. Nordlinger knocked a moment later.

"Well, the general stole my thunder," said Nordlinger. "If you do decide to stay an NCO, I've got a desperate need for a sergeant since I lost my last one to the peerage."

"Sounds like a story, sir," Jurgen said.

"Yup, seems like my NCOs get all the glory," said Nordlinger with a smile.

"War's not over yet, sir," said Jurgen with a smile.

"True, true. Well, the offer stands, if you're willing to transfer to the First," said Nordlinger.

"I'll think about your offer. Thank you, sir," said Jurgen.

"Keep in touch, and farewell, Wulf," said Nordlinger as he left.

Jurgen sat for a moment looking at the medallion. The GSG had been worn and well-loved, but that bit of metal and gold plating was the most precious thing to him in the entire universe. A war hero, and the grandest hero in the Unification Wars had given his GSG to him! A knock startled Jurgen.

"Hey Wulf," said Tobias, Mueller, and Vogel. It was the fireteam that had gone with Nordlinger. They wore battlesuits and looked none the worse for wear.

"Hello, gentlemen," said Jurgen.

"We just wanted to see how you were doing, since you were full of our blood and all," said Mueller with his Sud-Stahlburgian accent.

"Yeah, I figured you'd be okay with these two Stahlburgh boys' blood in you, but I'm a Hansaburgher and we bleed salt," said Vogel. "I figured you'd either adapt or start eating Reibekuchen exclusively."

"Looks like he's adapted," Tobias said with a smile.

"Thank you all for the blood," Jurgen said.

"We weren't using it," said Mueller. "After all those holes you put in that bastard Esperanza, we figured our blood was a fair trade."

"All right guys, we said our peace. Let's give Wulf some time to rest," Tobias said. "Don't be a stranger, Wulf!" The fireteam left, and Jurgen sat alone in the room quietly. He thought of Hot Dog and the major. They were the real heroes. Jurgen had just done what he needed to do. Like he had at home, like he did with his siblings, like he always did. He closed his eyes and tried to sleep. He was still so very tired.

A nurse woke Jurgen hours later when she checked his vitals. She poked and prodded long enough for Jurgen to wake up fully and then left. Jurgen sat in the dark of the Nakdong night and wondered what he would do with himself. He was a sergeant now, apparently promoted sometime between his killing Esperanza and yesterday. He mused on where his career should go. He expected to be an infantryman and maybe someday a senior NCO, but now the Academy was an option. He wasn't sure he could hack the skull sweating and ordering enlisted men about. Sometime while thinking about the future, Jurgen returned to sleep. Another nurse woke him. This time Lalande was up, and the light of day showed through the windows. The nurse left and Possum poked his head in camera in hand.

"Hold still," Possum said, snapping photos of Jurgen. "I need to capture the vibes of the moment. There we are, man." Jurgen frowned. He was sure his now medium length hair was a mess and he probably looked like a zombie.

"Hello, Possum," said Jurgen.

"Hey Lion! How's it roaring?" asked Possum.

"Beg your pardon?" said Jurgen.

"You're like, the Lion of Lalande, man. You are the next best soldier since Captain Orion punched out Kline the Kingmaker over

Heinlein!" Possum said, referencing an Eridani graphic novel.

"Never read the comic book," Jurgen said.

"Graphic novel, Leo," said Possum. "No matter, I've got my photos and you can thank me when I've got my novel. I'm calling it 'The Lion of Lalande Roars!' Now let me see here. Astral Clarity sent me this new tablet, and she also sent a ring. Looks like I'll be Mister Clarity soon. Although neither of us has promised exclusivity in our upcoming karmic bonding." Jurgen nodded at the odd man.

"There we are, now I slide the tab, and confirm and hit print, and confirm, and voila! Here we go," said Possum. He handed the tablet to Jurgen. The tablet was set in landscape mode and showed the Possum Press masthead with the title "Lion of Lalande captures enemy headquarters on Nakdong!"

Jurgen read the story. While the article wasn't entirely factual and Possum had slipped from white lies to fiction in places, overall Jurgen could live with what Possum wrote.

"Do you like my magnum opus?" Possum asked eagerly. "I've already got a dozen offers for syndication! *The Sheeplands Gazette, the Lochiel Looker, the Fomalhaut Formal*—Astral Clarity's dad owns that one though—and of course a half dozen news services here on Nakdong."

"Congrats, Possum," Jurgen said, encouragingly.

"Thanks, Panthera Leo Poomba. Now, I'm going to float off. My muse is calling me to the mess hall where my next soon-to-be-Nova-award-winning article awaits! If you have a hot tip, don't hesitate to message me!"

Possum left but returned a minute later. "Almost forgot the tablet. I lost one already, and Astral Clarity said she'd kill me if I lost another one. Bye!"

Jurgen surrendered the device, and laid back in the bed. He must have been feeling better as the hospital bed was now uncomfortable. At some point a nurse appeared to check his vitals. She offered him a tablet from the hospital's supply, and Jurgen started reading. At first, he looked at newspapers, but, later, he found a few non-fiction works on the Felgenland Unification Wars and specifically MacAllisdair. Jurgen felt a bond with the man who was a well-known hero and a reclusive geriatric living shuttered on his estate.

The books were scholarly and covered MacAllisdair's childhood and early military career as a privateer and pirate hunter. Jurgen tried to diligently read the books but skipped much of the material. Boredom set in and Jurgen pulled up the message service.

Jurgen discovered he had hundreds of messages — the result of months of being in a communications blackout. Mostly the messages were just junk. One message was from Mara, who sounded worried and kept saying she loved him and missed him. Another was from Olrich who mentioned that his mother had wasted Jurgen's dragon on a shyster who promised a thousand-fold increase in the money. Olrich had turned sixteen recently and wrote about possibly running away from home. Jurgen worried about his younger siblings and knew he would need to return home and set things right. He'd been avoiding his family, but reading the messages made him realize how much of a mistake he had made.

One message caught his eye as he was about to compose a reply to Olrich. It was from a Jenny Mercy and the subject read, "I'm sorry." Jurgen was tempted to hit delete, but didn't. He kept looking through the messages, deleting the junk, and checking for more surprises. After deleting a hundred or so messages, another one from Jenny Mercy came up. The message's subject read "Take me back, please." Jurgen deleted that one. Then, in anger he deleted Jenny's older message from Jenny and emptied the digital rubbish bin just to ensure he wouldn't succumb to temptation. Jenny had made her bed, and now she must lie in it. Jurgen couldn't take her back even if he wanted to. The state religion forbade divorce, and Jurgen wasn't into bucking the church for a woman who had fooled him once.

Jurgen continued to check his messages. He discovered another Jenny message that said, "I was wrong," then another from her that said, "Soldier, take me away!" He deleted those too. Finally, there was another one that said, "I miss you... Talk to me."

Jurgen's resistance wavered, and he considered opening the message. The devils of his psyche tempting him. *'Why not look at the message?'* the evil little voice said. He was about to open the message when he saw the message below it. The subject read, "Hello dreamboat." Jurgen checked the sender. The message was from "Hannah DeBeck, Star Lieutenant UNIS, *Spirit of Lena*."

Jurgen remembered that UNIS stood for Union Navy Interceptor Service, the main switchboard for all the interceptor communications. Jurgen had an electric shock flow through him as the name registered. Hannah was STELLAR SERAPH, the pilot he had rescued all those months ago. She had apparently contacted him shortly after VIKINGRAID. Jurgen had been pretty low after the action, ignored his messages and generally had felt sorry for himself and for the comrades who had died.

Jurgen opened on the message. The body said:

> Hello, Dreamboat or rather my hero, Jurgen,
> I don't know if you remember me, but I remember you. When I was alone in that jungle I remember your voice. Now, I'm alone, but in a totally different jungle. I'm the poster girl for the Interceptor Service, but that is a total lie. I don't deserve the honor; I was just doing my duty! Lana lost her life covering me. She was the real hero! I feel alone here, dreamboat. Everyone wants to be with the glamorous Valkyrie, but I'm not her! I'm just the girl next door from Antwerp-on-the-Neu-Rhine! I'm sorry to bother you. I remember how you were with me, and I could use your calm voice talking to me these days. If

```
you get this months later and have forgotten
me, then just delete this message. I made a
mistake.
Hannah
P.S. If you do remember me, you can come
rescue me any time you want
P.P.S. Forget that. I'm being an idiot
```

Jurgen checked the date. Hannah had sent the message in early February. Hannah sent another one in mid-March with the subject, "Forget about the last message." Jurgen was tempted to open that one as well. Instead, he decided to respond to Hannah's first message. He wrote:

```
Hello Hannah,
I remember you. In fact, I can't forget you.
You saved my life many times over and those of
my friends. They too would thank you profusely
for your sacrifices. I understand the feeling
of being a fraud. I am sure you'll know why
shortly. I am coming to rescue you. I will be
in Stahlburgh in a few weeks provided you Navy
types can stick to a schedule! Don't count me
out; keep your head down! I'll be there soon
and I'll gladly lead you back to your
interceptor where you can fly like the Angel
you are.
Sincerely,
Jurgen
```

Jurgen hit send. He might beat the message to Stahlburgh. However, if the message reached Hannah first, at least she would know he was coming. Suddenly, Jurgen remembered that she was one of the holy officers while he was an unclean enlisted man. Even if there weren't a war, he'd be untouchable to an angel like SERAPH.

Jurgen thought about the officers he knew, Laakso, Nordlinger, and even Bruckner. They all risked everything for the Union and the future. Jurgen caught the glint of the GSG around his neck. He'd risked his life once for a promise to a woman, and the Allfather had rewarded him. He'd take his chances for another, the beautiful pilot.

Jurgen felt his determination rising. He'd work out the skull sweat. He decided that he would never let someone tell him he was "no good" or "not worthy" again. He'd become an officer and be as good as all the others he'd known. When he made his way to Stahlburgh, he was bound for the Academy!

CHAPTER TWO
A Window Opens

Loss

As they drove through the countryside, Henry felt a pang of sadness. He missed the hinterland.

"Do you remember how we used to go fishing, father," Henry asked.

"Intensely, what I wouldn't give to have a pole in my hands, a nice breeze, and a peaceful lake full of trout," the protector said. "Alas, son, there are downsides to every job, even being the Protector of the Union."

"Why? Is it not possible to have a job that one loves that gives you perfect fulfillment?" Henry asked.

"That sounds like heaven in our flawed universe. Why not wish men to be angels as well?" the protector asked.

"I suppose," Henry said.

"I know this transition hasn't been easy for you, Heinrich."

"It hasn't, father," Henry replied. "My expectations were to be a general or end up as an executive at Campbell Industries. Work my forty-five-hour week and spend my weekends with my wife and family. Become one of the middle-classes."

The protector laughed. "And, I suppose then I would be a grand duke with a fellow fisherman by my side? Would my only concern during my weekly fishing trip be whether my companion would catch more fish than I?"

Henry smiled, "Sounds too easy, doesn't it, father?"

"We were never destined for such roles, son," the protector said. "Besides, the Terrans would have spoiled that dream quickly. There is so much that the commoners do not understand about the Directorate's motivations."

"If you can, enlighten me, father," Henry asked. The Directorate was a strange bogeyman to the Felgenlanders. To the average Felgenlander Terrans were clueless tourists.

"Sure, we are under no threat of Terran spying, and anything I would reveal is common knowledge. The secret ambitions of the Directorate are manifestations of their public statements. To say that another way, 'if your enemy tells you what they are doing, it is wise to believe them.'" Henry nodded.

"The Terrans... Where to begin... I want you to know, I learned all this on my own. Your grandfather heavily favored my brother, and as a result I never had the luxury of an apprenticeship like you. I had asked your brother to join us, since the electors may not select you, or the Allfather may take you from us. Mathias declined. He has taken an apprenticeship with old Schwartzenrode instead. He has decided to become part of the Assault High Command, and learning the *Kriegkanzlery*," the protector said. Henry thought about that for a moment. His brother had often declared he would decline the election for protector. Henry had never felt he was totally serious.

"Mathias is in love with the War Chancellery," the protector said, as if reading Henry's thoughts. "He sees you as the ensign bearer and marshal, and he as logistician. You will rally the people, he will keep them armed and fed. I'm sorry I digress, where were we?"

"The Terrans," Henry said.

"Ah yes. They are such a useless subject, but I'll start with Lena, since our revered grandmother continues to be such a thorn in their side after two centuries." The protector straightened his jacket, and cleared his throat after a sip of a water bottle.

"Lena Kocher was a member of the Society of the Human

Phoenix..."

"I remember them from my lessons. When Earth welcomed—the now extinct—aliens, the Society of the Human Phoenix became an underground group dedicated to freeing humanity from the Solar System," Henry interrupted.

"Yes, the aliens, who our people called the *Sammelvolk,* were never honest about their intentions with Lena's generation. *Sammelvolk* roughly means 'composite people', and the aliens, once established on Earth, quickly intermixed with humanity. The Society of the Human Phoenix suspected the *Sammelvolk,* had begun to transform our species through hybridization. The *Sammelvolk's* purposes for this genetic intermixing remain speculation even today. But their legacy is part of our current conflict. Lena—as every Felgenlander knows—was the one who decoded and transmitted the plans for the *Sternfomotor,* the star anchor, which gave humanity the basis of the wormhole technology that enables faster than light travel between the stars. She paid for that knowledge with her life. If I raised a thousand statues, that would not equal the worth of her actions. Without her, humanity —true pure humanity—would have perished and we would be Frankenstein's monsters, like many of the aqua-skinned *Sammelvolk* maxims of Earth."

"I understand that, father, but what happened to Earth after our people left? Why didn't the Society of the Human Phoenix revolt in a human overthrow of the *Sammelvolk*?" Henry asked.

"The Society members were a minority. Only about three percent of humans who wished to fight for change, just like in the ancient American Revolution, the Processing Age German Alternative, the Caliphate Age Texan Secession, and the current Martian rebellion. Those individuals were and are ants pushing boulders. In some of those instances, humanity won and ushered in golden ages, while in others, humanity lost and Terra embraced darkness. Terra is divided amongst various groups, ancient regimes, tribal alliances, ethnic groups, and of course the *Sammelvolk*. The Directorate claims it is a democracy, yet it holds no elections. They decry our system as a tyranny, but there is always a vote for our parliament members, the Dynasts government, and the Protector of the Union."

"But why? Why don't the Terrans rise up for their freedom?" Henry asked.

"Aesop once told this story, do you remember the tale?" the protector asked.

"Is this the debate between dog and wolf?" Henry asked.

"Yes, remember, the dog is well fed and cared for, but is a slave to his master, while the wolf may starve but he serves no man," the protector said.

"Aye, dangerous freedom over peaceful slavery," Henry said. "But don't the people of Earth see this?"

"They see profits in their financial statements. They have the newest electronic toys. They hear celebrities and athletes praise the regime. They ignore what they are told to ignore, and they slumber contentedly in their peaceful slavery. I, however, wish to take their toys, like the ancient creature who stole Christmas. I wish to see if the Terrans will sing in contentment if there are not profits in their accounts and the toys are gone," the protector said. Henry was flabbergasted.

"The children's story? The one you read on Christmas eve? That's your plan? Steal from the village? Father, you must be joking!" Henry said in disbelief.

"Oh, don't forget I will steal their food too! When the Earthlings are starving and tired, will they still praise the *Sammelvolk* or will the desperate populations of the coalitions that comprise Earth suddenly understand why the wolf prizes his freedom even though he can starve?" the protector said.

Henry sat dumbfounded. He looked out the window and saw the statue of his great-great-grandmother in the distance. They were in the capital, and would soon be at Assault High Command.

After a few minutes of navigating the traffic the limo pulled up to the hardened checkpoint. Daniels rolled down his window and flashed credentials. The guards looked into the limo, saluted, and then waved the vehicle forward. Daniels drove to the main entrance and parked.

Henry and his father exited the limo. Henry took a moment to look over the Assault's command building. The structure was an ancient bunker with an estate house above it. Like the tip of an iceberg, the estate house, despite its size, was only a fraction of the entire complex. The house and bunker had belonged to the old dictators before the protectors. Karl reused the structure, after removing the blood and bodies that he made while conquering the complex. Many a fortune hunter would have loved to explore the facility with the rumors of hidden rooms and caches of ancient treasures. Sadly, in the handful of times Henry had been to High Command, he had never even seen a secret door.

"To my brother-in-law, long may he live," said Field Marshall of the Assault Padraig O'Cruadhlaoich. "And my nephew too, I am honored." The Field Marshall stood amidst colonels, generals and his peers, the marshalls who comprised High Command.

"I knew I picked the wrong brother-in-law to run this place," the protector said with a smile.

"Oh really, well you can have my resignation if you're that worried," said Padraig. "I'll happily go back to the Emerald Vineyards and bottle the clan's wine."

"That would make Marta happy, and demoralize the Assault," the protector said. "With the war on, I'll stick with my unwise decision."

"Now, now, brother," Padraig said, "I have good news, hot from a data corvette no less. Please come in."

There was no need for introductions. The military brass had supported the protector and knew his son from the many reports on Henry's military career. The Field Marshall turned and led the group inside. When the group approached the main set of glass double doors, the two Assaultmen on ceremonial guard snapped to attention. They were a living decoration, and different units rotated through guard duty. As Henry stepped into the building he noted the guards wore the Line Guards insignia. With the war and the Assault regiments out of the Holsten Tor system, Henry suspected the honorary guard would come from the Line Guards for quite some time.

Inside the High Command reception hall were the typical displays and info boards. On the far wall were several portraits of the Field Marshalls of the Assault. Padraig recently assumed the position and did not yet have his portrait on the wall.

Aides handed badges to the protector and Henry, and much like USIS, they needed to electronically check in to the security system. After check in, Padraig escorted Henry and his father to the posh Field Marshall's conference room. When the gathering was seated, Padraig said, "Give us today's briefing, please, O'Malley."

A major, a few years senior to Henry appeared from the back of the room. He stepped forward and motioned to a holoprojector, which turned on to show an orbital view of Nakdong.

"Good day, Protector, Primus, generals, and sirs," the major said. His tone was formal and comfortable. "I will focus on our main combat theater in Nakdong and reserve the other police actions, anti-terrorist, and counter-pirate actions for the end, provided there is time."

Padraig nodded. The major continued, "We received urgent news via the data corvette *USWC Kodiak Bear* that we have neutralized all enemy activity on Nakdong. The report came yesterday at twenty-one-hundred hours." High Command broke into a cheer and the room took on a loud hum at all the sudden voices.

"I'll make a note to ask the Admiralty about the captain of the data corvette," said the protector. "I assume the knowledge was transmitted in system by our network?"

"Yes, the upgrades we have made to the carrier pigeon system have shown a definite improvement in communications," Padraig said.

Henry remembered a briefing on the carrier pigeon. While ships could make an instantaneous jump between two points in the universe, a jump was risky in a large gravity well. That meant ships needed to travel to the edge of a solar system to make their jump. In most systems, the habitable worlds sat in a Goldilocks zone that was fairly close to the star, so spacecraft had to travel weeks or months to move people between worlds. Those were the longest parts of the journey; the jump was instantaneous. Data traveled at the speed of light, but data couldn't be transmitted through the wormhole. The solution was ancient. A corvette—a data corvette—would carry the electronic information across the universe via the wormhole.

A previous First Star Lady, Alice Gordon, had concocted a joint Assault-Navy project to create the so called "carrier pigeon network." The project was a series of signal stations that would receive information at the most common wormhole transit points in a system. A series of signal stations would relay data from the edge of a system and terminated at Stahlburgh, or another Union world. The Assault had been the prime station builders. In larger hubs, the Assault also staffed the outpost. The project was ambitious, and constantly needed funding, but Henry and his parents believed the benefits were worth the costs.

"Sirs, here is the summary from General Meagher," said the major. "The general reports that after months of searching for the enemy leadership, an elite squad volunteered to locate and eliminate the enemy high command and Maxim Xiomar Zhan-Li Esperanza. Major Wilhelm Bruckner led the team. Unfortunately, the major died in the attack on the enemy command bunker. However, the team completed their objective, and Esperanza is dead."

Henry felt like he had been punched in his gut. Will had been his friend since childhood. They had enlisted together. Will had recently been promoted to major. Will's promotion made Henry feel like his career had stalled. Now, Will was dead and Henry, sat safely up range from the combat.

"I'll inform his mother," the protector said, "Bruckner was the *Markgraf* of the Bruckland. His people will need to select an heir."

"No, sir," said Henry. "Will had an infant son. The boy will need a regent, but the succession is clear."

"Well, that's at least a small condolence," said the protector. "Make sure his contribution is noted for posterity. Did anyone survive the attack?"

"Yes sir," the major replied, "The surviving officer was a Captain Frank Nordlinger, First Stahlburgh Rifles as well as Corporals Wulfjaeger and Tobias, and five other enlisted men. Nordlinger and Wulfjaeger's actions are all over the news services. An independent press outfit has been reporting nonstop on the operation."

"Independent press outfit? Who leaked the details of the mission?" one of the generals asked in fury.

"Seems like Major Bruckner brought the journo along. He's from a news service called 'Possum Press.'"

"Eh, never heard of that one," said the previously enraged general in confused tone.

"What's Wulfjaeger's role in this operation?" the protector asked.

"He singlehandedly charged into the command bunker and eliminated all of enemy high command, while heavily wounded. He's in the hospital; he'd lost almost two liters of blood."

"What about the battlesuit?" a new voice said. Henry looked and saw Alasdair Campbell in his Line Guard Uniform standing in the back of the room.

"Colonel, the suit took a beating. According to the suit's data recorder, it never alerted the Assaultman to the blood loss," said the major.

"You'll need to go back to the drawing room on that feature,

Alasdair," the protector.

"Yes, Lord Protector," Campbell said passively.

"The enemy forces folded and many units have come forward looking for amnesty. USIS has assembled a tiger team on sorting war criminals from the rank and file," the major said.

"Maybe we can build a deck of cards with the top fifty worst criminals, like they did in that ancient war," suggested the protector.

"I'll let the team know," said Director Graham, who had also entered late.

"Have Assault Intelligence coordinate," the Field Marshall added.

"Send Wulfjaeger's name over to the parliament; put him up for the GSG," the protector said.

"Of course," said the Field Marshall. "Thank you for giving the Assault a hero too, sir. I was getting worried that the public would think that the Navy was carrying this war. My sister wouldn't let me live that down."

Henry smiled. His aunt, and Padraig's sister, Siobhan O'Riordan—nee O'Cruadhlaoich—was the First Star Lady.

"You know how this goes, Paddy," said the protector. "The Navy gets the glory first in every action. We all know who takes the worlds and holds them. Today, though, the Assault gets its hero. We'll slap his face on recruitment posters across all our worlds. Now, anything else on Nakdong?"

The major continued the briefing, and Henry sat listening. The Union forces had Nakdong mostly pacified. The remaining revolutionary guards had relocated to Libertad. The Assault was deploying two regiments there, but the locals weren't supporting the remaining bad guys. They were eager to sell out the revolutionaries to the new government and the Union. The situation had become an intelligence operation, more than a military one. Henry knew he should be happy, since the Union had scored a victory, but he felt glum at his friend's death.

"Still no response from the Terran Directorate?" the protector asked, cutting the major short.

"No, sir. Intelligence gathered seems to indicate that the Terrans, when they slip our blockade, are massing at L 98-59. System charts indicate a habitable world in the Foxtrot ring. We're prepping a platoon from the Seventy Second for a reconnaissance operation, but, we have a logistics issue on Nakdong that's preventing deployment," said the major.

"What's that," asked the protector.

"The mecha-jaeger armor is stuck in maintenance. There weren't any repair parts sent with the initial thrust," the major said looking like a puppy ready for a beating.

"Not acceptable," said the protector. "Alasdair, do you know anything about this?"

"No, sir," said Campbell. "Our deployments and operations group has briefed both the Assault and Navy on the need to carry spares, even if there isn't a scratch on the armor. Environments will grind down the delicate servos. The wear and tear can't be helped due to the laws of thermodynamics."

"I need to know who pooped the bed on this one," the protector said.

"Ask Siobhan. She's the bus driver," said the field marshall curtly. Henry inwardly shook his head. This was typical for the Services. If the Assault had an issue, then the Navy caused the problem, and vice versa. Henry realized repair parts were just one incident that showed a military which wasn't ready for war. If the Service rivalry blame game didn't resolve, these mistakes would end up killing everyone in the Union.

"Look, gentlemen, we can't have any more of these mistakes," the protector said. "We're up against the wall here. I'm off to the Admiralty next. I'll hang those ladies on their own petards, but as a veteran of this service, I expect better from you all! Major..."

"Yes, sir," the major responded. He had snapped to attention and awaited the protector's fury. Such was the role of a briefer.

"Did Major Bruckner have access to the Mechs? Those units are designed specifically for bunker busting and other special operator assignments," asked the protector.

"No, sir. Bruckner could not use those resources," said the major.

"In other words, Major Bruckner is dead because he wasn't given access to the best tools in our arsenal. Good job, High Command! You threw away the life of one of our officers because no one thought to bring spare parts!"

"You're being harsh, sir," said the field marshal, trying to protect his men.

"How much is the cost for us to train a major? A special forces major? How many years do we need to wait to get that experience back?" the protector said raising his voice ever so slightly. "Heinrich, how many years for a major in the MjGAs?"

Henry straightened. His father was now going to use him as a rod to beat Assault High Command.

"Seventeen years until enlistment," said Henry.

"Excellent point, I'd forgotten those years," the protector said. "Please continue..."

"Assuming the Assaultman tests well in basic, he can go to the Academy immediately," said Henry.

"Did Bruckner go directly to Steinthal?" asked the protector.

"No, sir. He and I had a case of alcohol induced nerves," Henry said. Several of the High Command chuckled. The placement exam was close to graduation from basic and many an Assaultman would celebrate 'early' and come in hung over for the test.

"We each served a two-year tour. Will made sergeant first after eighteen months. Will was in the Seventy Second already, since he had passed the orbital explosives training and special operations screening process," said Henry.

"That's nineteen years, and I've got a special forces sergeant. Continue Heinrich..." said the protector.

"Will and I both applied to the Academy and were accepted. In the first year he was head of the class."

"What was his major?" the protector asked.

"Cybersecurity," Henry said. The general staff muttered. The top rank at the Academy often went to a humanities major as the sciences tended to have harder material for the cadets to digest.

"He was commander of cadets in our second year," said Henry. "We were both twenty-one standard-years old at that time."

"Twenty-one years lost. How much is the Academy education, Heinrich," asked the protector.

"If we dropped out or reneged on our commission, we would owe forty gold dragons or an additional twenty years of service as enlisted," Henry said.

"I could get forty enlisted men for that same cost," said the protector. "How many years did Major Bruckner serve before Nakdong?"

"He made major a few months ago, when he was twenty five. He was one of the best officers with whom I've ever served," Henry said, tears forming at the corner of his eyes.

"You knew him personally?" Campbell asked. The question was an odd one. Henry had not been formal about the major's name or rank. The protector nodded to Henry, as if to goad him to answer.

"Yes, sir," Henry said. "He was my best friend. We grew up together."

"Primus, I am sorry for your loss," Campbell said. "I will find out what happened at our plant. If Campbell Industries is to blame, I assure you heads will roll."

The tenor of High Command was somber, "If the Assault is at fault, someone will be making big rocks into little rocks on a penal colony," one of the generals said.

"We've got to get ahead of problems like this, gentlemen, before our Assaultmen die needlessly. Major, anything else of note," asked the protector. The room had gotten the message, and now, Raimond needed them to focus.

"Reconnaissance on high-population core worlds show that the Terran client states are producing more carbon in their atmospheres. Our analysis is the increased carbon is most likely from accelerated weapons production. We're coordinating with USIS on HUMINT for recruiting, troop numbers, and sudden shifts in the order of battle." The USIS director nodded, confirming the statement.

The protector stood. "We're done here. I'm off to the Admiralty to see what the Navy has to say. Fix the issues! Get the Assault to be the 'tip of the spear' like the damn *Marching Song of the Felgenland.* Right now, gentlemen, I see a ground force that is operating on luck and prayers. Those will be in short supply when the three hundred divisions of the Directorate Army are sailing towards Stahlburgh."

Henry stood too, digesting what his father said. He did the math quickly. There were around fifty thousand soldiers in a Terran division, multiplying that by three hundred meant there was almost fifteen million soldiers in the Terran army. The Assault on a good day could field five divisions and that included all the constabularies on the Union's four main worlds. The protector and Primus walked out of the command building and entered their limo. Daniels had left the driver's door open and was not present. He came running towards the limo, zipping up his fly.

"Do you need more time for a rest break, Daniels. I realize we're ahead of schedule," asked the protector.

"No, sir," Daniels said. "I took care of things. I misjudged my timing. I'd expected you to stay longer. I apologize, sir."

"Well, we've gotten good news. That's why we're leaving early. Now, to the Admiralty please, and roll up the window," said the protector. Daniels started the limo and sealed the window separating him from the passengers. The limo began moving.

"We're in trouble, aren't we, father?" Henry asked.

"I didn't want you to run away screaming on your first day, but yes. As things stand, we're underwater and drowning. When the military learns there is more to making war than parades and honors, then we'll be in a better spot," the protector said.

"We shouldn't have gone to war, if we weren't ready," Henry said.

"I didn't have a lot of options. The terrorist attack on you was the wake up call. Yes, I would have liked to wait five more years. I could have rebuilt the Assault. I could have hundreds of ships in space docks waiting for the Navy to command them. But you never go to war with the military you want. Rather, you go to war with the one you have, son."

"Is that why Fighting Mad Meagher is on Nakdong?" Henry asked. He remembered the court martial and the public outcry at the "renegade general of Asimov."

"Sort of. Now that he's pulled the rabbit out of the hat, so to speak, he can come back to Stahlburgh. He'll get his honorary title and disappear. If he had failed..."

"You would have had him shot and his name drug through the mud twice over," said Henry.

"I don't think Meagher or the regiments on Nakdong would have come back," the protector said. Henry grew quiet at the thought the protector would have thrown so many men and women into the meat grinder of war and so cavalierly.

"You would have sacrificed all those men and women?" Henry asked.

"In a heartbeat! The outrage, the fury that the loss would have caused would have raised twenty divisions and brought forth enough recruits for hundreds of Union Navy fleets," said the protector. "The loss would have taught the admirals, generals, and marshals a valuable lesson. We are not ready, and we must hurry to catch up. The Terrans have been making war for a century solid. They have five divisions that are not only battle-hardened but also experts at ground insertion and planet-wide operations."

"While we struggled to pacify Nakdong," Henry said.

"Exactly. Meagher should have walked all over Nakdong and had half of Libertad freed. He's a capable planner but a poor operational lead. Losing Nakdong would have been a shakeup. And when the fifty divisions that the Terrans really *can* field show up we would be hungry, agile, and ready."

"Wait, you said three hundred."

"Yes, son, on paper, but the Terrans suffer from the same human failings we do. People lie, cheat, and steal. Not every division that the Directorate says is under arms is loyal or could fight the Union with a chance of success. Terra also has to maintain troops in occupied territories. Otherwise those people might find the courage to become Aesop's wolf."

"Now, we're back to square one. But, can we win this war," said Henry.

"I'll answer that after we're done at the Admiralty," said the protector as the limo floated past the Admiralty's gates. Unlike Assault High Command, the Admiralty had a modern headquarters that was large and squat with massive tons of plas-crete as the prime material. There were massive gravity-pressed glass windows that allowed light to enter, though they were heavily tinted to prevented peeping toms. After all, there were beautiful Valkyries that roamed the Admiralty's halls. More importantly, in those Valkyrie's model perfect hands were the Union Navy's state secrets. The limo stopped and the protector and Primus exited. An oyster gray uniformed woman stood waiting for them. Henry noticed the officer bore interceptor wings and over her name plate that said, "DeBeck" was the emblem of the Silver Owl, the Union Navy's award for an ace.

"Lord Protector, please follow me," DeBeck said. She motioned the men forward and both men fell in behind the interceptor pilot.

"Good afternoon, Star Lieutenant. How have you been?" said the protector. "This is my son Heinrich, the Primus."

"Good afternoon, Primus," DeBeck said formally.

"Good afternoon, Star Lieutenant. My father has told me of your remarkable interceptor prowess over Nakdong," Henry said. He was trying to be less formal, but polite.

"Thank you, sir," DeBeck said stiffly. The trio entered the building and the security officer gave the protector and Primus their security badges. All three took off their headgear and tucked them under their arms. Henry looked around. The Admiralty had a similar interior color palette as Assault High Command with Eisenwald beach colored sand walls. Pictures, info boards, and awards showing off the glory of the Navy covered the walls.

"Take me to the First Star Lady's office first. I need to speak to her privately, face to face," said the protector. DeBeck signaled to the men to follow her, and she silently and efficiently guided the two to the private elevator and up to the First Star Lady's office. The elevator opened to a large reception space. Henry noticed the First Star Lady's secretary was not at her desk. Perhaps she was on lunch break? A sudden suspicion permeated Henry's mind on why his father was in a private meeting with his aunt. Henry would be left alone with the interceptor Ace, a young attractive woman.

"Thank you, Star Lieutenant," said the protector entering the admiral's office and shutting the door. Henry wondered how this interplay would go. Would DeBeck be too timid to talk to him. Henry looked at the pilot. She blushed, and looked at the floor, before looking at Henry.

She said, "I just did my duty, sir. I'm no hero."

Henry nodded, solemnly. He understood why DeBeck responded the way she did.

"Well, I can still thank someone who does her duty. I image you've saved hundreds of my brothers-in-arms' lives."

"You're welcome, sir," DeBeck said, with slight blush on her cheeks.

"What's your call sign? My father never mentioned that," Henry asked hoping to lower the tension.

"STELLAR SERAPH, sir," DeBeck said, less stiffly. "I don't suppose you Assaultmen get call signs or anything like that, do you?"

"I'm a MjGA; we get call signs," said Henry. Then he looked left and right like he was going to get into trouble, and said, "They're all ultra top secret, but since its just us, my call sign is 'TEUTONIC PRINCE.' But now that I've told you that, I will have to kill you."

DeBeck looked shocked, but then started laughing. She said, "I'm cleared for ultra top secret. I'll keep my lips shut, at least with your secrets."

Henry winked at the pilot. Her true colors were showing, and he could feel his heart rate pick up at the woman's mild flirting.

"I'd appreciate that. I don't often get to talk shop. Most of the young ladies I've met are too busy worrying about their hair or daddy's title. Not many women understand the military life," Henry said.

"My name is Hannah; DeBeck is mom and dad," Hannah said.

"I'm Henry; only mother and father call me Heinrich," Henry said.

"Henry, that's a cute name," Hannah said. "I saw the Seventy Second in action on Nakdong. Why aren't you deployed with them? Did you get injured?"

Henry paused for a moment. He wasn't sure what to say and the questions had inadvertently hurt him. He could feel his metaphorical quills bristle. The door opened and his father entered, cutting the discussion short. Following the protector out was his aunt.

"Henry, well I'll be, I haven't seen you in forever," his aunt said in her Sud-Stahlburgian drawl. "You coming along with your father? Or are you trying to chat up my best interceptor pilot?"

Henry smiled. "I'm coming along. Although Star Lieutenant

DeBeck is more interesting than a Navy briefing." Hannah smiled at the compliment.

The Star Lady said, "Assaultman's bias. You'll see, we've got all sorts of interesting things to talk about today. You boys are so terse, but we ladies love to chat about important women things like, nail colors, cute boys, dropping nukes on battlefields, and blowing up space craft."

The protector, Hannah, the First Star Lady, and Henry; went down a corridor and to the admiral's conference room. Henry and his father took their seats in the room's center. Admirals and captains entered. Hannah stood on the side of the room in parade rest. A commander appeared. She was a middle-aged woman, who had dark black hair pinned to the back of her head in a bun. She wore the same uniform and wings as Hannah, minus the owl.

"Commander Lenart will brief us, sir," said the First Star Lady.

"Good afternoon, sirs, *meine Damen*," said the commander. She used the Felgenland plural of ma'am, which gave Henry a moment of confusion.

"With the Assault's total victory on Nakdong, the Third and Fifth Fleets are ready to begin embarkation and ex-filtration to the war's next thrust. We are leaving remnants of the Tenth Fleet in Lalande to counter any Terran Navy threats. This leaves the Second, Fourth, Sixth, Seventh, Eighth, and Ninth Fleets set for patrol duty. The Eleventh Fleet is still struggling to prevent a breakout from Sol, and we've got the Twelfth Fleet in transit to beef up the blockade. The Thirteenth Fleet is staging at Tau Ceti, with the carrier, *Julia of Protelan* readying her three interceptor wings in case the Assault wants to pivot and land on Asimov again."

"Not on their dance card, but carry on commander," said the protector.

"Aye sir," the commander said. She was a pro and didn't seem ruffled by the contrary information.

"Fourteenth Fleet is running freighter capture, but the fleet is stretched thin. Fifteenth Fleet is in reserve in case Alpha Centauri declares for Terra. Sixteenth Fleet is in transit to Fomalhaut. We're shaking our sabers with that system government in case they go client state. Seventeenth Fleet is stretched over the rest of the middle-expansion systems."

"What about the Eighteen, Nineteen, and Twentieth Fleets?" asked the protector.

"Lack of personnel, sir," the commander replied. "The fleets are mothballed until we get more recruits. Thanks to STELLAR SERAPH, enlistments are up."

"Thanks, DRAGON LADY," Hannah said. The commander nodded.

"Any questions, sirs?" the commander asked.

"Why doesn't the Assault have spare parts for the MjGA's Mechs?" the protector said.

"I'm not aware of any refit or repair shortages," said the First Star Lady.

"And now we're at the crux of the problem, Siobhan. I have just come from Assault High Command. They're screaming at me because the Navy didn't pack their spare parts. Who am I to believe? Traditionally, if the Assault is under supplied, that responsibility falls on the Navy. If the problem is numbers, I am willing to open the Navy up to male recruits." The First Star Lady paused looking like she was seeking an answer.

"Clear the room," she said. Henry watched as all the Naval officers stood up and left. He was about to stand up, but the protector said, "No, Heinrich. You stay."

Henry sat back in his chair.

"Well, say what you want, Siobhan, as sister-in-law to her brother," said the protector.

"You're fooling yourself, Raimond. I have twenty fleets of garbage scows. I barely have enough ladies to fly interceptors, pilot transports, and command warships. Opening the Navy to men isn't going to fix the problem and will bring a host of others. Males can't take the interceptor gees and can't fit into the standard cockpits. Plus, you'll need all that testosterone to take a world like Asimov or Mars. If you bring in men, my admirals will quit in protest, and you'll be stuck with a knowledge gap. Something the Terrans will undoubtedly exploit," Henry's aunt stated. The protector sat silently listening.

The First Star Lady continued, "My gals aren't going to tattle on me, but yes, the Assault didn't get the supplies. I have the *Advantage* racing back and forth getting the parts and delivering them. Sternfahrer is one of the best, but Johanna is floating in a tub that's been in service since Grand Duchess Signe Bosdottir wore miniskirts and flirted with Assaultmen. How am I going to fight a modern war with an ancient Navy? The Navy's anthem goes on about 'Our ships and lines are mighty and grand,' but that's a huge lie. I can't get MacCarthy or Campbell to commit to a full roll out. Both men are from older families and fret that they'll have to hire women to fulfill the orders. I know that thought galls their old-Felgenlander sensibilities."

"I'm hearing a lot of excuses here, Siobhan. I don't have time to babysit the Navy or the Assault. The Services have got to get their acts together. The Terrans have over six hundred fleets, and the Directorate will have them all sailing here as soon as they can break our blockade around Sol," the protector said. Henry's aunt looked so frustrated she wanted to cry.

The tears welled up in the corner of her eyes, but she stood and said, "I'm a Sister of Athena! Niamh and Fiadh in uniform too. My family will bleed out our last liter for the Union. So will all the gals in uniform in our Navy." Henry had just witnessed his aunt pledge her life and her daughters' lives for the Union. Henry waited to see what his father would say.

"The time may come when that happens in this war, but as long as I'm protector, I'll get you the ships. You get STELLAR SERAPH out there recruiting. She can take Heinrich. I am sure a girl from the middle-classes being seen with the Primus will give many a young lady an incentive to enlist. Now, get the Navy's house in order, and don't short the Assault! They need you. I need you. The Union needs you."

"Yes, sir," said the First Star Lady. Then she snapped to attention and saluted.

Henry stood at attention. The protector stood and returned the salute.

Siobhan looked at Henry, it was clear she wanted a private word with the protector. She said, "Go on. Please be careful! I know you, Henry. You'll be in a drop capsule or a dropship shaking a rifle soon enough."

"Thanks Aunt Siobhan, you take care too!" said Henry exiting. When he left the conference room, he encountered a half dozen naval officers standing and staring at the conference room door.

"Primus," a brunette said to him. "One minute, Primus." Henry looked at the sub-lieutenant, whose nameplate said 'Callan'.

"Yes, Sub-lieutenant Callan, what can I do for you?" Henry said.

"Hi, I served with Star Lieutenant MacDonald. She has a message for you. It is several weeks old, but she asked me to give you the message when she heard that I was heading back to the Admiralty. She asked me to let you know that she's messaged you, but wasn't sure you received her message with the communications blackout."

"Oh, no. I've not gotten her message. But, I'll make sure to check again. Thanks for letting me know," Henry said.

"Well, I'm being a little self-serving. After all, I got to meet you," Callan said with a wink.

Henry smiled. "Thank you. I'll keep an eye out for Bonnie's message, now I need to get going."

Callan giggled like a schoolgirl, and said, "Bye."

Henry fast walked through the group of ladies who stood there listening. He passed down a corridor and soon found himself turned around and lost.

"First time I saved an Assaultman inside the Admiralty," Hannah DeBeck said approaching Henry.

"Hi, Hannah. You guessed it. I am lost. My orienteering instructor at the Academy is probably cursing my name now," said Henry. Hannah smiled and laughed.

"You know, I think half the Assault would kill to be lost in these halls, trapped with beautiful interceptor pilots and spacecraft commanders. Follow me. I'll show you the way out of the labyrinth."

Henry nodded and Hannah started leading him to the main entrance. He mused on her statement and couldn't find an argument against being trapped in the Admiralty. After a few minutes of zig zagging corridors, Hannah delivered Henry at the main entrance. The protector was waiting for him and talking to an admiral.

"There he is, Admiral Schultz, delivered by your gallant pilot. Her reputation for being fearless is true since she's willing to spend time with Heinrich," the protector said. Henry knew his father was teasing, but he turned red in embarrassment.

"I'm glad STELLAR SERAPH can save an Assaultman, even if he's in the Admiralty. We've trained her well. Don't be embarrassed Primus. Your absence offered me a opportunity to beg your father to appoint me to lead the next thrust," said Schultz.

"I said I'll consider the matter, Martina," said the protector. "Alexander Gordon may be your cousin, but I'm still the protector."

"Yes, Raimond, but Alexander can deliver you the political capital needed to revitalize the Navy. I know you want to build up the fleets. That is why I supported you in the election. That's also why Elias voted for cousin Alexander in the House of Dynasts," the admiral said. The protector looked at the admiral with a stern glance after her subtle threat.

"Now, consider away, oh mighty protector. If *you* don't give me my chance at glory, I'll go above your head to the patroness," the admiral said with a coy smile.

"I'll tell Siobhan you're the gal, then," the protector said. "Be thankful you are beautiful, well connected, charming, and above all cunning. Also, the patroness reports to me, not the other way around!"

"Of course, my wise and patient protector, sir," said Admiral Schultz. She then gave a large grin to the protector, having gotten her way.

"You see, Heinrich, you get a compliment and a sir after you've been shamelessly used. Now, let's leave before the admiral wants a new title for her dynasty," said the protector. He gave the admiral a wink and a slight nod.

"Are you offering," the admiral asked. "Did I mention you're beautiful and intelligent too?" Henry snapped to attention and bowed to the Navy officers. The protector turned and left, beating a hasty retreat. Both men put on their headgear, dropped their security badges into a collection box, and exited the building.

"Did the admiral really take advantage of you, father?" Henry said.

The protector smiled. "Once, before your time. Let's say she's an old friend, both she and her husband, Elias. Honestly, she only asked for what was her due. Martina wants to lead the next thrust, and she was already on my shortlist. I expected her to ask. I was ready for her to find me here at the Admiralty. That's a lesson for you, be ready to cash your favors. Now, we're headed back to the Villa. Tell me son, did you learn anything today?"

The limo appeared and Daniels parked, hopped out and opened the passenger door. Both men entered. The door shut and Daniels started on the way to the Villa.

"Yes, I learned a lot. First, we're in a war and we're not ready for it. Second, everyone is patting themselves on the back for a job well done, but they shouldn't," said Henry.

"A fair assessment," said the protector. "Anything else?"

"Finally, my father is a human being and my mother wasn't his first love," Henry said with a smile.

"A gentleman doesn't kiss and tell. Especially about women he might have met before your mother. Martina, however, wasn't a match. Your grandmother—my mother—Julia, couldn't stand Martina. That worked out in the end. Martina was, and is, very much married to the Navy. Now, did you find anything or anyone else interesting? Like an interceptor pilot, perhaps?"

"My father said a gentleman doesn't kiss and tell," said Henry. The protector merely smiled.

Henry continued, "I have learned that my mother and father are tenacious and cunning badgerers when they want to be."

"Remember your friend, Will. He died which is a sad thing for us all, but his death could have been worse for the Union. He and his family have an heir for their dynasty. His bloodline, with all his strength, continues."

"You and mother have Rolf, my nephew," Henry said.

"We have larger plans than one little baby boy can fulfill. The von Machthabers, and our ancestor clan—the Neu-Branfels—have always been small tribes. For our own tribe's good that needs to change," said the protector.

"Then why did you only have two boys?" asked Henry.

"Your uncle had three boys," Raimond said. "He was the Primus. We couldn't have had more sons or we would have been accused of out-breeding the prime family. You've seen how our true enemy treats us. You had a taste of that treatment with the assassination. Our true enemy isn't the Terrans, rival clans, or the bureaucrats. Our true enemy is the press, especially the corporate press, who are vicious in their ignorance." Henry remembered the assassination headlines. He was the victim but the press turned him into the monster.

"How do we fight the press?" asked Henry.

"We make our own news. Women like DeBeck, and men like Wulfjaeger will be our champions. Star Lieutenant DeBeck is a potential ally. The image of her standing by your side would give our family so much political capital. Her middle-class origin would make a match between you two into something from a fairy tale. Unlike the Dynasts, she doesn't carry a name or any ancient baggage. Her parents are engineers, common and decent folk. Think about that," the protector said. "Or does your heart lie elsewhere? I saw you talking to the ladies outside the briefing room."

Henry searched his own feelings. He had liked his time with Bonnie, but at present she and Hannah had spent the same amount of time with Henry. Hannah certainly seemed nice, but Bonnie had been too. If Henry had a correspondence with Bonnie, he could be more certain of how things stood between them. A coffee date was not a large enough peg on which to hang a relationship. Alternatively, Hannah was an Ace, and unless things changed, if Henry and Hannah moved forward, Henry would be known as the man who married the Ace. Henry wasn't sure that being a famous wife's husband was a reputation he wanted.

"Yes, you'd be known as the Primus who married an Amazon. The press would sell you as the fairy tale prince," the protector said, like he was reading his son's thoughts.

"I'd rather be known as the Primus who fought at the front," Henry said.

"That's my moniker," said the protector.

"No, father, you were only Secundus," said Henry, with a smile.

The protector smiled. "Savor this day, Heinrich. You've bested your father today. You are correct; I was only Secundus."

"Well, I've not fought at the front either," said Henry.

"True, if you were matched or even married, I could rest easier in sending you off. Above all, our family legacy must continue — just like that of your late friend, Will."

"I've heard you, father. I'll give you the answer you gave the admiral. I'll consider it. I will consider a coffee with Star Lieutenant DeBeck."

"I'll not be hoisted on my own petard twice. All I ask is that you spend a day with the charming interceptor pilot. As circumstances at home and on the front start changing, I'll make sure you're in the next thrust. Something dangerous enough to get you close to the front to shoot a pin rifle, but far enough away that you have a better than average probability of coming back," said the protector. "Does that sound fair?"

"I get to choose when we have the date?" Henry asked.

"Of course, you're a man, not a secondary school boy," said the protector. "Or, did you want me to drive you and play chaperone."

"No. Wait! Won't a chaperone be necessary? We're both unmarried youngsters," said Henry, suddenly remembering the unwritten rules of Felgenlander courtship and dating.

"You both are officers. I think Military regulations can chaperone you both. Plus, you two might be taken with each other more if there is some freedom in your interactions," said the protector with a wink. Henry smiled but turned red at his father's implication.

"You're a good boy, Heinrich. Just remember, a gentleman..."

"Doesn't kiss and tell," Henry said smiling. The limo stopped; they were in the Villa's motor pool. Henry felt sad that the trip had ended. Henry had spent more time with his father during the drive than he'd had in years.

"Goodnight son, I will let you know when the next apprenticeship session will be. I've decided to space out our sessions. If you shadow me every day, you'll never want to be protector. Keep up with your social engagements, and in the meantime, consider dating the pilot or explore another charming venture. Allfather willing, the Union will catch a break and we'll all be ready when the Directorate makes its move," said the protector as he exited the limo.

"Goodnight, father," responded Henry. Henry thought about all that had happened during the day. Henry then exited the limo. He was tired, hungry, and he decided to head back to the Protelan Suite. Henry walked to the elevator, and summoned the lift with his EVIL.

Entering the elevator, Henry selected the floor. His message service suddenly flooded with notices. Electronic communiques from his deployed friends were now being transmitted to Stahlburgh. Henry decided to ignore the messages until he was inside his apartment. The elevator moved slowly toward his floor. The EVIL continued to chime with incoming messages, taunting his willpower.

"How can I be protector if I let the EVIL dominate my life," Henry said to himself. The elevator reached the floor and opened. Henry strode towards the apartment he considered home. Entering the corridor, Henry looked up at the painting of MacLeod. He remembered Callan's message that Bonnie MacDonald had written him. Then he hurried into the apartment. Opening the door Henry saw his new valet hard at work scrubbing the kitchen.

"Hello, sir," said Markus. "The maids left this place in a terrible shape, so I decided to clean the stove."

"What a difference a day makes," Henry muttered to himself.

"What was that, sir," Markus asked.

"Nothing. Thank you, Markus. In the future, just call them or your uncle. The maids should clean the stove. You're my man, not my maid," said Henry.

"Understood, but I'm not afraid of a little dirt, sir," Markus said. "Shall I call for some dinner for you, sir?" As if by magic, Markus summoned Henry's hunger with the question. The Primus's stomach rumbled.

"Yes, any suggestions?" Henry asked.

"I believe Uncle Otto said you were an apex carnivore, so I would suggest a perfectly seared rib eye with garlic butter. I believe a side of eggs and some pork crackling would pair well with that, or perhaps bacon-wrapped asparagus?"

"Markus, you are heaven sent. Order two meals and feel free to join me," Henry said.

"Oh, no, sir. I've already eaten. However, after I've made the order, if we're done for the evening, I will take my leave and help my uncle in his duties," Markus said.

Henry raised his eyebrow in surprise and said, "No. I'll order my dinner. You've exceeded my expectations for the first day. You're at leisure. I'll see you tomorrow at zero seven hundred."

"Thank you. Goodnight, sir," Markus said leaving.

Henry dialed the kitchen on his EVIL and placed his order. Henry sat on one of the chaise lounges in the front room and began to tackle his messages starting from the beginning. There were many "mercy messages" from unknown addresses—all Assaultmen—writing him begging for favors. Some Henry read, others he marked for the Villa staff to answer. He knew some of the messages were from men who where now dead. He decided to sort those from the rest of petitioners and deliver the dead men's final words to their loved ones. He believed bearing those messages was the least he could do.

Thinking of the dead, Henry saw several messages were from Will. Each one reminded Henry of his loss. He started with the last one whose subject line was titled, "My friend, the road parts here for us." Henry it and read:

> Hello Dear Chum,
> This is the big one! After days of begging I've finally convinced the general to do something. I'm not going to lie; we're going on a suicide mission. If this mission is my end, I'll go happily knowing that I'll end up on the right side of the resurrection for my actions. I've had Colonel-Reverend Wilcott give me a proper penance. Short of a battlefield succubus tempting me away from my

dearest Yenna, my soul will be clean and pure when I meet Malcolm and our Savior. I know you'll be irritated with me, but I've made you Leopold's regent. That was Yenna's idea, she says that my mother wouldn't accept her in charge of the dynasty.

We can argue about who is in debt to whom at the Last Judgment. However, I would say you owe me since I went on the date with Yennifer in your stead. Although, you might claim that I owe you, since I married Yenna after finding her a charming woman. That was your loss and my gain! Please do keep an eye on her. But, if you two ever find a spark, my shade will haunt you through all your blissful years! On a serious note, please do keep an eye on her! I have her heart in my hands, and she mine. I think my death will break her heart forever. I told her of the sacrifice I intend to make. She understands as we both love the Union and our religion above all else.

For you, my dearest friend, I only have our fond memories. Remember that as your oldest and most loyal friend, I have always treasured your—sometimes—wise and eternally steadfast companionship. Now, I put the pen down and draw the sword!

Then it's aye! Aye! Hooray!

The Assault leads the way!

Major Wilhelm Markgraf Bruckner of Bruckland

P.S. I'll see you on the other side of eternity. I will put a good word in for you! You're my best friend and I know you need all the good references with the Lord!

Henry put down his EVIL, and stared at the fancy cook top stove, on display for guests, in his front room. The tears came down his cheeks in slow streams. When he had heard Will had died, the news seemed unreal, like a bad dream. Now, reading his friend's last words, reality hit. Henry felt a bright light in the universe had been snuffed out. Without Will, Henry felt his life was less colorful.

There was a knock on the door. Henry dried his tears on his sleeve and went to the door. A footman pushing a cart with his dinner stood in the hall.

"Please put the cart in the dining room, I'll be in directly," said Henry.

"Aye, sir," the footman said, before delivering the cart and then exiting the apartment. Henry was not sure he had an appetite, but he moved into the dining room with his EVIL in hand. He sat and began to eat.

Henry continued reviewing his messages as he ate the steak and picked at the sides. Henry found a message from Beatrix MacDonald, LvG UNIS. The message's presence cheered Henry slightly, and he read the subject which said simply, "Hi." Henry opened the message's body:

> Hello Henry,
> I had a nice time with you on the day war was declared. I hope you didn't feel I was forward for kissing you on the estate steps. That Clark woman unnerved me. She seemed like she was trying to sink her claws into you. I apologize if kissing you was forward. However, as a naval officer, I swore an oath to protect the Union and you—and your father—are a part of that oath. I hope you didn't think I was a hypocrite either. After going on about worrying that I would be in the tabloids as your girlfriend, but then sitting next to you in front of everyone. I also wanted to apologize about my interactions with Campbell. My family has a tortured history with the

Campbells, and especially Alasdair. Alasdair suddenly appeared and, well, we MacDonalds don't back down to a Campbell. I know that seems silly since someday I'll marry and be a completely different dynasty—totally loyal to my husband and his family. Gosh, I'm rambling… I hate communicating through the messaging service but I'm busy doing One-Hundred-Fifty-First wing ("the Killer Ladies!") missions, and can't voice call you. My squadron mate, STELLAR SERAPH made ace in VIKINGRAID. Don't think poorly of me, but I'm jealous, since she's going home to Stahlburgh. I'd love to get leave and go home as I've been promised good coffee by someone. Shoot! Got to go…
Best,
Bonnie

Henry looked for more messages from Bonnie and found another one with a subject that said, "Nevermind. Sorry, coffee may be off." Henry's heart, which had been slightly happier, felt heavy. Henry opened the message:

Hi Henry,
Look I am sorry for the last message and all the rambling. I hereby release you from your promise of coffee. I don't do this (run hot and cold) but Frank sent me a message. He said he lost a fireteam and their deaths shook him up. He said he realized he made a mistake. He wants to try again with me. We talked about Frank a little. Frank had already asked my dad to court me and my dad had accepted. I know dad seems like a tiger in public, but privately, he's really a big teddy bear. Well, my father and I can't easily tell Frank we're over without a scandal. Frank isn't from a

high family, but he has done all the right things for us to make a match.
Before we broke up, we had made a loose promise to each other and now Frank and his family are pushing for an engagement. Sorry, I don't know why I'm telling you all this except that I haven't received a reply to my earlier message. Probably because you think I'm a crazy redhead (which isn't true as I'm actually strawberry blond—the red comes from a bottle). Oh, sorry, I'm rambling in this letter again, just forget about the coffee, sorry again.
Sincerely,
Bonnie

Henry felt his heart drop. Bonnie hadn't given him a chance before she had seemingly rejected him. Henry sighed. First his heart had been hurt over his friend's death. Now his emotions had been pummeled by the ups and downs of Bonnie's messages. Henry looked at the food in front of him. The dinner was lavish, but the meal might have been sand for all Henry cared. Henry threw the plate's contents into the trash bin. He set the utensils and plate in his dishwasher. He looked again at his EVIL, to determine his schedule for the next day. Surprisingly, his schedule was clear. Henry didn't know what to do with himself. If Will were in the capital, but that wasn't an option now.

Henry went to the front room and flipped on the news on the holoset. The headlines celebrated the victory on Nakdong, and the newest war hero, Sergeant Wulfjaeger. Occasionally, the news service would mention Hannah, flashing her picture up on the holo. Whatever had been holding him back from contacting the beautiful pilot evaporated. Henry wasn't sure where he and Bonnie stood, but her messages sounded like she would soon be Frau Nordlinger. If she married Frank, he wished her well. Bonnie wasn't the first woman

Henry had lost. Hannah's picture flashed again, and Henry felt his pulse jump.

"An Assaultman shouldn't be afraid of a Valkyrie. The navy sings about holding our hands and carrying us upwards and all that," Henry said psyching himself up for the call. He checked the time. It was twenty hundred hours, two hours before lights out. Henry reasoned the hour wasn't greatest time to call a girl but still early enough to be proper.

Henry pulled up the voice connection on his EVIL, found Hannah's contact information in the directory, and dialed the number. The dial tone buzzed. Once, twice...

"I'm going to her audiomail," muttered Henry.

"Hello," said Hannah's voice.

"Hi, Hannah," Henry said.

"Hi, um who is this?" Hannah asked. Henry smiled, of course his number would be hidden.

"Hi. This is Henry, um... von Machthaber."

"Oh! Hi! Hi, Henry!" Hannah said suddenly more animated than she initially sounded.

"Hey, what are you up to tomorrow?" Henry said.

"I'm off duty. With the new Assault hero, I'm now yesterday's news. Fun fact: he saved me on Nakdong, so I'm in his fan club," Hannah said. The ball was in Henry's court.

"Want to go get a coffee? I know a great place near Kocher Square," Henry said.

"Is this a military function? Or, are you asking personally?" Hannah asked. The question was meant to be neutral, but Henry detected a bit of excitement in Hannah's voice.

"Strictly personal, I'd like to get to know you. No uniforms, strictly casual," said Henry.

"Awesome, casual clothes are great. I don't think gray is really a flattering color for me," Hannah said.

"I disagree, you looked very nice today," Henry said, the statement rolling off his tongue.

"So, you think I look nice, eh?" said Hannah flirtatiously. "Well wait until you see me tomorrow. What time?"

"Lunch time?" Henry asked.

"Let's meet at fifteen hundred. If things work out, I'll take you to dinner," said Hannah.

"Hey, isn't that my move?" said Henry.

"No, silly! The Assault only leads the way in the mud. Let's meet by the statue of Lena... You know your great-grandma..." said Hannah playfully.

"Sure, I'll see you then, Hannah," said Henry.

"Not if I see you first, dreamboat," said Hannah.

"Fair enough, bye-bye."

"Bye-bye-bye," said Hannah cutting the connection. Henry smiled, and looked at the picture displayed on her contact information. Henry smiled. He had a date with an angel.

Jurgen looked at the academy acceptance letter on his brand new EVIL. He had been one of the first Assaultmen to receive one. Before the GLORIOUSDEAD mission, Jurgen had been a pariah. Now, he was the Assaultman everyone wanted to know.

He again read the digital message. The acceptance letter stated he would be attending the Assault Academy at Steinthal in the Fall. There was a rider that mentioned he could attend the year after, if he missed his transit window to Stahlburgh. The hospital had discharged Jugen a week ago and he was currently on light duty while he waited for his ride home.

Jurgen's orders stated he would return to Stahlburgh as a Marine on the *USWC Advantage.* His orders had come down from Assault High Command. After receiving the GSG, Jurgen's bunk assignment changed. Assault Command moved Jurgen into a sergeant's bunk with the First Stahlburgh Rifles. Jurgen felt the move was a net plus, his new bunk was private, separated from the rest of the barracks by screening walls. If the barracks' constant noise hadn't been in the background of his new bunk, he'd consider his new accommodations quite regal.

Jurgen's EVIL chirped again. Jurgen was slowly getting use to sound of the device. He looked at the message notification which said: "Wulfjaeger report to Captain Nordlinger on the parade grounds."

Jurgen wondered what this order was all about, usually the messages referred to him as Sergeant Wulfjaeger. He hustled to the First's parade grounds. Jurgen couldn't keep an officer waiting after all.

Nordlinger had taken a shine to Jurgen, and after the fallout from the major's suicide mission, command had put the glorious dead into their own detachment. Nordlinger had casually commented that the glorious dead were like radioactive elements, useful but hazardous to the touch. Jurgen turned the corner and headed towards the parade grounds.

"Aye! Aye! Hooray! The Assault leads the way!" shouted the gathered Assaultmen on the parade grounds as Jurgen came into view.

"Attention!" shouted the newly promoted, Sergeant Tobias.

"Jurgen Wulfjaeger, report!" said Captain Nordlinger. Jurgen marched over and faced the officer, locking his heels and saluting.

"In recognition of your acceptance to the Academy, I am required to strip you of your sergeant's stripes," said Nordlinger. He waved his new EVIL over Jurgen's shoulders, and Jurgen's battlesuit displayed only his name "Jurgen Wulfjaeger." Jurgen felt naked. Even on day one of basic he'd had a title. On that first day his title was 'maggot,' but soon he'd crawled upwards to Assaultman, assaultman first class, lance corporal, corporal, and finally sergeant. Now he was a nobody again.

"In recognition of your acceptance, good conduct, and exemplary battlefield actions, I, brevet-Colonel Nordlinger of the newly constituted Eighth Stahlburgh Rifles, am proud to present the Eighth's newest *Feldfähnrich* or subaltern, Jurgen Wulfjaeger. As subaltern you are an officer and a gentleman. The Assault promotes on merit, therefore accept the respect and gratitude of your former enlisted colleagues as they salute you. May your former enlisted brothers seek leadership and guidance both on the battlefield and in the barracks from you, Subaltern Wulfjaeger."

Nordlinger then saluted Jurgen who hesitated before returning the salute. Being saluted was a strange feeling, like Jurgen cutting his steak with his left hand. Jurgen then turned, almost saluted the small gathering, but instead waited.

"Present arms!" Tobias said. Tobias stood in front of a small line. Mueller, Vogel, Brennan, and Ackbar—complete with two legs—

stood in the line wearing their helmets and in new battlesuits. Tobias and the line saluted waiting on Jurgen.

Jurgen felt the tears in his eyes and was glad he wore his helmet. The honor his comrades gave him deeply moved him. He returned the salute and dropped his arm to his side.

"Dismissed," Nordlinger said. He stepped forward and shook Jurgen's hand and said, "Welcome to the officers' ranks. When you realize you've fallen into a trap and want run away, I won't blame you," Nordlinger said with a laugh.

"No, sir, never in a million years," Jurgen responded. Nordlinger shrugged.

"Congratulations, sir," Tobias said shaking Jurgen's hand.

"Sounds strange, sergeant, but thanks," Jurgen responded.

"They tried to get me to go officer, but I realized that you can't make a silk purse out of a sow's ear. But you, you were already velvet, so I agree with command's decision, for once. Don't tell my NCO brethren, or I won't be allowed in the NCO club," Tobias said.

"Your secret is safe with me, sergeant," Jurgen said. Tobias patted Jurgen on the shoulder and moved on. Mueller was next. He had been promoted to corporal.

"Sir, well deserved," Mueller said, shaking Jurgen's hand.

"You as well, corporal," Jurgen said. The Glorious Dead had grown closer in the days after the suicide mission. Now, Jurgen was increasing the distance between most of them by becoming an officer. Mueller moved on after releasing Jurgen's grasp. Vogel came next, also wearing corporal's stripes.

"Well sir, I'm not sure I can shake your hand. I might get dirt on your pristine officer's hand," Vogel said with a gentle rib.

"I'll take my chances, since command obviously messed up and made you an NCO, corporal," Jurgen said sticking his hand out to the man from Hansaburgh.

"I see my salty blood has taken over, sir. Congrats, you are now the smartest officer in the Assault," said Vogel.

"You're on the squad channel, corporal, and I heard that," Nordlinger said.

"Sorry Colonel Nordlinger, Subaltern has you beat! He's an officer without a command. I'd say that's pretty dang smart," said Vogel.

"Subaltern, you are hereby ordered to supervise Corporal Vogel as he cleans the latrines," Nordlinger said. "A magnificent first command, if there ever was one."

Nordlinger, Jurgen and Vogel started laughing.

"Belay that order," Nordlinger said, "The corporal gets a pass for today."

"Aye, aye, sir," Jurgen and Vogel said in stereo. Vogel gently punched Jurgen on the shoulder and moved on.

Brennan approached, and grasped Jurgen's hand. "Congrats, sir, best of luck," said the new lance corporal.

"You too, lance corporal. Keep your head on a swivel with this bunch," said Jurgen.

"You as well. We'll all be marching behind you, after all, sir," Brennan said with a hint of mischief. He moved on leaving Ackbar.

"Congratulations, sir," Ackbar said.

"Thank you, lance corporal," Jurgen said to the man who never left his side after VIKINGRAID. "Are you staying with the Eighth?"

The others had become the core of a new regiment. Assault High Command had started filling the order of battle with combat veterans. Moving some into new units, in an expectation of new Assaultmen graduating basic. For now, the new regiments were paper tigers. Jurgen realized he'd be involved in fixing that. His message service had been flooded two weeks ago with interview requests from the news organizations. Between now and the Fall, Jurgen was sure he'd be selling war bonds as a new GSG. Jurgen realized the news had reached Stahlburgh when Jenny's messages started appearing repeatedly. The Assault had given Jurgen five gold dragons in victory pay. The money was a pittance considering the total intelligence haul that the Assault and USIS had dug out of the bunker. Jurgen didn't complain though. Five gold dragons was more money than Jurgen could expect to earn in a decade of honest work in Tavishire.

"No, sir," said Ackbar. "After they put the new leg on me, I received a transfer to the Second Stahlburgh Rifles."

"The Line Guards? What an honor!" said Jurgen.

"Aye, sir," Ackbar said, "I've been told I'll be attached to Special Projects. They wanted me as a dog handler, but I deferred on religious grounds. The new assignment is classified. I'm not sure what exactly I'll be doing."

"I understand. Best of luck," said Jurgen.

"Thank you, sir. *Inshallah*, we will see each other again," Ackbar said, moving along. Nordlinger approached again.

"Well subaltern, I owe you a beer. The O-club only has terrible, non-alcoholic stuff, but I'm happy to buy if you're interested?" said Nordlinger. Jurgen was about to respond when a cruiser came down on the tarmac past the parade grounds. Jurgen's EVIL chirped with an urgent tone.

"One moment, sir," Jurgen said, opening the message.

```
USWC Advantage has landed, Subaltern
Wulfjaeger to report to the cruiser
immediately for liftoff. EOM
```

"I'll need to pass, sir. New orders, I'm to report to the cruiser that just landed," said Jurgen.

"Understood. Next time we meet, remember I owe you one," said Nordlinger. Jurgen saluted the officer, who returned the salute.

"Farewell, sir," Jurgen said.

"Goodbye, Wulfjaeger, best of luck," said Nordlinger.

Jurgen then turned and ran to his bunk inside the barracks. He grabbed his duffel, which he had kept packed for this moment and surveyed the small room looking for anything he forgot. The room was empty. Jurgen opened the duffel to double check that the GSG medallion was in its clamshell and on top of his uniforms, underwear, and personal effects. He closed the duffel and slung the bag on his shoulders. Next, Jurgen headed to the barracks armory.

"Sir," the armorer, a sergeant said snapping to attention. Jurgen looked around, wondering if an officer had entered without his notice, and then he remembered his promotion.

"At ease, sergeant," said Jurgen.

"What can I do for you, sir?" the armorer said.

"I need my rifle, serial number 7X9Q2F3M5P8L," Jurgen said. The armorer nodded and returned in a moment with his rifle. The pin rifle was a brand-new Anderson and Campbell mark five. Jurgen had been assigned the new rifle and battlesuit in preparation for his marine duty and return to Stahlburgh.

"Nice firearm, sir. That's brand new, I just removed the machining grease yesterday. You're very lucky, I've got guys on patrol that have been begging for this model," said the armorer.

"Thanks, sergeant. Farewell," Jurgen said grabbing the rifle, slinging the weapon and turning to leave.

"Goodbye, sir," the sergeant said, returning to his duty.

Jurgen walked along the tarmac and watched Navy petty officers used auto-loaders to remove several spacecons from the cruiser. More personnel loaded spacecons with labels that indicated they contained food and water into the cruiser. Jurgen waited a moment for the heavy machinery to move out of his way. Other gray pressure-suited personnel had hooked hoses to the cruiser's bottom to dump gray and black liquid waste. A robot carried a canister marked with the trefoil radioactive symbol, led by a woman in a much bulkier pressure suit. Jurgen noted that his Geiger counter clicked, but the measurement was a fraction of what his suit had registered at VIKINGRAID. After a moment, the machines cleared and the cruiser began closing up hatches. Jurgen marched up the main cargo ramp, toward where a tall woman in a pressure suit stood. Jurgen wanted to know where to report for duty. Two meters from the woman, his HUD synced with the ship and identified the individual as *Behfelshaber* or Commander Johanna Sternfahrer, the *Advantage's Kapitän* or skipper.

"Subaltern Jurgen Wulfjaeger reporting as ordered, commander," Jurgen said. He'd never reported to the Navy before. When his battlesuit synced, it connected him to the *Advantage's* communications channels, giving him access to the various division channels and the sacred O-channel, the officer communications link.

"The title is captain, subaltern, I'm only a commander when I step off this ship," the captain said. "Now according to protocol, you ask permission to come aboard, and I say welcome aboard. However, since you seem to be a mudboot and not used to marine duty, I'm going to let that slide. My name's Sternfahrer. Since you're the new Assault commander on board, you get the privilege of privately calling me Joan. That's the only perk to the job, I'm afraid."

"I'm Jurgen, Joan, though most people call me Wulf," said Jurgen.

"I'm good with Jurgen. I have a cousin with that name. Now, go find Laser. Formally he is *Oberfeldwebel*, or Sergeant First Class, Timothy Enlow. Laser is the Assault NCO. He's been with me since I wore miniskirts. He can teach you how to be a marine officer until you are safe to be on a ship," said the captain.

"Yes, ma'am," Jurgen said.

"Laser's that way. You can't miss him. He's the only one wearing black in the corridor with the turrets," said the captain, waving Jurgen forward. Jurgen moved towards the bow of the large wedge that was the *Advantage*. The cargo bay ended with a hatch that was open to a long corridor. Inside the corridor were a half dozen figures in gray pressure suits and one in black, an Assaultman's battlesuit. Jurgen approached the black-clad figure, who stood a half head shorter than

Wulfjaeger.

The Assaultman saluted. Then, he said, "Look-ee here, we got ourselves a baby officer. Welcome aboard, sir."

Jurgen saluted back and said, "You Laser?"

"Aye, aye, sir! The one, the only, the myth, the legend," Laser said in a hinterland colonial accent.

"I'm Wulfjaeger," Jurgen said.

"Nah. You're sir to me," Laser said. "Ever been a marine before?"

"No, not at all," Jurgen said.

"Well then, let me show you what being a bold marine Assaultman is all about, sir," Laser said. "Follow along, I'll show you where O-country is, sir. Then you can store your stuff and I'll introduce you to the rest of the boys."

Laser guided Jurgen back to the bay, and then up a set of loading stairs, then down a corridor until the hall ended in a hatch guarded by two Assaultmen.

"Attention," Laser shouted and the two Assaultmen snapped to attention. Jurgen almost snapped to as well but realized they were standing at attention for him.

"Well, sir," Laser began in his drawl, "This here hatch is where we part ways. I'm not allowed past this bulkhead as I'm an unwashed working man. But, I've been told the compartment beyond here is all pretty and female. If you're missing some male company there ain't no regulation on you slumming with us enlisted men in the rear. Only thing you gotta watch out for is if the captain needs you."

"I'll be right back, Laser. I need to drop my stuff," said Jurgen. Jurgen passed the hatch and went into the officer compartment. Inside he saw a series of sleeping bunks. A large section was cordoned off by canvas shutters, and had a door. Jurgen realized the segregated section was for him. Jurgen looked to see if there were naval officers in the compartment. Seeing none, Jurgen stepped into his segregated bunk. For a shipboard berth the compartment was luxurious, compared to the three or four stacked bunks for an enlisted man on ship. His compartment contained a locker, into which Jurgen stuffed his duffel. Jurgen latched the locker closed, remembering that on ship everything had to be secured. There was a weapons cradle by the door for his rifle. Jurgen unslung the pin rifle and latched down the weapon. Jurgen continued to survey the room. The bed was a soft sided box that hung from the ceiling. Underneath the bed was a desk. Jurgen saw hinges on the locker and mini-armory. He realized the locker and mini-armory could fold up into the bulkhead along with the compartment's walls. In a combat situation Jurgen figured the nonessential items would be secured in the bulkheads. Jurgen then turned around and exited his compartment. Back in the officer's room he opened the hatch went back to where Laser stood waiting.

"I thought I was going to have to go in after you, sir," Laser said. "I've seen officers go in and come out in their skivvies, being chased by a half dozen man-eating Navy Amazons." Jurgen laughed. Laser had described every Assaultman's fantasy.

"He thinks I'm joking. I'm not joking sir," Laser said. The two guards' shoulders shook as they suppressed laughs. "Better start here. This is Maslov and Guitierrez, they came on board at Stahlburgh and are just out of basic. We got them guarding officer country. We give the new guys the hard jobs, sir."

"Gentlemen," Jurgen said.

"Sir," both men replied.

Laser just shook his helmet, "Don't call them that, sir. Next thing I know, they'll be having tea and crumpets and thinking themselves lords."

"Sorry, Laser," Jurgen said.

"I'll smack them around later; they'll figure out they're just apes," Laser said. "Come on, we got about thirty more Assaultmen I need to introduce you to. At this rate I'll be introducing you through the entire voyage," Laser said, moving aft.

"Why do they call you Laser?" Jurgen asked.

"Cause Assaultmen can't say *Lapua*," Laser said pronouncing the word "lapp-wah."

"That's an ancient rifle, isn't it?" said Jurgen with confusion.

"Yes, my great-great-great-grandpap, also named Timothy, had a beauty of a gun. It is a beast and my inheritance. I've taken that rifle with me everywhere," said Laser.

"So, Laser?" Jurgen said.

"Hang on, sir. Geez, even the baby-officers are impatient! I'm a storyteller from a long line of homespun yarn threaders," Laser said with mock irritation.

"Of course, my pardon," said Jurgen.

"Where was I? Oh yeah, grandpap. Well, he gave the gun to his son; however, stories diverge on how that happened. One family tale says the Lapua was lovingly gifted on old grandpap's deathbed; the other said grandpap fell afoul of great-grandma and poof! The gun disappeared before she could met it down," Laser said, ducking through a tangle of wires that a navy enlisted had pulled out for repair. "Well, somehow, the rifle got handed down until one of my honored hillbilly ancestors got mixed up in the Texas succession. Like a dummy, grandpa gets captured by the American Directorate forces. The "bad guys" confiscated the Lapua, of course. But good old General Scott hit the base, freed my great grandpa, and of course gramps takes the gun with him. Somehow, and family lore is murky on this, my great grandpa ends up on Titan just in time to hop on a colonizer to Alpha Centauri. After that, my kin ended up on Brandstadt, which is a light year past nowhere. We arrived just in time for good old Karl to roll in and liberate us from some client state that forgot we were ever a colony of theirs. Liberation was fine by all of us on Brandstadt, cause we liked the Union better anyway. Watch your head," Laser said, ducking past a ripped open bulkhead.

"And Laser?," Jurgen said.

"Oh yeah, so when I was seventeen I got my inheritance and joined the Assault. I show up on day one in basic with this rifle. The drill sergeant approaches, grabs my Lapua and snickers. He then said, 'This maggot's brought his own laser rifle! News flash, maggot, we use pin rifles in this man's Assault!' He sends my Lapua to the armory, and for the rest of basic everyone calls me 'Laser Rifle.' When we graduated, I ended up on a ship as a marine, and some of my classmates from basic were with me. They kept calling me Laser Rifle, but soon they got tired of my last name so then they just called me 'Laser.' Well, I served with them for a year, then I got a berth here on the *Advantage*, back when the grand duchess was the skipper. Now, Signe, she was something! Not that Goldilocks is bad, but 'Shattering Signe' was like a holy terror. She'd blast pirates if they didn't surrender when she showed up," Laser said.

"Wait, who is Goldilocks?" Jurgen said. Laser stopped and turned around, helmet swiveling left and right.

"That's the cap'n, but don't say that to her face," Laser said quietly. Jurgen didn't have the heart to tell him they were on an open comms channel.

"Come on, we're almost there. The Navy likes to stick us near the reactor. I've told them that ain't going to do what the ladies think the radiation will do, since I got kids and all. The ladies laugh and don't listen to me anyway."

"Attention!" Laser said opening a bulkhead and stepping through the opening. Inside twenty some Assaultmen fell out of their bunks and snapped to attention.

"This here is our new sir. Say 'hello' fellas," Laser said.

"Hello, sir," the men said in unison.

"Hello, and dismissed," Jurgen said. The men returned to their bunks. Four of them returned to playing cards, while others were exercising, cleaning gear, or just talking. Laser pointed to each one and named them, some by surname, others by nickname. After a while

Jurgen just nodded since he had forgotten who was who.

"They are good boys," said Laser. "Got to crack the whip on em sometimes, but hard workers otherwise."

"Wulfjaeger, report to the bridge," rang out in Jurgen's helmet.

"That's the cap'n, better git," Laser said, pointing to a ladder. Jurgen hurried and climbed upwards.

"Wrong way, sir," Laser said pointing down. Jurgen reversed and climbed down the ladder until he landed on a catwalk. The catwalk ended at a pressure hatch. Jurgen turned the hatch and entered the bridge.

"Shut the hatch," said the third officer, a Sub-Lieutenant Thomasin Pullings. Jurgen dragged the hatch closed and spun the manual wheel.

"Ship's secure, ma'am," said the first officer, a woman only a few years older than Jurgen.

"Thank you, Lieutenant Stourton," the captain said. She stood looking over the console that bore all of the navigation information.

"Subaltern, take your spot at the Assault station," the captain said pointing to a station at the side of the bridge. Jurgen went over and sat in the couch.

"Buckle up, sunshine," another officer said. She sat next to Jurgen and his HUD identified her as Lieutenant Nicolls. Jurgen fumbled with the straps.

"Midshipwoman Babbington, take us up slowly. I'll never hear the end of the Assault's complaints if we buzz the tower," the captain said. Jurgen felt the rumbling of the spacecraft as the engines powered up to reach escape velocity.

"First time on a bridge?" Nicholls asked.

"Lieutenant Nicholls, give the tower our flight plan and ask for fleet clearance. I'd hate to get a surface-to-orbit missile because someone lost our flight plan," the captain said cutting short the chance of conversation.

"Full throttle on the engines, Midshipwoman Babbington,

remember what I taught you," said the captain. Jurgen white knuckled his console as the ship continued the upward trajectory. After a few minutes Jurgen could feel the weightlessness of orbit. He'd trained for zero-gee in basic, so while he was unfamiliar with floating, Jurgen knew how to maneuver.

"All department heads are dismissed," said the captain. Jurgen watched as the rest of the officers released their safety webbing and floated off. Jurgen stayed and watched as the captain continued to mentor the young midshipwoman, who looked a year or two younger than Jurgen. After a few moments the cruiser entered a coasting trajectory. Jurgen then tried to remove the safety straps.

"Midshipwoman Babbington, please help our new Assault commander," said the Captain.

Babbington released her straps, floated over, and said, "First time on the bridge?" The communication connection was point-to-point.

"Yes, ma'am," Jurgen said.

Babbington giggled and said, "We're the same rank, so don't ma'am me... I'm Wilhelmina."

The straps floated free and Jurgen replied, "Jurgen, or Wulfjaeger, but everyone calls me Wulf."

"Oh, how rugged," Babbington said.

"He's free, now back to your station, Miss Babbington," Sternfahrer said.

"Bah-bye," Babbington said with a purr. Jurgen floated out of the couch and to the hatch, which he managed to open, float through and close without issues. He went up to the deck near O-country. He floated, turned around and slightly lost. Jurgen entered a medical bay, where a pressure suited naval officer hovered.

"Hello, are you lost?" the woman asked.

"Yes, ma'am. I am afraid I'm turned around," Jurgen said. The woman looked the same age as the captain and since she was in the medical bay, Jurgen assumed she was most likely the ship's surgeon.

"No 'ma'am' here, Assaultman, I'm Stephanie, or Doctor Gediegen if you want to be formal," Stephanie said.

"Subaltern Jurgen Wulfjaeger, Stephanie," Jurgen said introducing himself.

"A nice name, from the Valley of the First Farmers if I am not mistaken," Stephanie said.

"Close, Tavishire, but my people have been on Stahlburgh since Karl's conquest," Jurgen said.

"I'll note that, I'm a Biopsychosocial Humanist, I study humans, taking notes and looking for specific evolutionary or social divergence," said Stephanie.

"Uh, I thought you were the ship's surgeon," said Jurgen, thoroughly out of his element.

"Oh, I do that too. Do you have something ailing you?" said Stephanie.

"No, just lost."

"Ah, yes, that's right," said Stephanie. "Let me show you around. Did you have a particular destination in mind?"

"I was planning to go back to my berth and spend time studying. I am heading to the Assault Academy when we arrive on Stahlburgh," Jurgen said.

"If you are interested, I am willing to be your tutor. I've been working with Midshipwoman Babbington, but she isn't a good scholar," said Stephanie. "Well, except for male anatomy."

"Yes, please," said Jurgen. "I'm afraid my education was not that great."

"Well then, I'll have to remedy that. Let me show you back to officers' country. We're close to supper time."

Jurgen followed the doctor, and they made their way across corridors and past the Assaultmen guarding the hatch to officers' country. When Jurgen entered, he saw that his berth was still configured, but that someone had folded up the rest of the berths, and had extended the dining table from the ceiling. Jurgen noted that the officers wore their pressure suits without their helmets, which made sense when everyone was eating. Jurgen hit the quick release on his helmet and stowed it in his berth. Returning from his room, he noted that Nicholls and Babbington were staring at him, while whispering, and giggling. Jurgen looked at Babbington. She was a dark blond, with light brown eyes. She had a scar across her forehead that Jurgen felt detracted from her looks.

Stourton sat at the head of the table and motioned to the foot. "Subaltern Wulfjaeger please join us. As our Assault commander yours is the place of honor at the foot of the table."

Jurgen floated into the space and placed his rear on the seat. The seat magnetically attached to his suit locking him down on the chair. The stewardess was an ancient battle axe who had scars across her face. She grumbled about one more mouth to feed as she handed Jurgen a piping hot bag with a straw. Jurgen noted a space on the table to place the food, and like magic the bag stuck to the table.

"Careful, Cëllian over-boils everything," said Babbington. "I'd hate for your beautiful lips to get burned." Jurgen nodded solemnly, but he felt his cheeks burning at the compliment. He gave the Navy high marks, every woman he met had told him he was handsome or beautiful. Had Jenny given him even half the stares his Navy sisters had given him well... Jurgen suddenly thanked the Allfather she hadn't. He remembered Jenny's insistent messages and his fury in deleting them. He was in a better place.

"Pfennig for your thoughts, blondie," Nicholls said. Jurgen looked at Nicholls. She was good looking with a deep ebony complexion, coppery brown eyes, and wavy black hair.

"I like being called Jurgen or Wulf, ma'am," Jurgen said.

"So formal, Jurgen, I'm Nichelle. Wilhelmina said she's introduced herself," Nichelle said motioning to Babbington, "and the old lady over there," Nichelle pointed to Stourton, "is named Mia, but goes by lieutenant."

"I'm first officer," Mia said. "I maintain discipline on this ship."

Jurgen looked at Stourton. She was lightly tanned with deep brown hair and steel gray eyes.

"Out of my chair," Sternfahrer said entering the mess. Her helmet was off, and Jurgen got to see the captain's face. Sternfahrer was middle aged with blue-green eyes, fair skin, and golden blond straight hair that was gathered in a pony tail. If the captain were ten years younger or Jurgen ten years older, he would have tried his luck and asked the captain out. She had a model's look, but Jurgen sensed iron in her demeanor.

"Yes, captain," Mia said moving on to the bench with Nichelle and Wilhelmina. "Who is on duty?"

"Pullings," said the captain. "She is officer of the watch and Chief Bonden is the sailing mistress."

"Wait, captain, aren't you the sailing mistress?" asked Jurgen. The ladies all giggled at his question.

The captain scowled at her officers, and said, "An excellent question, Mister Wulfjaeger. I am mistress and commander of this ship by my commission as its captain. The sailing mistress is whoever is sitting at the tiller—what we call the piloting controls. I am sure you'll figure out our terms. If not, one of my officers can explain them to you... Not you Miss Babbington." Babbington for her part looked like a child who had learned Christmas was canceled.

"Now, to the protector, long may he live!" Johanna said, raising up a bag of a golden colored beverage. Jurgen reached out and found his drink, raising the bag up with the ladies, and said in unison, "Long may he live!"

The women sucked down their bags, Jurgen put the straw to his lips and pulled. A light fruity wine taste spread along his palette. When he swallowed the liquid burned his throat, and he coughed into the towelette that floated next to his meal. The women giggled and the captain said, "All you all right, Mister Wulfjager?"

"Yes, captain," said Jurgen after clearing his throat. "I haven't had anything more than one percent alcohol for almost two years."

"Oh, how terrible," said Babbington in disgust. "They make you fight and don't give you anything to drink?"

"No, Miss Babbington. I volunteered; no one makes me fight," said Jurgen.

"Quite right," Lieutenant Stourton said, "To our Spartan brothers, the Assault!"

"The Assault!" the ladies said again taking large pulls on their wine bags.

"To the Sisters of Athena," Jurgen said, taking a discrete sip. After his first sip he started to feel the alcohol's warm euphoria working across his body. If any of his dead brothers-in-arms could see him here sipping wine with a half dozen beauties, Jurgen expected they would trade the pearly gates for Jurgen's earthly paradise.

"I don't want to embarrass our new Assault commander," the captain said, "but he is our newest war hero."

"Oh..." the women all said giving Jurgen soft side glances.

"I did my duty, that's all, captain," Jurgen said, burning in embarrassment.

"A humble hero at that," said Stephanie, appearing. The doctor was carrying a tablet that displayed a medical journal. She attached the tablet to her pressure suit and floated over to the table.

"How many soldiers did you kill?" asked Babbington.

"Wilhelmina," said Stourton, "that's a rude question!"

"No, her question is fine," said Jurgen. "Personally, I'm not sure. I was at ground zero for VIKINGRAID. My entire squad was wiped out."

"I'm sorry for your loss," said the captain. "They all were brave men who volunteered to protect the Union, our condolences."

Jurgen nodded grimly. "They were the best."

"What was the flora like on Nakdong? I suspect you saw plenty of interesting species?" Stephanie asked changing the subject.

"Um, the plants?" said Jurgen.

"Yes, Mister Wulfjaeger," said Stephanie, confirming the question.

"There were large three or four meter round trees with palm like leaves everywhere. The foliage was thick, nothing like the vines and brambles of the fields of Stahlburgh," said Jurgen. Stephanie pulled her tablet off her suit and began writing with a stylus, taking notes.

"How about flowers?" Stephanie asked.

"Apologies, I have to leave for my turn as officer of the watch," Stourton said, sliding off the bench.

"There were some red flowers I saw pretty much everywhere, also a lot of purple ones," Jurgen said. Again, the surgeon scribbled furiously.

"I'd like to know about the fighting, did you run into any Terran units proper?" asked the captain breaking into Stephanie's questions.

"No, captain," Jurgen said, "the partisans on Nakdong could be fierce in groups, but unit on unit the Assault always got the upper hand."

Jurgen remembered Laakso and the child. He must have made a face.

Sternfahrer said, "If I've dredged up any bad memories I apologize. We fight a little differently up here. Like when the grand duchess was the captain, she looked at me and said 'Joan, never mind the maneuvers. Always go at them!' I'll never forget that battleship we fought in Alpha Centauri. The bloody thing was huge! Signe just sets the tiller, yells at engineering to 'give the old gal full power!' and the *Advantage*," the captain said patting a bulkhead, "jumped like a racing mare. We plowed right into that ship, Assaultmen racing into the enemy like the *Advantage* was on fire. Signe swoops into the enemy in her pressure suit firing two pistols like she was an ancient cowgirl. The enemy didn't know what hit them. The captain flies forward, with me in tow. I was like a scared schoolgirl. In the chaos, they hit old Signe, twice, once below her left breast and once on her thigh. She just shrugged off the shots; her Viking lineage wouldn't let her fall. Then in all that chaos, she bellows, 'Joan! Take the bridge!'"

"What did you do, captain," Jurgen asked. He listed to the tale spellbound. He had forgotten about the horrors he'd seen.

"I charged forward, a fireteam of Assaultmen and Barrette Bonden along in tow. We charged through a Centauran space marine line that was supposed to repel us. Honestly, the charge was reckless, but at the time I was worried more about what Signe would do to me if I disobeyed, than the enemy. We floated up to the bridge and took control of the ship. The enemy surrendered shortly thereafter. That ship became my first command. The Centaurans called the ship the *Stardream Inception* but the Admiralty had called the boat the 'Turd Storm' as the blasted thing had mauled or captured so many of our own merchantmen. Of course, the old protector—Allfather bless his soul—had to disavow the ship's capture. I sailed the 'Turd Storm' into Pentothia and sold the boat to the lizards. My cut of the purse was the best victory prize I had gotten—at that time. In those days we made lots of money, since old Signe was no slouch in commerce raiding," said the captain with a wild smile. "My victory pay bought the ball gown I wore at Signe's banquet. The dress was probably the best investment I ever made, since, I met Auggie, my husband. I was only a Cochrane, and he was a mighty Sternfahrer, from a family that had thrown in with the old protector early in Karl's ascent." The captain looked at her midshipwoman with that statement.

"What happened then?" Nichelle asked. Apparently, Jurgen had shaken a new story out of the captain.

"Auggie fell on his knees and proposed to me right there," said Sternfahrer. Jurgen and the other officers just stared. Johanna laughed and said, "Seriously, I had to practically hit Herr Sternfahrer over the head, tie him up, and water board him to pay attention to me."

"Really? That sounds fun," said Babbington. The lieutenants looked at the midshipwoman in disgust.

"Hey, some guys like that sort of thing," Babbington said defensively.

"No, no. Auggie played his hand close to his vest. He danced a dance with me and said goodnight," the captain continued.

"Then she chased after him like a desperate university girl," Stephanie said finishing her notes.

"Well Stephanie, my plan worked. We've been married almost twenty years now," the captain said.

"Is he in the Assault?" Jurgen asked. He couldn't see anyone other than a dashing Assaultman winning the heart of the magnificent captain.

"Not anymore. He did a tour as a young man, nowadays he's involved in far more dangerous profession, international finance," the captain said. "He, along with our nanny, also takes care of our children. He's a brave man." The assembled chuckled at the remark. A new face appeared in officers' country, Third Lieutenant Pullings. She had dark brown hair, fair skin, and light brown eyes. Jurgen could see a scar running from her chin down her neck. A wicked blade must have made the cut.

"Scoot over, Wilhelmina," said Pullings.

"Lieutenant Pullings, this is Mister Wulfjaeger," the captain said.

"Hello, ma'am," Jurgen said.

"My name is Thomasin," Pullings said, "We're a casual ship. Not some spit and polish outfit." The captain made a sour face at that comment.

"Well, we do clean up nicely, but we're a warship, a go for guns and come at 'em craft," Pullings said trying to extract her foot from her mouth.

"That's enough for now, Thomasin," the captain said. Jurgen had a nagging sensation he knew that name from somewhere. Suddenly, the memory of SERAPH's rescue came flooding back to him.

"You were STELLAR SERAPH's roommate," Jurgen said rather abruptly.

Thomasin smiled a brilliant, beautiful smile, "Yes, I was, and don't let Hannah tell stories. She was just as culpable in all those wild tales as she says I was. Wait, how do you know Hannah?" Jurgen smiled as all eyes were on him.

"She was shot down and I went on a rescue mission to get her back." If Jurgen had said he nursed three-legged puppies to health on weekends, he couldn't have gotten a better reception from the women.

"A Galahad!" Nicholls said.

"A new Hector!" Stephanie said.

"To our new Assault commander," the captain said.

"Here, here!" Pullings said lifting a bag of wine. Jurgen hadn't expected this reception and blushed. The women spent several more minutes toasting him, and Jurgen's memories of the evening blurred. He remembered floating into his bunk before black sleep consumed him.

Days passed on the *Advantage*. His tales of SERAPH's rescue made him many fans among the lieutenants. His hero status gave him a large amount of respect and latitude with the captain. She was patient with Jurgen, even though he was a neophyte on proper etiquette and spacecraft knowledge.

Stephanie, for her part, saw Jurgen as a tutoring project. She worked diligently in getting him ready for the academy. At first, Jurgen felt hopeless with all the work the surgeon had assigned him. After a week of one-on-one sessions with the surgeon, Jurgen's educational gaps started closing.

Studying was easy as life aboard the *Advantage* was fairly monotonous. The ship was coasting at several meters per second, attempting to reach the periphery of Lalande where she could deploy her wormhole rings and jump to Stahlburgh. Jurgen, being the Assault commander, had little to do, other than manage the Assaultmen. The enlisted were experienced marines, and Laser kept them working and out of any trouble. After he would complete his tutoring assignments, Jurgen would spend his duty hours with Laser. The NCO could make the hours fly by with his tall tales.

"That was when I was younger. Sammy told me I better behave or I'd end up in her garden. She said I'd be on the underside of the vegetables. I told her 'woman go make me a sammich!' When I reported the next day, my battlesuit helmet didn't seal because of the knot I had on my head," Laser said shaking his head.

"What did she hit you with," one of the Assaultmen asked.

"She dropped the cast iron pan with a toasted sandwich on my head. I probably deserved the pan to the head. The sandwich was worth the knot, though," Laser said. The others laughed and the NCO smiled. Jurgen laughed and made a mental note to never cross Mrs. Laser if he ever had the pleasure to meet her.

"Duty stations!" Pullings shouted over the speakers. "Pressure helmets on!"

The Assaultmen hopped up and moved to their assigned bulkhead. Laser and Jurgen moved towards the bridge. Laser would stand at his station guarding the bridge door and Jurgen would go to his station on the bridge.

"I bet we got a merchant! If the ship was a war craft the captain would have given the orders," Laser said. "Let's just ask the Allfather for a quick broadside that destroys the ship."

"Won't we lose victory pay that way?" Jurgen said.

"Yes, sir," said Laser, "but that is safer for us."

"Huh?" Jurgen said as he grabbed the holds and crawled along behind Laser. Jurgen had gotten better, but Laser was like a floating monkey.

"Oh boy! Combat goes like this: if the ship is a merchantman, the lieutenants are going to get all riled and the cap'n will show up. Ol'

Goldilocks will go at 'em and we'll have a boarding action," Laser said.

"Right, and that's good, we'll all get paid," said Jurgen.

"No," Laser said. "The Assaultmen will have to hustle to race ahead of the cap'n and the other girls, 'cause they are wonderful button pushers, but the ladies can't shoot a pin rifle and hit the broadside of a battleship!"

"Oh boy," Jurgen said repeating what Laser said.

"Exactly! If anything happens, stay with the cap'n. She rushes ahead in a paper-thin pressure suit. Now, the cap'n is a good shot, but she does some foolhardy things in combat. She'll need you watching her six, especially if she and the other officers start singing the song," Jurgen and Laser reached the bridge door, and Laser opened the door for the officer.

"What song?" Jurgen asked as he floated through the door.

"Their dang anthem! It gets the Navy ladies in a fighting mood," Laser said slamming and latching the door after him. Jurgen sat and strapped into the couch. The captain was already on the bridge giving orders.

"Have they changed course, Miss Pullings?" said Sternfahrer calmly and patiently.

"No, ma'am. They're not responding to our hails either," Pullings said.

"What signals did they flash? Did they run up false colors?" Sternfahrer asked.

"Nothing, ma'am. They have Protelani colors flying now," Pullings said. Jurgen had learned that every ship had a cryptographic signature called colloquially the "ship's colors." Every nation had their own signatures and keys. If the ship was flying the appropriate colors, then the signature and key would match. If not, they were flying false colors. Flying false colors was a ruse of war. Ships needed to send the appropriate national colors before commencing hostilities, anything else was piracy. Pirates were hunted by all vessels.

"Flash our colors," the captain said.

"No response," Pullings said.

"Lieutenant Nicholls open a voice channel," Sternfahrer commanded.

"Open, ma'am," Nicholls responded.

"Unidentified space craft this is the Union Space War Craft *Advantage.* Flash your true colors or prepare to be boarded!" the captain said.

"Flashing Terran Directorate colors, and they're firing missiles, captain!" Pullings said nervously.

"Have the missile defense guns fire a volley," the captain said, "We've got them out gunned and we too can fire missile volleys. Close with the ship, and Miss Pullings, give our enemies a chorus from our Anthem, please."

Pullings' mezzo voice sang out over the comms:

> "Sailing forth, we are the light,
> Sisters of Athena, we fight!
> Defending all, our solemn chore,
> For the Union's call, forevermore!"

"We're in deep poop now, sir," said Laser. "Orders?"

Jurgen paused for a moment and thought through what he had learned on the job, from Laser, and from the captain. The Assaultmen would need to be first at the airlocks, pin rifles in hand. A corporal or sergeant in each fireteam would have a bulkhead buster ready. The Assaultmen would either space dive to the hull or the airlock would crash into an enemy bulkhead. Either way, the Assaultmen would cut their way in. Then, the Navy NCOs and officers would direct the men, tactically, on what enemy command points the Assault should take.

Jurgen heard the orders to vent the ship, and his battlesuit registered the pressure drop in the compartment. The captain would order the airlocks opened a few hundred meters from the enemy. Sternfahrer was "going right at 'em" like she'd been taught.

Jurgen cleared his throat and said, "Okay men, we're taking this ship! The Navy may be the Sisters of Athena, but the Assault is the tip of the spear!"

"Then it's aye! Aye! Hooray!" said Laser.

"The assault leads the way!" The rest of the Assaultmen said over the channel.

"Not bad, sir," Laser said on a private channel, "Remember what I said. Stay next to the cap'n! She'll float off like a hawk and try to get herself killed!"

Jurgen almost said, "Aye, aye, sergeant," but then realized he was the superior. He settled for, "Understood. Watch out yourself, Laser."

"I been doing this for twenty years. We'll take the ship, sir," Laser said his voice less paternal or playful. Jurgen recognized that tone. Laser, like all his Assaultmen, was gearing up for the fight.

"Full thrust!" said the captain. She pulled out her service pistol and cocked the weapon.

"They're trying another salvo of missiles! They're firing anti-boarding guns too," Stourton said. The anti-boarding guns shot explosive rounds of ball bearings at a ship, attempting to penetrate the aggressor's hull. If a captain was stupid, their ship would suffer explosive decompression when the balls punched holes in bulkheads pressurized to full atmosphere. A normal ship had a paper-thin hull, but Jurgen had learned that the *Advantage's* hull had several large reinforced panels of gravity-pressed cermetal. The merchantman's weapons didn't have the kinetic potential to smash into the *Advantage's* hull. The merchantman was just outmatched by the warship.

"Give them a broadside with our bow turrets," said Sternfahrer. "Now, we'll make Mister Wulfjaeger's job a lot easier, since the enemy ship will be full of holes!"

"Aye, aye, captain," Stourton said punching the fire control buttons.

"We there yet, sir?" Laser asked. Jurgen realized that his NCO couldn't see anything in the well outside the bridge.

"Three hundred meters," Jurgen said.

"I hate waiting," Laser said without a 'sir', and Jurgen figured the man was grumping and forgot his channel was open.

"Two hundred meters to impact," Pullings said.

"Put an electromagnetic pulse charge along their dorsal aft side," said the captain. "That will give them something to worry about while we make our attack."

"Aye, aye, captain," said Stourton, who punched another one of the fire control buttons. Jurgen watched as the specialized missile, a robotic drone, arced out into the merchantman's dorsal spine. The drone attached on the long stem that connected the forward cylinder that was the main hab and bridge to the rear with engineering and the main engines. The drone glowed brightly and then went suddenly dark. The engineering compartment's lights went dark too.

"Scans are reporting no power in the aft decks, captain," Pullings said.

"Time to claim a bridge! Mister Wulfjaeger, please inform the Assault they are on the clock," the captain said.

"Move out men!" Jurgen said over his command channel.

"Aye, sir!" came back over the channel.

"I'm heading with the force to engineering. You take bridge, sir," Laser said, "that's where the captain will run!"

"Good hunting!" Jurgen said, releasing his buckles. Placing his hand on a bulkhead, Jurgen could feel the vibration of the *Advantage* rubbing against the merchantman.

"Pullings, you have the bridge," the captain said, "Open up, Laser!"

The hatch opened and the captain, Stourton, Nicholls, and

Babbington floated out. Jurgen stayed at the end of the Navy officers' column. He planned to jump into the lead in the wider corridors that led to the airlocks. Laser was already gone when Jurgen floated through the hatch. The ladder up was a tight squeeze, but the space opened to a large central corridor.

"Stourton and Nicholls take engineering, Babbington you're with me. Heads on swivels, ladies! That means you Wilhelmina! Staring at Mister Wulfjaeger's posterior is a good way to get killed," the captain said, coaching her most junior officer. Jurgen used the opportunity to float past and take the lead. As he floated to the airlock, he pulled his service pistol and cocked the slide, loading a bohrium round into the chamber. Unlike on a planet, space fighting was more art than science, and using two hands often meant that gun play was secondary to floating off.

"Oh, remember your magnets," Laser said. "No, you go left!"

Jurgen switched on the pressure controls for his boots. The boots, if in contact with a hard surface, would magnetize. If the surface was magnetic—like most deck plates—the boots would stick. As an infantryman, Jurgen had turned off the magnets in his boots, and then forgotten about the setting.

Jurgen floated through the inner door of the airlock and into the blackness ahead of him. The enemy ship's internal lights were off. Jurgen felt like he was sailing from a well-lit room into a black cave. He flipped on his external lights and flooded the enemy compartment with light. Babbington turned on her lights, creating a shadow across the compartment. A cacophony of voices came over the Assault channel; Jurgen muted the channel to concentrate.

"No, lights off Miss Babbington. Mister Wulfjaeger is playing human torch. From the looks of this compartment, the Assault has already cleaned out this section. There is an open hatch, if you would lead, please, Mister Wulfjaeger. Jurgen grabbed a piece of hull and pulled. He floated forward a few meters, illuminating the way until he came to a T-intersection.

"Left, Mister Wulfjaeger, I have a hunch the bridge is that way," the captain said.

"Yes, ma'am," Jurgen said. As he turned the corner, he felt several hits on his armor and the shots pushed Jurgen back. Jurgen fired his pistol into the darkened corridor at the muzzle flash. The weapons maker had designed the Anderson-Campbell 2311 service pistol to be as "reaction less" as possible, meaning that the shots wouldn't add to Jurgen's velocity. He watched as the bohrium pin tracers found the area where the muzzle flashes originated. Jurgen grabbed a bulkhead, stopped, and then pulled himself to the area. For being so quick, the fight was one of the most terrifying Jurgen had ever experienced. Jurgen's helmet scanned the visible spectrum but there wasn't enough ambient light to generated an artificial picture. The fight was like shooting in a cave armed only with pistols and flashlights. Jurgen illuminated some shapes in front of him. His suit registered the shapes as three Assaultmen with no vitals. Beyond the Assaultmen, were a half dozen pressure-suited forms. Ice crystals rattled against Jurgen's helmet. After a second's pause, Jurgen realized that the crystals were the blood and body matter of the Assaultmen and enemy crew.

"Keep moving, Mister Wulfjaeger. You've eliminated the only remaining enemy," said the captain. The trio moved forward past the floating dead bodies.

"Sir, get on the A-channel," said Laser. "We've got a team ahead of you; they're in a hot mess!"

Jurgen unmuted the channel and a cacophony of voices blasted his ears. He made a fist to call a halt. Babbington floated ahead of him.

"Wait, Miss Babbington," said the captain.

"Got them pinned down in the bridge," an Assaultman said.

"I can't stack up. They're laying down covering fire every time we try to get close," another said. Red emergency lights came on. Jurgen's battlesuit immediately adjusted to compensate, trying to give him the clearest picture. The scene around him was a macabre horror. Forms lay twisted in unnatural positions and plumes of frozen liquid shot out from the bodies like icicles. Jurgen had seen plenty of dead and wounded, but the sudden images almost made him throw up.

"Problem on the bridge, captain," Jurgen said.

"Well then, let's go fix the problem, Mister Wulfjaeger," said the captain as she took off ahead of him. He wanted to shout "wait," but decided to race the captain. Sternfahrer holstered her pistol and was pumping both of her arms like a pull up queen. Eventually, Jurgen had applied enough force to start accelerating ahead of her, when he saw the corridor terminated in a ninety-degree turn.

Jurgen kicked his feet in front of him and hit the wall. The boots magnetized and he was able to "run" sideways along the wall. He ran three meters and fell "down" behind the fireteam that was outside the bridge. The team was using a bulkhead from an intersecting corridor as cover.

"Sit rep," Jurgen said.

"Every time me, Thurston, and Maddox try to make a move the enemy starts shooting," a corporal, the fireteam lead, said. The captain and Babbington floating into the makeshift foxhole. Jurgen had forget up and down. The view disoriented him since he was technically floating "sideways" in a corridor and staring towards another corridor that led to the bridge.

"Captain, how much damage would a grenade cause if I tossed it into the bridge," Jurgen asked.

"Nothing that isn't repairable," the captain said. Jurgen pulled an EMP grenade out of a utility pouch that he had prepped when he came aboard. The EMP wouldn't kill the crew, but the shock would paralyze them momentarily. It would also neutralize the bridge controls. Jurgen pulled the pin, which magnetized to his armor, and threw the grenade towards the bridge. The grenade sailed downward, looking like a rock dropped into a well. It passed through the open bulkhead and exploded with a large electrical bolt. Lights went out across the ship. Jurgen was up and walking down the walls towards the compartment. He raced, "upside down" in his mind, with the deck plating above him and the ceiling as his floor.

Jurgen burst onto the bridge. His helmet illuminated the scene. He fired several rounds into any pressure-suited form that moved. One enemy twisted and then stilled. The rest of the crew floated with their hands on their heads. The command crew had surrendered.

"In the name of the Felgenland Union I now take this ship as a prize of war. Come along peacefully, and I will ensure you and your crew are dropped off at a neutral world at our convenience," Sternfahrer said. "I am Captain Johanna Sternfahrer of the *Advantage.* Where is your captain?"

A form moved forward, "I'm Biko Abara, captain of this vessel, *Stellar Anvil*. I offer my word for me and my crew's parole." Abara made the statement passively. Sternfahrer's terms were fair, and the merchantman's crew had been no match for the *Advantage.*

"What's your cargo, Captain Abara?" Sternfahrer asked.

"Rare earth metals, Captain Sternfahrer. I will not provide any more information on our source or destination," Abara said firmly.

"Captain, I need you back here on the *Advantage.* We've got trouble," Pullings said.

"Miss Babbington, you've got your first command. Get the bridge up and working. Mister Wulfjaeger, take the captain and his bridge crew over to the *Advantage* and throw them in the brig. We'll make room in the crew mess for the rest of the ship's crew. Now, let's move! Lieutenant Pullings says there's a need for us on the bridge," Sternfahrer said, and with that Johanna floated off at great speed.

Jurgen trained his pistol on the enemy command crew. They floated along slowly, sullenly even. After several minutes of prodding and even firing a warning shot, Jurgen got them into the *Advantage's* airlock just as the outer doors began closing. Jurgen wasn't sure what was happening, but he was able to push the enemy to move faster now that he was in friendly territory.

An Assault fireteam appeared. One Assaultman said, "Captain needs you on the bridge, sir." Jurgen left his charges to the fireteam and floated as fast as his arms could propel him to the bridge. He entered and slammed the door shut.

"Have they flashed their colors yet?" Sternfahrer asked Pullings.

"No, captain," Pullings said. "They popped up at ten light minutes away when you crossed over to the merchantman."

"How many still on the *Stellar Anvil*?" Johanna asked.

"Nicholls and Babbington are on the *Stellar Anvil*, along with Laser and twenty-five Assaultmen, a handful of the engineering division and our forward deck division," said Pullings.

Stourton entered the bridge and said, "At my duty station, ma'am."

"Lieutenant Stourton, tell Lieutenant Nicholls she's in charge of the *Stellar Anvil* and to make sail for..." Sternfahrer pulled out a chart and looked at jumps, for a friendly port at which to drop the *Stellar Anvil*.

"Protelan, we'll collect them there. Apologize to Miss Babbington on the loss of her command," said the captain.

"The ship is flashing its colors, captain," said Pullings. "The ship is a Terran Navy Cruiser! Their captain is sending an audio message."

"Put the message on overhead! Action stations!" Sternfahrer said.

The audio crackled in Jurgen's ear, "Felgenland Union cruiser, this is the Terran Directorate War Craft *Formidable.* Release the *Stellar Anvil* and we'll allow you transit the system."

Sternfahrer swore over the ship command channel. "Dang spit and polish captains let one get through the blockade on Sol! Pullings, let me know the status on the *Stellar Anvil*, especially how soon she can jump! Stourton, take fire control! Pullings, flash our colors! We're going to fight!"

Jurgen pulled up the Admiralty data sheet on the *Formidable.*

Assuming the intelligence was correct, the enemy ship had almost five hundred sailors which was almost twice the number on the *Advantage.* The enemy cruiser was so new that Jurgen could almost smell the paint on the hull. The captain, a woman named Lian Mei, was a veteran with over thirty years' experience. Jurgen felt like the fight was certainly tilted in the *Formidable's* favor.

"Captain, Nicholls says they are thirty minutes away from command of the helm. After they get command, she will try an emergency jump," said Pullings.

"Time to range on the *Formidable*?" the captain asked.

"Twenty minutes at current speed. The enemy will have both ships in range then," Pullings said.

"We need to buy some time! Full thrust. Let's see how tough the Terrans really are," Sternfahrer said. Jurgen's mouth was dry, and he took a pull on the internal spout of his battlesuit's canteen. He wished Laser was aboard. Jurgen could question him about the battle. Instead, Jurgen kept quiet and watched.

"Put up a clock. I need to know when we're in weapons range; also give me the repair clock for the *Stellar Anvil*," Sternfahrer said. Jurgen could see the corner of the captain's display and he watched the clocks. The time to engage showed four minutes and thirty-seven seconds, the time to repair showed twenty-eight minutes and thirty seconds. If the *Advantage* could hold out for about twenty-five minutes of battle, then the *Stellar Anvil* could hopefully slip away. If not, Jurgen might be dead and the *Stellar Anvil* and its rare earths would be headed to Sol to help the Terran war effort.

Every second seemed to be an eternity, but eventually the *Advantage* was in range.

"Fire every missile on the starboard dorsal racks. Give me an anti-missile broadside and then switch to bohrium penetrator rounds. After the salvo, give me full port thrust. We'll slalom into the enemy! They won't expect that," Sternfahrer ordered.

"Missiles away, captain," Stourton said punching the buttons. Jurgen watched the display with the missile tracks.

"Enemy has fired their port batteries; they are wheeling away. Firing the anti-missile turrets," Stourton reported. Jurgen put his hand on a bulkhead. He wouldn't be able to hear anything, but he could feel if the enemy missiles hit due to the hull vibrations. If an enemy missile got lucky, the explosion would be the last sensation he'd have in the universe. As his hand touched the bulkhead, Jurgen smiled and thought, 'so much for a lazy cruise home.'

"Three of our missiles made their way past the enemy's screen. The *Formidable* is taking damage in her cargo bay and main engineering. Two enemy missiles made it past our screen. The turrets are tracking them but can't get a lock. They're going to hit," Pullings reported. The lights and displays went out and Jurgen felt the vibrations through the ship. A dull red emergency light came on.

"Where is the enemy? Damage report? Get me displays!" Sternfahrer roared.

"Captain, enemy is on a backwards track ten kilometers off our port side. They're coasting and the *Formidable* doesn't look like the ship has main engine control," said Pullings.

"Damage?" Sternfahrer asked. The displays came back up rebooting.

"The first missile hit the main cargo bay. Petty Officer McNulty and Chief Bonden are working on locking that down. The second missile hit our water tank; Petty Officer Jones is working on stopping the leak. Weapons are ready," said Pullings.

"Ma'am, Nicholls has reported she has the helm and will be jumping momentarily," said Stourton.

"Give the *Formidable* a thank you for the dance, full missile spread, ventral port side, and follow the salvo with an anti-missile barrage," said Sternfahrer.

"Captain, the *Stellar Anvil* has dropped her jump rings and is making the leap to Protelan! The *Formidable* is firing!" said Pullings.

"I want a reaction burn! Pull the nose up ninety and a full burn on all engines! Let's shake some missiles. Fire all anti-missile batteries!" said Sternfahrer. Jurgen watched the display as a mass of red lines headed towards the *Advantage* and a mass of blue lines arced towards the *Formidable*. He felt the gees as the ship accelerated.

"Six got through!" Pullings said excitedly.

"Theirs or ours?" Sternfahrer said anxiously.

"Ours! Impact on the ventral side, and two look like they cut into the dorsal side. Lights are out on the *Formidable*," said Pullings.

"Three enemy missiles still incoming, captain," said Stourton. Jurgen felt their impact in the hull as the lights went out, but the displays stayed up.

"Damage report! Where is the *Stellar Anvil*," asked the captain.

"*Stellar Anvil* is away! Their jump gate just folded through the wormhole," said Pullings.

"Audio message from the *Formidable*, captain," said Stourton.

"You've won this round, *Advantage*. Next time you won't be so lucky," the audio said.

"The *Formidable* is jumping away," said Pullings.

"Damage report," said Sternfahrer.

"We don't have a tiller. We've been hit in the emergency computer core and the main data bus from Engineering has been smashed. I'm on my way back to get an estimate of repairs," said Stourton floating from her couch. Jurgen checked his display; the Assaultmen were helping the Navy to patch holes and get systems back on line. Jurgen wished he could wipe the sweat off his brow. After the fight, he wanted to be off the ship. He had never felt so useless in combat before.

Part Three

Sailing to Destiny

CHAPTER ONE

Endings and Beginnings

Emissary

Henry ran Markus ragged that morning. The valet took the constant change of Henry's clothing in stride. Henry wanted Markus' validation on his outfit choices, but the poor young man had never been on a date and couldn't help. Markus did, however, offer encouragement.

In the end, Henry settled on a red turtleneck under his cream Sheeplands wool sweater, a pair of khaki trousers, and a pair of brown causal loafers. The look was popular with the young up and comers in the Felgenland. Krueger drove the Primus close to Kocher Square and made a discrete drop off three blocks away. Today, tourists packed Kocher Square. Henry wasn't worried about his safety. The square had wall-to-wall cameras and Line Guards at every intersection. As he arrived the clocks all over the square read fourteen-fifty. For a date, he was early, but for an Assault officer, he was on time.

Henry had debated bringing flowers, but decided against a bouquet. According to conventional wisdom, flowers were a gift for the third date. He went to the giant statue's pedestal. There was a queue to go up into the statue's arm. Ticket scalpers offered "deals" if Henry wanted to go up. Henry shook his head 'no.' A few made a continued attempt until a Line Guard shooed them off. Henry moved front of the statue. There was a Line Guard next to an info board, and a few meters past the info board, was the Eternal Flame of Freedom.

Henry read the info boards as he waited for Hannah. They gave some information on the Society of the Human Phoenix, the primitive star anchors, and humanity in the time of first alien contact. Henry had studied this material with his private tutor, like all the highborn. His instructor for this topic had been a dynamic priest who was now a seminary dean. He especially remembered the priest's lessons on Lena.

Henry looked up at his grandmother's statue. She was like a mother to all in the Felgenland. Henry then turned to scan the crowds. In the distance heading towards the crowds at the statue's base was Hannah. He could see that she wore sun glasses, a black leather jacket over a cream-colored blouse with loose feminine trousers and high heels. Henry waved to her and she waved back. Moments later she joined him at the Eternal Flame of Freedom.

"Hi," said Hannah. "Sorry I'm late. The bus got delayed due to traffic."

"You're early. We were meeting at fifteen-hundred; it is now only fourteen fifty-seven," said Henry.

Hannah smiled, "You know how the military is. If you aren't ten minutes early, you're late."

"Well then, let's get that coffee," Henry said. Hannah nodded and walked next to him. The crowd ignored both the Primus and the war hero. Henry smiled at the thought that if the crowd had recognized either of them, the walk would be much longer and more involved.

The couple crossed the plaza, towards a smaller pedestrian street. As they approached, they saw the sign for Kayley's Kaffeekultur. Henry opened the door for the blond pilot who wore her hair in a wavy half-up-do like a movie star. As Henry followed Hannah inside, he caught the scent of her perfume. It smelled of roses, jasmine, and pear. Henry stood next to Hannah in the line.

Hannah stood looking at the menu. Henry had already decided to get a black coffee, so he began people watching — taking the opportunity to observe the commoners and not rush his date.

"Oh, so many options, I can't seem to make a decision," said Hannah.

"What do you usually drink?" asked Henry.

"Tea," said Hannah, "but a fancy coffee sounds pretty good."

The queue had moved quickly and Henry and Hannah were at the head of the line.

"What can I get you two?" the barista asked.

"Black coffee, Eisenwaldian," Henry said.

"What would you recommend?" Hannah asked.

"Our special today is the Stellar Brewtini, in honor of the war's first hero and Ace, STELLAR SERAPH," said the woman. "The Brewtini is a shot of espresso with some coffee liqueur, a light amount of vanilla vodka, heavy cream, ice, and cocoa powder."

Henry just smiled at the drink. He was used to the randomly named items that were called Primus' this or that. Hannah looked like the woman had suggested she drink cyanide.

"I'll have a bottle of water," Hannah said. The barista nodded and charged Henry. Henry gave her a griffin and the woman gave him change. Henry and Hannah moved into the queue for the drinks.

"No coffee?" Henry asked as they waited for their drinks. "You can't call it a coffee date without, you know, the coffee."

"I know, sorry, I just... get tired of being the poster girl for everything," Hannah said.

"I understand. I felt the same way when my father, you know, changed jobs," Henry said, purposely being coy.

"I never thought about that," Hannah said. "I don't know if I could become a perpetual public figure."

Henry nodded and was about to say something when the barista shouted, "Eisenwald black and bottle of water."

Henry retrieved the drinks and handed the sparkling water to Hannah.

"Oh drat," she said, "I wanted non-carbonated water."

"Sorry, let me go see if I can exchange the bottle," Henry said.

"No, I'll drink the water," Hannah replied quickly.

"Do you want to sit here or wander?" Henry asked looking around the crowded coffee shop.

"Let's walk... if that's okay?" Hannah asked looking up at the Primus. In her ten-centimeter heels, the top of her head was almost even with Henry's nose. Henry led the way to the door, which a middle-aged man held open after having entered with his middle-aged female companion.

"Thanks," Henry said as Hannah and he exited. Outside, Henry led Hannah to a picturesque little park with a good view of the Lena statue.

"I miss the *Spirit of Lena*," said Hannah wistfully. "We have a photo of the statue hanging in the main pilot's mess."

"Why did you join up?" asked Henry changing the subject slightly. He wanted a safe question, since coffee wasn't going to generate much conversation between the two.

"I wanted to leave Antwerp-on-the-Neu-Rhine. I had thought about going to university. Mom wanted me to be an engineer and dad wanted me to be a ballerina," Hannah said. "I wanted to do something that would help people. The Navy gave me an opportunity do something worthwhile. In basic, I aced the ratings test. Not to brag but I did pretty well on the pilot's addendum too. I only threw up once." Henry smiled at Hannah's comment.

"Since you asked," said Hannah, "why did you join up? You, um, didn't really have to, since..."

Henry finished her thought. "My father is who he is? The Cognatii and all that?"

"Yes," Hannah said.

"Well, I didn't really have a choice. My father served and of course, my grandfather was a military man of a sort," Henry said. Hannah nodded.

"I never expected to be where I am now. I really expected a military career to open doors with Campbell Industries or a smaller defense contractor. I wanted a lifestyle similar to those of the middle-classes."

"Oh, I never expected that from you," said Hannah.

"Why?" asked Henry.

"I see all those folks who hang off your father's every word. I figured you wanted to follow in his footsteps, being the eldest and all. I don't know if you could adjust to the middle classes. You probably have tons of servants," said Hannah.

"Not really. Now that I am Primus, I have a valet. However, he's there to help me organize my day, which is usually full of official functions. My father has his majordomo, who takes care of our home and who has served our family for many decades. He is like an uncle. My mother has, well, a lady's maid would be the closest thing to call her. But my mother's lady isn't a full-time employee either. The Villa has staff, but they take care of the estate. The house is a massive undertaking, with security and maintenance being paramount," said Henry.

"Servants, staff, estates... that all sounds complicated. I don't think I could get used to that," said Hannah.

"Neither did I. I grew up in the country, where our house has a butler. That's it. My mother and my father cooked when I was growing up. We seemed like everyone else then. I didn't want the life in the fishbowl, here. What about you, any servants?"

Hannah smiled. "No, none. Mom was employed part time after my little brother came along. When I was a teenager, she went back to work full time. Dad worked his forty-five hours a week. On the weekends, he would set up a campfire in our backyard fire-pit. Occasionally, neighbors would come over for a grilled meal. Afterward, we'd do banana boats..."

"What are those?" asked Henry.

"The best campfire treat," said Hannah. "You split a banana in half and add marshmallows and chocolate flakes. Then you wrap them in foil and cook them until everything melts together. Oh, so good!

Banana boats are my favorite desert. What's yours?"

Henry motioned to keep walking as a large group of tourists came towards them, led by a tour guide. After walking a block away, Henry stopped.

"To answer your question, I love Steelwood-Forest Tiramisu. The cake comes from a bakery in the town — Grief-im-Waldorf, near where I grew up. The dessert is like a regular Tiramisu but has nuts and a cherry filling on top," Henry said.

"That sounds okay," Hannah said. "But, I'm not sure coffee and cherries make a good combination."

"If you ever come to our country house, I'll happily get you a slice. That cake may change your mind," Henry said.

"Who said we're getting to dinner, much less visiting your country estate," said Hannah.

"Yeah," Henry responded, "I can see things haven't gone well today. In my defense, I didn't expect the coffee shop to have a flavor named after you. I really hate when businesses randomly name things after people."

"I'm not surprised. STELLAR SERAPH is an exciting person right now. Thankfully that's going away. Since Jurgen has been in the news there haven't been that many stories about me. Plus, you aren't doing that poorly. I am hungry. If you want to do dinner, I'm game," said Hannah with a smile.

"Okay, I'll pay if you pick," Henry said.

"No, we go *splitten.* We'll each pay for ourselves. That's the only way to have a real date," Hannah said.

"Fair enough, but you pick," Henry said. He and Hannah spent the next half hour wandering and looking at menus. The cuisines available in the Union was varied, especially in the capital, where the foreign embassies influenced the options. The couple ended up in a Tau Ceti-based restaurant. While searching for a restaurant, their conversation had been sparse. Henry figured that Hannah was either nervous, hungry, or bored. They each looked at the menu. Henry used his EVIL to order their meal. Henry ordered a plains-fed hamburger, and Hannah ordered the signature salad that was topped with strong fish. When served, they ate their meal in silence. A waiter appeared and cleared the plates.

When waiter left, Hannah asked, "Do you like movies?"

"Occasionally, I mean, if I wanted to see something I can get a private screening... well... at home. Why? Do you like movies?" Henry asked.

"Oh, yes. I really like Lukas Stahl. I loved him in the *Last Message.* Did you see that one? He was the perfect husband. I doubt you would watch the *Last Message.* That was a total girl's movie," Hannah said.

"Sorry, no, but I remember him in *One Eighty Nine.* He was a good Caspar Röist. Actually, I don't really watch many movies. I spend my free time reading, and occasionally I'll play a video game," Henry said. "I'm a pretty big fan of a real-time strategy game, *Battle for Planet Thermopylae.* But, I never get the CAA faction to win against the Hipponike faction."

"Sorry, I don't like video games. Plus, I knew you were going to bring up *One Eighty Nine*, all the boys like that movie," Hannah said.

"Well, the book was much better. Hans Droit did a superb job in weaving the tale and the history together," said Henry.

"Wait? There was a book too?" Hannah said in disbelief.

"Yes, do you have any favorite books?" asked Henry.

"Not really, I like experiencing things, like movies, oh, and the opera," Hannah said.

"The opera? I went a long time ago. The opera bored me to death," Henry said. "My uncle and cousins are the artists in the family. I tried playing music and painting. Sadly, I just make noise or a mess." Hannah smiled.

"Well, opera is divine, but I understand. I get that it isn't for everyone. What do you like to do, if you're being active?"

"I like to hike, fish, and hunt. I'm good with a crossbow, but my favorite is hunting with a black powder rifle. There is something challenging in using ancient weapons," said Henry.

"I feel bad for the animals. You're an Assaultman and they don't have combat training to shoot back," said Hannah. Henry suspected Hannah made a joke, but the joke fell flat for him. An uncomfortable silence ensued. The bill came and they each paid.

Hannah stood. She said, "I had a good time. Thanks for helping me get away from the base. Thanks, also, for the non-coffee-coffee and dinner."

Henry stood as he said, "Thanks, we should do this again. I had a good time."

"Absolutely," Hannah said. She seemed stiff like she was unsure of what to do. Henry extended his hand, and she shook his outstretched hand in a ladylike gesture.

"Goodbye, Hannah," Henry said, as they both walked to the entrance of the restaurant.

"Bye-bye," Hannah said. They parted. Henry summoned Krueger and the driver picked him up.

"Well how was the date sir," asked Krueger.

"Strange, not as terrible as some I've had with aristocrats, but kind of awkward," said Henry.

"You know, sir, lots of regular folks get hung up around the so called 'high and mighty.' She might be one of those types. I used to be too, but after being around you and the protector, well you're just like the rest of us," the driver stated.

"I appreciate the vote of normalcy," said Henry.

The driver laughed. Then Krueger said, "Yeah, compared to your old valet you're a swell gent."

Henry laughed. "High praise indeed, sergeant."

The ride back to the villa was as uneventful as things got in Henry's world. He had settled into life in the capital, but he was lonely. He had a decent time with Hannah, but nothing seemed to click. He decided to put the ball in her court. He'd call her and if she was interested, she could pick the venue.

Henry scrolled through his messages on his EVIL but nothing caught his eye. Henry watched the late April sky clear as Eisenwald came over the horizon. He wondered if maybe a vacation would shake up his routine. He now felt like the Bundstadt was home. But the Villa was a lonely home, and at times, like a human zoo. The limo returned to the Villa and Henry put his loneliness aside as he went up to his apartments.

"Well, sir, success?" Markus asked.

"I feel like I had the fish on the line but couldn't bring the hook back to the boat," said Henry.

Markus said, "Well, as you're an avid fisherman, you know there are..."

"Plenty of fish in the sea?" Henry finished the statement. Markus nodded and laughed.

"Goodnight, Markus," Henry said, dismissing his valet for the evening.

"You too, sir," Markus replied, going to his own room. Henry was at least happy with the valet, Markus seemed to be the only human with whom he could talk that didn't want something in return. Markus didn't have the same history that his uncle, Weber, had with Henry. What Markus lacked in tenure; he made up with diligence in his duties. Henry tired of his wool-gathering and decided to go to bed.

In the weeks that followed, Hannah did contact Henry to suggest another date. She invited Henry to a new opera, *Cosmic Serenade.*

Henry suggested they go to the premiere and sit in the protector's box. Like many things in the capital, the protectors had sponsored the opera many decades ago. Hannah had deferred. The opera sounded a tad girly to Henry, and very high profile, but Hannah had booked tickets and suggested they go incognito as commoners. Henry was keen to try the opera again. Perhaps the performance would give them something to discuss. Henry was also drawn to the idea of living like "the other half," especially since Henry had only experienced the capital as the Primus. Hannah had suggested the opera's second week on May the ninth, a week away.

Today was Saturday, and Henry had found a book on art history and was reading about several of the lesser-known paintings that were part of the Villa's immense collection. At first, Henry's reading was like work, but soon the history made the book a page turner. During the latter half of the book, Henry noticed he had an oil painting of Kenneth, *Graf* Gilbraith-on-Heather hanging next to one of the Bonnie Dundee. Henry suspected he would have to talk to Maximilian, and swap the old canvas of Kenneth for one of the new *Graf*.

Henry had promised his Uncle Paddy to leave the new *Graf* alone in exchange for a posting when the new front opened. The Assault's departure from the Lalande 21185 and Nakdong seemed as slow as the buildup had been. The redeployment seemed ineffectual and slow to Henry, but he was stuck playing armchair quarterback, a position where everything seems easier.

The protector had also made vague promises about the front. Henry tried not to pester his father since the protector was stretched thin trying to manage the war effort. On days of extreme boredom, Henry was tempted to ask his father to just skip all the meetings and go fishing, but he didn't. While Henry had relished the first few sessions of his apprenticeship, soon the apprenticeship turned into just another series of boring meetings. Military officer and bureaucrats would make excuses, blame others, and complain.

Going to USIS was an exception. The intelligence officers were trying to uncover what was actually happening. Were the Terrans preparing to mount an offensive? Could the Union subvert any of the military or government blocks? Henry would watch as the USIS officers argued hotly in the meetings. Often, USIS members were escorted from the meeting to cool off. The USIS officers seemed to feel the sword of Damocles hanging over their heads, unlike the military services.

The Navy seemed to have stepped up its game. The Navy had a massive recruiting operation underway. Hannah's poster was everywhere. As a result, young women, many from the countryside, were flocking to sign up in the hope they could be a gallant Valkyrie like the posters portrayed Hannah. Henry wondered if he felt compelled to go on another date with her because her face was everywhere. Had he been affected by the propaganda?

Henry's EVIL made three long chirps and Henry jumped off his chaise lounge like he'd been electrocuted. Three chimes indicated a summons. The Assault could be calling him up!

He looked at the EVIL, only slightly disappointed.

`Come upstairs, love father.`

Henry put down his book and left his apartment. Pausing, he wondered if he should remove Kenneth's picture, or have a servant replace the canvas later. Opting for later, Henry reached the elevator as the doors opened. Two ministers from the Commons stood in the elevator.

"Primus," they said acknowledging Henry.

"Good evening, gentlemen," Henry said. They looked at each other unsure what to say. Their non-response made Henry slightly uncomfortable, but the elevator doors shut and the elevator continued upward.

Henry entered the protector's public apartments and saw a war zone. Ministers, military officers, USIS bureaucrats, and the protector's privy council were clumped throughout the expansive room. Some argued, while others hovered over documents on the flat surfaces.

Weber waded through the crush and said, "This way, Primus, the protector has called a halt to sessions until he can get you briefed."

Weber guided Henry through the groups. The scene was much livelier than the usual meetings he attended.

"What's going on, Weber?" asked Henry.

"Have you seen the news?" asked Weber patiently.

"Nope, I do a news blackout on the weekends," said Henry.

"Well, then your father will have to explain," said Weber mysteriously. Henry knew better than to try to pry information from the majordomo, and he counted the seconds until he could see his father. He did not have to count long, as Weber opened the doors to the private gallery and the protector. Henry stepped into the glass hall and looked at the flashing lights racing all across the capital.

"Hello, my son. I was relieved to hear you were in the Villa and safe," said the protector.

"Hello, father. What is going on? Your apartments seem a bit—lively—for a Saturday."

The protector laughed for a moment, stress leaking out with every chuckle.

"Well, that is one way to state things. We've had an incident today."

"I gathered, what happened?" asked Henry impatiently.

"Alasdair Campbell has been assassinated," said the protector.

"What?!" Henry said, unwilling to trust his ears.

"The same group who attacked you, got him at Midlothian Spaceport. He was in his private slip and they ambushed him. The Line Guards got there first and dispatched the terrorists. Only one survived and is in custody. However, poor Alasdair didn't survive the attack. He died en-route to the hospital. I know you and he didn't get along."

"No, I was just being... hasty. He seemed like he was trying to look out for me, but..."

"He had his own way of doing things that seemed contrary to your instincts. I know. I know," said the protector.

"Listen, father, what is this all about?" asked Henry.

"There are groups trying to orchestrate a civil war here in the Union. There are reports from Lochiel, Eisenwald, the Sheeplands here on Stahlburgh, and even some of our colonies that certain families have returned to the old ways of raiding and thieving," said the protector.

"What?" said Henry. "Don't they realize there is a war on? We need everyone focused on Terra!"

The protector smiled. "Praise Malcolm and Jesus, you are my boy through and through!"

Henry turned red in embarrassment and a tinge of anger. "I'm not a child, father."

"No, you're not. Thank God! You are an astute man whom I value as a fresh set of eyes. Someone I trust implicitly. Someone I need to deliver the truth when everyone else speaks lies," said the protector.

"Huh?" said Henry, confused.

"Heinrich, we're in a delicate time. Someone is trying to tip the Union into chaos. They want to see if Humpty Dumpty can put himself back together again. But we're not an egg! We're steel! We are a dragon! In the Sheeplands, folk are spilling blood and full of passion. There is so much that is happening now, and as much as 'terrorists' are supposedly behind all the violence, we both know who pulls the strings."

"The Terrans," said Henry.

"Yes, my boy. This is the Terran's modus operandi. Create internal chaos, engineer a takeover, start a 'revolution,' and create a client state," said the protector. "I was wondering why the Terrans were holding back; now we know. This is their play. Remove me and place their puppet in my spot."

"Why?" Henry said.

"You don't have to waste a soldier's life if your enemy collapses on its own! Even better if the former enemy becomes an ally," said the protector. Henry nodded. The Terran's play made sense the more he thought about it. Both men were silent.

The protector broke the silence and said, "The Directorate made a miscalculation though."

"Oh, really?" Henry said.

"They expected our spies to be as complacent as their spies. USIS is not idle. They are moving as fast as they can, and we have our own countermeasures. When the time comes, the Terrans will be fighting plenty of so called 'allies,' and we'll strike at them directly. We'll bring them into the fight ring for a title bout," said the protector.

"What can I do?" asked Henry, eager to be a part of something war related.

"Angus's daughter's name, what was it again? Belinda? Bethany?" asked the protector.

"Beatrix, but she prefers Bonnie," said Henry.

"That's what I thought, which is why I am sending you as my emissary to MacDonald Hall," said the protector. "I know very little about the MacDonalds. They are not part of the cadre of *Hawks*. What I do know of them is secondhand from their enemies. The Isles, their demense, are an insular province and could decide to breakaway."

"What? Wait? I thought I'd be moved to the front," Henry said with some surprise.

"Heinrich, you're a MjGA. Pretend the MacDonalds are a primitive tribe from another world, and just as dangerous."

"Sure, you want me to win their hearts and minds?" asked Henry.

"And do some intelligence gathering," the protector said. "This is a sensitive mission. The MacDonald is my vassal, which causes... complications... in our relationship. He could go rogue and be a nation unto himself. You, however, have been noted with his daughter, and you are not a friend of the Campbells, Gordons, or Buchanans.

The five families may have been first, but they were never one happy family. Your grandfather, like a good dad, knocked their heads together and made them all behave."

"Wait, you mentioned the first families. What about the Frasers? They have an animus against the MacDonalds too," said Henry, remembering his history.

"I will deal with the Frasers, directly," the protector said. "Now, grab some clothes. You're off to MacDonald Hall. Dress warmly. They're in the extreme north."

"When will I be back? I was expecting to go to the theater with Hannah next Saturday," said Henry.

"I'm not sure. It's your call on whether you need to cancel with Hannah. As an aside, how are things going with her?" asked the protector.

"Not great," said Henry. "Unlike some of the ladies you and mother have tried, the date wasn't terrible, but we didn't have a lot of chemistry."

"You've only had one date. The first one is usually the worst," said the protector. "I remember those days. Everything is awkward."

"Well, then, I need to get the MacDonalds sorted and get back here in less than a week," said Henry. "Farewell, father, you can count on me."

"I know! That's why you, your valet, and your driver are going. This isn't a public event, so keep your appearance there quiet. That also means Hannah doesn't have the need to know about your visit," said the protector. "Now, my son, goodbye."

The protector embraced Henry, and after a moment they separated. Henry turned and left. The public apartments were still chaotic. Before leaving, Henry decided to say goodbye to his mother. He detoured into the private rooms, passing through the double set of doors that separated public and private spaces. As he entered, two miniature schnauzers rushed towards him barking. The dogs got closer and the alert barks turned to puppy barks of happiness. Henry got down on his knees and the dogs climbed on him, attempting to lick and sniff his face.

"Hello Otto, hello Hildegarde," Henry said petting the puppies. He missed the packs of dogs that his family had in the country. Henry realized that he hadn't been completely truthful with Hannah. Schloss Machthaber at Greiff-im-Wald, was a small village. The main house only had a butler, but there were outbuildings including the kennel. Otto and Hildegarde flicked their cropped ears and wiggled their docked tails in excitement. Henry continued to pet them. He had given up one of their pack mates a few years ago to Special Projects. At the time, giving away the puppy was a heart wrenching sacrifice due to Henry's career. Often, Henry wondered where the dog was. He hoped the dog was well cared for.

"Hello, Heinrich, how are you, son?" the patroness said appearing at the noise of the dogs.

"Hello, mother," said Henry standing and hugging his mother. She squeezed him back. The schnauzers scratched at their legs.

"Otto and Hildy, down," said the patroness. The dogs dropped. Henry smiled, but knew better than to disturb the dogs.

"It has been a while since you visited. Is everything okay?" asked his mother.

"I'm heading up to MacDonald Hall; I wanted to say goodbye to you," said Henry.

The patroness looked relieved and said, "I expected you to be saying goodbye for the front. I am glad you came to visit before leaving."

"Someday, I'll have to say goodbye for the front. Otherwise we all will be hypocrites," said Henry.

"Yes, you and your father have said as much," the patroness replied, "I'd never have been a good Spartan woman. I have nightmares about you arriving home on your shield."

"I've been trained," said Henry, but his mother persisted.

"But Heinrich, if you arrive wearing your shield, that's even worse! You will always be a protector who fought the Terrans. You will never earn their trust. Earth is old, a place of humanity's birth and heritage. Taking up arms against them and winning would be as bad as your death."

"Mother, the Directorate hasn't given us a choice in the matter," said Henry.

"Yes, but you shouldn't be so gleeful to march off. You're like your father in that matter," said the patroness.

"And nothing like the woman who got into a fist-fight with Grand Duchess Henrietta of Bavaria-on-Salzheim. The courtiers say that three men had to grab each of you to pry you apart," said Henry with a smile.

The patroness smiled with a memory, and said, "That woman! She deserved a punch to the nose! She insulted your father! She insulted your grandfather! All that made her get on my last nerve! Well, you might be a little like me too."

She hugged Henry and said, "Maybe I worry too much! You're a smart man, you'll figure your way out of this war. Now, I've heard you went out with that pilot, DeBeck. What happened? Do you like her?" Henry always hated recapping his dates with his mother as she seemed to imply the date's failure was his fault.

"The date didn't go well; she isn't a coffee drinker. I think she doesn't like my hunting, but she may have been joking. We're different people," said Henry.

"Her loss," said his mother. The response was a different tack and surprised Henry. "Your father seemed more set on her as a match. I wasn't sure she could handle life here in the fishbowl. She may be a glorious Amazon, but not every Navy officer can turn into a Grand-Duchess of Haldersmere. Oh, now there's a woman with a daughter."

Henry laughed and said, "Astrid is engaged! Even if she weren't, there is a queue for her hand everywhere she goes."

"Engaged eh... I'm sure we could get you at the front of the line if you wanted," the patroness said.

"I'm letting the Allfather sort this out for me. The more I try to make a rock into an egg, the more teeth I break," said Henry, using an old Felgenland proverb.

"Well, then I will say my prayers for you. I always do," said the patroness.

"You're the patroness, mother," said Henry. "What don't you have?"

"Peace, my eldest married, my friends and their husbands content. Now, I am praying for poor Margrethe. She just lost Alasdair, and yet she seems so stoic," the patroness said. "All right, you've said your goodbyes. Go before events carry you somewhere else. I love you, my brave son."

"I love you, mother. Now, goodbye. The faster I go, the faster I can come back," said Henry. His mother hugged him and then he left, after giving Otto and Hildegard a rub on their tummies. Henry made his way back to the public apartments.

"Henry, one moment, your father wants you," said Weber. Henry stood outside the door to his father's private conference room and heard yelling from within. Henry could make out only part of the conversation.

"Daniel, I told you to lean on him, not threaten!" the protector said.

"Anointed! I did what the Spirit commanded! The man did not bend the knee and needed the rod," said the other.

"By the Allfather, you... Huegel... play a dangerous game with people. I need Fraser to come round to our side, not raise a flag of rebellion. Kenneth was a swine, but his son could be different," said the protector hotly.

"The apple doesn't fall from the rotten tree," said the other man. "The cancer must be excised. How else can the body function, Anointed?" Henry had never heard his father so irritated with a bureaucrat or vassal.

"Go... just go..." said the protector. Half a heartbeat later an angular man in a black suit opened the door. His eyes locked with Henry's and, for a moment, Henry thought the man might challenge him. For whatever reason, Henry wasn't going to move aside for the man.

"Heinrich, this is Daniel von Huegel, by courtesy called *Freiherr* of the Barony of Knockhill. He is an auditor of the House of Dynasts for his father, James *Markgraf* von Huegal," said the protector. "Daniel, this is my son, the Primus."

"Honored, sir," said Daniel, snapping his heels and bowing.

"Likewise, Daniel," said Henry. Daniel rose to his full height and was slightly taller than Henry. Henry still hadn't moved.

Daniel said, "With your leave, sir, I must go. I have pressing business elsewhere."

"You are excused," Henry said with some sternness. The tone surprised Henry, for he only used that voice as an officer when giving commands. Daniel bowed again and left moving subtly past Henry. Henry entered and Weber closed the door.

"Father, who..." began Henry.

"When you're done with Angus, we'll talk," said the protector. "I almost forgot, here is my signet ring. You're my emissary now. Keep the ring. You'll need the ring, as—per a discussion with your mother—I'm going to bring you increasingly into the government and my decision making. Perhaps you'll see why I keep stalling on sending you to the front. Especially if you hear how poorly we're handling this war."

Henry took the ring and said, "Thank you, father, I said my goodbyes to mother. Send my best wishes to Mathias and his family."

"Yes, now go. Your valet has your things; your driver is waiting; and a dropship is at the spaceport ready for liftoff," the protector said, sending his son into potentially hostile territory. "Be careful, my son."

"Goodbye, father," Henry said, turning and opening the door. Weber stood outside waiting.

"This way, Primus," said Weber. The two moved through the crowded public apartment and into the hall.

"How's Markus working out, sir," asked Weber casually as they waited for the elevator.

"Very well, I'm very impressed with him. Why?" asked Henry.

"Markus has asked his parents for permission to join the Assault. I was afraid you were unhappy with him and were looking to sack him, sir."

"Quite the opposite, Weber."

"I see. He is seventeen. I am sure the allure of a uniform and swinging a rifle for Allfather, Union, and Protector has gotten into him like a case of Tau Ceti Malaria, sir."

"I'm not the best judge of whether a young man should join the Assault but didn't you serve too?" asked Henry.

"Of course, I served, but... well..." said Weber but was interrupted by the elevator doors. He and Henry entered, and Weber pushed the button to the motor pool.

"I'm not young, sir, and Markus is my protégé. I intend to position him as the next majordomo, much like my uncle did with me. A war and an Assault career can create unexpected complications for my plan," said Weber. "My bones creak in the morning, and I get tired of the cook complaining about Assaultmen stealing 'her' beer. Such complaints and challenges are for a younger man who has more energy."

"Whatever you need to do, I understand. I also understand Markus' position. I wish him well if he joins the Assault. From what I understand, the Union needs every man and woman in a uniform if we are to keep a Terran boot from our throats," said Henry.

"Your father was wise to apprentice you. I'll let Markus' parents know I have no reservations about him joining. I can wait out the war. I'll rest a little easier knowing Markus will be following officers like you. He'll have a better chance of going to the front and returning.

You make an old man pleasantly comfortable with the future," said Weber.

"I was trained by the noblest of steeds, a veritable Chiron," said Henry.

Weber smiled. Then he said, "You are too kind, Primus. But I thank you. Now, I am, afraid you may be short a valet when I tell Markus of our discussion."

The elevator door opened. Markus stood waiting with Krueger. Henry headed toward Krueger while Weber signaled for the young man to join him and then they spoke privately. Henry waited by the vehicle.

Markus approached Henry and said, "Sir, your things have been packed — the appropriate uniforms, several of your favorite outfits, and all your toiletries. I apologize, but I will not be going with you. I quit effective immediately. I am bound to serve the Union, and look forward to following you and your brother officers on the battlefield."

"I understand, Markus," said Henry. "You have been a magnificent valet, especially compared to your predecessor. You will always have a place here in the Villa. Best of luck in your training and good hunting. I look forward to seeing you as a part of the Assault brotherhood."

Markus bowed, turned, took off his jacket, and handed the garment to his uncle. Weber wore a bittersweet smile as he accepted the jacket but quickly arranged his features in a neutral mask. Henry nodded and Weber smiled.

Henry turned to Krueger, and said with a wink, "You planning to leave me too?"

Krueger smiled. "No sir, my battlefield is the Bundstadt traffic. I know where I'm needed. Besides I've done my time, I was a marine over Asimov."

"I missed meeting you there, sergeant," Henry said as he entered the limo. Krueger shut the door and entered the compartment.

"I think I was the one that missed all the excitement. As you know, the infantry and the MjGAs got mauled terribly. I am surprised Meagher didn't swing for incompetence, but hey, the old man pulled off operations on Nakdong. I read the other day that he's getting a title."

"Yes, he did," Henry said.

"Did they say who the next theater commander will be?" Krueger asked.

"My money is on General Klaus-Wilhelm von Eisenbach. He's been vocal during meetings at Assault High Command. He comes from Hansaburgh with a military lineage. He was also a MjGA. Made his name with his strategic brilliance in the Cygnian peacekeeping action," said Henry. "You plan on winning a command pool?"

Krueger laughed. "I've got five griffins in on the betting, but no, I wouldn't use that knowledge for evil. I'll wait until the betting gets hotter first."

"I'm glad to know you have some standards, sergeant," said Henry with a smile.

"I know, the modern Assault, standards included!" Krueger said as horns blared and he cut off someone as he merged into traffic. In the distance Henry could see a large billboard advertising "Primus Ale" from a brewery in the Valley of the First Farmers. The beer was a red ale and the billboard was a holographic projection of beer poured into a glass. Next to the billboard was another holographic projection of a giant golden turnip being eaten by a cartoon like sheep, with the caption, "Grab a royal treat! Royal Neep — the Sheeplands' favorite whisky!"

Henry laughed as he imagined his friend, George Stewart, growing richer by Henry just looking at the advert. The limo drew closer to the spaceport and Henry readied his EVIL for the checkpoint scan. The limo passed the public gates and went into the private part of the spaceport. Krueger stopped at a checkpoint and rolled down the windows. A sergeant in the Line Guards scanned Krueger's tablet, while a corporal swept the limo for bombs.

"Good evening, sir," the sergeant said as he scanned Henry's EVIL. Henry, for his part, held the device out of the window to speed scanning.

"Thank you, Primus. You're clear. Happy flying," said the Assaultman. Krueger toggled the windows up and drove forward. There was parking by a slip space marked number three. The limo floating into the spot, Krueger killed the engine and simultaneously opened the trunk.

Krueger opened the door for Henry, and collected their bags. Then, the sergeant shut and locked the doors.

"Ready for transit, sir," he said to Henry. Henry made his way to the slip entrance where a navy petty officer stood waiting.

As Henry approached, she said, "I'm Chief Petty Officer Köhler, follow me this way, Primus." Henry and Krueger followed the navy NCO to a well armored and flight ready dropship.

"Boarding a dropship isn't nearly as exciting without enemy fire," said Henry.

"We'll see what your reception is like at MacDonald Hall, sir," Köhler said with a wry smile. Henry laughed. He instantly liked the NCO. As they climbed the ramp to the dropship's cargo bay, three fireteams of Assaultmen snapped to attention. Krueger entered, dropping their bags into a secure bin. He then sat in the back next to where Köhler would sit.

"At ease," Henry said, reflexively. He entered and sat on one of the benches. The seat was harder than he remembered. Then, Henry realized he wasn't in his battlesuit. He hadn't changed and wore his a casual weekend attire. Henry hoped the informal dress would suggest a more relaxed meeting with the MacDonalds. The ramp closed and the dropship started the liftoff. The Assaultmen were an honor guard, but also would maintain security. Henry wondered what his father had sent him into.

"Strap in, sir," said Köhler. "We're going orbital and then dropping back in a hyperbolic shot to Broadford. There will be a car there to take you to Dunvegan and MacDonald Hall, or as the locals call the place, Dunvegan Castle. If you want to watch our flight, your tablet can connect to the navigation system in a read-only mode."

Henry connected his EVIL and watched the flight. After a few minutes he was weightless. An officer entered from the pilot and co-pilot cabin.

"Hello, Primus. We meet again," said the officer. Henry's EVIL identified the pressure-suited speaker as Sub-Lieutenant Callie Callan. Henry remembered the name but couldn't place the face. Callan opened her faceplate and Henry recognized her from the Admiralty.

"Hello Sub-lieutenant Callan, nice seeing you again," Henry said.

Callan smiled with a slight giggle and said, "I volunteered. I wanted to see if you got in touch with Star Lieutenant MacDonald."

Henry had a hunch the Sub-lieutenant might be making a play for him. He decided on a polite fib in order to not have to fend off the Amazon.

"Yes, she sent her messages and looks forward to a coffee with me when she returns," said Henry. Callan looked a little bit taken aback at the statement. Henry felt bad hurting the young woman's feelings, but after his date with Hannah, he wasn't sure if he could handle another awkward date.

Callan nodded. Then she said, "Well, I'm happy my fellow Sister of Athena has done so well. Please keep in touch and enjoy your flight. The pilot will be in to introduce herself. It's rare for either of us to escort a VIP." Callan shut her faceplate and went forward. In a moment, the pilot came back. She wore a pressure suit and the EVIL tagged her as Lieutenant Commander Anneliese Hartmann.

"Welcome aboard, sir," said Hartmann.

"Good day, Lieutenant Commander. To be ferried by such Valkyries is quite the honor," said Henry.

"Well, just remember TAWNY TULIP was your pilot, sir. That's my call sign, especially if you need help on the battlefield. Otherwise, call me Annie," said Annie.

"Thanks Annie. Nice meeting you," said Henry. With pleasantries exchanged he wanted to have time to contemplate the upcoming visit.

"Can I get a cam shot?" said Annie. "My husband and my wing won't believe me otherwise, sir."

"Sure," said Henry with a smile, unbuckling. "Do you want a self capture too?"

"Wow, yes please, sir," Annie said, taking her photos. Henry realized he had made a fan and was happy to oblige. When he was seated and strapped in, he looked at the dropship's plot. The map showed the dropship was three quarters of the way through the trip and starting the descent into Stahlburgh's atmosphere. Henry smiled. The trip had been pleasant so far, and the MacDonalds weren't shooting at him, yet. The dropship came down over the northern ocean and then turned southwards, flying just above the waves. Henry suspected the pilot was "hot dogging." As soon as he started to worry, the dropship elevated to a safer altitude.

"Sorry, sir," said the pilot. "We're training up here and got carried away."

Henry forgot the incident as the dropship passed over the large isle of New Armadale and he could see New Skye, the MacDonald's seat of power. The MacDonalds and the MacLeods had landed in the Sheeplands, a little ways north of Inverkelly. The MacDonalds had controlled the entirety of the Sheeplands for about twenty years, until the Campbells started poaching vassals. Then, the Ó Gallchobhoir tyrants came to Stahlburgh and within fifty years had enslaved or enforced vassalage on everyone. The old tyrants pushed the MacDonalds into the north. Today the MacDonalds only held a fraction of the Sheeplands, and all of these isles. The isles were a large archipelago with almost a billion hectares of land. They were a nation in their own right and joined the Felgenland Union under Karl. Their rivals, the Campbells, had more land, but fewer vassals than the MacDonalds. The MacDonalds comprised several clans and held many alliances externally. Only the Gordons had more alliances, but held less land than either the MacDonalds or the Campbells. The Buchanans were vassals of the Gordons and the Frasers were bound by an alliance to the Campbells.

The dropship went up momentarily and then dropped down in an automated landing path. Several moments later, the dropship was taxiing on a runway to a private slip space. The Broadford spaceport was modern and immaculately clean. Each slip had a skyway, which connected to the large central terminal.

"We're going to have you exit via the orbital connection, sir," said TAWNY TULIP. "One moment, please."

The dropship moved towards the skyway, the connection came out and thumped against the side airlock. Callan came from the pilot compartment and she and Köhler began to operate the airlock. The door opened and then they worked the skyway to ensure a smooth deck transition for Henry.

"Clear now, sir," Köhler said. Henry stepped through the hatch into the skyway. He moved fifteen meters through the skyway arm and into the main part of the terminal. Henry had arrived in the Skye Isles.

A delegation waited for Henry a few meters away. At the group's head was a young man with blondish red hair and he wore what Henry would call "Sheeplands' finery" of a Prince Charlie jacket, full plaid in what Henry assumed was a MacDonald tartan, wool socks, and gray spats over black dress shoes.

"Primus, I don't know if you remember me, I am..." the man began. Henry did indeed remember the man, who was Bonnie's cousin.

"Crown Prince Drostan MacDonald, a pleasure to see you," Henry said. Henry had decided to turn on the charm. He made Drostan smile from ear to ear. Henry extended his hand, which Drostan shook.

"MacInnes, get the Primus' things," Drostan said with a hint of irritation. A vassal retrieved Henry's travel bag from Krueger, who had appeared from the dropship, bags in hand.

"We have a limo waiting for you. You won't need a driver," said Drostan. Henry recognized the signs of a hostage grab, and his reaction would set the tenor for his visit.

"Of course, I have heard of the legendary MacDonald hospitality, but I never expected to be the recipient of such largess. Sergeant, you are at leisure until I return," Henry said. Krueger gave the delegation the evil eye but nodded to Henry. Drostan motioned the gathering to make a space and then motioned a woman about Henry's age to come forward. She wore traditional Sheeplands and islands garb. She wore a bright blue beret on her brown hair with a cream-colored blouse and a voluminous tartan skirt in the same tartan as Drostan.

She bore a bottle of whisky and said, "Welcome to the Isles, Primus."

"Thank you," Henry said accepting the bottle from the shy woman.

"Primus, this is my wife, Crown Princess Caitlin. She comes from the MacQuarries over on the island of Speur-Coisiche," Drostan said. "Unlike our cousins in the south, we value our womenfolk."

"Aye, sir, we welcome this visit. The last time a Primus visited us was forty years ago," Caitlin said. "Your arrival is a momentous occasion." Seeing the crown princess reduced Henry's concerns about the likelihood that the MacDonalds would throw a black hood over his head and toss him in a dungeon.

"Come along, sir," Drostan said, escorting Henry towards the exit. Everyone was on their best behavior. Henry started to relax, which reduced the MacDonald retinue's tension.

"What do you think of the spaceport?" asked Drostan.

"Amazing and beautiful," said Henry. "How old is the facility? This place looks brand new!"

"She's going on five years old now. We renovated the older parts. As heir, my goals are to renovate, rehabilitate, or modernize everything," said Drostan, with a hint of pride.

"Your hard work is paying off. At this rate my father will ask for your help in the Bundstadt," said Henry.

"I have offered, sir," said Drostan. "But the protector has kept the MacDonalds at arms-length." The group moved towards the exit slowly and Henry realized that there was no rush. The islanders would set the pace.

"The war has made the protector busier than my grandfather ever was," said Henry.

"Sir, I'll be frank. My clan, specifically my uncle, did not vote for your father. We supported the losing side. I recognize we are being punished for that," said Drostan.

Henry's face became a frown. Punishing a political rival did not sound like his father's behavior. Whatever misgivings had occurred, Drostan was apparently willing to own them.

"Crown Prince MacDonald," Henry said, using Drostan's formal title, "I do not know what history has occurred between my father and your clan, but I come here with fresh eyes to see where the MacDonalds stand."

Drostan's face was a mix of relief and worry. He said, "Then you are not here in an official capacity to assume a regency or conservatorship?" Henry couldn't help himself and laughed. He regained his composure when Drostan's face grew red.

"I'm sorry, Crown Prince MacDonald. I apologize. I am here as my father's emissary. This is a friendly visit, nothing more. Again, I apologize for my outburst," said Henry.

Drostan continued to grow red, and said, "No apology necessary. I was operating under incorrect information." Drostan glared at some of the retinue. He continued, "The proverb holds true: bad news travels faster than good. I'm discovering that there are some in the Union who would like to sabotage our relationship with the protector. But, this is a friendly visit and that business can wait."

After that statement, Drostan seemed to relax. Henry and the group exited the spaceport to find several vehicles waiting for them. Drostan guided Henry to the foremost vehicle; the hoverlimo bore the Union flag on one side and the Kingdom of the Skye Isles on the other.

"After you, sir," Drostan said opening the door. Henry entered, and Drostan and Caitlin followed. A retainer shut the door and the limo started forward leading the convoy.

"Well, sir, you may not know this, but our chief export is fish. I'm happy to report that our catches have been up this year; we've seen an explosion of cod, mackerel, herring, and haddock. We're careful so set limits and prevent overfishing, though. I want my grandson catching fish in these waters, after all," said Drostan.

"Were these native or variform species?" Henry asked. He had done some digging but most of the scientific records didn't specify whether a species was native to Stahlburgh. MacLeod, being a pirate, had not dedicated time to discovering and classifying the native species.

Drostan beamed in appreciation of the question. "Why? Are you a fisherman?"

"Yes, absolutely. I spent many a summer in creeks and rivers searching for elusive trout and bass. The protector taught me himself," Henry said. Drostan smiled again.

"The protector himself needs to visit. We have the best fishing in the Sheeplands and Isles, and perhaps even on all of Stahlburgh. I caught a sea trout last year that was fifty some centimeters. I donated the monster to our fishing museum," said Drostan.

"Wow, what a size," Henry said. "That sounds like a story."

"Caitlin and my cousin, Beatrix, were with me. The ladies scolded me for taking the fine catch. They catch and release, but I know what luck is. If the Allfather guided that fish on my hook..." said Drostan, but Caitlin scowled at him. There was a moment's pause.

Caitlin broke the pause asking, "Are you a hunter as well? I was under the impression that the protector's family was not interested in such pursuits."

Drostan looked at her with irritation, as if to quiet her.

"Yes, very much so," said Henry. "We donate our meat, so I've never eaten my own kill. However, I did field dress a deer once. A hunting guide is pretty invaluable there."

Drostan smiled and said, "There the ladies have me, I'm not as excited about hunting game as they are. But, Caitlin and I were engaged on a hunting expedition. Her clan have caribou on their island..."

Caitlin interrupted Drostan and said, "Sir, we hunt the caribou for two weeks yearly. The event is a grand celebration as many outside hunters come to help us keep the herds in check."

"Excellent, that sounds like fun and good husbandry," Henry said.

"As a representative of my island, I welcome you and your family and friends to join us, sir," said Caitlin.

"Thank you," Henry said. Drostan smiled at his wife. Henry's apprehension faded; so far things were going outstandingly well.

"What else is there to do? I get the impression you all are quite into the outdoor activities," said Henry.

"If you're up for it, there is hiking and, of course, camping," said Drostan.

"I joined the Assault as a way to keep doing that," Henry said.

"That's right. I had forgotten your and the new protector's military service," Drostan replied. "I am glad you are here, Primus. You give us an opportunity to discover what is true and what is fiction about your dynasty."

"I see that fiction has been beating the truth out of the door," Henry said.

"Aye," replied Drostan. "There haven't been any shortage of fanciful tales about you and your family."

"Perhaps when we get to MacDonald Hall, you'll share them with me over a drop of this whisky," Henry said patting the bottle.

"We call the place, Dunvegan, and that bottle is one of our best, almost as old as settlement on Stahlburgh," Drostan said pausing. Henry worried he had offended the crown prince somehow.

Drostan continued, "I'll probably catch hell, but if you're opening the whisky, I'll share a dram with you." Henry looked on as Caitlin scowled and said nothing. Henry then realized from whom Drostan would "catch hell."

"Are you married, sir?" Caitlin said changing subjects. Henry mused that perhaps Caitlin was looking for someone she could contact in case he and Drostan got out of hand with the whiskey.

"I was hoping to invite your wife to see our home, for next time, sir," Caitlin said, realizing what Henry was thinking.

"No, I'm not married," Henry said, "I went on a date someone recently, but well the date was complicated."

"I've seen that," said Drostan. "My cousin, she's the catch of the Isles. She's had her ups and downs. Who is that fellow she called it quits with recently?"

Caitlin looked embarrassed, like she was tattling on a confidant by saying anything in front of Henry. Drostan just stared at her.

"Frank Nordlinger, she said he was running hot and cold, but that's Uncle's business," Caitlin said, trying to silence her husband.

"You remember my cousin, from the Campbell's celebration of himself." Drostan said.

"I do, poor Alasdair, pity the terrorists got him," Henry said.

"Wait!" Drostan said, "he's dead?"

"Yes, I expected that news would be everywhere by now," Henry replied. The limo wound around the highland mountains that dropped into the ocean. The trip was long, and made longer by the terrain.

"I apologize, Primus, but don't spare us the details. We're an... insular... region, but some things even an islander notes." Henry related the details and watched as his guests grew pale.

"If the details are too much," Henry said, stopping.

"No, Primus," Drostan said, his reserve in place. "Are you really here on a friendly visit? We have always been wary of the protector and his family because of the lack of honesty in their motivations." Henry wondered what had changed with the revelation of Campbell's death.

"Yes, I am an emissary and come here in friendship," Henry said trying to reassure his hosts. Drostan rolled the window up between driver and passengers.

"Primus," said Drostan nervously.

Henry stopped him and said, "Call me Henry."

"Henry," Drostan said, "I swear on my life and the lives of my wife and children. We MacDonalds had nothing to do with Campbell's death. Allfather have mercy on his soul." Henry nodded inwardly; this was a prime piece of intelligence. Henry tucked the information away for later. He was sure his father would debrief him.

"Why did you tell me this?" Henry asked. "I haven't made any accusations. In fact, no one has."

"Henry," Drostan said, with the tone of a drowning man looking for help, "things have been... tense... in the Sheeplands. The Campbell and his allies have raided our lands. The raiders have killed animals and have not even butchered them! Left them to rot! The raiders have spoiled the crops. In some counties there has been privation due to these raids. The MacDonalds do not ask for help, only for understanding."

"Understanding?" Henry asked.

"Since MacLeod's landing, our clan has walked the plains, hills, and mountains of Stahlburgh. We named most things. When others of the Scottish diaspora came here, we welcomed them at first. Even the Campbells, with whom we had our differences in Old Scotland. The Campbells quickly became rapacious; defying agreements and stealing our vassals. How? By putting a family or clan to the sword then outright stealing their food. After all, every high lord knows a starving man is a desperate man and a desperate man will bind themselves in servitude for food. This thieving came to a climax when the Campbells put our distaff cousins, the MacDonalds of New-Glencoe-on-the-sea, to the sword. Then they installed a lackey."

"This was a repeat of history from Old Scotland, sir," Caitlin said. "Something we MacDonalds cannot overlook a second time."

"And now, the Campbell is dead, after he mocked me at his banquet, which is why I swear I had no hand in his death," Drostan said. Henry vaguely remembered the incident. He'd seen men—and a few women—grab pistols or swords for less. At the time, Henry had felt Drostan showed great discipline.

"I remember words being said, but Bonnie certainly didn't yield an inch to Campbell, and you showed great restraint," Henry said. "I had no notion that the MacDonalds would be involved at all. I too have had my share of terrorists shooting in my direction. Unlike Alasdair, I had less able shooters." Drostan again visibly relaxed.

"Speaking of that night, I apologize for coming on so strongly Henry," said Drostan, remembering his actions.

"No need to apologize. I too have asked after a man's desires with an attractive kinswoman," Henry said brushing the incident off. Caitlin looked at her husband with a slight smile. Drostan gave her a husbandly look. The car went quiet, and Henry looked out of the window. A large imposing manor loomed. He had arrived at Dunvegan.

Tavishire Revisited

After the fight with the Terrans the crew needed a few days to make repairs on the *Advantage*. Eventually, the *Advantage* dropped her rings and jumped to Protelan. On Protelan, Jurgen never had a chance to get off the ship, as he was busy directing the Assaultman who ensured the *Advantage's* security in port. Nicholls and Babbington returned from the planet and handed the prize purse over to the captain who threw a gigantic party after the *Advantage* sailed from Svansdocka. Jurgen got drunk, but only after ensuring the man-eating lieutenants were well past their ability to strip him out of his battlesuit. He somehow floated into his bunk and slept like a baby.

After the party, things had returned to the typical shipboard routine. The *Advantage* sailed out past the safety margin in Protelan, and jumped to Holsten Tor. Jurgen still had weeks of sailing ahead of him, but he was back in his home system. His EVIL chimed with more messages. Many were from Jenny, which he'd delete on sight. A few were from Mara, with her standard "I love you, I miss you." Olrich had gone silent. There was one from SERAPH. The subject said:

```
I'm in the jungle deep, and maybe kidnapped.
```

Jurgen opened the message which read:

```
Hello my brave Hero,
I saw your message. I'm here waiting just like
last time. I see your handsome face
```

everywhere. You're a celebrity, even if you don't know that yet. You've eclipsed me, which is fine, as I was never a hero—unlike you. I'm such a fraud. I went out with the Primus, and never felt more like a phony. He's a nice guy. I just don't really have anything in common with him. I don't know why he wanted to go out with me!

I shouldn't talk about the date, but I need you to come rescue me! I'm lost again.

Bye,

Hannah

Jurgen didn't know what to think about this email. He had sudden flashbacks of Johnny Mercy and his poaching of Jenny. Jurgen's feelings came in waves. He wanted to respond to SERAPH and tell her he was there, and then he wanted to tell her he wasn't coming because he she was using him. He stared at the message over and over again during the next few days. He didn't know what to think. Should he write her back? Should he not? If the Primus was dating her, how could he compete with a Cognatii? With a week until Stahlburgh, he vowed to ignore the message and clean out his remaining messages. He was worried about what would happen when he landed.

As he looked at the message list again, one stood out, and Jurgen checked the message's credentials to see if the message were a fake or a hoax. The message's sender was a Douglas Ian MacAlasdair, (GSG, OoSC, OFM (Ret.)) The subject read, "An invitation from an old man."

The message intrigued Jurgen, and he quickly opened the it.

Dear Feldfähnrich Jurgen Wulfjaeger,

Hello. You don't know me personally, but I want to change that. I am Douglas Ian MacAlasdair. Yes, the same one that is in those damn lying history books. First, call me

```
Doug, 'cause that's what the few remaining
friends I have call me. Second, as a once poor
boy from Tavishire I feel a we poor fools need
to meet and stick together. I want to invite
you to the house. We've got lots to talk
about. You'll see you'll have the leave.
Schwartzenrode and I go way back. He'll take
an order from his old CO and follow like the
grand old Assaultman he is. Once you arrive,
you'll stay with me, of course. I'll fill you
in further upon arrival. I hate these damn
machines and would rather have a face-to-face.
See you soon.
Sincerely,
Doug
P.S. Consider this a polite request, but if
you're an orders type—that can be arranged
too!
```

The next message was from Assault High Command giving him two weeks of leave upon the *Advantage's a*rrival. If Doug's message was a fake, the fakers had good timing.

The *Advantage* made planet fall a week later. The night before there had been a send-off as the ship's current orders were ending. Jurgen had said his polite goodbyes to all and promised to correspond. The lieutenants had become sisters of sorts. The change had been subtle, but after the captain regaled her officers with Jurgen's exploits on the *Stellar Anvil,* the navy officers had a deeper appreciation for him.

Instead of leaving with the Assaultmen when they landed, Jurgen had stayed on board to ensure that unloading had gone smoothly. Sternfahrer would be the last person to leave, and she was busy making sure the ship could sail again as soon as the Admiralty cut the *Advantage* new orders. The Navy had leaked the *Advantage's* scrape with the *Formidable* to the press and Sternfahrer had become a minor celebrity. She wasn't perturbed by the situation, though. Her greater fame would mean more officers and enlisted women would seek berths on her ship. Another bit of good news was that the Navy had promoted Sternfahrer and was a *Kapitän, unterer Dienst* or Captain—junior service. Sternfahrer had explained that once an officer made captain—by rank—she was on a list with all of the Navy's captains. As the other captains retired—or died—she'd move up in seniority. That gave her opportunities for better commands, and eventually—provided she survived and didn't quit—she'd be an admiral. Jurgen remembered the bags of wine the two shared at the news. Jurgen watched as the last spacecon was loaded, and the Navy NCOs left the *Advantage.*

"Captain, permission to depart the ship?" Jurgen asked approaching the captain and saluting.

"Granted, Mister Wulfjaeger. Your presence has been a true pleasure, Jurgen. You'll always have a home here, if you get tired of stomping around in the mud."

"Thanks, Joan, I may take you up on that. I've got two years and then I'll need a job. In the meantime, Laser has everything in hand, when you've got new orders. I think he was a little sad to see me go. He said I was lucky since he made so much money on the *Stellar Anvil,*" Jurgen said.

"I suspect when the war's over, he'll go back to his little world a rich and exceedingly happy man," said Sternfahrer.

"I can see him now, shooting the Lapua at anything that crosses his garden. Well, I need to get going. I have to head home and take care of some family business," said Jurgen.

"Best of luck, Jurgen," said Sternfahrer.

"You too, Joan," said Jurgen. He grabbed his things and ran to the main terminal to catch the departing train. He just made the train just before the doors closed; he was on his way to Tavishire.

He went to the conductor to buy a ticket. His bank account had cleared his victory pay. His share of the booty was one thousand four hundred and twenty golden dragons. He was rich, perhaps even rivaling the Mercy clan in money. Jurgen planned to buy a better house for his siblings, but past that, he wasn't sure what to do about the money.

The conductor saw him in his battlesuit and said, "Well, sir, I don't know why you're asking me for a ticket. The protector declared all active-duty military ride free. Since you're in a battlesuit, I'd say that counts as active duty."

Jurgen nodded and thanked the man. Jurgen found a spare compartment. He sat down on the bench and put his head back. Jurgen felt odd sleeping in gravity. He tried to get comfortable but he felt like weights pinned his arms and legs. Somewhere between adjusting to the gravity, staring out the windows, and the setting of the Holstensonne, Jurgen drifted off to dreamland.

"Sir, wake up sir," the conductor said. Jurgen popped up, checking for his duffel and helmet. Both were tucked neatly under him, right where he had left them.

"Sorry, sir," the conductor said, "We're at the end of the line."

Jurgen nodded, thanked the man, and grabbed his things. He marched off the train and saw he was at the end of the line, a village over from Tavishire. Tavishire wasn't on a line, but rather a bus ride away. Jurgen went over to the ticket counter for the bus. Again, he didn't have to pay because he was active duty. He was told the bus would be along "shortly" and that he was welcome to wait. The hour was late, and Jurgen asked the station to call a cab. While he waited for the hovercab, he wrote a short note to MacAllisdair. Doug had known he was coming, but Jurgen gave him fair warning. Doug's response was succinct, "Come in upon arrival."

The taxi approached and the driver honked his horn. Jurgen approached. The cabbie opened the trunk and passenger compartment. Jurgen stowed his duffel but held on to his helmet. The cabbie nodded, got out to shut the trunk and door.

"Where to gov'nor?" the cabbie asked.

"MacAllisdair estate," Jurgen said.

"You a relation," the cabbie asked putting the taxi into drive. The fans on the hover vehicle whined in the background.

"A brother of sorts," said Jurgen. The cabbie looked at Jurgen through his rear-view mirror, suddenly realizing who was in the cab.

"Oi! You're the Lion of Lalande!" the cabbie exclaimed. "Wow! A bona fide war hero in my cab!"

"I just did my duty," Jurgen said, feeling a little uncomfortable.

"Can I get a picture? I'll wave the fare! The missus won't believe this!"

In an earlier day, Jurgen wouldn't have blinked at trading a picture with the cabbie for the fare—which in his youth would have been a luxurious expense. He weighed his options.

"I'll still pay the fare, but sure, you can have a picture. Did you serve?" asked Jurgen.

"No, sir," said the cabbie. "I had a bad leg after conscription. Damn duke worked us to the bone and I got injured."

Minutes later the cab floated into a giant demesne. The gates were open and waiting. The cab wound through ornate gardens following the concrete path up to the large estate house. Jurgen couldn't make out the details, but the house looked spooky and deserted at this late hour.

"Are you sure you want to pay the fare?" The cabbie asked. The fare was one griffin and thirty pfennigs. Jurgen nodded, throwing the man a five-griffin coin.

"Keep the change. Now, you want a photo?" asked Jurgen.

"Thanks! Sure!" said the cabbie, providing a full-service experience by getting out, opening Jurgen's door, getting his duffel, and ensuring Wulfjaeger had all his things. The cabbie posed with Jurgen and snapped a half dozen photos most with flash. Jurgen waited as the cabbie got back into the taxi and drove off. Darkness consumed the front garden, and Jurgen's night vision slowly returned. He looked for and found the main door. However, as he approached the entrance, he saw a small sign that said, "Broken. Go to side door" with an arrow pointing to the left side of the house. Jurgen followed the broken concrete path around the house. In the darkness Jurgen couldn't tell the house's condition, but the path and gardens looked like they had seen better days.

Jurgen followed the broken path. Rising above, Eisenwald came over the horizon bathing the landscape in its reflected light. Jurgen looked out and saw a pasture with sheep down the hill below. A chicken coop sat down there too. A dog's lonely bark rang out. Jurgen walked a few more meters and came to a small servant's door. He touched the handle and the door opened.

"Hello!" Jurgen shouted. A dog's bark echoed through the building and a large white Great Pyrenees came bounding toward him and knocked him down. At first, the dog barked, but after smelling Jurgen's battlesuit, it opted for licking Jurgen's face.

"Ignatius, heel!" a voice said. The dog immediately stopped licking Jurgen and went to his owner's side. An old man with shaggy hair and a grizzled beard stood there holding an ancient slug thrower. The man wore a ratty green jumpsuit.

"Subaltern Wulfjaeger?!" the man said in a half command half question.

Jurgen reacted on instinct. He snapped to attention and said, "Aye, aye, sir!"

"At ease! I'm Doug, and this here is Ignatius, or Iggy, when he ain't licking strangers," Doug said. "Welcome to my crumbling estate. We're past taps. I'll show you your bunk and we'll talk at reveille. Let's move out." Jurgen picked up his duffel and helmet and eyed the Pyrenees, who remained at the old man's side. Doug didn't talk as he led Jurgen around the kitchen, where Jurgen had entered, down a long hall that was built for entertaining, and into a very open conservatory that had two separate staircases up to the second floor.

"Remember, Subaltern, always the right stairs, never the left," Doug said, offering no official reason.

"Why's that field marshal?" asked Jurgen.

"No! No! No! Name is Doug. I ain't a field marshal anymore," grumped Doug. "Curiosity, now that's a good trait for an officer. The left stairs are busted. You walk up 'em, the staircase is likely to collapse."

"Yes, er, Doug," Jurgen said as he climbed the right set of stairs.

"Adaptability, another good trait. Karl's pup is doing pretty well based on his baby officers," Doug said. They wandered across the platform to which the two staircases attached and down another corridor. This one had photos. Many of Doug and a woman Doug didn't mention. Jurgen assumed the woman was Doug's wife. There were also two boys. Doug stopped at one photo. "This here is Ian. He's gone: he died over one of those science fiction writer worlds. Assaultman to the core, I miss him. He had a son. I never see the boy anymore; he's named Doug too. Little Doug is on Lochiel with his mother, who remarried."

Jurgen looked at the photo; the man looked as old as Jurgen was. There was another photo next to Ian's.

"Who is this one, sir?" Jurgen asked.

"Ain't a sir, no more, just Doug," said Doug. "That's Rob. He's a meathead. Lives on Hansaburgh with his live-in something or another —not wife. Doesn't call, doesn't write. He and I had a fight and I cut him out of the will."

"Sorry sir—err, Doug," said Jurgen.

"Forget about him," said Doug. "Here's your room. The barracks is dusty, but the blankets are clean and the bed still stands. If you get cold, use that fancy suit. I doubt that will happen. If you want, Iggy can stay with you too for warmth."

"I couldn't do that to you... Doug," said Jurgen. "I'll manage."

"Good, I'd hate to find out the Assault went soft on me after I quit," Doug said. "Goodnight, subaltern," said Doug. "Breakfast is zero eight hundred sharp — an hour past reveille."

Jurgen entered the room. Doug wasn't kidding on the dust. But after a few minutes of fighting with a stuck window, Jurgen got fresh air into the room. He fluffed the sheets and looked at the bed. While it wasn't his bunk on the *Advantage,* the bed wasn't the straw sack he slept on as a child. He pulled off his battlesuit and stacked the suit on an armchair in the room. He pulled off his suit's under layer and laid out clothes for the next day. He opted for a sweater and some bib overalls with his ankle boots. He crawled into the bed and fell asleep.

Jurgen awoke to the cock crowing. He checked his EVIL's chronometer. The time read zero six twenty, ten minutes before his alarm. He rose, did some calisthenics, and got dressed. He arrived in the kitchen at ten until eight.

"Perfect timing, subaltern," Doug said as he rummaged through his refrigerator. There was an honest to goodness cast iron pan on the gas stove. In the pan were four eggs and a half dozen slabs of ham. The eggs and ham smelled heavenly, and even better, breakfast wasn't served in a bag with a straw.

"Thank you, s... Doug," Jurgen said.

"Careful, almost slipped up and called me, sir," said Doug. "How you want your two eggs?"

"Sunny side up," Jurgen said. Doug smiled.

"Straight up Assault style. How many eggs you eat as a boy? I bet you got them on Sunday," Doug said.

"No, Doug," said Jurgen.

"Figures. I seen your mom out selling those eggs, I guessed you never got any..."

"Doug, um, why did you ask me here? We aren't kin, or clan."

"We're more kin than you think. For one, we got the blood of our brothers running in our veins. Oh yeah, I heard about you being a few liters short of full. Welcome to the club; so was I," said Doug.

"Thanks, Doug," said Jurgen.

"Then, there is Tavishire. I grew up here. When I was out fighting with Karl I couldn't wait to get back here. We won our war and I came here to rest my bones. I'll be buried in the large churchyard, until the Messiah comes and hauls my old bones out of the grave," said Doug.

"So what? Lots of folks come from here," said Jurgen.

"True, how many of them won a GSG?" Doug said. Jurgen didn't respond and Doug said, "Ah, exactly. Plus, now you got my GSG, which makes you my project."

Jurgen thought about that statement.

"I can smell the smoke, caught your imagination, eh," said Doug. He flipped an egg out of the pan and the Pyrenees, Iggy, caught the egg as the morsel tumbled towards him.

"Why?" Jurgen asked.

"Ain't got a son to give that GSG to. The one real grandkid doesn't know me, and why not? I liked the story about you in the Sheeplands Gazette," said Doug.

"The story is fiction mostly," said Jurgen.

"Yep, but a good story... The Union needs its stories. We need our heroes. What do you know about me, for instance?"

"You were a field marshal, a master tactician, who maneuvered his enemies into a big canyon at the Battle of the Landing, and got Schwartzenrode to climb the obsidian cliffs to form a pincer on the old tyrants. All the while watching the battle with Karl."

"Wow, that's great, who is playing me in the movie? Hopefully it won't be that wimp Lukas Stahl!? That kid looks like a puffed-up marshmallow," said Doug.

"The story is that much fiction?" asked Jurgen, surprised.

"Well, if I dig at the tale, I can get the truth out of the story. I really don't remember all the details on the Battle of the Landing. We landed, thanks to Alaric, who timed his rebellion just right. Al was like a Swiss clock. The doors opened on the dropships and Karl was off, way too fast for a space emperor. One good sniper and old Karl would have met Malcolm and Jesus that day."

Jurgen looked surprised.

Doug saw the look and continued, "Yeah. People these days forget Karl was an emperor once. He was an emperor when they were in vogue. Karl gave that title up for the Union, but if you go to Hansaburgh they call him *Kaiser* still. Anyhow, Karl runs off with the First Regiment. He loved those boys, and they would have followed that old man to hell and back. The Second was just the Second then, not Line Guards. They go charging after Karl. I'm in direct command of the Third, and I am supposed to be the supreme commander, so I do the only thing I can do, and run after Karl. Alaric Campbell was in command of the fourth and he stays put where the dropships landed — which was fine since he was guarding the ships. Bob, that's what we called Rob MacDonald, commander of the Fifth. Old Bob looks at me, not sure what to do, and I yell 'Charge!' and point to Karl. The rest of the regiments take off then. How's that for strategic genius?"

"You all fell out like the Navy on shore leave?" said Jurgen.

"Pretty much. Schwartzenrode along the way gets this wild hair to climb the cliffs and go around the back. Karl is on the radio goading him on. Old Adolphus was just a stupid kid then. Schwartzenrode then says to his men in the Ninth, 'Who here thinks they are a hero? Cause only heroes will dare follow me today!' I'm like, 'Addie are you drinking again?' 'cause what he said was so stupid. But, what the heck, the dang speech worked!"

"Then, they climbed the mountain?" asked Jurgen.

"Yup, but what they don't tell you is the Addie lost half his men on the cliffs. Those boys fell, and the few that didn't get cut to pieces were pretty messed up. No statues to them though."

Jurgen remained quiet. He thought of Laakso, Hertzog, Bruckner, Hot Dog, Metal, and dozens of others.

"Yeah, I can see you know how that is," said Doug. "Anyway, Addie and his crew make their way across the worst part of those cliffs and start shooting the old tyrants, which messed with those devils' world. Those maniacs had put up an effective screen that our ladies in the Navy were having a hell of a time trying to break. The old devils' screen was so dangerous, our regiments barely made planetfall in the dropships. Bless the pilots, those gals were so dang busy keeping us alive and getting us to the ground. A lot of them bought the farm going back up."

"What happened then?" Jurgen asked.

"The tyrants panicked. The dictators killed a general or two in their army. Then the regulars went on strike on the battlefield. Karl marches in and strings up anyone with more acorns than a captain, and the rest is history. Except for Karl gave a ton of pensions, gave Schwartzenrode a fancy title and me the GSG plus *Freiherr*, even though for half the fight I'm trying to manage my boys, get them to wipe their butts and fire at the enemy, instead of each other. Sound like something you've seen?" asked Doug.

"Pretty close," said Jurgen.

"Well, now we come to the best part. Here are your eggs and fried ham," Doug said, spooning out the meal on a plate. Doug made a quick cross and then ate. Jurgen followed suit. Both men ate the breakfast in silence. Iggy whined and sat waiting for the other half of his breakfast. When Doug was finished, he tossed some ham to the dog who gulped the pieces down in mid air.

"Thanks for breakfast, Doug," said Jurgen, standing.

"Not so fast, I know what you're going to say next. Sit down, I'm an old man and need to warm up to my proposal," said Doug. Jurgen sat down, and waited.

"Who's got your back, boy?" asked Doug.

"What do you mean, Doug?" asked Jurgen.

"In the Assault, you got friends in high places?" asked Doug.

"No, Doug, other than maybe Captain Nordlinger," said Jurgen.

"Captain ain't going to do you no good," Doug said. "Sounds just like I figured. Do you got your skull work down?"

"Yes, Doug, I had the surgeon on the *Advantage* help me," Jurgen said.

"Well, that's good. You're smart enough to ask for help. I'll give you some backup from on high. Addie owes me a favor or two, and there might be a pup or two who has some laurels I can call on if you run into a scrape," Doug said. "After all, a good officer needs to break the rules from time to time, and a legendary officer has to be able to get away with his rule breaking. I been reading the papers. Meagher shouldn't be called 'Fighting Mad' he should be called 'Mess Making Meagher.' The Union is going to need officers with moxy."

"Okay but what's my end of the deal," said Jurgen.

"I need someone to keep this place from falling down on me. I seen you and your little brothers and sisters out floating around. I watched your fights, even put a bet or two on 'em. I can see that demonic mud pit from my library on a good day."

"Huh, okay," Jurgen said, never knowing he had a secret fan. "What's the catch about my siblings helping you?"

"I want 'em to live here," Doug said. "I'm an old man, and the room and board would be their wage. There are some in the village who would think I've got other designs on them. If I was twenty years younger, I'd probably put someone in the ground that would even whisper that. But as I am a bag of bones and well over one hundred, they're going to wag their tongues... if you accept."

"Why? What about your kin? Why not ask them?" said Jurgen.

"Ain't happening. Little Doug gets the place provided he's seventeen. Otherwise meathead and his whatever-not-wife can make a play for the place. I got a capital lawyer that says they ain't getting a pfennig. Now, Little Doug is still in short pants with mom and step-dad on Lochiel, but this place needs new blood or will fall apart. I aim to sort of 'adopt' you and your kin, like I should have a long time ago. With your kin here, you can save the Union's rear end. I'll make sure your little brothers and sisters are with their real..." Doug trailed off. Jurgen wondered if there was another story, one he was missing.

"I'm still not following. Why do you want them here?" asked Jurgen. Doug took a deep breath, Jurgen wasn't sure why the old field marshal was holding back.

"I been watching you for a while. And while I said got one good son and one bad son, I actually lied. I had two good and two bad," said Doug.

"What are you talking about?"

"The story is long. Who you named after?" Doug asked.

"My uncle, Jurgen," said Jurgen. Doug got up and wandered off for a moment before returning with another photo. This one was of a young man, who looked almost exactly like Jurgen.

"There he is, your uncle, my youngest boy," Doug said a tear coming down his cheek.

"Wait, how's this possible?" Jurgen asked. He never had met his paternal grandparents or heard anything about them. All Jurgen knew about his grandparents was that his maternal grandfather was the poor village reverend who baptized him.

Doug produced another picture; this one was of a beautiful woman. She had golden blond hair, the same color as Jurgen's, and she wore a white blouse and long calico skirt, which covered her feet.

"Jemima Wulfjaeger, she was some from backwater shire on Hansaburgh. She and I fell in love," said Doug. Jurgen just looked strangely at the old man.

"Back in the day, I was a big deal, and of course, like a wild stallion I had gotten married. Unfortunately, that one was a nag. Well, you know how that goes, you can't get divorced. The nag spent all my money on this estate and herself. Then, she up and moved out to a place in the capital. I was happy to be rid of her. We stayed that way, divorced in all but name until she died almost twenty years ago," Doug took a pause to breathe and keep control on his emotions.

"Well after the nag left, I met this fine little filly named Jemima. She came here to be a maid. I never had a wrong design on her. She cooked, she cleaned, and one night she ended up in my bed and there she stayed. We had your pop and his brother, your uncle. My poor filly died with our third, who would have been your aunt," said Doug, pausing as tears rose in his eyes.

"I, of course, had this other family. After Jemima died, Ian and meathead, who were teenagers, started craving a father and wanted to come back and live with me. Ian came home first. A spell later then came Rob, the meathead. Ian pretty much figured out the two boys that were here belonged to Jemima and me. Rob, the meathead, took longer to put two and two together. When Rob finally figured it out, he started lording his status over on your dad and uncle. How he and Ian were my 'real' sons. Four boys in a house without a woman is not the best of worlds. Ian was hurt by meathead's comments. I guess Ian felt I had thrown him and Rob away. Your dad and your uncle, on the other hand, felt like they were second best," said Doug.

"Wait, what about the village? Did anyone else know?" Jurgen asked.

"You know how that is, son," Doug said. "Can't keep a secret in the village. All the head men knew. Mercy, MacTavish, Thackeray, even old Bauerhof, and of course the Reverend McFadden knew. Only time the reverend said anything was on Sunday when he'd call down fire and brimstone on me from the pulpit. Every sermon he had was on adultery. But we'll come back to him shortly." Jurgen nodded. He still couldn't think of the field marshal from his history lessons as his paternal grandfather.

"One by one, they all moved out. First Ian, who ran off and joined the Assault. He was like a prize goose to that recruiting sergeant. The great officer's son. Ian made the cut first chance and was off to the

Academy, but he died just the same in Tau Ceti. Probably doing something heroic, I never looked how he fell, all these decades later his death is still too painful. After Ian, your father and uncle moved out. Both got conscripted by *Graf* Bauerhof but did well too. The old count didn't work them like dogs and they weren't loafers. Anyway Rob, the meathead, got bored or tired of me and ran off to momma, and has stayed away ever since. Mission accomplished, he made my life miserable," said Doug.

"My dad and uncle?" Jurgen asked.

"Got done with their tax time and roamed the shire. Eventually, Jurgen gets a hankering to join up with his half-brother, Ian, and runs off. Did just that, ended up just as dead too, but saved a whole mess of Assaultmen's lives in the process. You might hear about his exploits. He wasn't a GSG, as he died and we don't usually award GSGs to dead enlisted. Call that a crime, but that was never how Karl wanted to give awards," said Doug, taking a moment to compose himself. "Then there was your father. He had been working on Mercy's farm, doing well. Mercy had come back from the Sheeplands with his beautiful bride, but somehow your father, Magnus, fell out with her. I suspect because Magnus was dating McFadden's daughter."

"My mother," Jurgen said, filling in the pieces.

"Yup, Peggy, old Mercy's wife, was a queen bee. She didn't tolerate a whole lot of female shenanigans from the help's women. Where your mother was a preacher's daughter and practically looking for help from the devil to get even with her father. This is all just this old man's opinion, but I think your mother drove Magnus to the bottle and your family to ruin. I built their cottage — the one you all lived in — for my son, Magnus. I gave him what I could, but your momma, well..."

Jurgen nodded and then said, "Should I call you grandfather now?"

Doug shook his head, "You can't really, as no one would accept you. Those that know the history won't like you're father's illegitimacy, those that don't will think you're up to no good with me.

Just call me Doug. I'll call you subaltern or, if you want, Jurgen."

"Jurgen is fine, Doug."

"Listen, I made lots of mistakes in my life, but never with an officer's hat on. I want you to succeed, and by the look of things, this war is going to need officers who stop listening to men who won't lead from the front. I intend, in my unlimited golden years, to make sure I can squeeze out one last drop of my blood for the Union! You, my unrecognized grandson, are that AB+ blood drop."

Jurgen smiled, noting that Doug had the same blood type. Things grew quiet, except for Iggy's snoring.

"I can smell the smoke. What are you thinking about, Jurgen," Doug said.

"Life, how strange it all is," said Jurgen.

"Well, get your class A's on. We're going to pay momma a visit and then we'll bring the family home," said Doug.

"Why class A's?" Jurgen asked.

"That is the uniform of the day, for respectability. You go change. I'll be right with you after I make a few calls," said Doug. Jurgen went up to his room and changed into his Prussian blue class A uniform. He buttoned the jacket and adorned the uniform with the Golden Segreant Griffin. The mythological beast's dull yellow color contrasted against the deep blue, almost black, color of his jacket.

The award landed over his heart. Jurgen realized the GSG wasn't just a famous war hero's medal, the GSG was his grandfather's award. He went down to the kitchen. Iggy was still sleeping and Doug stood by the door waiting.

"You look good, Subaltern, real respectable. Now, let's roll," Doug said. He and Jurgen left the kitchen and Doug led them to a beat-up old outbuilding. Inside was an equally beat up hovertruck.

"Doug, is this truck roadworthy?" Jurgen asked.

"This truck is a twenty five, best year Campbell's Carriages ever made!" Doug said climbing into the truck. Jurgen climbed into the passenger side. Doug turned on the ignition and engaged the fans. The truck lifted up, even though the fans were making light scraping sounds.

"Something is scraping," Jurgen said.

"I got a fix for that," Doug said as he turned on the radio and used the music to cover the sound. Doug put the truck into drive and they left through the back side of the estate down the hill and into the village. The truck floated through the vehicle paths, curving around the main square with its boxing ring, and out towards the track that ran parallel to Jurgen's house's footpath. Doug stopped the truck, and climbed out. Jurgen followed suit, noticing three other pulling up behind Doug's hovertruck. One he knew from his fighting days.

"Jurgen, my boy!" said Baron MacTavish. "What a pleasure to see you! Feel like going a round or two in the pit after this? I've made some mighty large bets and would love to have your knuckles deliver on them."

"No, thank you, baron. My boxing days are over," Jurgen said.

"I understand. After you've graduated to Assaultman, I am sure the thrill of bare-knuckle boxing is tame in comparison," said MacTavish. Jurgen smiled and nodded, his officer cap bobbing up and down on his head.

The next person to leave their truck was the count, a younger man. The old count had conscripted Jurgen, the new one was a complete mystery to Wulfjaeger.

"Hello, Barons MacTavish, MacAllisdair, and Mister Wulfjaeger," the count said. Jurgen nodded politely, amused to be given a "Mister Wulfjaeger" from the noble. Before the Assault, the count would have probably not even noticed him. The final truck's doors opened, and John and Johnny Mercy exited.

"Why are we dealing with these peasants, father?" Johnny asked in a snide manner.

"I'm not dealing with peasants. I am here for the field marshal. He's called in his markers," John said.

"That crazy old man?" Johnny said. Jurgen must have straightened at the comment and caught Johnny's eye. "And him, the woodland trash!"

"Be quiet!" John the elder said. If Jurgen could have become invisible, he would have raced over to Johnny and renewed his bare knuckle brawling pro-bono.

"Thank you for coming," Doug said. "You all know the law. When someone makes an endangerment claim, the local noble or magistrate must be present along with three elders of the village. Subaltern Wulfjaeger is here for his siblings. He is full blood kin to all of them, and he will be their guardian until they reach their majority at seventeen."

The count nodded and said, "Exactly. Mister Wulfjaeger, are you fully prepared to attend to their needs? An Assaultman's salary is not... financially flexible... enough to take on minors."

"Yes, your grace," Jurgen said.

"He's lying," Johnny said petulantly. Jurgen and Johnny had a fight over two years ago, but Jurgen thought the man would have been over that by now.

"Oh, really," the count asked.

"Johnny, what are you doing?" the older Mercy asked angrily.

"This peasant doesn't know his place, father," Johnny said. The older Mercy looked at the two barons and the count in a way that showed he had washed his hands of this affair.

"Can you elaborate on that, Mister Mercy?" the count asked.

"This poor piece of woodland trash doesn't have a griffin to his name. I don't know what game he is playing here, but he should have stayed gone," Johnny said.

Jurgen moved to the count's side, and said, "If Johnny doesn't think I have any money, he can claim the coins in my pockets; provided he is willing to face me. I have a right to face my accuser, right, sir?"

The count nodded, understanding the rivalry between the men, and said, "Yes, Mister Mercy. I think what Mister Wulfjaeger is asking is fair."

Mercy hesitated, looking at his father who made a sweep with his head as if to motion the young man towards the count. MacTavish smiled with relish at what he knew was coming next, while Doug watched on silently.

As Mercy approached, Jurgen put his fist in his pocket and pulled out the coins. The handful of gold, silver, and bronze coins came tumbling out of his pocket and spilled on the ground.

"If Mercy wants, he can count the coins afterwards," Jurgen said, "and my apologies, sir."

"Apologies for..." the count began, but Jurgen did a half step and cold cocked the younger Mercy. The short quick punch sent the younger Mercy to the ground.

"Did the thought ever occur to you to shut up and mind your own business, little Johnny?" Doug said. Doug looked at the older Mercy who watched impassively, not willing to make this his fight. Johnny sat on the ground dazed, around him were a dozen gold dragons, more money than the village saw on a market day.

"That's settled. Does anyone else have a concern about Mister Wulfjaeger?" asked the count. None of the other men uttered a word. "Let's approach the house," said the count. Jurgen approached the gate first. His mother and four of his siblings stood watching. Mara broke free from her mother's grasp and shouted, "Jurgen, Jurgen!" She ran and embraced her brother, crying.

"Hello, scamp," Jurgen said, hugging her. "I'm here to take you home."

"No, you won't," said his mother. "These are my children. You can't." She stopped speaking when she saw Doug. She grew afraid.

"Mother, you may live in this house until you are dust, but I am taking my family with me," Jurgen said.

"He put you up to this, that devil!" said Jurgen's mother pointing at Doug.

"Interesting choice of words there, Cassie," Doug said, using Jurgen's mother's nickname. "Did you worry about Ol' Scratch as you watched your husband drink himself to death? How about fifteen years ago when you all starved and had to go to the next county to eat, because you and daddy didn't see eye to eye?"

"He's a vile adulterer!" Cassandra said. "You can't let him take my children; They are mine!"

"Wait," Jurgen said, "Where is Olrich?"

"He's gone," said Mara. "He ran off chasing after you, after she lost your dragon."

Mara's look was pure spite at her mother. Jurgen put a hand on the thirteen-year old's shoulder. Frederick, Duncan, and Agatha, all slowly moved from their mother's side and crowded around their oldest brother, hugging him.

Jurgen stared at his mother and said, "He was sixteen, too young to leave."

"He wanted to be as useless as you and become a killer like him!" Cassandra said pointing to Doug.

"Now, now, Cassie," said MacTavish. "Go inside, this will be easier for you if you just let the proceedings happen."

"You too, William? I thought we were kinfolk?" Cassandra said. The MacTavishes and the McFaddens were kin back in the time of the shire's founding.

"All the grounds being established, I wish to ask the children what they think is best," the count said. Doug looked irritated. Jurgen nodded, while old Mercy and MacTavish tried to look impartial.

"Miss, you are?" the count asked.

"Mara," Jurgen's oldest sister said.

"Miss Mara, whom do you want to live with, your brother or mother?" the count asked.

Mara didn't even blink, "Jurgen, he's the better choice."

The count nodded and asked Freddy, who was eleven, the same question.

Freddy said, "With Jurgen, sir. He never beat us."

The count again nodded and asked Duncan the same question.

The nine-year-old responded, "With my brother, when he lived with us, we always had food." Finally, the count turned to Agatha, and asked her.

The seven-year-old looked between her mother and Jurgen, but said, "I want to go with Mara. She combs my hair and helps me bathe." Cassandra turned red in fury.

"You can't take them! Who will do the laundry? Who will sweep the house?"

"Woman, you could have had a brand-new house with all the conveniences with the money you wasted," Jurgen said. "We're done."

The count nodded and said, "Frau Cassandra Wulfjaeger, I hereby emancipate your children. If you truly want them back, you can earn them back. Otherwise, they are free to live with whomever they choose."

"Attested," Doug said.

"Attested," repeated MacTavish. Both old men looked at Mercy who nodded and said, "Attested."

"With the witnessing of three parties, this emancipation is completed. Good day," the count said leaving the side garden of Jurgen's former house. Jurgen turned and followed the count out passing by Doug, MacTavish, and Mercy. Mara and the others followed along, Jurgen led them past Johnny Mercy who still sat on the ground. Duncan and Freddy, like the poor boys they were, saw the coins and ran to scoop them up.

"Get in the truck," Jurgen said, and the children climbed into the bed. Jurgen doubted anyone would complain, even though the bed was not the safest of spots.

Doug moved towards the truck and the elder John Mercy said, "We're even now, MacAllisdair."

"Fine," Doug said climbing in the vehicle.

Jurgen moved to the other side. As he opened the door, MacTavish shouted, "I didn't expect to see you in action, Wulfjaeger! If I had known you were swinging, I'd have laid some money down!"

Jurgen climbed in and hung his head out saying, "I hope you live long enough to see the next one, baron!" MacTavish roared and clapped. Jurgen pulled his head back into the truck and Doug started the vehicle, engaged the fans, and drove off. They rolled into town again, and Doug stopped at the little general store and grocery.

"Why are we stopping again," Jurgen asked.

"Your brood will eat up my rations in a day. We need to lay in supplies," Doug said. "Something a good officer is keenly aware of."

"Aye, aye, Doug," Jurgen said, stepping out from the truck. His siblings piled out amazed at the thought of entering the grocery store to buy more than a singular milk carton.

"You're paying since you can fling enough gold around to tempt even a saint," Doug said with a grim smile.

"I can afford the food," Jurgen said.

"Cause of Lalande? If that's the case I might just re-up. Raimond pays way better than his father," Doug said.

"No, I berthed as a marine," Jurgen said.

"Say no more, you got yourself a lucky ship and a lucky cap'n," Doug half said and half asked.

"Yup, Sternfahrer on the *Advantage*," Jurgen said grabbing a shopping cart for their food and entering the store.

"Signe Bosdottir's middie? Wonders never cease," Doug said. Jurgen was about to push the trolley forward when his eyes scanned the lines to pay. Ten meters in front of him was Jenny and she was headed his way.

Jenny walked right up to him and said, "If you kiss me now and carry me away, all is forgiven."

Jurgen just looked at her. Her light brown hair was greasy. She reeked of tobacco and looked like a million kilometers of bad road. Jurgen suddenly wondered what he had ever seen in the woman in the first place. She might have been the pick of the village in days past, but the Holstensonne had definitely set on that time.

"I think you made your bed, Jenny," Jurgen said, trying to move forward, and on.

"Wait," Jenny said, "that came out a little harsh, let me try again..."

"No, you're married to Johnny. I wish you two a long life together," Jurgen said.

"Um, he's not as exciting as you were," Jenny said.

"Get used to less, I suppose," Jurgen said.

"Look, I made a mistake. Can't you just forgive me and take me back?" Jenny asked.

"Marriage doesn't work that way, Jenny," Jurgen said. "I am not risking my soul over someone who ran off on me once."

"You know, you were never that great to begin with!" said Jenny angry and hurt.

"Then, why do you want me back now," asked Jurgen, "because of the uniform? The officer boards? Or the news services trumpeting my name?"

Jenny became furious and said, "You are woodland trash and will never be anything more than that. Jurgen Wulfjaeger!" She turned and stormed off, forgetting her groceries.

"I can see we need to work on your relationships with women," Doug said. "Your mother and an ex-girlfriend in the same day. I don't feel so terrible about my own female relationships anymore." Jurgen stared at the old man, and then Doug began to laugh. After a moment, Jurgen smiled.

"I guess my ability with women runs in the family," Jurgen said, which made Doug laugh even harder.

"What does that mean?" Mara said eying both men.

"Where are your brothers and sister?" Jurgen asked. Freddy, Duncan, and Agatha appeared just then, arms full of every candy they never had been allowed to have.

"We're rich, we can afford candy," Freddy said fishing the golden dragons from his pocket. Jurgen smiled, his younger siblings never seemed happier.

"Are you going to tell me? Or do I have to punch you? You never duck, so I am pretty sure I can take you," Mara said with a mischievous grin.

"Douglas Ian MacAllisdair, meet Mara Wulfjaeger, also known as Scamp. Scamp, meet your grandfather," Jurgen said. Mara just stood there with an odd look on her face. Freddy was checking out candy bars on the self-checkout, and Duncan was racing back to the candy aisle and returning with arms full of more treats. Agatha had chocolate over her mouth and sat plucking bar after bar out of the paid pile.

"They are all riding in the bed," Doug said, "at the rate they are going, I expect them to start throwing up any time now."

Jurgen, with some gentle coaching from Doug, was able to rally his siblings, get them to bag the purchased candy, and force Duncan to put back the rest of the sweets. Jurgen and Doug went aisle by aisle in the little store and collected the staples needed to feed everyone for a few days. Freddy and Duncan surrendered the money they had collected with a solemn oath from Jurgen that he would hold "their" money in trust. Jurgen suspected "their" money was to be spent on sugary drinks, ice cream, and treats. Agatha had stuffed herself, and with the Mara's eagle eye, arrived in the ladies' rest room in the nick of time. By the time the girls had finished, Jurgen and Doug were ready to pack up and move out.

The boys helped load the truck. Mara and Agatha sat in the cab, while Jurgen decided to ride in the bed. The trip to the estate was uneventful, and Jurgen had the joy of hearing his brothers ooh and ahh at the sight of the estate. In the daylight, the manor and grounds didn't look nearly as worn down, or in need of coats of paint. In the noonday Holstensonne, the move seemed doable. Doug had begun a running conversation with Mara along the way and seemed to be holding his own. As the truck touched down at the kitchen door, Jurgen was ready to be on firm ground.

"Why don't you have a wife?" Mara asked.

"She's gone," Doug said climbing out.

"You could get another one," Agatha said.

"Not on my dance card," Doug said.

"Why not?" Agatha asked.

"I'm too old and tough," Doug said.

"You sound like a bad hot dog," Agatha said.

"That's exactly what I am," Doug said with a chuckle.

"No, you're not!" Agatha said, "You're like Santa Claus!" Doug looked at Jurgen with an expression that was a mix of joy and terror.

"I never had any girls," Doug said. "I need you to watch my six!"

"You're doing fine, Doug," Jurgen said. Then to his siblings, Jurgen said, "Okay, unload!" The children got out and began to unload the bags and bags of food. In all his life, he had never seen his siblings so happy. Even Agatha didn't mention Cassandra, not even once. Iggy made a racket at the sound of the truck.

"You have a dog?!?" the boys asked. Doug nodded, moving to open the door. Ignatius bounded out and barked at the boys who giggled in delight. Jurgen could remember the endless asking for a dog, only to be told they couldn't afford one. Iggy quickly adapted to the new human puppies and found the boys had a particular skill at scratching all the hard-to-reach spots.

After the unloading and storing of groceries, Doug took the children on a tour of the house with Iggy in tow. Freddy and Duncan began by asking where they would sleep, while Agatha and Mara would ask "Who's that?" at every picture they passed. Jurgen ducked out to change into his casuals that he had put on that morning. Fully clothed, he put his EVIL on and checked the device. It showed only a message from SERAPH. The subject said, "Are you here yet?"

```
To my hero,
I know I've seemed really odd. I made a
decision; I am breaking off whatever I have
with the Primus. He's a nice guy, but his life
isn't for me. We were supposed to go to the
opera, but if you're available, I would like
to take you instead. I owe you after all, and
well… I keep thinking about you.
I understand if you aren't interested.
Sincerely,
Hannah
```

Jurgen wasn't sure what to do and decided to consult with Doug. Jurgen realized he was in brand new territory with his siblings, with Doug, and with Hannah. Doug had stepped into the role of surrogate father, or at the least, a kind mentor. Jurgen appreciated the guidance.

He went down to the kitchen to see Mara scrubbing, Agatha chopping vegetables, and Freddy and Duncan peeling potatoes. In the center of the kitchen, Doug seasoned steaks and sang old Assault marching songs.

"Putting them all to work, I see?" Jurgen said as he appeared.

"They volunteered, like good Assaultmen," Doug said defensively.

"This place is filthy," Mara said, happily washing the wall's baseboard.

"He's feeding us steak and chips!" the boys said.

"We're having a salad too, like rich people," Agatha responded. Jurgen remembered that leafy greens weren't always on the menu. Jurgen resolved to focus on his siblings for the moment.

"What does that paper say, Frederick?" Doug asked as the boy pulled out the local free paper from the shopping bag with the remaining potatoes.

"Peer of the Union killed," Freddy read with hesitation.

"Poor bugger, what was his name," Doug asked.

"Alasdair Campbell," Freddy said. Then, he read a few more lines of the article.

"Alaric's pup," Doug said, "Old Al, he was a real honest pleasure. Al mixed things up with highborn and commoner alike. He was as close as I got to a friend, other than Addie, who was like a little brother to me."

"And Alasdair?" asked Jurgen.

"Couldn't stand him. He was like his mother, a conniving weasel. Alasdair's mum was the nag's best friend, probably convinced her to leave Tavishire," Doug said. Freddy held up the paper looking for the cartoons.

"Whoa, Frederick, what's that article on the back say?" Doug asked.

"Wool prices expected to spike," Freddy began.

"No the other one," Doug said. Jurgen was impressed the century-old man could see the article.

Doug smiled and said, "I got me some new-fangled peepers ten years ago when the cataracts started getting so bad. I can spot the veins on the back of an eagle's feather as the bird sails overhead."

"Barony of Loch Urquhart defects to Gilbraith-on-Heather, Sheeplands in turmoil!" Freddy said.

"I'd hate to be that poor son of a bi..." Doug started but quieted looking at the children. "A beautiful woman," Doug said covering.

"Why?" Agatha asked. Why had become her favorite word.

"Well, I don't know about the new protector, but Old Karl would have Gilbraith's head on a pike for disrupting the way of things. I'd hate to be that poor kid if he hadn't had the protector's blessing on that transfer. Read more of the article, Frederick," Doug said. The statement sounded like an order to Jurgen but Freddy beamed with pride at the attention. He continued to read the article and Jurgen began to agree with Doug. The current count of Gilbraith-on-Heather was in deep trouble now. Dinner was ready soon, and Jurgen looked at the ten perfectly seared steaks, the fried chips—crispy on the outside and mushy in the middle—and the towering salad with lettuces, onions, and veggies. The meal was more food than his siblings had seen in a week. Even by his now inflated standards, Jurgen found the dinner opulent.

Fifteen minutes after Doug, Jurgen, and his siblings had bowed their heads in prayer, the group finished the meal. Iggy enjoyed the little left over steak and rough bits that the boys had fed him. Agatha and Mara happily did the dishes and Doug sat back, looking full and happy.

"Everyone has sleeping arrangements and we'll begin the chain gang in the morning," Doug said with a wink.

"What's a chain gang?" Agatha asked.

"Mister Doug means that we'll be working on getting the estate in order," Jurgen said.

"Oh," Agatha said, drying a dish. Freddy and Duncan were lying next to their new best friend, and all three looked like they were ready to sleep right there on the kitchen floor. Eventually, after the girls dried and stored the dishes, Jurgen hustled his brothers and sisters upstairs to their rooms, saying goodnight to Doug, and Iggy. As the children went to bed, Jurgen had time to think about his next move. He had a little more than a week and a half left of leave. He wanted to figure out whether he wanted to see SERAPH. An opera sounded interesting, as he'd never been before. But his heart was still sore from Jenny. Jurgen thought of her vitriol and her comments echoed in his mind.

A wild laugh started in his gut and moved upwards at the thought of her; disheveled, smelling of smoke, and angry at him for not throwing himself at her. He thought of her now-husband, and surmised Johnny was probably getting an earful from his old lady on how he was "half the man as Jurgen Wulfjaeger." Like a bright spot after a storm, Jurgen realized that whatever Jenny said didn't matter anymore. In a week and a half, he'd be back on duty, and provided Doug and the kids didn't kill each other, he wouldn't have a worry in the universe. He booted up his EVIL, not sure exactly what he wanted to say.

```
Hello Hannah,
I've been home now for a twenty-five hours
dealing with some family business. But, I can
bushwack my way to you in the capital. I've
never been to an opera and would be excited to
go. I'm sorry about things not working out
with the Primus, but only so much. You'd have
made a great future patroness, but I
understand being a symbol of the Union isn't
for everyone. I am happy to be home and have
some ground under my feet. You Navy ladies
really are crazy. Send me the ticket and I'll
meet you at the opera.
Sincerely,
Jurgen
```

Jurgen hit send and put the EVIL on the chair with his battlesuit. He was ready to crawl into bed. The entire day had been an insane mess, and he was tired. As soon as he was naked and under the covers the EVIL started chirping. He got up, wondering who in the world was pinging him at this hour.

"Send me your coordinates!" the message said. The message was from "Hannah DeBeck" with SERAPH's personal contact number. Jurgen debated whether he should. He wasn't sure what SERAPH was planning. He tried to go back to sleep, but his mind kept rolling the message over in his head. Finally, he jumped up, grabbed the EVIL, copied the geo-coordinates, and sent them to Hannah. A message popped up moments later. "See you tomorrow!" Jurgen crawled into bed and wondered what adventure he had just signed up for.

Jurgen had a restless night. He tossed and turned. In his dreams he kept arguing with his mother and Jenny. In the morning, Jurgen awoke, tired and feeling like a zombie.

"Getting your mud foot back, I see," said Doug as Jurgen appeared. He was the last one up. The boys had set the table and waited eagerly for breakfast. Doug supervised the girls with the stove. They were cooking a dozen eggs spread over three pans, plus a hash in another big pan. The meal was an extravagant breakfast for Jurgen's siblings who had usually only had boxty with an occasional maize ear.

"Aye! Aye! Hooray!" Jurgen said. Doug harrumphed and poured a cup of coffee—black—for Jurgen.

"I was thinking the boys and I would clean out the attic," Doug said. "The girls have volunteered to launder the sheets, curtains, and anything cloth."

"Are they ready to do all that scrubbing?" Jurgen asked.

"No, he has a machine! Like a real family!" Mara said excitedly.

Doug nodded and said, "The dang thing is older than you are, subaltern, but you know how things are. An old Assaultman keeps the march too." Jurgen smiled. A hover-taxi horn sounded, and Jurgen suddenly remembered SERAPH said she was coming.

"Are you expecting anyone, Pawpaw?" said Agatha.

Jurgen didn't have time to wonder about Agatha's use of the term as he said, "My friend from the capital wanted to visit. I apologize. I was going to say something first thing this morning, Doug."

Doug smiled and said "As Karl used to say to us general officers, '*Fühl dich wie zu Hause*'. Your friend is always welcome." The taxi door slammed and Ignatius started barking like the devil had arrived. Jurgen slipped outside, keeping the Pyrenees at bay inside the kitchen.

"Hi hero," Hannah said, standing a few meters away with a small day pack.

"Hello, SERAPH," Jurgen said. She walked over. Jurgen noted she wore a kerchief for her hair, a waist length brown jacket with a red T-shirt underneath, black leggings and hiking boots. Jurgen smiled at SERAPH.

"What?" she said playfully.

"You look like a hiking travel poster for big city folk," Jurgen said.

Hannah laughed and said, "You look like a stereotypical First Farmer — sweater, bib-overalls, and boots. You need a shock of wheat and a Homburg hat to complete the look."

"Guilty as charged, SERAPH," Jurgen said.

"Call me Hannah. I'm not in the cockpit," Hannah said.

"Sure, I wouldn't want the real angels to get jealous," Jurgen said. Hannah smiled. She stared at the estate and waited for Jurgen.

"Oh, this isn't my house," Jurgen said. "And please come in, I'm staying..."

"With a friend of the family," Doug said appearing.

"Hi," Hannah said.

"Hello, Jurgen's very attractive friend," Doug said as only a one-hundred-year-old man could.

Hannah laughed and said, "I take that as a compliment from a spry man of eighty such as yourself."

"Marry this one, subaltern," Doug said with a wink. Hannah laughed and so did Jurgen.

"Hannah, this is Doug. He's an old fart," Jurgen said.

"Guilty as charged, ma'am," said Doug. "Do you have a last name, Miss Hannah?"

"DeBeck," Hannah said.

"Oh, you're the heroic Valkyrie," Doug said. "I knew you looked familiar."

"And you bear a strange likeness to a statue in the capital," said Hannah.

"My much nicer and better mannered doppelgänger," Doug said. "We don't talk about him around here."

"I understand. I feel the same way about that Amazon," Hannah said.

"Well, seems like today is war heroes or better to play," Doug said. Suddenly the door burst open and Ignatius came running out barking.

Hannah looked a little worried until Doug said, "Ignatius, sit!" The dog plopped his rear immediately.

"Sorry, he's an excitable boy," said Doug. "If you give him a dog biscuit, he'll tell you where the family jewels are." Ignatius looked at Doug with pitiful eyes, and Hannah laughed.

"Come on inside. You might as well meet the rest of them," Jurgen said. Hannah entered and was mobbed by Jurgen's siblings.

"One moment!" Jurgen finally had to shout as everyone began talking at once.

"Hannah, this is Mara," Jurgen said pointing. "This is Freddy, Duncan, and that's Agatha. These are my siblings. I have one more, Olrich, who..."

"Joined the Assault," said Mara, "he's in basic."

"An Assault family. I feel outnumbered," said Hannah.

"Why is that?" Agatha asked.

"I'm a Navy interceptor pilot," Hannah said.

Mara smiled looking between Hannah and her brother while Agatha said, "What's that?"

Jurgen smiled and said, "Plenty of time for that later. We all have chores. Get going."

"Sorry, I suppose I should have asked if you were busy," said Hannah.

"Not at all. You are welcome to keep me company," said Jurgen. "Today, I'm on roof repair, and stairwell reinforcing duty."

"An Assault officer getting his hands dirty, what will they say in the O-club," asked Hannah.

"They'll say I was following the field marshal's orders," said Jurgen.

"Well then, I'll help!" Hannah said. "I'd hate to get a bad evaluation sent from the field marshal to the First Star Lady. They might make me sell more war bonds, and I'd never get back into the cockpit."

Jurgen smiled. He realized that he had done the right thing by sending the coordinates. Hannah was nothing like his mother or Jenny.

CHAPTER TWO
Fate Calls

Dunvegan

"Ah, Primus, a pleasure to meet you," roared Angus MacDonald, the High King of the Skye Isles, as Henry entered the large front great hall. Henry looked at the space, the heating bill alone was probably more than a poor man's yearly wage.

"The pleasure is mine, your Highness," Henry said, he as strode forward extending his hand. The action wasn't proper etiquette, as Henry should have stood and waited for the Great King to approach. Henry humbled himself ever so much to gauge the man's reaction. Angus reached out and grasped Henry's hand firmly.

"An islander greeting, what a pleasant surprise," Angus said shaking Henry's hand. Henry matched firmness and pressure. After a moment the men broke contact.

"You know, my boy, had you stood for election, I might have favored you over your uncle," Angus said casually.

"I've done that well, eh, your Highness?" Henry said.

"The name is Angus, and yes, my nephew is firmly in your court, especially after your reception at the spaceport and the news," Angus said.

"Well then Angus, call me Henry. I apologize for coming at such an ill time, but I am an Assaultman. I go where the protector orders me," Henry said.

"It's aye! Aye! Hooray!" Angus said with a smile, "Yes, I too served. My father, Robert Bruce MacDonald, was one of your grandfather's chief lieutenants."

"I heard of his gallant action at the Battle of the Landing," Henry said. "I've always been interested in his rebellion before that. In my studies, I saw tremendous heroism in his stand against tyranny, especially as he saw those same tyrants cut his father down as a child."

Angus puffed up in pride, and said, "Henry, you have been given a magnificent education, at least in our history. Not many remember those events in the Union. Let's head to my library. You, Drostan and I will take a dram—to ward off the cold—and we can talk history and some politics." Henry bowed his head slightly in assent. Angus began to walk the Primus back through the hall and into yet another large chamber.

"These are meeting halls, one for our subjects and the other for our vassals. I apologize they are so cold. They cost a fair griffin to heat, and well," Angus said but was interrupted.

"My uncle is a miser," Drostan said catching up to the men. "Hopefully he isn't boring you with tales of yesteryear. Remember, Uncle, we must look forward, not backwards, otherwise we'll be as bad as our cousins, the Sheeplanders."

"Drostan, you know you can be replaced. Maybe the kingdom needs a female heir after all," Angus said grumpily.

"See how he is," Drostan said with a smile.

"There are days I am willing to give Bonnie the crown just to see what you'd do," Angus said.

"My sweet cousin would have a rebellion in a fortnight," Drostan said.

"Marshaled by you no doubt," Angus said.

"No, Uncle, I'd be manning her defenses with a smile on my face," Drostan said with a wink to Henry. "After she put down the rebellion, she'd have to deal with all the costs, then there would be the modernization plans she'd need to enact in order to keep up with the islanders on Lochiel. Then, there are the constant headaches of the fishermen's guilds, and finally, my dear, beautiful, cousin would be besieged by suitors all wanting to marry the beautiful queen of the isles, with her immense fortune."

"Fortune, what fortune," Angus sputtered in mock anger.

"Exactly," Drostan said.

"You look like you are doing well for yourselves here," Henry said in confusion.

"We are," Drostan said, "but before the war, we mainly exported goods to Terra. Now that is not an option as there has been an embargo..."

"Suggested by the devil himself," Angus said. "Apologies, Henry, but I am glad that backstabber is gone."

"Alasdair?" Henry suggested.

"Yes," Drostan said, "Uncle, Henry had the privilege of sitting next to Bonnie at Campbell's banquet."

"Eh, what's that all about? You know Henry should you desire to court my daughter, you need to ask me," Angus said, his expression serious. Henry turned red. He hadn't tried to put Bonnie in a tough spot.

"A happy misunderstanding, Bonnie had an issue with her shoes. I offered her my arm and walked her to the front of MacLeod Hall. I had released her arm..."

"When you were accosted by one of Campbell's lackeys," Angus said with a smile. "My daughter is an Amazon, Henry, and she told me she had no hesitation in charging to your defense. You should feel fortunate, not many outsiders gain the loyalty of an island woman." Henry smiled. Bonnie had mentioned the incident to her kin, and Henry relaxed. Neither Bonnie, or Henry, had offended anyone in their actions.

"She was instrumental in my deliverance from a very belligerent *Graf* Gilbraith," Henry said.

"Aye, and now his spawn is poaching my baronies," Angus said.

"Speaking of which, I will leave in the morning for the capital. Drostan, as my heir, I expect you to entertain our guest."

"I am sorry to see you leave so soon," Henry said. The men had moved through the larger chamber's doors and were now in a three-meter-wide east-west corridor. Henry suspected this was the private family area of the castle.

"The affair with the barony is all politics, Henry," Angus said, "But, I had hoped that in this new age we could move beyond the pettiness of the past."

"That is why I am here, Angus," Henry said. Angus smiled a genuine smile and nodded.

The men walked down the the corridor to a series of ornate doors on the south side. Angus went forward and pushed a button to open the doors.

"Gilbraith claims his library is the grandest on Stahlburgh, but the University of the Isles at Portree says otherwise. Behold, Henry, the finest library in the Union." Angus said with pride. The doors opened and an expansive seven-meter-tall library opened. Henry estimated the room was forty meters deep by almost one hundred meters long. The back wall was glass that looked out at the dark foreboding northern ocean. Only a three meter wide part of the wall was solid. Hanging and illuminated on that part was *MacLeod's Landing on Stahlburgh*. The painting drew Henry's eyes like a moth to a flame.

"Impressive," Henry said moving close enough to see the details.

"This is one of three originals," said Angus. "There are supposed to be three ways to distinguish the first drafts. Each original had different marks showing they were original."

"Outside my apartments in the Villa is a version that my family received as a gift. It stands out among the other paintings," Henry said. "Of them all, this canvas is my favorite."

Angus smiled, and said, "The story is only a legend, but supposedly any man who finds joy in this painting is a full member of clan

MacDonald, whether he realizes it or not. This painting drew both Martin Fraser and Alaric Campbell. Their children..."

"Whisky time, Uncle?" Drostan asked.

"Only one dram, Drostan. Otherwise you'll get me into trouble," Angus said, "I have an early flight tomorrow, and I'll be... Well, I don't want to deal with the my niece-in-law complaining if her husband is beyond redemption tomorrow."

"I've promised Caitlin only a dram," Drostan said with a smile. "Besides, I have brought up the *Red MacDonald*, you've always said you were saving that whisky for a special occasion."

Angus looked like a man painted into a corner. He said, "Aye, this would count. Pour out the libation into three glasses." Henry looked between the two men, and then back to the painting. He was trying to see if he noticed anything that looked out of place from what he remembered. Angus came over and handed Henry a small glass, of neat whisky.

Angus raised the glass and sniffed the whisky, savoring the aroma, "Henry, you are about to taste history. This whisky is the first distilled on Stahlburgh. The MacLeod himself drank half the cask, a red oak. Drostan has been eager to taste this Felgenland whisky since he could drink at seventeen. Enjoy a taste of the past."

The three men lifted the small glasses and drank. Henry's mouth burned and the liquor tasted akin to the glue on a postal envelope. He swallowed and dared not spit out the thirty-five milliliters of liquid for the whisky's cost. He also did not want to cause offense. Henry saw Angus sat with a meditative look on his face, and Drostan had his mouth closed.

"Oh, sweet Allfather," Drostan said, "That was terrible!"

Henry relaxed. He wasn't the only one who was not impressed.

"I honestly remember the *Red MacDonald* tasting better," Angus said, smacking his lips, "I was just seventeen so maybe I didn't know any better. I apologize Henry."

"No, the whisky was fine. I was worried I was the only one who didn't find the dram delightful," Henry said. "In whisky, I am a bit partial, as my friend brews the *Royal Neep*."

"Aye, Stewart knows his stuff, for being Campbell's man," Drostan said. "Shall I fetch a bottle?"

"Might as well," said Angus. "Only one more, though, a nightcap for me, and palate cleanser. I really remember that whisky being better. The folly of youth I suppose." Drostan left and Henry continued to look at the painting.

"Looking for the clues is of no use, lad," said Angus. "The other legend is that only a MacDonald woman can tell if the painting is a real or fake. If Bonnie were here she could explain the legend. Perhaps she mentioned the legend to you during the banquet? If I haven't already, I apologize if she was forward with you."

"Not at all, we had met twice before. We did discuss the painting, the one in the Union History Museum, in fact," Henry said. "She was very quick to help me with Gilbraith, and of course with Campbell."

"You don't sound like a fan of the late Alasdair," Angus said. "I have my issues with the Campbells, but they stem from land and vassals."

"He's not my favorite peer," Henry said.

"Well, since you let my heir know of his death. I will share a bit of intelligence with you. The young Gilbraith has poached a barony of mine. While Loch Urquhart is a poor province and of no real worth to me. The theft, however, must be called out. I intend to challenge the theft with your father. Do you know how he will respond?"

Henry felt a pit of dread in his stomach. Angus was asking him to answer a question on behalf of his father and Henry had no idea how his father would react.

"Angus, I will be honest with you. I don't always understand the way my father's mind works," Henry said with complete candor.

"I understand. I too had such a father. Don't worry, Henry. I will not any incorrect counsel you give me against you. Your father is a stranger to me and my people. You have influenced many in the Isles with this mission. There now seems to be one Machthaber that recognizes what the MacDonalds have done, in the past and present, for the Union."

"All I know Angus, is my father is a man of reason. Your tremendous speech for the war opened the door for this visit," Henry said.

"You liked the speech?" Angus said with a hint of pride.

"Very much so," Henry said.

"Bonnie helped me draft that speech, and I am immensely proud of her for that," Angus said. Henry nodded.

"*Royal Neep*, gentlemen," Drostan said coming back with three glasses.

"Gentlemen, where are they?" Angus said with a laugh. Henry laughed as well.

"If this were just us, Uncle, I would have said island tinkers, but Henry seems to be a cut above on that account," Drostan said.

"Boy, do I have you fooled," Henry said with a smile. Both MacDonald men laughed.

"Well then we're in good company," Angus said.

"To good company," Henry said. All three men tipped back the dram.

"Much better," Drostan said.

"If Stewart ever wanted to defect, we would make him a prince in a heartbeat," said Angus.

"George is a good man. I remember that he too wasn't fond of Kenneth. Seems like Kenneth went after George's fian... Well, its complicated. Let's say Kenneth was apt to pick fights he couldn't win," said Henry.

"That he did," Angus said. "You didn't even have to hear him drone on in the Dynasts chambers."

"There are perks to being part of the chancellery," said Henry.

"Aye, speaking of which, how goes the war," Angus asked. Henry was again on a knife edge here as Angus was the loyal opposition to the current government.

"Not now, Uncle. Remember your bedtime!" said Drostan. "I'll show Henry to his apartments. If he's willing to indulge in another nightcap, we can talk fishing, because, Henry likes to fish."

"Well, I can see I am being shuffled off. Union politics loses to fishing," Angus said with a wink. "That's how things should be, if you ask me."

"Goodnight, Angus. I look forward to your return," Henry said.

"Goodnight, Uncle. Henry says that now, before he really knows you," Drostan said.

"Goodnight, Henry. Goodnight, Drostan. Bonnie will be a great queen. I'm strongly leaning that way tonight," Angus said turning and leaving.

"I will support her to the utmost! She will need my help getting this kingdom into the twenty-fourth century," Drostan said. Angus merely waved.

"He's already declared me publicly," Drostan said. "He teases, but he knows there are hold-outs that would deny women the right to vote if they could. Bonnie would be an excellent queen, for all of about five minutes. Then the clans would hoist another, more distaff MacDonald on their shoulders. We aren't a small clan and there are plenty of potential competitors."

"Sounds tenuous. We Machthabers are small, maybe too small for the Union," said Henry.

"Well, at least you know where the daggers in your back are coming from," Drostan said.

"No," Henry said with a pause, "We Machthabers always stab each other in the front."

Drostan laughed, and said, "Yes, I can see that. Your father for instance?"

"Yes," Henry said. "Not that my uncle didn't do his own share of stabbing too."

"What of the future? Are you and your brother," Drostan asked.

"We're on different paths. He and I have worked out succession between each other. There are still eight others," Henry said, "although one is my infant nephew."

"Yes, but a Primus and Secundus united together, my, what a block that would be — something worth throwing support behind," said Drostan.

"You sound like you are politicking for me," Henry said.

"I won't lie, a fisherman as a protector, that would be something," said Drostan with a smile.

"You already have one, my father," said Henry.

"I'll believe that when I see him with a pole. On that note, let's retire. If you're up for fishing tomorrow, we can go out on a boat or find a pleasant river and dip a lure in. Consider the trip a state function," said Drostan.

"I see I am going to have all the diplomatic challenges tomorrow," Henry said with a smile.

"Yes, with the empire of fish, but fear not, we MacDonalds will stand side by side in your quest to commune with the big one. A mythical beast that is worthy of taking home to the capital," said Drostan. "Follow me, and I'll show you to the state apartments." Henry smiled and nodded, following Drostan. When he first set out Henry wasn't sure what to think. Now, he was fishing and drinking with the MacDonalds. Henry's visit wasn't over, but the trip was looking successful, so far.

Drostan lead Henry seemingly from one end of the castle to the other. At the western end there was a large round tower which housed the state apartments. The tower was a quarter of the size of the Villa in the capital. It was a veritable keep within the castle.

"A man could get lost in your state apartments," Henry said.

"If that happened, we'd flood them and stock them for you, then you'd have a good excuse not to return to the capital," Drostan said with a laugh.

"When do the hydraulic engineers arrive?" Henry asked with a chuckle. Drostan led Henry up two flights of spiral stairs to the main apartment. He opened the grand doors. Inside Henry's duffel sat strategically in front of the dining table.

"Goodnight, Henry," Drostan said.

"Goodnight, Drostan, fishing at zero six hundred?" Henry asked.

"We start at seven, but if you're game, I'll have breakfast sent up before then," Drostan said.

"Thank you," Henry said. Drostan bowed and left. Henry grabbed the duffel and looked at his room options. There was a grand bedroom with an incredibly posh king-sized bed and an en-suite bathroom. On a floor above, there were three bedrooms with queen-sized beds and bathrooms. Henry figured there were more bedrooms below and on the two floors above. He could have slept in any one of them, but opted for the king bed. He opened his travel bag, and rummaged through the suitcase for his EVIL, which he had stowed in the bag upon landing.

He opened up the suitcase, laid out clothes, ruggedly outdoorsy wear for fishing, and then flipped on the device. As per usual the device's message buffer filled. Mostly of the messages were junk — carbon copies of unclassified government meetings, and the usual marketing spam.

The EVIL chirped three times, a priority message. Henry opened the priority message.

```
Confidential Message: Protector's Villa
Switchboard.
```

Henry placed his thumb on the device and the message decrypted.

```
Henry,
Gilbraith has stolen a barony from the
MacDonald. Be advised they may seek
retribution, be on your guard! Have guards
posted in case of trouble!
RvM-POTU
```

Henry looked at the message and laughed. If the MacDonalds were seeking retribution and looking to kill him, well, he'd hate to see what a real enemy would do. Angus had discussed the event and shared the intelligence. This gave Henry pause. Was he being maneuvered or used? A voice to voice would be necessary, Henry thought. He pulled out the small kit USIS had given him.

Henry pulled out the small USIS encryption module. Unlike a grid, the signal wouldn't perfectly protected with the device. Sometimes speed trumped security.

"Protector's Villa switchboard, how may I help?" the operator said.

"I need to speak with the manager. I have a dried-up pizza with no cheese," said Henry using a code phrase.

"Who is speaking?" asked the operator, as was protocol.

"TEUTONIC PRINCE," Henry said.

"Directing your call right away, sir," said the operator. The voice call clicked once, twice, and then the protector answered.

"Are you safe?" the protector asked.

"Completely, father. Stand down," Henry said.

"Thank the Allfather. With what has been happening, I am surprised the entire Sheeplands hasn't exploded in violence. The Dynasts are all coming in to the Bundstadt. What are you seeing on your end?" asked the protector.

"People who were afraid I was coming in as a regent," Henry said.

"What?" the protector said, "Why?"

"I don't know. The MacDonalds' intelligence here is hit or miss. Angus told me about Gilbraith. The new count is opening old wounds here, but as much as Angus looks angry, he's not. The barony is a stand on principles for the MacDonalds, nothing more," Henry said.

"Thank the Allfather twice over," said the protector.

"Yes, the trouble isn't here in the isles, but the MacDonald's vassals have reported raids on their lands too," said Henry.

"Good to know. I'll direct Domestic Branch to start working that. Are they treating you well, son?" asked the protector.

"Terribly, father. They made me drink a two-hundred-year-old-whisky, some *Royal Neep*, and are abducting me tomorrow to go out on a boat and fish," said Henry.

"I'll pray for your safe return to the capital. In how many years will that be?" said the protector dryly.

"You know, you could join me! Drostan caught a fifty-centimeter sea trout. He doesn't believe you're a real fisherman either," said Henry.

"If I could, I'd have a dropship deposit me there in a few hours," said the protector. "Keep your eyes and ears open, I will meet with Angus tomorrow."

"Always, father," said Henry.

"This was good work. Enjoy the fishing. We'll talk when you get back," said the protector. "Goodbye."

"Goodbye, good night," Henry said, cutting the connection, and then turning off and packing up the USIS device. Henry then traded his clothing for a pair of loose pajama shorts, and crawled into the bed.

"By the Allfather," said Henry, "this bed is almost as good as zero gee." With that, the Primus fell asleep.

The sun was up when Henry's EVIL buzzed. Henry rose and looked at his chronometer. The time read zero four thirty. Henry realized with the extreme northern latitude that the Holstensonne would be up earlier than in the Bundstadt near the equator. Stahlburgh had only a fifteen-degree tilt, compared to Earth's twenty-three degrees. This gave

Stahlburgh a wider milder climate and long uniform seasons. For Henry, this meant a nice cool summer day of around seventeen or eighteen degrees centigrade. Henry put on his undershirt and strapped the EVIL on his arm. Then, he found his undershorts and trousers and put them on. With enough clothing that the servants bearing his breakfast wouldn't be scandalized, he decided to pay attention to the EVIL.

There were the usual messages and one from Bonnie. The subject line said:

```
Hi, let's try this again.
```

Henry opened the message.

```
Hi Henry,
I'm sorry about the last message. I was
foolish, and well, Frank is completely out of
the picture. I'd like to talk about good
coffee, since I am stuck drinking Navy brew.
The Navy brass claims the coffee is from a
bean from a volcanic island on Eisenwald, but
the coffee tastes more like a can pensioners
would buy. A little bird (my sister-in-law)
told me you were visiting my home, and I'm a
little sad I could not be there to show you
around and go fishing with you. I hope you
write back. I never got a response before, and
for all I know there could be messages waiting
for me because of the Navy censors. Again, I
apologize for the confusion. Let's try this
again.
Sincerely,
Bonnie
P.S. If the deal is still available, I should
have leave soon and will try to catch a ship
```

`back to Stahlburgh as soon as a I can.`

Henry laid on the bed and thought for a moment, crossing his arms underneath his head. He wasn't sure whether he needed to respond immediately, or wait and see. Henry enjoyed his time with Bonnie, and there was the mystery of the painting he wanted to sort out. Henry just didn't want to get his hopes up again only to have Bonnie react to something Frank would do and change her mind.

"Sometimes all of this would be simpler if I were a commoner," Henry said. His parents wouldn't be so set on a perfect match. He could marry a girl that caught his fancy and he hers. The match could be as simple as picking a girl out of a pew at the local church. Henry rolled that thought around and realized that the streaming vids were full of complicated relationships and most of the characters were in the middle classes.

Henry stood up as the automatic curtains on his room's window opened. The room was dark when he'd entered, but now the chamber was brightly lit by the glow coming from the east. After the curtains finished opening, Henry looked out across a broad expanse of water from the Nordsee or the Northern Ocean. Dunvegan was on a peninsula, so the north, east, and west were all ocean facing. Henry looked at the waves rolling peacefully. The view promised a good day on the ocean and potentially good fishing.

Henry's mind went back to Bonnie. All these weeks he had forgotten about her. Most likely, he thought, as a defense mechanism. He had enjoyed her company, and she seemed nonplussed around him, unlike Hannah, who Henry felt was guarded or uncomfortable around him.

The thought of Hannah made Henry reconsider the opera. The last time he went, as a young teenager, he attended Verdi's *Ernani* with his parents. Henry found the love quadrangle dull and boring. He thought of his previous experience and the opera Hannah had suggested, and decided that the opera and the date wasn't a compelling enough enticement to meet back up. Hannah was nice, just not someone Henry could be comfortable around. Henry opened his EVIL and typed out a message.

> Hi Hannah,
> I apologize but I am on official business for the protector and will be out of the Bundstadt through this weekend. I'll have to cancel on our date, sorry. I'm happy to send money for the ticket, since I am canceling. Let me know if that works.
> Best,
> Henry

Henry looked over the message three times before hitting send. The statement was loose enough that it didn't imply a need to meet back up but didn't preclude that opportunity. Just like in fishing, Henry would throw out the lure, and if the fish were interested, she'd bite. If not...

"Plenty of fish in the sea," Henry said to himself. A knock at the door roused Henry from his thoughts. He looked at the time, his EVIL showed zero five hundred. Henry rose and headed towards the main doors. He wondered who was at the door this early.

"Breakfast sir," the servant said.

"You're a little early, I'd have expected breakfast at zero six hundred," said Henry.

"Aye, sir. I'm here at zero six hundred," the servant said wheeling in the food. Henry looked at his EVIL and hit the sync button. Magically the time changed to zero six hundred. The servant pulled the main dish off the cart and placed it on the dining table before wheeling the trolley out with him.

"So much for this EVIL being ultra-modern," Henry said, irritated at having the wrong time zone. He checked the local time on a Union time and weather site and sure enough Dunvegan was an hour ahead of the Bundstadt. He'd have a discussion with the *Markgraf* or his son Daniel about the EVIL's flaw when he returned to the capital.

In the meantime, Henry consoled himself with checking out the breakfast. Inside the serving dish were smoked salmon, kippers, a bagel with cream cheese, capers, oat cakes, and several hot and cold sausages. There were also a glass of apple juice, breakfast tea bags, an insulated carafe of coffee, and a travel mug. The meal was a feast for a family. Henry grabbed a bagel, salmon, and some capers for his breakfast.

Henry was tempted to check the news services, but he contented himself with the messages on his EVIL. The radioactive political fallout in the Sheeplands continued, as the Barony of Loch Urqhart's defection to the new *Graf* of Gilbraith-on-Heather dominated the headlines. The MacDonalds and their surrogates were publicly calling for the young *Graf's* head. The Assault had left Nakdong, leaving behind a garrison for the protection of the Lalande system. Some of the regiments would be cycled back to Stahlburgh to bring in fresh recruits. Others were being cycled to the next front, which Henry knew from the top secret discussions at Assault High Command would be L 98-59 Foxtrot. The Assault and Navy knew the Directorate Navy was massing there, and the leaders of both services wanted to catch the Terrans napping. If everything went according to their plans, the Terran Navy would be hobbled, and the Terran Army would be stuck on L 98-59 Foxtrot without a ride home. Henry thought the plans looked solid, but plans could always look good on paper. Henry pulled open his message service and hit reply to Bonnie. His subject said "Coffee."

> Dear Bonnie,
> The offer is still open, although I am having trouble locating good coffee around Dunvegan. The stuff the servants gave me is okay. Maybe I've grown used to the roasters in the

capital. I'm happy to take you there, or anywhere else.
I've been staring at MacLeod's Landing on Stahlburgh and I can't see a difference between the version in Dunvegan, the one in the protector's Villa, and the one in the history museum. Your father says only a MacDonald woman can tell, so if coffee goes well, I'd like you to come over to the Villa and see the other painting. I hope you are on leave soon, that way I can treat you to coffee and you can help me solve the mystery of my painting!
Best,
Henry

Henry hit send, powered off his EVIL and prepared to go fishing. He decided to let the universe go to hell in a hand basket without worrying about anything. He packed up his things and placed the EVIL in the top of his travel bag. Henry then left the apartments, at their entrance Drostan met him. Together, both men made their way through Dunvegan to the docks where the fishing crew awaited.

Henry had a long day at sea; and enjoyed himself immensely even though he hadn't caught anything of note. Drostan was a gracious host, who saved politics and his worries for the castle. Henry was happy that Drostan realized that fishing was serious and while they were on the water, the fate of the Union could wait. After hours of fishing, Henry headed back to the state apartments to change. Drostan had invited Henry to Drostan and Caitlin's apartments for an informal dinner.

Henry entered the state apartments and saw that everything was as he remembered. He pulled his business casual clothes from his travel bag. His EVIL sat there tempting him to turn on the device, yet Henry resisted. If he turned on the device, he'd probably lose the half hour he'd need to get ready. Clothes ready, Henry hopped into the shower. The water was chilly at first, but rapidly warmed up. Henry scrubbed, washed, and toweled off. No longer smelling like fish or sea, Henry clothed himself. When dressed, he combed his hair, attempting to make a good impression. He wished he had a Dynastic attaché from the chancellery. He'd have sent the poor soul off for something he could offer at the upcoming meal. Henry checked the time and started down towards the central part of Dunvegan Castle. Along the way, Henry realized that he didn't know where he was going.

"Impeccable timing," said Drostan. Again Drostan met Henry at the entrance to the state apartments. "If you come back, I'm going to have to teach you how to be on time in island time."

"Apologies," said Henry, joining his host early. "I can't help myself; the Assault taught me if I wasn't ten minutes early, I was late."

"Well, to calculate what time you *actually* need to be somewhere on island time, you take the time, and add a half hour. Then you can arrive five minutes before that time and everyone will consider you on time," Drostan said with a smile.

"Sounds complicated," said Henry smiling.

"Everything in the Isles is complicated, why should time be easy?" Drostan said with a wink.

"The fishing was easy," Henry said.

"True, but we didn't get you your monster fish," said Drostan. "I'm officially a failure as a host."

Henry laughed. "Quite the opposite. I, however, am a terrible guest, I have nothing to give your charming wife for your supper invite."

"Don't fret. You haven't tasted dinner; you might regret saying yes," said Drostan with a mischievous grin. "I kid, Caitlin is a surprisingly good cook, for a Chieftain's daughter and a tomboy fisher woman."

"I see," said Henry in surprise. Caitlin had appeared to be a demure Sheeplander-Islander woman.

"Aha, she fooled you," said Drostan. "Welcome to the club."

"Oh," Henry said, "sounds like a story."

"Sure, after we're seated," said Drostan. The men began walking through the castle and passed through a security checkpoint then went up an elevator. The doors opened and there was a similar corridor leading to two ornate doors, just like the state apartments.

"I apologize, this section has been lived in unlike the state apartments," said Drostan.

"I couldn't tell the difference," said Henry.

"Good, I'm glad you don't see all the hand prints and wax coloring tool marks my children have made on these walls," said Drostan in reply.

"I imagine some family historian will find those invaluable in their research," said Henry.

"Now you sound like my cousin," said Drostan, opening the door. Inside three children stood in a line. They stood boy, girl, boy. The eldest had reddish-brown hair; the others had light brown hair. To Henry, they were spitting images of Drostan.

"Henry, this is my eldest and heir, Robert," said Drostan, announcing the boy of seven.

"Good evening, Primus," said Robert.

"Good evening, Master Robert MacDonald," said Henry using the proper formality with the boy.

"Good job, Robby," said Drostan. "He's named after my grandfather, Angus's father. He was an amazing man, and we hope Robby will also make his mark on Union history. Next is my dove, Alyth."

The girl looked almost as old as her brother. She curtsied and said, "Good evening, Primus. Welcome to our home."

"Good evening, Miss Alyth MacDonald," said Henry with a half bow. Alyth giggled as Henry was the first adult to bow to her.

"Hello, Primus," said the littlest one. He was a boy of maybe four. "I'm Finlay! I'm going to grow up and be a general like my great-grandpa! I'll guard you when you're protector. If any Terrans look at you funny, I'll shoot them in the butt."

Henry bowed and said, "Master Finlay MacDonald, I look forward to your service. I expect many an Assaultman will cheer to follow your banner."

"Okay, Fin," said Drostan. "You, Robby, and Allie have to go to bed."

Drostan said as an aside to Henry, "they ate earlier and are getting an early bedtime so Caitlin and I can have some adult time." Henry nodded and smiled.

"Good night, Primus," Robert said as he passed into his bedroom. "Good night, Primus," Alyth said as she too went to her room.

"Good night, sir," Finlay said, saluting. Henry returned the boy's smart salute.

"Sleep well! Remember, an Assaultman fights best when he is are alert."

"Yes, sir!" the little boy shouted and ran to his bedroom in the nursery.

"They are charming," said Henry.

"Why thank you," Caitlin said appearing from the kitchen. The apartments were spacious and had all of the comforts that Henry's place did in the Villa.

"I'll make sure they are tucked in," said Drostan, leaving Henry with his wife.

"No nannies?" said Henry in surprise.

"No, my kin don't believe in letting others raise their children. That was something I was adamant about with Drostan. He agreed. Both he and Bonnie were tossed about with nannies and governesses growing up. In poor Bonnie's case, she was in with the nannies due to her mother's premature death, Drostan..."

"Drostan what?" said Drostan returning. "I knew you two would be talking about me."

"Knows when he's being talked about," said Caitlin with a smile. "Now, please set the table, Dross." Drostan nodded dutifully and headed into the kitchen.

"I'm serving you mince and tatties, Primus," said Caitlin. "The dish isn't fancy fare, but I am sure you and Drostan will appreciate the home cooking, after being on a boat all day."

"Contrary to popular opinion, I grew up in the hinterland on beef and potatoes. Anything similar to that will make me happy," said Henry.

"Our Primus is a country boy? Drostan, you liar," said Caitlin.

"Huh?" said Henry.

"He told me you were a high and mighty type and only ate the finest of beef and the rarest of potatoes," said Caitlin. "That's okay, Primus, I suspect Drostan was angling for Cullen skink or a curry out of me."

"You don't get the servants to cook for you?" asked Henry.

"Only when we've had a busy day," said Caitlin. "I want my children to know the joy of a mother's home-cooked meal." Henry nodded, remembering many a meal fixed by his parents. Drostan came out with the plates, placing them on the broad dining table that sat away from the door. He pulled silverware from his pocket and placed the utensils in their correct spots. Drostan went into the kitchen again and returned holding a pot with two cloth hot pads. He placed the pot on a waiting trivet and ran back to the kitchen.

"Almost ready," said Drostan. He returned in a moment with three wine glasses in one hand and a bottle of red in the other.

"Shall we," asked Henry, offering his arm to Caitlin.

"Uh oh, watch out, Henry, that's how I ended up overboard," said Drostan. Henry escorted the crown princess to a spot at the table and held her chair out for her.

"Escorting you is the least I can do with my hostess," said Henry to Caitlin as he seated her.

"Thank you, sir," said Caitlin. "Drostan should take notes. After I said, 'I do,' he forgot how to spell gentleman, much less act like one." Henry sat at his spot to the right of Drostan and across from Caitlin.

"Gentleman wasn't part of the vows," said Drostan as he sat down. "I also remember you saying 'love, honor, and obey.'"

"I only promised the best two out of three," said Caitlin with a smile. She ended the discussion by crossing herself and bowing her head in prayer. Henry and Drostan did the same.

"Let's eat," said Drostan spooning out mashed potatoes to everyone and then dowsing the potatoes with minced beef and gravy. Henry noted the meal was simple fare, but hearty and good. After being on the water all day, Henry had to keep his appetite in check, otherwise he would have gobbled his meal. Drostan didn't hesitate to inhale his meal. Caitlin looked at Drostan and smiled at her husband's vigor in eating the meal. Henry looked down at his plate and attempted to stave off a pang of jealousy at Drostan's loving wife. The emotion passed after another forkful of the delicious food.

"We're sitting, and I'm drinking your lovely red wine. Now, you mentioned a story?" asked Henry.

"Aye, and then we'll get Caitlin to clean up so we can talk politics, once we've completed all our important business," said Drostan.

"What story are you going to tell the Primus, Drostan," asked Caitlin. "The one about how you fell overboard scrambling after the selkie?"

"Yes, specifically how one selkie has cursed me to live under her thumb, raise her children, and generally wear down my carefree nature," said Drostan with a wink at Henry.

"You see what you have here, Primus," said Caitlin, "a bold liar. Look at how shamelessly he says such things in front of his future liege."

"Hey, I might be passed over," said Henry. "Nothing is done with the protector until the cathedral rite."

"Well, if I have a say, and I will, mind you. I know who I'll support," said Drostan. "Now, to the story of how this selkie captured my heart and won't take her sealskin back, since she lives the high life here in Dunvegan."

"One second, what's a selkie?" asked Henry. He had heard stories of mermaids from his mother's people, but the stories had been sanitized and scrubbed down for his young ears.

"Ah, well, when the Scots of the diaspora came here with old MacLeod, we brought our myths with us. One of those is of the selkies or seal folk. We believed that there are 'mythical maidens of the sea,' creatures that could take human form as beautiful maidens."

"And handsome men," added Caitlin.

"These maidens shed their seal skin and if a lucky fellow finds the skin, he can force the selkie to marry him. Usually after the man dies, she takes her skin and leaves land," said Drostan.

"Ah, thanks," Henry replied.

"Now, once, a long long time ago," said Drostan.

"Eight years ago during the midsummer fishing festival," said Caitlin with smile.

"There was a dashing, not—yet—recognized crown prince, whose wicked cousin made him take her to the festival, for he was seventeen and had many a tavern to conquer," said Drostan.

"Bonnie was sixteen and not legal to drink so she didn't want Drostan to have too much fun without her," said Caitlin translating.

"Well, our hero gets on a fishing boat that was leaving at the very last moment and, left his evil, fun-killing cousin behind. As he was nursing his broken, sober heart, what should appear, but a beautiful selkie! Being a gentleman, our hero offered his arm to the beautiful selkie and immediately went overboard, as she tried to take him into the deep with her," said Drostan.

"He wasn't paying attention and my uncle knocked him overboard. In my uncle's defense, the sea was rough, and Drostan was oblivious to what was happening on deck," said Caitlin.

"You don't understand, Henry, the magnificent beauty of this creature had transfixed me!" said Drostan with a smile.

"What happened next?" asked Henry. Caitlin rolled her eyes at Henry's encouragement of her husband.

"I almost drowned when she took me to her lair," said Drostan with a smile. "But the noble fishermen, my subjects, threw lassos and rescued me."

"I jumped overboard and got a life preserver underneath him, then my uncle and father hoisted him back on board. We had a good day fishing and he asked to court me when we got back to port," said Caitlin. "Now, before any more horse manure gets spread, I need to clean up. I'm wearing my nice shoes and not my wellies, Drostan."

"She just doesn't want to admit she jumped in after me because I struck her fancy," said Drostan.

"I felt sorry for you," Caitlin said from the kitchen. Henry smiled. There were worse ways to start down the road to marriage.

"Now, after a good day of fishing, wine, and a tall tale, let's get down to business," said Drostan. "We're especially fortunate that my uncle isn't here as that would complicate things."

"Sounds fair," said Henry. "Let the horse trading begin."

"Henry, you've exceeded my expectations," Drostan began. "For being a 'Great Kingdom,' we're a gigantic, chaotic, relatively poor province. As I said previously, we rely on exports, which the Union has now banned. My uncle and I are trying to run a tight ship, but we need help! Angus and I have over one hundred vassals, some direct, others indirect. Angus has their respect, which can curb their worst excesses, while I am trying to modernize everything. Rebuild infrastructure that time or our climate has worn down. We don't need funds. We need trade, and we need allies." Henry nodded and sat silently thinking.

"Take fishing, for example," said Drostan. "We don't have the capacity to keep up with Lochiel, which is a water world with huge schools of variform and native fish. In agriculture, we don't have the growing season of the Valley of the First Farmers or Eisenwald. We drill for petroleum, but even there we're behind the production of Hansaburgh and even some of the colonies. We're a province that produces commodities without a market!"

"I can't make a market materialize for you, Drostan," said Henry sympathetically.

"No, don't mistake me. I'm not looking for a solution, just a patron, if only to tell of my troubles. Rightly or wrongly, we see your father as partial to the Campbells or the Gordons. Both of those clans are heavily invested in manufacturing and infrastructure. Markets that are now booming. All I am asking for is a friendly ear in the capital. My uncle had a meeting with the protector today. The meeting was less than we had hoped for. The protector said Gilbraith's theft will stand, and we will lose yet another vassal. I know our wealth and vassals seem boundless, but we don't have that much to spare. Every loss further impoverishes our province, potentially causing a death spiral for the kingdom. If this continues for a generation or two, the kingdom is no more, which means instead of one block, thousands. All those conflicting interests could destabilize this region."

"I see. Well, I don't have a tremendous love for the Campbells. I have yet to meet the Gordons, Buchanans, or Frasers. But I've seen that you are committed to your demesne, your province, and the Union. I am comfortable being your ear in the capital. Just remember, we Machthabers walk along the knife's edge and that not everything you bring to me will go your way. No protector, in training or otherwise, can give one family everything they want," said Henry.

"That's wise and true. From what I am hearing, you sound like you are willing to scratch our back and watch our backside too. For that, we will return the favor tenfold. Stahlburgh is noted for our tumultuous clans, but the Union has plenty of cutthroats beyond the capital world," said Drostan.

"I've been told as much," said Henry.

"The pirate families of Lochiel make us look tame and compliant. The salt families of Hansaburgh revel in their antiquity and Germanic aggression. Those of Eisenwald are as unforgiving and venomous as anything that grows in their jungles. Then there are the hungry upstart families in the colonies. To that, I say, when you have the oath of a clansman of the Sheeplands or Islands you have a brother for life," said Drostan offering his hand.

"I was your brother when you said we were going fishing," said Henry shaking Drostan's hand.

"Convinced so easily? Henry, I can see you'll need a good adviser, one that understands the necessity of fishing and whisky," said Drostan.

"I haven't won any elections yet," said Henry with a smile.

"You've chosen well as a first step. We MacDonalds have hundreds of proxies. Remember, we will watch each other's backs," said Drostan. The light began fading as the Holstensonne went down over the horizon.

"Now, I won't be called a terrible host. It is time for you to return to your apartments, and for me to go to bed," said Drostan.

"Yes," Henry said, feeling suddenly tired from the seriousness of the conversation and the long day. Henry stood and followed Drostan. As they entered the main nexus of Dunvegan, Henry saw Krueger standing there with a MacDonald man.

"Sir, urgent message from the protector," said Krueger. He handed Henry a sheet of paper. Henry read the message, which said, "Return immediately. New developments have occurred, and you've gotten your wish."

"Drostan, apologies," said Henry, but was cut off by his host.

"You must return immediately," said Drostan. "I am glad you were able to come fishing and to dinner."

"And you'll need to come to Schloss Machthaber along with your family. You've been an excellent host and I wish to return the favor, as one should do." Drostan nodded and smiled.

"If I can pry my selkie from the sea, we'll be there," said Drostan. "Farewell, Henry. I look forward to seeing you again."

"Thank you for a delightful time and I will see you again, Allfather willing."

"Amen, goodbye," said Drostan. He then turned to his servant and said, "Hamish, please help the Primus gather his things and show him the way out."

"No need, your Highness," said Krueger. "I've retrieved the Primus' things, and the dropship has received clearance to land at the Hall, so we're just waiting on Herr von Machthaber."

"You see, Henry, we're an isolated province. Next time, don't leave so suddenly," said Drostan.

"Father found out I was having too much fun," said Henry.

"That sounds like my wife and my uncle, farewell."

"Again, thank you, goodbye," said Henry. Krueger marched towards the exit and Henry fell in line.

"Issues?" asked Henry.

"Everything, nothing," said Krueger. "The usual, hurry here, wait, now rush there. Here's your EVIL, sir."

Krueger handed Henry his EVIL, and Henry turned the device on. Upon powering up, the device chirped three times. Henry watched his message buffer fill. When the messages stopped, Henry scrolled through them looking for the priority message.

```
From: Assault High Command. To: HPT
v.Machthaber, Heinrich K.A. Subject: Report
for Active Duty
```

Henry shook his head inwardly. After all these months and when he was finally comfortable with his new job, Assault High Command pulled their head out of its rear and called him back up.

"Got the call, eh, sir," said Krueger. "I suppose I'll be getting the same soon too. Just as well. I've had my fill of traffic in the capital. At least if you're in traffic at the front, you can shoot the cars ahead of you."

Hamish left Krueger and Henry at the large doors to Dunvegan. Outside a dropship hovered with the drop ramp a meter above the ground.

"Come on, sir," said Krueger breaking into a trot. Henry followed him, noting that without weapons fire running to a dropship wasn't nearly as exciting. Henry climbed into the compartment and the pilots buttoned up the hatch and throttled the engines. Within moments, the dropship was high over the ocean. Henry read the duty summons again; the message was as he expected. He looked through the rest of his messages. There was a message from Bonnie, which said.

```
Coffee in a few weeks?
```

Henry wanted to read that one, but as more messages spooled in his buffer a more important one caught his eye. The sender was "Mahjong's pizza."

```
Did you order anchovies?
```

Henry opened the coded message.

```
Today's Special!
Leeks and anchovies! Due to a plumbing problem
all our pizzas are on sale. Call us now to
secure your deal!
```

Henry quickly deciphered the code. Leeks meant someone had leaked information. Anchovies were dead fish or bad guys. The plumbing problem meant the Villa wasn't secure. Pizzas on sale meant urgent. Call now to secure your deal meant call on the secure channel.

"Secure sat link, please Köhler," said Henry.

"Sure, sir," said the NCO, handing Henry a phone. Henry dialed the secure number that came up on his EVIL's one time pad. The number buzzed and Weber answered.

"Primus, I hope you are safe," said Weber.

"In a dropship," Henry replied.

"Very good, sir. Your father was worried; there have been incidents. We've locked down communications at the Villa. I wanted to ensure you were okay," said Weber.

"What happened? Is my family okay? What's going on?" asked Henry.

"The protector and his family are in secure locations. *Markgraf* Gilbraith is unaccounted for..."

"Wait, I thought he was just a *Graf*?" said Henry.

"That's a long story, sir," said Weber. "The Prime Minster was attacked, much like your incident, but he got to safety. There have been more raids in the Sheeplands, and USIS Domestic Branch has new intel. The protector was waiting until you returned to tell you, but the field marshal has won the day. You're headed to Steinthal, sir. I wish I could go with a knight in painted armor such as yourself. You will need a noble steed on the field of battle!"

Henry could hear the pride in the majordomo. Henry said, "Thanks, Otto. You're too good for us."

"I only wish to do my utmost duty to serve, sir," said Weber, a little choked up. "Be careful, and if you see Markus, make sure he comes back safely, sir."

"Always, goodbye, Otto. Tell mother and father goodbye too."

Henry hung up the connection and looked at his EVIL. The flight plan confirmed what Weber had said was true. Henry was headed to the Assault Academy, the central rally point on Stahlburgh. The flag had gone up, and he was sailing for the front. Where that voyage would end, like the Assault Anthem said, "barracks or grave," only time would tell.

Henry stripped off his casual clothes in the middle of the compartment, for all the Assaultmen and the Navy to see. Markus had packed his class A uniform. Now he rummaged through the travel bag for the uniform and threw them on as fast as he found them. He was just ready to put on his shoes on when the dropship started to free fall. Henry strapped in, one shoe on the other under his left thigh.

"We have a spot in the landing, Primus. I twisted the ATC to let me cut the line," said TAWNY TULIP.

"I sense a but," shouted Henry.

"Not going to lie, the landing will be a little fast and rough," the pilot replied.

"You girls know how to show an Assaultman a good time," said Henry.

"Aye, aye, sir," said the pilot and Callan in unison.

"Drinks are on us, if you ever set foot on the *Julia of Protelan*, sir" the NCO, Köhler said.

"Appreciate the offer, Chief," said Henry. "If you ever set foot on the *Bismarck,* I'm buying."

"You reporting on the *Bismarck*, sir?" asked Köhler.

"I'm the marine commander," said Henry. "Just got my orders."

"Congratulations, sir," said Köhler. The dropship then dropped again. The vehicle righted and Henry could see the landing lights outside of the window. The sky was full of spacecraft. Off in the distance was the Fortress, the Acdemy's main schoolhouse. The Academy would typically be empty since it was May. Henry remembered his time there. He was always busy: busy studying, busy with extra-curricular activities—in Henry's case the drill team—busy with trying not to be busy. Now he was returning for the rally. The dropship came down, hovered off the landing pad, and the rear door opened. Henry grabbed his travel bag and ran down the ramp.

"Good hunting, sir!" the company in the dropship hollered. Henry cleared dropship's jet wash and the vehicle hovered over to the taxi line to take off.

Henry looked around the small brightly lit spaceport. Past the lights Henry only saw absolute darkness. Henry scanned looking for the order in the chaos of enlisted men and officers moving to and fro. Henry was saluted by subordinates and gave salutes to superiors. Moving a few meters towards the main exit, Henry saw the processing area and joined the line with the rest of the recently arrived.

"Sir," the enlisted said in front of him. Henry nodded. The pace picked up. Within minutes, he was at the main desk. A master sergeant sat with a scanning device and an oversized Assault-hardened tablet.

"Hello, sir. Identification number, please," the sergeant said.

"One-one-seven-bravo-November-six-nine-three-nine," Henry rattled off.

"You are headed to the *USTC Bismarck;* she's above us in orbit. Sir, I need you to go to the armory to checkout a battlesuit, and grab a rifle. Then follow the green signs to the large dropship in the green landing zone. You'll see a chief there. She'll get you set to go up. Any questions, Captain?"

"No, sergeant," Henry said.

"Good hunting, sir," the sergeant said tapping something into his tablet. Henry followed the signs to the armory. Henry could have gone to the armory on autopilot, but after the long day, he was tired, and the signs were reassuring.

Henry marched into the armory and joined the short queue. Soon, he was fitted for a battlesuit. The armory sergeants were efficient, using hot air blowers to mold the heat reactive internals for a snug fit on the suit. The process used to take an entire day. Campbell Industries had gotten the process down to a half hour. Henry felt the residual heat in the suit as the armory sergeants buckled him in and dropped his helmet over his head. The suit detected the heat, started up the air conditioning and vented the internal air.

"Here you go, sir, one Anderson-Campbell 2353 mark five. Here's a new Anderson A17. It's a modular weapon and your armorer on the *Bismarck* can offer you attachments. We just shipped a crate up yesterday. Any questions, sir?" the armory sergeant asked. He was like an assembly worker and wanted to make his quota.

"No, sergeant," Henry said eager to get up to his duty station.

"Good hunting, sir," the sergeant said. "Next!"

Henry looked for and found a neon green line sprayed on the floor. As he followed the green line towards the loading area, Henry saw large tarmacs with dropships going up and down.

"Hurry up, sir!" a Navy chief shouted from the rear of a large "battle wagon"-style dropship. Henry ran to the ramp, climbed aboard, and found a jump seat in the rear.

"Up we go!" said the chief, as Henry's helmet linked into the dropship channel.

"Buckle up back there," said the pilot. Henry threw his back against the seat and the jump seat magnetized to his armor. He was secured to the hull and ready for takeoff. The dropship rocketed upwards pulling some gees. Henry felt his suit compensate, but the stress on his body was unwelcome at the late hour. After a minute or two, the dropship's engines grew silent. Henry felt the weightlessness. No matter how terrible things might be, he'd be sleeping in zero gee tonight. Henry comforted himself that zero-gee always made for a comfortable bed. Henry booted his EVIL, which now sat in a cradle on the suit. He had a new model suit, rifle, and pistol. Henry hoped they'd perform as well as the tried-and-true models he had known his entire career.

The EVIL connected to the flight console. His clearance as an officer afforded him two small perks: a peek at the flight plan and a feed from the external cameras. The battle wagon dropships didn't have a front window; they were essentially tanks with rocket engines. The pilots flew by wire and used a combination augmented reality and a glass cockpit to drive the ship. The windowless cockpit was newer technology, adapted from the interceptors who also flew windowless. Henry remembered the briefings at the Admiralty on how the window was a weak point. MacCarthy had argued to remove both the window and the pilots from future designs. The Navy had compromised, the pilot stayed and the window went. Henry had felt the argument was like a debate between two comic book geeks on whether the Union Orbiter was superior to the Dark Crusader. Now, seeing the new dropship, he could evaluate firsthand. Henry sighed; he missed the window.

"Arrival in thirty, get ready mudfeet. I need you all to haul your butts off my ship. I'm turning right around to grab more of you," said the pilot. Henry wasn't going to argue. He was tired and ready for his berth. Everything had moved so fast. Hurry up and wait, indeed. Henry didn't have half of his deployment kit, but he wasn't going to sweat the lack of kit. Like all troop transports, there would be a store for essentials, and he'd grab what he needed. The dropship connected with the *Bismarck.* Henry could feel the docking collar rubbing on the hull of the dropship. The airlock door opened.

"Out, out, out," commanded the pilot. The Assaultmen hopped up on the bounce and queued to exit. Henry waited, ensuring he was last off, as was proper for an officer. The Assaultmen were herded by a petty officer in a gray pressure suit.

"Hello, sir. Go straight to the bridge. The captain is waiting for you," said the petty officer as Henry approached. Henry's suit hadn't synced with the ship so he couldn't respond with her name.

"Thank you, petty officer," was the best Henry could do. He moved forward floating a dozen meters and into a line of Assaultmen.

"Make a hole!" Henry shouted over the Assault channel. The Assaultmen squeezed their suits against the side of the corridor bulkhead, allowing Henry to squeeze through the tight opening.

Henry moved a dozen more meters and saw a ladder that went up and down.

"Where's the bridge?" Henry said, and a Navy enlisted pointed down. Henry pushed his suitcase downward. The travel container slowly floated down as Henry slung his rifle and floated down the ladder.

"Reporting for duty, captain," said Henry, moving onto the bridge. The displays and consoles were ripped apart, and Navy personnel and some contractors were working furiously to put things back together. A naval officer in a gray suit turned and looked at him. Henry's suit synced finally and he got the name and rank of his new commander.

"Group leader, glad to have you on board," said *Kapitän, unterer Dienst* Erika Schwarzwald. Henry realized she was using a literal translation of his rank *Hauptmann*. Henry saluted. On a ship there was only one captain, and that was Erika.

"Permission to come aboard?" said Henry.

"Granted. Now stow your gear and then get back here. I've got mudfeet floating around this fancy garbage scow like lost sheep on market day in the country," said the captain.

"Yes, captain," said Henry.

"And Group Leader, you can call me Erika in private. We'll both need the informality to keep each other's sanity," said the captain.

"In private I'm Henry, ma'am. I expect you'll elaborate later?"

"Yep, after you and I exist in the same universe," said the captain. "Now go and get back. O-country is up three ladders and twenty meters forward."

Henry floated out of the cramped bridge. Outside his hovered travel bag. Henry grabbed the bag and shot up the ladder only slowing to hang around the ladder three decks up. He rolled around the ladder and floated down to the hatch to O-country.

"Attention," the senior of the two Assaultmen guarding O-country said.

"At ease," Henry said as he floated by. Henry opened the hatch and entered. O-country was huge with several large compartments for a half dozen junior officers. Henry looked at the compartments and tapped his EVIL. The usual shipboard systems that would give him a marker to his berth weren't working.

"This way, sir," said a Navy sub-lieutenant. She pointed to the farthest compartment, where the hull slanted downwards. Her name hadn't registered either on the EVIL, and Henry began his device was broken. Henry nodded and floated to the end compartment. It was actually a compartment within a compartment. Henry realized the sub-compartment was his as the Assault commander. There were two other bags stored in the Assault officers' mesh container rack. Henry brushed past the berths and entered the sub-compartment. A canvas wall separated his "room" from the other officers. He stowed his gear and locked his rifle into place in the officers' mini-armory. He was on the *Bismarck* and headed to the front.

Special Projects

Noontime had come, but Jurgen felt like he had been working on Doug's place for only a few minutes. He and Hannah discussed all sorts of things. Being the daughter of two engineers, she was keen to discuss mathematics. Jurgen had brought up the subject, as he was having trouble with his Academy pre-work. Jurgen hadn't done well in the one-room schoolhouse that was the Tavishire "free school." Most of the shire's middle classes sent their children to Saint Norbert's, a religious school near the border with the Valley of the First Farmers. The "free school" was not great at turning out scientists and engineers. Hannah was happy to explain pre-calculus to Jurgen. With such a pretty tutor, Jurgen was tempted to take an engineering discipline at the Academy.

"That's a trap," Hannah said. "I have a degree in aerospace engineering only because I wanted to be a pilot. I'd have taken classical ballet if I could have."

"That seems like an odd degree for the Naval academy," said Jurgen.

"Well, when you think about it for a moment, ballet makes sense: the physical conditioning and the body control. If you're floating in a war craft, having grace and body control makes a lot of sense," Hannah replied. "I'd suggest philosophy. Then, you'll be able to handle the course load and can focus on being an officer."

"I like the tutors for engineering better," Jurgen said with a smile.

"I'm pretty sure they don't look like interceptor pilots at the Assault Academy," Hannah said. Jurgen banged in some boards to strengthen the stairs.

"That's not going to work," Hannah said as she put her weight on the first stair.

"Is that your engineering opinion?" Jurgen asked.

"Yup, Doug's going to have to replace the stairs," Hannah said.

"Here I was worried you two were up to hanky-panky," Doug said, suddenly appearing. "Instead, you two are doing honest work."

"The stairs are *kaput*, Doug," Hannah said.

"As I feared," Doug said. "Tear 'em down."

"Aye, aye, Doug," Jurgen said with a smile.

"Found something your good at, eh, subaltern?" Doug said.

"Hey, Doug," Hannah said, "what did you take at the Academy?"

Doug laughed, and then said, "Back in my day, you got a commission because Karl thought you were 'officer material,' I never did a lick of skull sweat for a commission. Just fought a bunch of pirates as a sergeant. Karl thought I did a good job and said, 'Boy, you're now an ensign, don't mess up.' A decade later I've got laurels and stars. Why?"

"Jurgen wants to take a science degree. I told him take philosophy, the Academy is hard enough," Hannah said.

"Ha, why not poetry?" Doug asked. "Then you can be a *Kriegskanzler* like old Addie."

"A warrior poet could be, kind of sexy," Hannah said.

"I'll think about that," Jurgen said. "I'll be back, got to get a sledgehammer." Jurgen left leaving Hannah and Doug there.

"You on leave," Doug asked.

"Sort of I'm technically AWOL," Hannah said. "But no one will be looking for me until tomorrow."

"Taking a risk for our subaltern there, aren't you?" Doug asked.

"Everyone keeps saying I'm a heroine," said Hannah. "I'm not, and I'm tired of selling war bonds and getting others to pledge their lives for the Union based on my lies."

"Listen, young lady," said Doug sternly, "you are as much a heroine as I am a hero. Maybe more, since you downed those enemy interceptors where I just played nursemaid to a bunch of whiny Assaultmen."

"I keep seeing her interceptor exploding, Doug! She jumped out and grabbed the missile that was meant for me!" Hannah said tears forming.

"Yep, and there'll be a lot more of that before the war's over," said Doug wisely. "You'll never get past that guilt, but you can use those emotions. Make the Directorate pay for all the death they are dishing out. I can't give you any better advice. My enemies got their heads on a pike for fighting us. This war isn't going to end the same way. Still, I can name friends who should have been there at the end to see some justice."

"How do you keep going?" Hannah asked. She wiped her tears trying to gain some composure.

"I live for the ones who didn't escape the meat grinder," Doug said. "I've seen what you are going through. You can't shake a rifle much less a stick at the Directorate in the place you are. I'll make some calls and get you off the AWOL list, I know a space mermaid or two."

"Found the sledgehammer," Jurgen said returning. He looked at Hannah's face and then at Doug.

"I miss something?" Jurgen asked.

"I got some dust in my eyes," Hannah said. "Let me take a few whacks at the stairs."

"Sure," Jurgen said. Hannah took the sledgehammer and a pair of safety glasses and started to hit the stairs, which shuddered at every smack.

"When you heading back, subaltern?" Doug asked.

"I was planning on heading back in a day or two," Jurgen said. "I wanted to be sure everything was settled here. Why?"

"No real reason, just wanting to see when we'll all reach our equilibrium," Doug said.

"Well, I know Hannah will need to head back soon," Jurgen said. "I was planning to head back with her."

"Yeah, well, I am willing to stay a day or two. I have some leave, and provided the Admiralty doesn't get irritated with me, I'd like to use it, if that's okay, Doug," asked Hannah.

"If you can tolerate all the old crusty testosterone, a mutt, Jurgen and his siblings, you're welcome to stay, one old fraud to a heroine," said Doug.

"I'd be honored, and if you could make a call or two, that would make things easier," Hannah said, heaving the sledgehammer.

"Of course, I know a few lieutenants who climbed up the ladder to admiral. Some of those ladies will even pick up the call when I dial them," said Doug.

"Well, I am glad that's settled," Jurgen said. Hannah kept hitting the stairs, which finally shuddered and collapsed in a big dust cloud.

"They really were close to collapse," Doug said. "I'll have to get the local carpenters over here for an estimate."

Hannah looked like she had been dipped in dirt. Her face was filthy, but she was smiling.

"Should I get up on the roof?" Jurgen asked.

"No, I'll make my calls. You two go do something fun," Doug said.

"We could see a movie," Hannah suggested.

"Sure," Jurgen said, "You know, I've never even been to the local cinema. The theater is a shire over in Thackeraysville."

"Let me get cleaned up. Is there a shower I can use?" Hannah asked.

"I've got a guest room, downstairs. No guarantees on how clean the room is," Doug said. "Follow me, you can sleep in the guest bedroom provided the spiders don't eat you."

"I think I can handle some arachnids," Hannah said.

"I can get Maya and Agatha on cleaning duty if the room is terrible," Jurgen offered. Doug escorted Hannah down to the guest room, and Jurgen went along to see yet another part of the house. The guest room was clean and surprisingly spider free.

"Iggy must be making rounds in here looking for protein," Doug said. Hannah brought her day pack in and did an inspection. Nodding her head, she shooed the men out of the guest bedroom so she could change and shower. Doug and Jurgen went to the kitchen, the heart of the house.

"She needs a lot of support, subaltern," Doug said, tossing Jurgen a wet washcloth.

"She's tough, but VIKINGRAID hit us all hard," said Jurgen wiping down his face. "I was so tapped out that I went on the suicide mission you read about in the paper."

"Yep, been there, got the scars," Doug said. "The good thing is they get better. Like I said to Hannah, I got closure on my war. I was able to see the decomposing heads of the Ó Gallchobhoir tyrants. I witnessed the Union's birth. Karl came into his glory. Stahlburgh grew, things got better. The current war may not end that way. You and she will have your scars. But if Karl's pup pulls this out, we'll have peace and freedom for another generation."

"What happens then?" Jurgen asked.

"You get to be an old man and train the next generation to safeguard freedom. Then they take your place when your old bones are laid next to mine. The generation that messes that up, well, they're slaves to the next power that is hungry and wants to control the universe." Hannah entered a few moments later. She wore a casual light brown dress with her jacket and some sandals.

"You look really nice, young lady," Doug said.

Hannah smiled and said, "Thanks Doug. Coming from a mature sixty-year-old, such as yourself, I take that as a wonderful compliment."

"You know, you keep talking like that space mermaid, and I might forget about not getting another wife. Blonds have always treated me pretty well," Doug said. Hannah smiled and pulled out a tablet.

"Okay, movies playing at the Silver Swan cinema," Hannah said, "*Love in the Algorithms* is a love story about two programmers from Lochiel finding love in the Bundstadt. What do you think, Jurgen, Doug?"

"I'm out. I can't stand romantic comedies," Doug said. "I fall asleep at the movie theater too. Old age hasn't made that better, either."

"I'll pass on that one," said Jurgen. Hannah tapped her tablet, "Oh! Lukas Stahl is in this one, I can't believe the movie is out!" Doug made a thumbs down sign as Hannah looked at her tablet.

"What's the movie?" Jurgen asked.

"*Sleepless in the Sheeplands*," said Hannah. "Josef is a baron whose father has wasted his inheritance, while Maggie is a poor shepherdess who struggles to make ends meet for her family. When Josef gets lost in a fog, he stumbles upon the stunning Maggie and is immediately struck by her beauty and falls hopelessly in love."

"Hard pass," Jurgen said. "What an unbelievable plot line! We'll probably go and find out that Maggie is a mysterious baroness and that spies and terrorists threaten Josef's barony."

"Well, I though the movie sounded good, plus Lukas Stahl is Josef!" Hannah said. Jurgen stood behind Hannah and read over her shoulder.

"What about that one?" Jurgen said pointing at a movie poster on the tablet.

"*The Cowboy Engineer*? The mayor of a steampunk ancient Earth town struggles to survive after he loses his wife from deadly frostbite as a new ice age daws. Everything changes for him when a beautiful airship captain brings needed coal and other supplies to his isolated western town," Hannah read. "Okay, but since you're picking that, you can pick up the tab. This movie looks like a stinker to me."

Jurgen nodded and said, "Sure. Mind if I take the truck, Doug?"

"Nope, I'll hold down the fort," Doug said.

Jurgen held the door to the kitchen open for Hannah, and then followed her through and closed it. Jurgen opened the truck door for

Hannah, more for worry that the rusty door might fall off, than out of a sense of chivalry. Jurgen then went to the driver side and climbed in. He started the ignition and powered the fans.

"Ugh, Jurgen, the fans need aligned; they are scraping," Hannah said.

"Yeah, Doug just turns on the radio really loud," Jurgen said.

"Well, if we can get some tools, I am willing to fix the fans for him," Hannah said.

"I suppose we can, Hannah."

"The fix isn't that hard to do. I've been working on hover vehicles with my father since I was a teenager." Jurgen put the vehicle into drive and left the estate.

Jurgen guided the truck out of the village and down the county road to Thackeraysville. Hannah just sat in the passenger seat with the wind blowing through her hair. After twenty minutes, the truck came into Thackeraysville's outskirts. The town was doing better than Tavishire and there was a small suburb.

"Oh, how cute," Hannah said. "This place is adorable!" Jurgen nodded, concentrating on the road. The road curved around and there was a large shopping center with a chain clothing store, restaurants, a grocery, and a cinema. Jurgen pulled the truck into a parking space and shut the fans down and killed the ignition. He hopped out hoping to get Hannah's door, but she opened the door on her own. Thankfully, the door didn't fall off. She and Jurgen headed towards the box office. After buying two tickets, a beer for Jurgen, and a glass of wine for Hannah, they went into the movie. As the film opened, Hannah put her head on Jurgen's shoulder. Jurgen could smell the roses, jasmine, and pear of Hannah's perfume. As the film progressed, her head moved closer and closer to his chest.

As movie grew to a close and the beautiful airship captain and rugged cowboy kissed, Hannah reached up and kissed Jurgen. The kiss was gentle and timid, unlike the few times Jenny had kissed Jurgen.

Jurgen returned the kiss, touching the pilot's face. As the lights came on, they pulled away.

"That movie was terrible," Hannah said.

"Agreed," Jurgen said. "I only liked the end."

"Huh? How could you? She was totally not his type, and their romance felt clunky and forced," Hannah said.

"No, the kiss," Jurgen said.

"Oh," Hannah said with a smile, "I figured I'd try out a kiss with you. I've had a good time with you, and well, you are my hero."

Jurgen leaned in to kiss Hannah again, but his EVIL chimed three times. Hannah's tablet rang three times too.

"Well, how's that for timing," Jurgen said leaning back.

"Someone in the military better be calling us in for a full-on invasion of Stahlburgh, or I'm going on a rampage at the Admiralty. You wouldn't believe how competitive and petty those women can be! They can smell when one of us has a date, I swear!"

Jurgen checked his messages.

```
From: Assault High Command. To: SBA
Wulfjaeger, Jurgen Subject: Leave Canceled,
Report to Line Guards Barracks
```

"Weird, I'm reporting to the Line Guards barracks in the Bundstadt," Jurgen said. "I was supposed to be on leave for another week and a half, and then I'd be floating around Steinthal until classes start in September."

"Huh? Oddly I've been transferred to something called ORBITAL SCEPTER in orbit over Stahlburgh," Hannah said. "But at least I won't be going anywhere. Well, that's what the message indicates at least."

"Let's get out of here. I've sent my confirm. We need to get back to the house and let Doug know what's going on," Jurgen said. Hannah nodded. They left the theater and got into the truck. After twenty minutes they had arrived at the house. Doug was waiting for them outside.

"You got the call," Doug said. "Get packed up."

"How'd you..." Jurgen started to say but was cut off.

"Jurgen, who do you think used to make 'the call?' Load up, since an ex-marshal can't get you out of 'the call.' Besides, I don't think you want out of this one. Good hunting to the both of you."

Hannah went in to fetch her things, and Jurgen did likewise. He stripped into his underwear and threw on his battlesuit, without his helmet. He tossed his clothes into his duffel, and threaded the helmet through the duffel's straps. After almost twenty minutes, he was ready to go. He went downstairs. Hannah was packed and waiting alone in the kitchen.

"I've gotten us a taxi," Hannah said. "Doug was going to take us to the station, but I couldn't do that to him. Plus, someone has to watch the children." Jurgen took his opportunity and moved forward to kiss Hannah. He was passionate but gentle, and she wrapped her arms around his shoulders. They kissed for a moment and then parted.

"What was that about?" Hannah asked.

"I figured I'd try out a kiss with you. I've never kissed an angel before," Jurgen said. "Well, except for this one time watching a movie."

"What does this all mean?" Hannah asked.

"I don't know. I'm not sure what will happen with the war, but I'd like to take this as far as our hearts will let us," Jurgen said. Hannah smiled.

"What?" Jurgen said.

"I am glad the other guy, your friend, didn't rescue me," Hannah said.

"Why? You'd be kissing Roscoe now?" Jurgen said with a smile. A horn honked; the taxi was outside.

"Saved by the horn," Hannah said with a smile. "Let's go."

Hannah and Jurgen went out and met the hover taxi, which sat with the trunk open. Jurgen stuffed his and Hannah's bags into the trunk and headed for the passenger side.

"We're headed to Tauber-over-the-Roten," Hannah said. "There is an alternate spaceport there. If we're in luck, we can hop a transport. Or, if we're really lucky, I can requisition a trainer and get us to the capital in no time."

"Sound like you've done this before," Jurgen said.

"Not with a cute war hero who kissed me, but otherwise yes," Hannah said. "We used to do training flights to all the alternate spaceports. Some are in pretty rugged spots. LUNA liked to head to Tauber-over-the-Roten; she had an old beau somewhere around there. I'd tag along and then grab the transport back."

"Why?" Jurgen said.

"Well, flight hours and usually I was covering for her," Hannah said sadly. "I didn't do a good enough job in the end, I guess." Jurgen leaned over and kissed her.

"You saved me a dozen times over, and you'll save thousands more. You are my hero."

"Well then," Hannah said wiping tears from her eyes, "I suppose that makes us something special, heroes to each other."

"Yes," Jurgen said. They both sat heads touching. The taxi floated along until the vehicle reached the hinterland military facility. An Assaultman stood at the vehicle checkpoint. Jurgen paid the cab fare via his EVIL and grabbed their bags. Jurgen snapped his helmet on his head and handed Hannah her bag, as they approached the checkpoint.

"Identification, please," the guard asked. Jurgen presented his EVIL and Hannah her tablet. The guard nodded and ushered both into the facility.

"We'll need to go to the tower. I'll get a pressure suit there," Hannah said. She directed Jurgen towards the large, squat building with a glass tower on top. They both entered the building. Hannah left Jurgen at the entrance, while she headed towards the back. After about fifteen minutes, she came back.

She wore a gray pressure suit, her backpack slung on her shoulder and carried her helmet in her hand.

"We're in luck; I nabbed a trainer. We can take the interceptor back to the capital. Seems like today is my lucky day. A hunk gave me a couple kisses, and now I'm flying off to the capital and beyond," said Hannah.

"That's the plan then? Fly to the capital?" Jurgen said.

"I can drop you at the Line Guards, and then I'm going orbital," said Hannah. "I'll send a message when the dust settles. If you're worried, I can slather some lipstick on and tag you with kisses. I'd worry another Sister of Athena might take that as a challenge though." Jurgen hit the release on his helmet and kissed Hannah again. They stood together for a moment and then she said, "Come on, handsome. We better get moving before the tower cancels my flight."

Hannah put her helmet on and Jurgen did the same. They went out to the tarmac and Hannah tapped her tablet. A two-seater interceptor cockpit opened. Hannah went and opened the cargo hatch, and said over the point-to-point, "Load our stuff in here. I need to do a pre-flight check."

Jurgen stuffed the bags into the small space. He shut the hatch and stood waiting. Hannah was going over every centimeter of the trainer, looking for anything that was out of order and checking gauges and tanks.

"We're good. Climb into the back, that's the instructor seat," Hannah said. Jurgen climbed into the seat. The couch was small, and Jurgen's armor made the fit tight. He felt like a giant in the cockpit and worried he'd accidentally bump something.

"Hannah, I'm a little cramped back here," Jurgen said as his helmet switched to the interceptor's main comms channel.

"Sorry, the Navy makes things woman scale. Can you manage? The flight should only be a few minutes; I've plotted the fastest hyperbolic," Hannah said as she sat in the pilot's station and shut the cockpit door.

"I just don't want to bump anything important," Jurgen said.

"No problem," Hannah replied, "I'll turn off the instructor's seat. There... The controls are zeroed out, bump away, my beautiful Spartan," Hannah said.

Jurgen didn't have time to muse on what Hannah said as she started the engines and began throwing analog switches in the trainer. Navigation lights flashed and the trainer's ramjet-scramjet engines roared. The interceptor started rolling forward. Hannah was busy piloting the vehicle along the taxiway, towards the long runway. After a moment she pulled up parallel to the runway and throttled the engines. Then she rolled into position. Jurgen couldn't hear her conversation with the tower as his helmet wasn't patched in. Either way in a moment Hannah went from waiting to pushing the throttle to full. The interceptor rocketed forward and flashed over the fields of the Valley of the First Farmers. She pulled the stick back, and Jurgen could feel the gee forces press against him.

"Hang in there, Jurgen," Hannah said.

"I'm good, although not a fan of multiple gee forces," Jurgen said.

Hannah laughed and said, "That was a beginner's gee pull. I've done way more than that. I'm going to need to toughen you up!"

"When you drop out of an orbital capsule, you can toughen me up," Jurgen said.

"You've dropped from space? You're braver than I thought," Hannah said. "I don't do space drops in vehicles without engines."

"Yup," Jurgen said, "the Ninth dropped over Lochiel in training before Nakdong. We were gearing up for another operation that fell through, then we were sent to Nakdong."

"Sounds down right terrifying, floating in a capsule, then heat shielding down to a planet," Hannah said. Jurgen could feel the weightlessness of space as they floated over Stahlburgh.

"Honestly, the drop wasn't that bad. I wasn't fond of the high-altitude reentry, but once my parachute opened the drop was just a breathtaking experience," Jurgen said. Hannah pitched the interceptor nose down and fired the thrusters. The interceptor started to descend back into the atmosphere.

The ground flattened as the interceptor descended. Jurgen could see the Bundstadt off on the horizon as he and Hannah rocketed towards the city. Within moments the interceptor was circling the city.

"Something's going down, the ATC has me in a holding pattern," Hannah said.

Five minutes later Hannah said, "We're landing. The tower wants me to practically do a touch and go. We've got a short window if I want back up in the air. Sorry, beautiful, no goodbye kisses allowed."

Jurgen smiled and said, "I'll take a rain check on that."

The interceptor dove down to the small airstrip attached to the Line Guards barracks. Interceptors and dropships were lined up ferrying people and cargo up and down. Hannah entered the glide path, touched down, and rolled off the airstrip tarmac and on to the taxiway. Minutes later she rolled the interceptor into a taxiway connecting some small hangars.

"Bye, bye, Jurgen," Hannah said. Jurgen unfastened himself, hopped out, and grabbed his duffel from the small cargo hatch. He put Hannah's bag in the cockpit, in case she needed to disembark via cockpit only. He shut the hatch.

"Bye, Hannah. Best of luck. Write you soon," Jurgen said as Hannah shut the cockpit. The interceptor's engines throttled and Hannah turned onto the taxiway to take off. Jurgen watched as her interceptor taxied to the take off point. She flared her engines in a test and then rolled into take off. After a moment's pause, she kicked the throttle into afterburner and in a flash the interceptor was high up in the sky and then gone. Jurgen felt a small pang of sorrow at seeing her go. Then coming back to his surroundings, he realized he needed to find out where he was going.

The Holstensonne was setting and night was approaching. The base went from twilight to brightly lit as lights kicked on. Enlisted of all ranks ran to and fro. Jurgen would salute as they saluted him. Returning a salute still felt odd, but Jurgen was becoming more comfortable with the action.

"When the time comes to go to school for all this I'll be a natural," Jurgen said with some satisfaction. He decided to follow the crowd and soon saw a sergeant at a desk who processed Assaultmen who were queued in front of him. Jurgen joined the line. When he approached the sergeant, Jurgen presented his EVIL. The sergeant scanned the device.

"Hello Subaltern Wulfjaeger, you need to step over here," the sergeant said. Jurgen wondered what this was all about. He wasn't used someone giving directions and expecting him use his own initiative. A thin dark haired Assault captain approached Jurgen. The captain wore a class A uniform and no battlesuit. Jurgen snapped a salute which the captain returned.

"Captain Harold Baker. You are Subaltern Wulfjaeger, right?" the captain asked.

"Subaltern Jurgen Wulfjaeger reporting, sir," Jurgen said in response.

"Good, follow me," Baker said, leading Jurgen through a maze of barracks into a large Quonset hut that had several APCs and spacecons inside.

"Wulfjaeger meet your new command," Baker said.

"Uh, sir, I think there's a problem," Wulfjaeger said. "I'm supposed to be at the Academy."

"No. There's no problem at all. I *asked* for you," Baker said. "I read the official accounts. Any Assaultman who has your tenacity is who I need in Special Projects. We've got a war to win, and if we don't have a bag of nasty tricks, well, we're all dead men." As Jurgen and Baker were speaking, Assaultmen entered.

"Perfect timing, I'll introduce you," Baker said. "Men, listen up. This is your new commanding officer, Subaltern Jurgen Wulfjaeger. Now, line up and sound off!" The men moved to stand in a line. They all wore battlesuits and Jurgen's helmet hadn't been keyed in on their identities.

"Corporal Lucas Bitner, sir," the first man in line said.

"Lance Corporal Liam Munster, sir," the second said.

"Lance Corporal Jari Pertti, sir," the third said.

"Lance Corporal Ismail Ackbar, a pleasure to see you again, sir," Ackbar said clicking his heels.

"Where is Keller?" Baker asked.

"Here, sir," an Assaultman said, he came in and stood next to Ackbar, next to him was a small creature in a dog-like battlesuit.

"Sergeant Jason Keller, sir," said Keller. After a moment, he added, "This here is Moray... No, I'm not introducing you as the Alpha! I'm the alpha!"

"Huh?" Wulfjaeger said, "What's that all about, sergeant?"

"Moray is the heart of our special project," Baker said. "A dog that has been equipped with Terran bio-networking augments. At ease men!"

The men relaxed. Jurgen asked, "Wait! I'm not the greatest Stater, but aren't the bio-networking augments against the statutes of the State Religion? I vaguely remember something about disfiguring the soul and the destruction of the human-being by Artificial Intelligence."

"A frequent question, right captain," a female voice said. A Navy enlisted woman appeared, wearing Navy gray coveralls. She was tall, almost as tall as Jurgen, with platinum blond hair and green eyes.

"Subaltern, meet Specialist Rosamund Burkhart," Baker said,

"Burkhart is on loan from the Navy for this project. To answer the question, subaltern, the church wisely realizes that augments corrupt our inner humanity and taint our immortal soul. That is why they are illegal for people. If you don't have an immortal soul like Moray, well, then, there are no issues." Jurgen cringed inwardly. He was now commanding a nine-kilogram Frankenstein's monster.

"Sir, Moray isn't a monster," said Keller. "He protects us." Jurgen looked at Keller. Could Keller read his thoughts? Moray trotted over and put his battlesuited paws on Jurgen. Jurgen wasn't sure what to do.

"Moray, come!" Keller said. "Sorry, sir. Moray doesn't always understand the chain of command." The dog returned to the line.

"Captain, did we scan Mister Wulfjaeger," Burkhart asked.

"I'm sure he's clean unlike that midshipwoman that the Navy sent," Baker said.

"Protocol is protocol," Burkhart said. She approached Jurgen and waved a device across his body.

"He's clean," Burkhart said after a quick review of the results.

"Of course he is," Baker said. "The Assault hasn't had a compromise."

"Yet," Burkhart said. "Now, subaltern, you need to strip. Even as new as that battlesuit is, we have newer, better equipment."

"Right here?" Jurgen asked.

"Yup, we're all friends," Burkhart said.

"One moment, any questions for the men, Wulfjaeger," Baker asked.

"No, sir," Jurgen said.

"Dismissed," Baker said. The men went back to their work, only Ackbar remained.

Jurgen began peeling off his battlesuit, and Ackbar gave him a hand.

"You'll be happy to trade suits, sir," Ackbar said. Jurgen waited and Burkhart came back with an almost identical battlesuit.

"I don't see a difference here, Ackbar," Jurgen said. Ackbar helped

Jurgen put on the new suit. The HUD booted up as Jurgen put on the helmet.

"Welcome to Special Projects, Subaltern Jurgen Wulfjaeger!" the faceplate said. Jurgen scanned the room, the faceplate identified Burkhart, Ackbar, and Baker.

"I get the identification system, but what's so nifty about this suit?" Jurgen said.

"Grab a rifle," Burkhart said. Jurgen went over to the mini-armory and pulled out a rifle.

"Initializing new weapon... ... ..." the faceplate stated. "Weapon ready."

"That's a training weapon. That rifle doesn't shoot live rounds, just compressed air and paint. Aim the rifle at the target on the far end of the bay," Burkhart said. Jurgen put the weapon up to his shoulder. As he did so, the scope sight appeared in his helmet. Unlike his previous suit, his new battlesuit started calculating windage and was auto-adjusting for drift and wind speed.

"Nifty, but we're inside," Jurgen said. Burkhart hit a button on a tablet and large fans started moving the air around the bay. The wind began to whip up to sixty kilometers per hour, which Jurgen's helmet noted.

"Go ahead and shoot the target, sir," Burkhart said. Jurgen put his finger on the trigger, and the battlesuit began fine adjustments giving Jurgen a direction to move to achieve a perfect dead center hit. Jurgen squeezed the trigger and the paint round shot out hitting the target almost exactly in the center.

"The wind tunnel makes the paint rounds drift after they've been fired," Burkhart said, "but when we go to the live fire range, the shots are dead accurate, down to the millimeter."

"Work time?" a message came up on Jurgen's HUD. "I am *best* at work!"

"Who's pinging me?" Jurgen asked.

"Sorry, sir," Keller's voice came across the detachment's channel. "Moray likes to go to the range."

"That mutt needs to learn some comsec," Jurgen said, clearing the message that was being repeated over and over.

"We're working on that, sir," Keller said.

"Okay, subaltern, do you see the button off to the left on the lower side of your HUD. The button looks like a cloud and light bulb with a no circle over the entire icon?" Burkhart asked.

"Yes, specialist. How do I press that one?" Jurgen said.

"Snap your fingers with your off hand," Burkhart said. Jurgen snapped his fingers on his left hand. The icon highlighted.

"Well, what did the button do? I don't notice anything different," Jurgen said.

"Check your feet," Burkhart said. Jurgen looked down and didn't see anything except for a vague visual distortion. The suit had cloaked him completely on the visible spectrum.

"Not bad," Jurgen said. "But what about infrared or some of the other combat spectrums?"

"Switch the HUD and see," Burkhart said. Jurgen flipped through several standard combat visual scanning frequencies. In some, the suit had a reduced profile, while in others he was invisible.

"That's just ducky. Now I can sneak into the mess hall after hours," Jurgen said after a chuckle.

"The cloak isn't perfect, but we keep getting better and better at covering our signatures," Burkhart said. "If you were, say, infiltrating an enemy base, you could maybe make your way in and out before the enemy knew you were there. There are other use cases we're working out. That's what the detachment is here for, testing."

"What is up with the dog?" Jurgen said.

"He's your sniper," Baker said. "Just wait until you start training. Moray is the toughest and most dedicated—so far—of all of you."

"We'll see about that," Jurgen said. From what Jurgen had seen,

Moray was no Ignatius.

"Well, that's that," Baker said. "I'm off. Burkhart or Keller will show you your bunk. We have an officer shack in the back of the large Quonset hut bay. I've officially got a bunk there, but I don't stay there often, so you'll have the shack to yourself, subaltern."

"Nice, thanks, sir," Jurgen said dropping the rifle in the mini-armory and grabbing his stuff. "What about my old suit?"

"We'll send the suit back to the armory in a day or two. The biggest pain about this job is that we have to move randomly. Too many Terran eyes are looking here on Stahlburgh. I tried to lobby Assault High Command to move us to Lochiel or Brandstadt, but no luck on that front," Baker said. "Now, I'm off, heading up to ORBITAL SCEPTER. You coming along, Burkhart?"

"Yes, captain. Let me grab my pressure suit," Burkhart said, putting down a tablet and some tools.

"Sir, I'll show you the O-shack," Ackbar said, motioning Jurgen forward. The lance corporal made a zig zag through all the spacecons in the hut's large bay. Eventually after several lefts-then-rights, Ackbar motioned towards the O-shack. The O-shack was a converted spacecon that had two entrance doors, one on each side. Jurgen entered the closest one and saw there were two bedrooms. A partition was folded but could accordion across to the opposite wall in the middle of the container.

"Thanks Ackbar," Jurgen said over the comm. "I'm going to get settled, I'll catch you at chow time tomorrow."

"Aye, sir, goodnight," said Ackbar wandering off. Jurgen dropped his duffel on the farthest bed. Neither bunk looked used. He scanned the room. There were two desks with holo-displays into which someone could hook a tablet. Each desk had office supplies, including ink pens and paper. There was a red physical codebook on one of the desks, the closer one. There was also a physical classification manual on the same desk. The opposite desk had a series of data sticks, some colored red, others blue. There was an older, wired and corded audio call device in the center of the room. Jurgen suspected that was some sort of spook phone. There was a large holo display above the phone, probably for monitoring the news services. Across the container's middle was a small coffee mess. Jurgen nosed around in the selection. The beans were better than the mess hall, which was a plus. Moving to the center of his new home, he saw there was an armor stand next to his bed.

"Not bad accommodations," Jurgen said to himself. "I had worse on the *Advantage*."

Jurgen unpacked his duffel and stored his effects in the container's small locker and trunk. He pulled off his battlesuit and arranged the armor on the stand. Jurgen was home, for however long this container would be home.

He pulled out his EVIL and opened the message buffer. Doug had written; he was doing well as a new grandfather. He gave a few words of encouragement and ordered Jurgen to come home safe. Jurgen penned a reply, "Aye, aye, sir!" and hit send. Then, Jurgen wrote a light-hearted note to Hannah, expressing his hopes for a future date, soon. Jurgen put the EVIL on the small nightstand that was attached to his bunk, and then rolled over to sleep.

Over the next few days, Jurgen realized his purpose with Special Projects. He was the secretary, writing reports on the Assaultmen and their training. Occasionally, he'd throw on his battlesuit and go to the range. He was there to observe as the sergeant, the dog, and the corporals had all the fun. For being attached to a "black" project and consorting with spooks on a daily basis, the duty assignment was really boring. Hannah had written him and was apparently in the middle of her own secret assignment. She, at least, seemed like she was having more fun. The little she would say said everything. On a positive note, the nature of the detachment was very flat, and everyone from the captain down to the dog were informal with each other. The captain, especially with Jurgen, came and went being addressed as Baker. Jurgen returned to being Wulfjaeger, and surnames sufficed for the Assaultmen too. The weeks rolled on until the end of May, in typical Assault fashion things suddenly changed. Jurgen was working on a report when Captain Baker came in shouting.

"Gather up people," Baker said. Jurgen hopped up from his desk, he didn't need an invitation to get away from paperwork. Jurgen left the O-shack and walked to the large sand table that was along the south side of the massive Quonset hut.

"Gather up, folks, we have a visitor," Baker said. The detachment gathered around. Even the dog joined the group, before curling into a ball. Jurgen stared at the dog.

"That's Moray's thinking pose," Keller said.

"He's snoring, Keller," Jurgen said.

"He thinks best when sleeping, Wulfjaeger," responded Keller defensively.

"Listen up," Baker said. "This is USIS Chief Hendrik Olson, head of Domestic Branch. He's got a potential op for you all."

"Hello, all," Olson said hesitantly, "as the captain said, I am Hendrik Olson, and I work on domestic issues for USIS."

Jurgen nodded. He was the only one whose face was visible, as he was not wearing a battlesuit.

"USIS believes there are subversive elements sponsored by the Directorate inside the Union attempting to start a civil war. These elements were the ones who hit the Primus, killed Alasdair Campbell, and attempted to assassinate Alexander Gordon. Due to some triangulation of signals through SIGINT, we've got a series of potential sites where we think these subversive elements are hiding. For the record, we're calling them Ultra-Violets, as these terrorists are espousing extreme violet rhetoric. That's just a smoke screen though. The Ultras are backed to the hilt by the Directorate. Directorate electronics, weapons, even combat gear, rations, and, oh yeah, boots.

Any questions?"

"How do they walk with those Terran boots? Aren't they made for the webbed feet of those Earth inbreds?" O'Brien asked. The Assaultmen snickered.

"Uh, the boots aren't made for webbed feet," Olson said.

"Where do you think they are operating from?" Jurgen said.

"At present we believe there are two main groups. We've got one working here in the capital and one out in the Sheeplands. Both groups are dangerous, and we want you to go in and take them out. Whenever and wherever we get a break, we'll deploy this detachment for a kill shot," Olson said. "The thought at USIS is we'll keep an Orbital Drop team for one terrorist group and you all will take out the other."

"What is an Orbital Drop team?" Ackbar asked.

"Those are our paramilitary security forces. We use them as low-profile retrieval teams when assets are stranded in hostile territory," Olson said.

"Why use us then?" Bitner asked.

"We're tight on resources too. We can only spare one team as the rest are off world," Olson said.

"Sounds complicated. Let's ramp up training. We'll be ready," Baker said. "Now, we're all hands on-deck. That means more of you on the range, Wulfjaeger, in a command slot, and less paperwork."

Jurgen pumped his fist and said, "Yes, excellent!"

"Now, Mister Olson," Baker said.

"Actually, I'm Doctor Olson," Hendrik said, then meekly. "I can also go by Chief..."

"Chief Olson here will set up the sand table with what he believes the group's assets are and likely scenarios," Baker said. The detachment would run through every scenario on the table. Every time they ran the scenario the setting was an urban combat environment. Jurgen tried to absorb all of the details, and he found himself taking notes on his EVIL.

"We're taking a break," Baker said as everyone grew tired. They had been working the scenarios on the sand table for over four hours. The Assaultmen rose and went to get chow from the mess hall. Baker came over to Jurgen.

"What do you think?" Baker asked quietly.

"The table is all well and good, but we need range time. I can't see us doing this op without any casualties, either us, or some of the collateral," Jurgen said. After the first scenario, Olson had thrown wrench into the works with civilians who would casually wander through what quickly became a battle zone. The dense urban scenarios in the capital were especially full of civilians who Olson played as having too little sense and too much curiosity.

"You aren't leveraging Moray," Baker said.

"The mutt? I've seen him at the range; he's nothing special," Jurgen said.

"Uh huh," Baker said passively. Jurgen had learned the captain never argued. If he disagreed, he would just say "uh huh" and leave the subject at that. Jurgen went for lunch and the Assaultmen came back. The detachment spent the rest of the day working on the sand table with Olson running scenarios. Jurgen started to suspect that no one had any good intelligence on the Ultras as his day ended. He ran to the mess hall, loaded up on food and came back to the O-shack to eat and work until lights out. As he entered, he saw Captain Baker in the shack at the other desk.

"Hey, Baker, working late?" Jurgen asked, dropping the take away food on his desk.

"Yes, and staying tonight, we're going to get up early and run through some range exercises. I'm not happy with the idea of USIS paramilitary teams doing our work," Baker said.

"Sounds like a plan," Jurgen said.

"We'll need every man, and dog, ready to go if and when we get the call," Baker said.

"Aye," said Jurgen.

"I know Moray seems, unorthodox, but he's got the potential to turn the tide of the war in a lot of ways," said Baker.

"I'll believe that when I see him in action," said Jurgen.

"Care to make a little wager?" asked Baker.

"Sure, five griffins? What's the bet?" said Jurgen.

"Moray versus the detachment," said Baker. "First exercise tomorrow."

"We get him before he gets us? What side is Keller on?" asked Jurgen.

"Keller sits out the exercise. We don't want to confuse Moray," said Baker.

"Okay, you're on," Jurgen said. Jurgen ate his dinner and both men worked on paperwork until lights out. Jurgen climbed into his bunk and was out to the world.

In the morning, Baker was up and in a battlesuit. A rare occurrence as the captain was almost always too busy to suit up. Jurgen rose, stretched, and put on his battlesuit. Both officers went to the sand table, where the Assaultmen, Moray and Burkhart were waiting.

"Load up in the APC. We're going to the junk house," said Baker. "Pertti, you're driving." The detachment climbed into the APC, and Pertti started the engine. The APC rolled across the base to an area that looked like a small junk yard. The Line Guards called the area "junk house" because of all the nooks and crannies made by the large scrap piles. There were old ship bulkheads, rusted-through spacecons and dropship parts. Occasionally, the Line Guards would pick through the debris and, shift the junk house around. As a range went, the junk house represented an urban warfare environment where bad guys could find places to hide and take shots at the Assaultmen.

"Work?" a message appeared on Jurgen's HUD.

"Keller, the mutt can't cheat like that," Jurgen said.

"Sorry, Wulfjaeger. I'll let Moray know he's on a different channel today," Keller said.

"Okay, here is the scenario," Baker said. "Moray is an Ultra enemy who's gone into a junkyard to escape, since someone let a squirter through. If Moray gets away, he will kill civilians and cause more mayhem. Your job is simple: get Moray before he gets you. Any questions?"

"No, sir," said the men.

"We're ready, Baker," said Jurgen.

"Great Wulfjaeger, line the men up on the blue line. Moray get ready on the red line. Keller you're out. I'm muting you so you can't help either side. Three, two, one, go!" said Baker, playing a whistle sound on the channel.

Jurgen took off finding cover, he hand signed for his corporals to surround the junk house and create a net for a field of fire.

"What the... I'm out," said Munster angrily.

"That's one," said Baker. "I'm muting you, Munster, since you're dead."

"Bitner, keep an eye out. When he pops up, get the mutt," said Jurgen.

Jurgen watched as the range weapons shot paint at a spot where junk had tumbled.

"Did you get him," asked Pertti. Pertti spun around shooting rapidly.

"What! The mutt got me!" said Bitner just before he was muted.

"Work together," said Jurgen. "Ackbar flank left wide, Pertti right, I'll go up the center." Ackbar hopped up from his cover and paint splatted his helmet.

"The animal got me," said Ackbar sitting down. Pertti started squeezing off rounds. He had a bead on Moray, but the dog was too fast and too chaotic to lead as a target. Pertti seemed to be a half second behind even with the fancy targeting.

Jurgen poked his head out and tried to catch Moray in a crossfire, and the dog shot at him. Jurgen rolled back.

"Almost got him," said Pertti. "Malcolm's beard! I'm out of ammo and need to reload. Cover me, sir."

Jurgen rolled around and saw the dog trying to get the drop on Pertti. Jurgen smiled as he trained his sight on Moray. He was about to squeeze the trigger when the dog jumped, turned and shot Jurgen in the face. Without missing a beat, the dog charged forward and double tapped Pertti.

"You owe me five griffins, Wulfjaeger," said Baker. "Do you want to try double or nothing?"

"No, Baker, you've made your point. Come on, guys. Let's set up with holograms," said Jurgen. He tossed out some drones that would simulate terrorists and the Assaultmen went over to a hanging sprayer that would clean the paint off their battlesuits.

The next few exercises went better for the Assaultmen. Keller and Moray were a powerful force multiplier as both could "smoke out" the bad guys from hiding places. Lunch time rolled around and Baker called a halt.

"Not bad," said Baker.

"Baker, you should know we're not the important ones here. This is Moray's world, we just happen to live here," said Keller.

Baker laughed and said, "The way he's been working, Moray deserves to be an emperor. Grab an MRE bar and let's set up again."

Jurgen popped his faceplate and gobbled the MRE bar. The bar was chicken or fish, dry and not very tasty, but chock full of calories. Keller pulled Moray's faceplate up and gave the dog food and water. Jurgen still couldn't believe the mutt had beaten him. Moray came over and put his paws on Jurgen's legs.

"Moray says he's the officer now, since he whooped you all this morning," said Keller with a chuckle.

"He can join me at the Academy in the fall, if he can hack the classwork, I'll salute him and call him sir," said Jurgen.

"He says that's not fair, because he can't read," responded Keller.

"Not my problem," said Jurgen with a smile.

"Okay, seems like everyone is rested," said Baker. "Let's go again."

The detachment spent the rest of the afternoon training. Sometimes they would go against each other, sometimes they'd fight drones, and sometimes they would split Keller and Moray versus the rest. As the Holstensonne started to wane in the June sky, Jurgen realized he was getting tired.

"In the APC, on the double. We'll head back to the Quonset hut, then you're dismissed," Baker said abruptly. The detachment loaded up, and the APC rolled out, Pertti drove once again. In ten minutes the APC had rolled into the large Quonset hut, and the doors shut behind them.

"Baker, you aren't going to like this news," Burkhart said approaching the group.

"What now?" Baker asked.

"We're needed at ORBITAL SCEPTER. The brass said we'll be needed there for the next week," Burkhart replied.

"Well, I'm happy I've got the subaltern to run the exercise. When do we leave?" Baker said.

"Now," Burkhart replied, "the dropship is waiting for us, I've been trying to raise you for the past hour."

"No comms was a necessary evil, let's go. Wulfjaeger, you have command," Baker said leaving with the Navy specialist.

"Orders sir?" Ackbar asked.

"Chow time. Come back, clean and stow your gear, and get some rack time. We're back in the saddle tomorrow," Jurgen said. The Assaultmen lumbered off slowly. Jurgen could tell they were tired. Jurgen went to the O-shack and dropped his armor, and then decided to hit the mess hall. He picked up his EVIL, which he had left when they went to the range and checked the device for messages. The message checking gambit was risky as he might not make his way to the mess hall if he got sucked in by the device. There was a message from Hannah, the subject was "Guess what?" Jurgen slid the EVIL on his arm and decided to read the message while walking.

```
Hi Jurgen, my beautiful Spartan,
Guess what! I am at the Line Guards base,
doing an overnight, as I am working on
something hush hush. Where are you?
Kisses,
Hannah
```

Jurgen suddenly felt like he was electrified. Hannah was on base! Jurgen booted the calling application. The tone rang, rang, and then finally connected.

"Where are you, sweetie? No one knows who you are here. I'm beginning to think you don't exist," Hannah said.

"Meet me in the mess hall," said Jurgen.

"You mean the galley, Assault boy," Hannah said playfully.

"Yes, the place you stuff your face," said Jurgen.

"We're dainty in the Navy. We don't stuff our faces; we suck down our bags, like proper ladies," said Hannah.

"Don't remind me. I still have bad dreams about all the wine," said Jurgen.

"Oh, never mind. I see you. Bye for like three seconds," Hannah said hanging up. Jurgen looked around and saw Hannah fast walking at him. She wore her class A's and Jurgen though she looked like a movie star.

She threw her arms around him, kissed him, and said, "Hey, sodger, long time, no kiss." Jurgen kissed her for a few minutes and then they stopped.

"I asked the Allfather for an angel to drop from the sky, and all I got was a lousy pilot," said Jurgen playfully.

"Behave, or I'll find another subaltern to go to dinner with,"

Hannah said.

"Oh, you're taking me to dinner? I guess I am a pretty cheap date, since the Union is footing our dinner bill," said Jurgen.

"I'm Dutch by heritage. We don't say we're cheap. Instead we say we're thrifty," Hannah said. "Come on, my stomach is rumbling, and I'm eager to have a solid meal."

Hannah and Jurgen entered the galley or mess hall and grabbed plastic trays. They wandered the expansive food selection. Jurgen chose Assaultman Curry, and Hannah went for a Valkyrie Special Salad that came from the salad bar. They sat down, bowed their heads in prayer, and then began eating.

"You look hungry. There is barely a spaetzle left in that curry, honey," said Hannah. Jurgen smiled and nodded.

"You should talk," he said, "I think there is only a leaf of lettuce or two in that bowl."

"I've been sucking bags. What is your excuse?" said Hannah with a smile.

"Training, I have a d... an Assaultman, who is an excellent sniper. We had to go a few rounds against him, and he put up a good fight," said Jurgen.

"What's his name? He sounds dreamy," said Hannah, with a sly smile.

"Moray," said Jurgen.

"That's an odd surname," said Hannah.

"Yup," said Jurgen with a smile. "Look, next time I get leave, I want to meet your parents."

"Oh ho," said Hannah in surprise. "Where is this coming from? Aren't you happy just fooling around?"

"Kissing via message isn't cutting the mustard. If we get married, we can stay in the married quarters at the Academy. I think with your Ace and my GSG we can probably find a nice posting that keeps us together," said Jurgen.

"Marriage, eh?" said Hannah a little pensively.

"Well, I mean, if your mom and dad have no objections, and the war," said Jurgen.

"Relax, beautiful. As long as you aren't carrying me off to the chapel right now, I'm not saying no. Besides Mom is dying to meet you, and Dad is making grumpy papa bear noises, but I think secretly he's happy I am dating a blond boy, just like him," said Hannah with a wink.

"And mom has brown hair?" asked Jurgen.

"She swears her hair is light brown, but if she stands for five seconds in the Holstensonne, her locks go golden... supposedly," said Hannah with a giggle.

"Well, Doug is the closest I really have to a parent. I am sure you figured out he's my grandfather," said Jurgen.

"I knew he was kin somehow. In the right light you two look alike," said Hannah.

"Are you saying I look older than a century?" said Jurgen playfully.

"No, I'm saying he looks almost twenty-two like my beautiful boyfriend," said Hannah.

"Good recovery. Now that chow time is over, where are you headed?" asked Jurgen.

"I can't say, sorry, dear, but what I am doing is super exciting," said Hannah. "I promise."

"I understand. I can't talk about what I am doing either, but if you knew, you'd probably fall down laughing at the absurdity," said Jurgen.

"Like Assaultman Moray?" said Hannah.

"Him especially," Jurgen replied. Hannah's arm buzzed, and Jurgen noted she now wore an EVIL.

"Hey, you got one!" Jurgen said pointing to Hannah's wrist.

"Yeah, and this thing really is evil! I can't get a moments peace with the device. I miss my tablet; I could 'forget' the device in places," Hannah said. She flipped her wrist and looked at the EVIL.

"Oh drat, I have to go! See you later, boyfriend," Hannah said standing up.

"What no kiss?" Jurgen said.

"Sorry, no time, I'm really late. You can eyeball me in this uniform as I am leaving. I'll make everything up to you later," said Hannah with a wink.

"Bye, bye, girlfriend," said Jurgen as Hannah walked off. She sashayed in an exaggerated manner, playing things up for Jurgen's gaze. After Hannah disappeared, Jurgen decided to hit the chow line one more time looking for a snack or dessert. He settled on a strudel and grabbed the treat to go. He walked back to the Quonset hut as the Holstensonne was setting. The lights of the base came on, and he stopped to admire Eisenwald rising over the horizon on the pleasant June evening. In the skies, above there were tons of shooting stars. Navy transports, war craft, civilian spaceliners, and satellites all floated up in the void. Jurgen entered the Quonset hut, which was quiet. Everyone was tired, the training had been hard that day. Jurgen entered the O-shack, took off his uniform, and crawled into bed, placing his EVIL by his head, just in case. He closed his eyes and went to sleep.

Jurgen stirred as his EVIL made a three loud chirps, the notification for an urgent message. He picked up the EVIL and looked at what the device said.

> FLASH TRAFFIC! FLASH TRAFFIC! Second Stahlburgh Rifles Special Projects Detachment to report for deployment in thirty minutes on Tarmac Bravo in the detachment APC. THIS IS NOT A DRILL! FLASH TRAFFIC! FLASH TRAFFIC!

"Ah, for crying out loud," Jurgen said to himself rising and tossing on the battlesuit under layer. "The moment Baker leaves we get called up."

Jurgen hauled the battlesuit chest plate over his head, and then put the lower half. He had to backtrack for a moment as he had the order backwards. After grumping about being sleep deprived, he fitted the two parts together and found his helmet. Putting on the helmet, Jurgen attached his EVIL to the suit and found the intercom button.

"Attention! Special Projects Detachment up and at 'em, we have fifteen minutes to get our butts on Tarmac Bravo! Come on, gents! This is what they pay us the big coins for!"

The enlisted men moved faster than Jurgen, and he was happy to see Munster fall out of a spacecon and open the armory. The men grabbed rifles and got ready to move.

"Load up in the APC!" Jurgen said over the intercom. The troops started moving. Keller and Moray climbed into the back first, Munster entered the driving compartment, and Pertti climbed into the cupola. Bitner took the loading station at the door, and Ackbar was on last with the large medical supply container. Jurgen marched towards the APC and climbed the ramp, as Bitner shut the hatch. The APC started moving as Jurgen climbed into the commander's station. His battlesuit synced with the APC and he was ready to rumble.

"Call coming in for you, sir," said Pertti from the cupola.

"This is Wulfjaeger, go for communication," said Jurgen.

"Good morning, subaltern. I hear you boys need a lift. I'll be catching your APC and we'll do a hyperbolic. Make sure the hatches are sealed and you boys are all suited up. TAWNY TULIP out," said the pilot.

"Hatch check!" Jurgen shouted on the d-channel, the detachment channel.

"Secured!" said Bitner from the back.

"Secured!" said Munster from the front.

"Okay, hang on," said Jurgen. A moment later a loud clank echoed in the APC. All the Assaultmen's stomachs dropped as the APC was hoisted into the air.

"You can kill the engine and go into neutral. I've got you boys," said

TULIP over the d-channel.

"You heard the lady," said Jurgen. He looked as more traffic flashed in.

```
FLASH TRAFFIC! FLASH TRAFFIC! Second
Stahlburgh Rifles Special Projects Detachment
en route to Gilbraith-on-Heather. Subaltern
Wulfjaeger to report to First Gilbraith
Volunteers Colonel Maximilian Fraser upon
arrival. EOM
```

Jurgen acknowledged the message, and did what the Assault always did when there was a lull between action. He closed his eyes and started to doze. When he arrived in Gilbraith-on-Heather, he'd get his orders from the colonel. He hoped the colonel was ready to rumble. Jurgen's detachment was certainly ready. As Jurgen was about to nod off, he heard snoring on the d-channel.

"Who is snoring on the channel?" said Jurgen testily.

Keller replied, "That's Moray, Wulfjaeger. He says he needs his beauty rest, or he'll start to look like us apes!"

Epilogue

The First Star Lady's limo parked in the motor pool. She jumped out and approached the Villa's elevator. Her brother stood waiting for her there.

"Siobhan, been a while," said the Field Marshall of the Assault.

"Paddy, we should do this on a day we don't have to deliver bad news," said First Star Lady.

"Who will take the news worse? Him or her?" asked Paddy.

"If you have to ask, you've forgotten our childhood, with big sis always bossing us around," said Siobhan. The elevator opened; Weber stood in the lift. He looked tired and worn.

"They are waiting, sir and ma'am," said Weber. The First Star Lady and Field Marshal of the Assault entered. Weber nervously pushed the physical button. The majordomo's eyes were red, whether from lack of sleep or tears neither military officer could tell. The elevator door opened.

"They are in the private gallery," said Weber. The sun was coming up on a crisp Tuesday in October. For once, there wasn't a cloud in the sky, and the Holstensonne's rays came streaming in the protector's public apartments.

"No sense putting this off," said Paddy. Otto watched as the military officers left the lift. He stepped a meter away from the elevator, close enough to hear the conversation, but far enough away to not be seen as a nosy servant.

Otto knew the arrival of the flag officers meant trouble with the front.

"Good morning, Lord Protector," said Paddy and Siobhan together.

"Good morning, Paddy, Siobhan," said the protector.

"Where is Marta?" asked Siobhan.

"I'm here, sister," said the patroness. She was clad in a long robe that covered her night gown.

"Sir and madam," began Paddy. "As the Assault officer in charge I regret to tell you that your son, Heinrich von Machthaber has been lost over L 98-59 Foxtrot." The patroness began to cry loudly both the Field Marshal of the Assault and the First Star Lady closed their eyes.

"Details, give me details!" said Raimond sharply. Siobhan stepped forward.

"Sir, the fourth fleet entered L 98-59, and contrary to naval intelligence, did not see any presence of the enemy. The eighty ships of the attack fleet began to encircle L 98-59 Foxtrot. After a bombardment, the transport *Bismarck* was given clearance to disembark, the Fifteenth Stahlburgh Rifle Regiment. The transports *T.Roosevelt* and *Churchill* followed her. When the *Bismarck* hit the orbit drop line, the point of no return, the orbital guns on L 98-59 Foxtrot started. The *Churchill* was able to make a quick turn around. But both the *Bismarck* and the *T.Roosevelt* were hit. Admiral Schultz ordered the one hundred and fifty first interceptor wing to knock out the batteries. That's when the Terrans launched their attack." The patroness held a corner of her robe against her face trying to control her sobbing. The protector standing in his uniform shirt and trousers, looked like a man hollowed out by life.

"And," said the protector.

"The Terran Directorate First Fleet, called 'Pride Fleet,' came out from the pole of the small moon, L 98-59 Gamma Beta. The two hundred ships of the Terran First Fleet clashed with the Union's Fourth Fleet. Between the hammer of the Terran First Fleet and anvil of the orbital guns of L 98-59 Foxtrot, the Union Fourth Fleet stayed and fought like true Sisters of Athena. Admiral Schultz commanded the captain of the *Chrysodory*, the Admiral's flag ship, to charge. Captain Bauer obliged her admiral and the *Chrysodory,* the *Aegis*, the *Pegasus*, and the *Thetis* made a wedge and attacked the Directorate First fleet. The *Spirit of Lena* came under attack and had to recall her fighters. If the *Advantage*, *Supremacy*, *Ascendancy*, *Sovereignty*, and *Zenith* hadn't provided a screen, the fleet carrier would have been destroyed. At the same time, the *Bismarck* and *T.Roosevelt* plummeted down into the atmosphere and broke up." The patroness began sobbing loudly again. The protector went to his wife and put his arms around her.

"Go on, we both want to know the rest," said the protector softly.

"Admiral Schultz, sensing the fight was lost, held the *Chrysodory* as a rear-guard, sacrificing herself and the ship to protect the rest of the fleet. As the Directorate First Fleet launched a fleet salvo at the battleship, the crew of the *Chrysodory* were heard singing the Union Navy Anthem, specifically the last verse. All hands were lost."

"The fleet carrier," said the protector.

"Dropped her jump rings and made an emergency jump. *The Spirit of Lena* was lucky, and made her way back to Stahlburgh. She was shy two wings, sir."

"Can you give me a summary of the battle," asked the protector. He was still in shock at the news and the flag officers realized they would need to recap again later.

"Our losses were heavy. Of the eighty ships that entered L 98-59, only fifteen made their way out," said the First Star Lady.

"And the Terran First fleet? How many losses," asked the protector.

"Five, sir," answered the First Star Lady.

"Only five? By the Allfather, that wasn't a battle that was a slaughter," said the protector savagely.

"On that note, I tender my resignation as First Star Lady, effective immediately. I will take up a post on the Seventeenth fleet, raise their flags and sail to L 98-59 Foxtrot," said the First Star Lady.

"I will need to consider your resignation, so, for the moment, consider that on hold. Paddy, you're up, I hope you have better news, did anyone get out?" said the protector. He was a parent looking for a ray of hope from the gravest of news.

"Sir, we don't have any determinations at this time. Both the Admiralty and Assault High Command are deciphering the radio chatter we collected from the action. I will say this, I had reports from the *Churchill* that some of the Assaultmen had hit the tubes and were ejecting. That's the best news I can give."

"And the bad news," asked the protector, cutting off the marshal.

"Raimond, I'd rather," Paddy said looking at his sister.

"No, she stays. She's been sick with worry since Heinrich missed his check in," said the protector.

"All right, the best guess I can get from the Assault's SIGINT survey during the battle is that there are five divisions of Terran Army on Foxtrot. There are a series of planetary batteries that make any landing impossible. In addition, there are five wings of Terran interceptors and a full battalion of mobile artillery. If we can't land ten regiments in less than thirty minutes, we don't have the beach head to fight on Foxtrot."

"Go on," the protector said, his eyes starting to water.

"Alpha company under the command of Major Declan "Deke" O'Brien of the Seventy Second volunteered to go in on reconnaissance. We had them ready to go, and Sternfahrer on the *Advantage,* as beat up as the ship was, volunteered to insert them. Sternfahrer made two passes on Foxtrot but couldn't shake the batteries and had to abort. Deke and his boys never made capsule-fall off the *Advantage,*" said the Field Marshal of the Assault.

"That the end of brief, Field Marshal?"

"No, sir. I saved the worst for last. Assault Signals Intelligence caught a packet as the *Advantage* made her pass. Kalo Portrand was sending a message to the Directorate's Maxim of Defense. We're decrypting the body now," said Paddy. "My replacement can brief you. I too submit my resignation effective immediately."

"Who is Kalo Portrand?" asked the patroness.

"Portrand is the colonel and CEO of the Crimson Command. They are the ones who USIS says started the revolution on Lalande, and have been suspected of running death camps on Mars. The Crimson Command is a top tier mercenary unit. They are well paid by the Directorate to do dirty jobs, and we suspect they have the contract for Henry's head, Marta," said Paddy.

"When will the press know about this?" asked the protector.

"We're briefing in thirty minutes," said the First Star Lady.

"I will hold your resignations for the moment, but don't be comfortable. I may fire you both. For now, you are dismissed," said the protector.

"I'm sorry, Marta," said Paddy.

"Marta, he's a tough kid, I am sure," said Siobhan.

"Dismissed," said the protector. Otto quickly wiped the tears from his eyes. He not only had lost a noble knight; he had also lost a nephew. Weber straightened, putting the handkerchief away and escorted the military officers out of the Villa.

*

"Geo, be a dear and get me some juice," the woman said.

"You want me to leave our bed of marital bliss?" the man said. "Only for you my wonderful, wild, womanly, widow, wife..."

"You can't say that three times fast, I'd wager," the woman said. "Speaking of three times, do you want me to wear my special nightie? I feel the need to... stimulate... you again."

"I shall return with your juice, my wonderful, wild, womanly, widow, wanton, wife," the man said. The woman sat up, listening as bells started chiming.

"Extra! Extra! *USTC Bismark* Lost! Assault and Navy's Initiative

Crushed! *Primus* Feared Dead in Failed Attack! Extra! Extra!" a news boy shouted. The woman heard a crash of glass in the small kitchenette. She rushed out clad only in a flimsy nightgown. The man had dropped the glass and it had shattered on the tile floor. Glass was everywhere, and the man looked like he had seen a ghost.

"I'll clean that up, Geo. Hold still," the woman said.

"Gheegee, did you hear the newsboy? Tell me I'm hearing things," said the man.

"Let's get the glass cleaned up first, then we can worry about the news." The woman grabbed a cloth towel and began to gather the glass. Her husband stood naked in front of her, and she maneuvered around his legs, only briefly staring at the scar where the new leg had been fused to his old stump.

"I think I got all the glass, but be careful, Geo," Gheegee said.

"I'm having a hard time thinking of glass now, dear," the man said. His voice wavered and tears were coming down his cheeks.

"Geo, what's a matter?" Gheegee said worried about her husband.

"Darling, I don't want you to hate me, but I may need to go back to the Assault," Geo said. Tears fell from Gheegee's eyes.

"I would never hate you for that, quite the contrary! You are my knight-in-painted-armor, my Saint George the Gallant! But why are you suddenly saying this to me?" Gheegee said, tears still wet on her cheeks.

"You remember my old unit? The one Hans and I served in?" Geo said.

"Yes, why?" Gheegee asked.

"We never talked about who we served with, but the now Primus was our comrade. He saved both Hans' and my life several times over. I don't think I could ever make up that ledger, and Hans, well, he'll have to have that discussion with Henry at the resurrection," said Geo.

"I never knew you and my late husband served with a Machthaber. Now, the news makes sense. Come on, let's get you dressed," said

Gheegee.

"Yes, yes," responded Geo.

"I will get dressed after you're ready, you can drop me at Stewart Castle, Saint George, although I am the one fighting the dragon there," said Gheegee.

Geo started putting on clothing and said absently with a chuckle, "Dragon, well Helen isn't that bad."

"Says the man who is constantly over at his liege's home hiding from his sister," Gheegee stopped. "Wait! What about Max and Isobel? Who will let them know this terrible news?"

"I suppose I will, after I drop you off. You're very wise, wonderful, wild wife. I had never expected Max or Isobel to have a care in the world having been on honeymoon for so long," said Geo.

"Enough talk, Geordie Stewart. You must hurry up, that's the Assaultman's way," said the woman.

"Spoken like a true Assaultman's wife, Gisela Stewart," said Geordie. Geordie sped towards the march of Gilbraith-on-Heather and made excellent time, after dropping his wife at Stewart Castle.

As they parted Gisela said, "Saint George the Gallant, goodbye. Don your uniform, my knight-in-painted armor and slay many dragons! Come back to me soon, my love."

Helen appeared as well and said, "Goodbye, brother. Come back or I'll inherit the barony!" Geordie laughed. He grabbed the hard copies of the news he had printed out, and drove off. He put the posh hovercar rental on auto and opened his dialing program. He entered Alexander Gordon's number.

"Office of the Prime Minister," said the receptionist. "How may I help?"

"Tell Alexander the *Royal Neep* is calling; he'll know who that is," said Geordie. After a moment the line clicked.

"Geordie, old boy, to what do I owe the honor?" said Alexander.

"Uncle Alex, if there ever were ever a favor to call in. I'm doing so now," said Geordie.

"Okay, how can I help, nephew?" replied Alexander.

"Get me in touch with the Field Marshall of the Assault," said Geordie.

"Is this about the *Bismarck*?" asked Alexander.

"Yes," said Geordie. "Can you connect me?"

"You know, for my late sister's boy, you ask for a lot... This one is going to cost you," said Alexander.

"How many cases," said Geordie with a smile.

"Well, my favorite nephew, I want five of the reserve. You'd be surprised at how the Buchanans, Campbells, and the other Gordons drink your libations! They are like fish that swim in your bottles," said Alexander with a laugh. "How do you think I ended up as President of the Dynasts?"

"Done! Now, the Field Marshall," said Geordie.

"Hold on," said Alexander. After five minutes with Geordie being on hold, the line clicked.

"Padraig O'Cruadhlaoich speaking," said the field marshal.

"Lieutenant George Stewart requesting to return to active duty, field marshal."

"You're medically out, Lieutenant, and I may be out too. The judge hasn't made a ruling on that though," said the field marshal. He sounded old and tired.

"I've got a new leg, one of the best, I can pass the PT test. Put me back in, sir."

"I wouldn't even take this call, if it weren't for Alexander," said the field marshal.

"Both my uncle and I can be quite persuasive when we need to be, sir. Since you feel you are on the way out, there is nothing stopping you from reversing the administrative discharge. Then, the chips can fall where they may."

"I see I'm not getting off this call without you getting what you want," said the field marshal. "Get my nephew back, and then we're even."

"That was my intention, field marshal," said Geordie. "I'll let my uncle know how cooperative you've been."

"Thanks," said the field marshal flatly, ending the call. Geordie turned to look at his destination. The large estate house rose before him. He was going to have to say goodbye to his friends in order to save another.

Henry and Jurgen will return in...

Heir to the Union

Maximilian and Isobel Fraser will return in...

Blood and Passion in the Felgenland

See more details on our publisher's site https://woodenhookstudios.com!

Thank you so much for reading *Protector of the Union.* I hope you enjoyed this novel. I need your support as an independent author working for a self-publishing imprint! If you enjoyed this manuscript, please rate my work on platforms like Amazon, Barnes & Noble, and Goodreads and encourage others to read my work!

Here's a little bit about why your support matters so much! I retired from the IT Security industry at the beginning of 2024, and I have decided to make a full-time career out of being an author. My vision is to write novels that project my optimism about the future with Christian faith and charity. To that end, I started my imprint (or press). As a self-published author, I am a "one-person show" where I must write, lightly edit, publish, market, and schedule signings for my works. Unlike a press-published author, I don't have teams of people making the "magic happen."

While being an author has been a dream of mine, I don't exist in a vacuum. I have daily struggles with all of the same issues that everyone else has (to date, I haven't made it on a best-seller list or had any movie deals), and that is where you can come in! A five-minute review means the world to me, as I can use the review (and your kind words) to generate traffic so more readers can be entertained by my stories.

Your feedback is not just important, it's the lifeblood of my growth as an author. I read every review, and after years of using customer satisfaction scores to guide my professional growth, I'm eager to learn from your insights. Your critique, if you didn't resonate with the work, is especially valuable. It's a gift that helps me hone my skills and deliver better stories to you. Your voice matters, and

I'm here to listen.

Once again, I want to express my heartfelt gratitude for your support. As a solo author, I rely on your word of mouth and feedback to reach more readers and expand my fan base. Your role in this journey is not just significant, it's everything. Thank you for reading my work, and stay tuned for more! The best is yet to come!

Best Regards,

Eric C. Holtgrefe
eric.c.holtgrefe@woodenhookstudios.com

Kickstarter Backers

Kickstarter Backers of this Book
And to much thanks is given!
Unio Omnia Obligat!

Union Supporters Tier

R.L. Akers

Parliament Tier

Kurt Adam
Mark Goodfellow
David Holtgrefe
Marcia Holtgrefe
Matthew Holtgrefe
Robert Kochems

DRAMATIS PERSONAE

House Machthaber: The protector, his family, & retainers

LENA KOCHER	Liberator of all humanity, member of the subversive group "Society of the Human Phoenix," Karl's great-grandmother, her statue dominates the capital
STEFAN NEU-BRANFELS	Lena's husband, Karl's great grandfather
KARL VON MACHTHABER	The founder and first Protector of the Union
JULIA SVENSDOTTIR	Julia of Protelan, Karl's wife, the first Patroness of the Union, Ruprecht and Raimond's mother
RUPRECHT VON MACHTHABER	Primus under Karl, Karl's eldest son,

leader of the doves

RAIMOND VON MACHTHABER Secundus under Karl, second Protector of the Union.

MARTA VON MACHTHABER Raimond's wife, second Patroness of the Union, Henry's and Mathias' mother

HEINRICH VON MACHTHABER Sextus under Karl, Primus under Raimond, Raimond and Marta's eldest son, goes by Henry

MATHIAS VON MACHTHABER Septimus under Karl, Secundus under Raimond, Raimond and Marta's second son

TANJA VON MACHTHABER Mathias' wife, Rolf's mother

ROLF VON MACHTHABER Octavus under Karl, Tertius under Raimond, Mathias and Gisela's son

STEPHAN VON MACHTHABER Arch cardinal (chief cleric) of the Central Christian Orthodoxy

JOHANN STRASS	Heinrich's first valet, the Margrave of Kildromey on Lochiel
OTTO WEBER	The protector's majordomo, served under Karl and continues with his successors
MARKUS FLEMING	Otto Weber's nephew, Henry's second valet

Clan MacDonald: The First Family on Stahlburgh

H. MALCOLM MACLEOD	Ancient pirate, ancient leader of Stahlburgh
FLORA MACLEOD-MACDONALD	H. Malcolm's niece, painter of *MacLeod's Landing on Stahlburgh*
ROBERT MACDONALD I	One of Karl's generals at the Battle of the Landing, former Great (or High) King of the Skye Isles
ANGUS MACDONALD	Great-grandnephew of MacLeod, Great King of the Skye Isles

DROSTAN MACDONALD	Angus' acknowledged heir and Crown Prince
CAITLIN MACDONALD	Drostan's wife, formerly a MacQuarrie from Speur-Coisiche, Crown Princess
ROBERT MACDONALD II	Drostan and Caitlin's eldest, a young boy
ALYTH MACDONALD	Drostan and Caitlin's middle, a young girl
FINLAY MACDONALD	Drostan and Caitlin's youngest, a toddler
BEATRIX MACDONALD	Angus' daughter, Star Lieutenant in the Union Navy and interceptor pilot, goes by Bonnie

Clan Campbell: The Second Family on Stahlburgh

ALARIC CAMPBELL	One of Karl's generals at the Battle of the Landing, former Grand Duke of Inveraray and the Argylle Islands
ALASDAIR CAMPBELL	Alaric's son, current

	Grand Duke, head of Union's foremost defense contractor, Lieutenant Colonel in the Line Guards and Commander of the Battalion of the Presence
MARGRETHE CAMPBELL	Alasdair's wife, Grand Duchess
JASON ALARIC CAMPBELL	Alasdair's eldest and heir

Clan Gordon: The Third Family on Stahlburgh

ALEXANDER GORDON	The Union's Prime Minister, President of the House of Dynasts, sixth Duke of Huntly-on-the-Aberdeen, fourth most powerful man in the Union

Clan Fraser: The Fourth Family on Stahlburgh

MARTIN FRASER	Known for the loss of his hand to the old tyrants, third Earl of

the Bonnie Dundee and Gilbraith-on-Heather

KENNETH FRASER — Martin's grandson, fifth Earl of Gilbraith-on-Heather, father to Archibald and Maximilian

ARCHIBALD FRASER — Kenneth's eldest son

MAXIMILIAN FRASER — Kenneth's second son, sixth Earl of the Gilbraith-on-Heather, protagonist of *Love and Honor in the Felgenland*

Clan Buchanan: The Fifth Family on Stahlburgh

Not mentioned in this novel

Members of the Chancellery

ADOLPHUS SCHWARZENRODE — One of Karl's generals at the Battle of the Landing, now War Chancellor and former Field Marshal, the second most powerful man in the

	Union
RUSSEL BERTRAND-HOYT	The Chancellor of State, the third most powerful man in the Union

Notable Members of the High Peerage

SIGNE BOSDOTTIR	Steward (Arbiter) of the Election, Grand Duchess of Haldersmere (on Hansaburgh), Admiral and Raimond's close friend
ASTRID BOSDOTTIR	Signe's daughter, Captain of the *Bearded Axe*, technically ranked Commander in the Navy
WILHELM BRUCKNER	Margrave of the Bruckland (on Hansaburgh), Henry's best friend

Military, Diplomats, and Other Figures (by order of appearance)

OLIVER TROCHTER	Assault Ensign, Advocate

for the Defense at the tribunal

CHRISTIAN BERGDORF	Assault ensign, Advocate for the Protector at the tribunal
CARL TUCKSON	Felgenlander independent news man with over thirty million followers
JURGEN WULFJAEGER	A poor man from Tavishire, exemplary Assaultman
THOM LAAKSO	Assault Ensign, Jurgen's commanding officer on Nakdong
JOHN HERTZOG	Assault Staff Sergeant, Jurgen's Non-Commissioned Officer (NCO) on Nakdong
MARICELA FENG-LING SOLARA	Counterrevolutionaries (contra) fireteam lead
AUGUST SUTCLIFFE	Assault Sergeant, called "Auggie"
HANNAH DEBECK	Navy Sub-Lieutenant and

	interceptor pilot, call sign: STELLAR SERAPH
ROSCOE CANNON	Assault Corporal, Bravo fireteam lead, Jurgen's friend
LANA STRÖHE	Navy Sub-Lieutenant and interceptor pilot call sign: LUNA JETSTREAM
THOMASIN PULLINGS	Navy Sub-Lieutenant, Third Lieutenant on the *USWC Advantage*
JOHANNA STERNFAHRER	Navy Commander, the *Advantage's* Captain, formerly Johanna Cochrane, known as Joan or Goldilocks (for her hair and prize money)
JOHN CLAYTON II	Assaultman First Class, nickname "Metal Kid" for his taste in music, later shortened to "Metal"
JOHANNES NEUKLANG	Felgenlander opera composer, famous for his *Singularity Cycle*

BENJAMIN MACINTOSH	Assault Lance Corporal, First Lochiel Dragoons
LUKAS STAHL	A-list Felgenland Union actor, heartthrob known for dramatic roles that appeal to women
SOPHIE VAN DER MEER	A-list Felgenland Union actress, a rare beauty
FREDERICK KRUEGER	Assault Sergeant, Henry's driver
BJORN HALVORSEN	Major in the Protelani Space Marines, military attaché for the Protelan Republic to the Felgenland Union
GALENOR VON ADLER	Count of Westhaven-on-the-Lindenau, Director of the Museum of Union History
JULIA SCHNEIDER	Chief Curator of the Museum of Union History
FRANK NORDLINGER	Lieutenant, then Captain in the First Stahlburgh

	Rifles, dated Bonnie MacDonald, part of the Glorious Dead
MARTHA CLARK	"Friend" of Kenneth Fraser
DONAL MACTAVISH	Baron and leading man in Tavishire
JENNY MERCY	Formerly Jenny Hunt, Jurgen's ex-girlfriend, Johnny Mercy's wife
MARA WULFJAEGER	Jurgen's oldest sister and favorite sibling
OLRICH WULFJAEGER	Jurgen's oldest brother
CASSANDRA WULJAEGER	Formerly a McFadden, Jurgen's mother, called "Cassie"
JOHN MERCY	The elder Mercy, richest man in Tavishire
JOHNNY MERCY	The younger Mercy, John and Peg's son
MARGARET MERCY	John's late wife, Johnny's mother, called "Peg," formerly a Douglas
DOUGLAS IAN MACALLISDAIR	Known as "Doug", made a Baron by Karl after the Battle of the

Landing, formerly the Field Marshall of the Assault and a major Union hero

THOMAS FRANCIS MEAGHER — Assault General, known as "Fighting Mad Meagher," found guilty of dereliction of duty in a court martial after Asimov, made commander of the First Division at Nakdong

GRETCHEN HAAGEN — Publican of "The Golden Cock" in Tavishire

ISMAIL ACKBAR — Assaultman First Class, later a Corporal and medic

MARION FLATERTY — Lance Corporal, Third Lochiel Dragoons, called "Wayne"

ISLA MACLAN — Navy Star Lieutenant, callsign: AURORA GUARDIAN

PADRAIG O'CRUADHLAOICH — Field Marshall of the Assault, Duke of Emerald-Hills-on-

	the-Cork, eldest brother of Marta von Machthaber, known as "Paddy"
EWAN FRASER	USIS Subversion Division Chief, cousin of Gilbraith
MOLLY FRASER	Ewan's wife, USIS Subversion Division Deputy Chief
GEORG LACHELN	USIS Synthesis Division Chief, legendary Intelligence Officer
JAMES GRAHAM	USIS Director
JERRY SLOMONG	Martian rebellion money man, also known as "George Reynolds"
WILLIAM MACKINTYRE	USIS Collection Division Chief
HENDRIK OLSON	USIS Domestic Division Chief
JAMES VON HEUGEL	Secretary for Dynastic Affairs in the House of Dynasts, Margrave of Neu-west-Silesia-on-Meer
DANIEL VON HEUGEL	James's son and dynastic

	auditor
JOACHIM KRAUSE	Sergeant in the Seventy-Second Grenadiers, man enough for an entire fireteam, one of the Glorious Dead
ANDREW TOBIAS	Corporal from the First Stahlburgh Rifles, one of the Glorious Dead
ENRICO ANDREAS	Corporal from the First Stahlburgh Rifles, one of the Glorious Dead
FRANCIS HOLZHAUSER	Assault Sergeant First Class from the First Stahlburgh Rifles, known as "Hot Dog," NCO of the Glorious Dead
POSSUM	Journalist for Possum Press, "it's just me, man, I'm Possum"
ASTRAL CLARITY	Possum's financier, girlfriend, and later karmic-bonded partner
JAVIER XIANGWU SUNO	Maricela's father and the former Prime Minister of the Lalande System

XIOMAR ZHAN-LI ESPERANZA	Dictator and head of the Directorate-backed Revolutionary Government of Lalande 21185
TOBY BRENNAN	Lance Corporal from the First Stahlburgh Rifles, one of the Glorious Dead
JOHANN MUELLER	Lance Corporal from the First Stahlburgh Rifles, one of the Glorious Dead
MARCUS VOGEL	Lance Corporal from the First Stahlburgh Rifles, one of the Glorious Dead, from Hansaburgh
COLIN O'MALLEY	Assault Major, Assault High Command briefer
SIOBHAN O'RIORDAN	First Star Lady, Marta and Paddy's younger sister, a member of the O'Cruadhlaoich family
ANTHONY DANIELS	Assault Color Sergeant and the protector's

	driver
ELAINE LENART	Navy Commander, Admiralty briefer, callsign: DRAGON LADY
AIDAN MACCARTHY	Marquess of Galway-on-the-Meer, CEO of the defense contractor MacCarthy Naval Industries Limited
NIAMH O'RIORDAN	Union Navy Star Lieutenant, Siobhan's eldest daughter, Raimond's niece
FIADH O'RIORDAN	Union Navy Sub-Lieutenant, Siobhan's middle daughter, Raimond's niece
CALLIE CALLAN	Union Navy Sub-Lieutenant
MARTINA SCHULTZ	Union Navy Admiral, Fleet Admiral for the L 98-59 Foxtrot thrust, cousin to Alexander Gordon, Union Elector
ELIAS SCHULTZ	Grand Duke of Hamburgh-on-the-Neu-Rhone,

	Martina's husband, Dynast, Elector
YENNIFER BRUCKNER	Wilhelm Bruckner's wife
LEOPOLD BRUCKNER	Wilhelm's son and successor as Margrave of Bruckland
TIMOTHY ENLOW	Assault Sergeant First Class and senior Assault NCO on the *Advantage*, goes by the nickname "Laser"
MICHAEL SCOTT	Famous Processing Age General from the XXII century's failed War of Texas Succession
MIA STOURTON	Union Navy Senior Star Lieutenant and first lieutenant of the *Advantage*
NICHELLE NICHOLLS	Union Navy Star Lieutenant and second lieutenant of the *Advantage*.
WILHELMINA BABBINGTON	Union Navy Midshipwoman, bridge officer trainee
STEPHANIE GEDIEGEN	Union Navy Lieutenant,

surgeon of the *Advantage,* a Bio-psychosocial Humanist

MAIDEN CËLLIAN	Union Navy Petty Officer, Sternfahrer's stewardess, and personal cook
BARETTE BONDEN	Union Navy Chief Petty Officer, Coxswain of the Captain's yacht on the *Advantage*
HANS DROIT	Bestselling Author of *189: The Papal Defense*
OTTO	Alpha male of the protector's Schnauzer pack
HILDEGARDE	Alpha female of the protector's Schnauzer pack
HENRIETTA VON SCHLIEFFEN	Grand Duchess of Bavaria-on-Salzheim (Hansaburgh), counter-pugilist of the patroness
KLAUS VON EISENBACH	Assault General, Baron of Bremen-on-the-Saltz

MARIA KÖHLER	Union Navy Chief Petty Officer for Henry's dropship to the Skye Isles
ANNELIESE HARTMANN	Union Navy Lieutenant Commander and interceptor pilot, pilot of Henry's dropship to the Skye Isles, call sign: TAWNY TULIP, also known as "Annie"
JULIUS MACINNES	Baron of Armadale Island, retainer to the MacDonalds
IGNATIUS	A Great Pyrenees, Doug's dog, also known as "Iggy"
JEMIMA WULFJAEGER	Mother of Magnus and Jurgen, Doug's love
MAGNUS WULFJAEGER	Jurgen's father, Doug and Jemima's oldest son
JURGEN WULFJAEGER	Jurgen's uncle and Magnus' younger brother, Doug and Jemima's youngest son

JOSEPH THACKERAY	Baron of Thackeray Shire
FLORIAN BAUERHOF	The old Count who conscripted Jurgen
WILLIAM MCFADDEN	Priest of Tavishire Parish, Jurgen's maternal grandfather
IAN D. MACALLISDAIR	Doug's eldest son with "the nag"
ROB ROY MACALLISDAIR	Doug's second eldest with "the nag," "Meathead"
HUGO BAUERHOF	The current Count of Chemnitz-on-the-Zschopau, Jurgen's home county
FREDERICK WULFJAEGER	Jurgen's middle brother, called "Freddy"
DUNCAN WULFJAEGER	Jurgen's youngest brother
AGATHA WULFJAEGER	Jurgen's youngest sister
HAMISH MACDONALD	Drostan MacDonald's personal servant
ERIKA SCHWARZWALD	Union Navy Captain - Junior Service, Captain of the troopship *Bismarck.*
HAROLD BAKER	Assault Captain, Second

	Stahlburgh Rifles, Special Projects Leader
LUCAS BITNER	Assault Corporal, Second Stahlburgh Rifles, Special Projects Detachment
LIAM MUNSTER	Assault Lance Corporal, Second Stahlburgh Rifles, Special Projects Detachment
JARI PERTTI	Assault Lance Corporal, Second Stahlburgh Rifles, Special Projects Detachment
JASON KELLER	Assault Sergeant, Second Stahlburgh Rifles, Special Projects Detachment, former MjGA, Moray's handler
MORAY (SAID "MURRAY")	Special Projects K9, Miniature Schnauzer Sniper with cropped ears and a docked tail, former pack mate of Otto and Hildegarde, Henry's former puppy

ROSAMUND BURKHART	Union Navy Specialist (Petty Officer) on loan to the Second Stahlburgh Rifles, Special Projects Detachment
DECLAN O'BRIEN	Assault Major and MjGA commander of Alpha Company, Seventy-second Grenadier (MjGA) Regiment. Known as "Deadly Deke".
KALO PORTRAND	Colonel and CEO of the Crimson Command, Ltd.
GEORGE STEWART	Assault Lieutenant, Seventy-Second Grenadier (MjGA) Regiment, Baron of Breakin, known as "Geordie" and "Geo"
GISELA STEWART	Baroness of Breakin, George's wife, known as "Gheegee"
HANS VON BERG	Assault Lieutenant, Seventy-Second Grenadier (MjGA) Regiment, Gisela's late husband

Sons and Daughters of The Frontier

In Stahlburgh the heart of the Felgenland, our fortunes aligned,
A union born of hope, we were all entwined.
We're the sons and daughters of the frontier,
In this land of freedom, we hold traditions dear.

Gray skies ignite with starlight at night,
Faith guiding us through darkness as we struggle and we fight.
We're the pioneers, carving out the sky,
United by our freedom until we die!

(Chorus)
We hear the echoes of our past,
In the old songs we sing and stories held fast.
We're the sons and daughters of the frontier!
Carrying on Lena's legacy, holding it dear.

Through the valleys and hills, where the shepherd hums his song,
To cities and the factories, our union is strong.
We've forged our future in this rim land,
Where unity prevails and justice takes a stand.

A beacon of freedom, shining far from old Earth,
Guiding the lost and offering solace to those of worth.
The stars will fade, but we will always stand strong,
In the Felgenland Union, we'll always belong!

(Bridge)
From dawn till dusk, our toils are hard won,
In the Felgenland Union, with the Protector we are one.
Together challenges we face with unity and might,
We'll carry our destiny across the stars tonight!

Together serving the Allfather above,
Our hearts beat, held fast with love.
We are the guardians of the settler's dream,
A testament to unity, and our people's theme.

In unity we stand, united we thrive,
With Lena's spirit guiding us we arrive,
Together marching towards the dawning light,
Together we shall conquer this endless night.

(Chorus)
We hear the echoes of our past,
In the old songs we sing and stories held fast.
We're the sons and daughters of the frontier!
Carrying on Lena's legacy, holding it dear.

Beneath the Allfather's watchful eye,
We've built our home, our dreams soaring high.
In Stahlburgh we thrive, the heart of the frontier,
United by freedom, our Union so dear.

In fields and in factories, where the people's voices show,
The Felgenland Union is where the strong grow.
Through hardships and trials, our spirit will never break,
In this land of opportunity, our people together awake.

(Chorus)
We hear the echoes of our past,
In the old songs we sing and stories held fast.

We're the sons and daughters of the frontier!
Carrying on Lena's legacy, holding it dear.

United together, all our foes will fall,
Assaultmen and the Navy, the Felgenland's wall.
Oh come you sons and daughters of the frontier!
Remember together, we'll all hold Lena's vision dear!

Marching Song of the Felgenland

March along men, sing our bars, we're the Guardians of the stars,
We're the brave, we're the true, we are the mighty few.
We're the Assault, proud and bold, protect the Union we're told,
We're the last wall, against our might the foes will fall!

First to fight for what's right,
In the skies and on the ground,
With our courage as our might,
Our enemies' bones make our crown.
Proud of every step we take,
Fighting till the mission's done,
We guardians rise and wake,
We will shine like the Holsten sun.

[Chorus]
Then it's Aye! Aye! Hooray!
The Assault leads the way.
Count off your cadence loud and clear!
For where e'er we go,
You will always know,
The Assault is the tip of the spear!

From the depths of distant worlds,
To the heights of azure skies,
With our banners unfurled,
We will answer the weak's cries.
Frontier men of a new age,

Always ready, brave and true,
Victory and honor is our wage,
The Assault the proud and few.

[Chorus]
Then it's Aye! Aye! Hooray!
The Assault leads the way.
Count off your cadence loud and clear!
For where e'er we go,
You will always know,
The Assault is the tip of the spear!

In the face of every foe,
With our hearts and minds aligned,
Our faith in the Allfather does grow,
We never leave a man behind.
The Protector is our guide,
We forge a path anew,
Together standing side by side,
The gold, black and red are true.

[Chorus]
Then it's Aye! Aye! Hooray!
The Assault leads the way.
Count off your cadence loud and clear!
For where e'er we go,
You will always know,
The Assault is the tip of the spear!

Now rest ye mighty men, the battle is now done
Your bravery, and courage is shown for all.
Whether barracks or grave calls you, the fight is won,
As your pin rifles fire, the Union will not fall.

Sisters of Athena

By star and nebulae, we chart our course,
No matter the system or the g-force,
In the silence of space, our weapons sing,
The Union's freedom, our lives do bring!

Like Valkyries we ascend,
Bearing our warriors, hand in hand,
This duty never ends,
We soar high, united we stand.

[Chorus]
Sailing forth, we are the light,
Sisters of Athena, we fight!
Defending all, our solemn chore,
For the Union's call, forevermore!

With the strength of countless suns,
Our ships stronger than guns,
We shall shield our home, our kin,
Our will to fight will always win.

[Chorus]
Sailing forth, we are the light,
Sisters of Athena, we fight!
Defending all, our solemn chore,
For the Union's call, forevermore!

[Bridge]
From Stahlburgh to the void, we pave the way,
Like Amazons we guard and boldly stay,
Ready for every challenge, we are prepared,
For the Union's people from death are spared!

In the dark void, we do stand,
Our lines and ships mighty and grand,
Like the angels our ships do fly,
interceptor Aces in space and sky.

[Chorus]
Sailing forth, we are the light,
Sisters of Athena, we fight!
Defending all, our solemn chore,
For the Union's call, forevermore!

Through asteroid fields and nebulas' glow,
Our resolve and courage will grow,
In the cockpit or on the bridge we fight,
Our valor and glory we'll write!

[Chorus]
Sailing forth, we are the light,
Sisters of Athena, we fight!
Defending all, our solemn chore,
For the Union's call, forevermore!

Women answer our call far and wide,
Stand tall Sisters of Athena with pride,
We are the Union Navy, strong and free,
Our courage calls throughout all history!

www.ingramcontent.com/pod-product-compliance
Lightning Source LLC
LaVergne TN
LVHW100502110826
845146LV00002B/482

* 9 7 9 8 9 9 0 0 4 5 9 8 9 *